FIVE RITES

OTHER INSTALMENTS:

Four Troubles
Three Strikes
Two Roads
One Truth
Zero Hour

OTHER WORKS BY THE AUTHOR:

50 Years to Paradise
Scifact 2525
Things Happen In Threes

FIVE RITES

LEIGH DAVID

The Book Guild Ltd

First published in Great Britain in 2018 by
The Book Guild Ltd
9 Priory Business Park
Wistow Road, Kibworth
Leicestershire, LE8 0RX
Freephone: 0800 999 2982
www.bookguild.co.uk
Email: info@bookguild.co.uk
Twitter: @bookguild

Copyright © 2018 Leigh David

The right of Leigh David to be identified as the author of this
work has been asserted by him in accordance with the
Copyright, Design and Patents Act 1988.

All rights reserved. No part of this publication may be
reproduced, transmitted, or stored in a retrieval system, in any form or by any means,
without permission in writing from the publisher, nor be otherwise circulated in
any form of binding or cover other than that in which it is published and without
a similar condition being imposed on the subsequent purchaser.

This work is entirely fictitious and bears no resemblance to any persons living or dead.

Typeset in Adobe Garamond Pro

Printed and bound in Great Britain by
CPI Group (UK) Ltd, Croydon, CR0 4YY

ISBN 978 1912362 295

British Library Cataloguing in Publication Data.
A catalogue record for this book is available from the British Library.

There is nothing
more difficult to carry out,
nor more doubtful of success,
nor more dangerous to do,
than to initiate a new order of things.

#Unit

PROLOGUE

The Organisation

Organisation: a group of people working together to achieve a shared goal.

The Organisation doesn't have an official name. It doesn't need one. It used to be called the Brotherhood.

Those who lived through, what some called, the Bonaparte betrayal doubted whether their beloved Brotherhood could survive. Elders worked tirelessly to revive their precious order but the wounds were deep. New life was eventually breathed back into it and it was given a new name: 'the New Brotherhood'. A new brotherhood for a new era. For forty years the Organisation went by that name but it fell out of use for reasons which will become obvious.

***

There's a saying in the Organisation which goes, "If you need a good man to do a job hire a woman." Females are more dedicated and ruthless than men, better communicators, more self-sacrificing and less self-promoting.

Reigning supreme over the Organisation is the Chair. The

Chair for the period this instalment is concerned with is a Madame Chairman who usually goes by the name of Margaret Rotheram.

***

The Organisation of the late twentieth century numbered north of one point one million globally. The number who knew its mission was approximately four thousand.

THE FACE OF MIKHAIL MOROZOV

London, 5th May

2158 BST.

Svetlana Morozova sits cross-legged on her fashionable shabby chic sofa waiting for husband Mikhail to return home. To kill time she's reading a magazine. She wished she still smoked. It's late, he's late and she's irritated; she's angry; she's controlling her nerves and gathering her courage for what must be done this night. *Mikhail always calls if he's coming home late*, but so far there'd been no call.

Damn him, he always screws things up. She didn't mean that. A small portable TV is droning away in the background atop an upcycled 1960's credenza. It's only on for company. She's paying little attention to it. She hates being alone in the flat. In fact, as a twin, she hates being alone full stop. She tosses her magazine to the floor, gets up from the sofa and goes into the kitchen to make herself a mug of green tea.

She seldom drinks coffee or non-herbal teas and rarely drinks alcohol as her father died from alcoholism in the old Soviet Union. Well, that's the story she'd given Mikhail. She normally takes her tea from elegant china cups sitting on saucers. She looks at the mug she's holding and shudders at the logo of Chelsea Football Club emblazoned on it. "How ugly." All her beautiful chinaware, along with everything else she owns, is packed in preparation for her imminent flight from this life. With husband Mikhail out of the flat she'd been packing all day. It'd been a much longer than intended assignment and she wanted something to show for it. *Where the hell is he?* The flickering light from the TV reached into the kitchen through the serving hatch of the on-trend 1960's apartment which she and Mikhail have shared for three years in chi-chi South Hampstead, NW6. She peers through the hatch for no particular reason. What she sees on the TV screen turns her blood to ice. *Mikhail?* She can't believe what she's looking at.

Mikhail? He's moving on the screen; talking; now he's kneeling. There's a man dressed in black standing over him holding a huge curved sword. She runs into the lounge and turns up the volume on the TV to hear the voice of a BBC News reporter on location outside Scotland Yard. He's saying this is the fifth abduction in recent weeks, all from the London area.

The reporter went on: "The video recording of this latest kidnap victim was sent to the BBC earlier today along with several other recordings containing messages from all five abductees, apparently confessing to being agents of both the CIA and MI6." The video recording continues playing in the background while the BBC News reporter talks over the moving images behind him, summarising them as their actual content are "the subject of a police investigation and therefore cannot be fully aired at this time". The reporter goes on to say, "… this latest kidnap victim of so-called ISBJ is a Mr Mikhail Morozov who claims to be a Russian émigré, single and of no fixed abode. In his video recording, Mr Morozov has clearly suffered a beating; he appears disoriented; he's shabby, cut and bleeding. During his video statement Mr Morozov is heard to say that he is partially crippled and in need of regular medication for his various ailments. The other abductees can clearly be seen blindfolded and tied together in the background. In an uncharacteristic move by the Russian Embassy, it issued a statement categorically denying any knowledge of the existence of

Mr Morozov either as an émigré or as a defector. In a statement from so-called ISBJ accompanying the video, they restate their aim to execute, by beheading, seven of what they are referring to as 'Western agents of Islamic oppression' in the week leading up to Ramadan to 'highlight the West's criminal and genocidal persecution of Muslims over many centuries'." The BBC News reporter finished off with "… and that's all for the time being from outside Scotland Yard so now it's back to you in the studio". Back in the studio the news anchor continued, "We will of course keep you updated with any developments in that story. And in other news today…" Svetlana lowered the sound but left the TV on in case there were any further updates.

Under her breath she thanked her clever Mikhail for the messages contained in his description of his condition and circumstances. As he'd claimed to be of no fixed abode nobody would be looking for her until after she was long, long gone.

The telephone rings. She tentatively picks up the receiver. The brief conversation is in Russian. She knew that back home they must have got as big a shock as she had when they saw Mikhail on the BBC News, which is monitored 24/7 for obvious reasons.

Svetlana's immediate concern was that the Russian Embassy must have had advance knowledge of the kidnap story in order to obtain authority to make an official statement of denial concerning the émigré status of Mr Mikhail Morozov. She knew full well what it would take to obtain the authority to make such a statement. This was something that went right to the top in the Kremlin. It could not possibly have been a local decision. Why they'd made any statement at all was baffling. There really was no need. Then a terrifying thought occurred to her. Perhaps the Kremlin was sending the kidnappers a message. Perhaps it wants them to look into their prisoner's past. *If they find out what's in Mikhail's head they'll burn everybody.* That thought sent a shiver spiralling down her spine: *The Kremlin must be relishing their opportunity for revenge.* She knew that mass arrests and executions would already be underway back home.

Things would not bode well for her if she returned to St Petersburg. But she hadn't planned to go back there anyway, at least not in the short term. She needed time to think, to plan. *Damn Mikhail, he always screws things up.* The timing could not have been worse as far as she was concerned. She'd sacrificed enough and now it was her time but it was looking as though she'd have to wait before she could have her time.

A question popped into her head just as she opened, and then closed behind her, the door to the apartment for the very last time. *How did a bunch of amateurs manage to kidnap Mikhail Morozov?* It was unbelievable to her. *Maybe it's his age?* she thought, laughing a little laugh. *Mikhail Morozov, a man who for decades has been… how should it be called?* How would Svetlana describe what Mikhail did for a living? For a living? That's funny. She'd give it some thought, but not much. It was hard to explain what Mikhail did; what he was involved in even. His abductors could not possibly have known his true identity otherwise this night would have ended differently. The video recording from ISBJ would have contained a very different message. There wouldn't have been any BBC News broadcast about the abduction of a certain Mr Mikhail Morozov, that's for sure.

As it was though, Mikhail's face was out there and, without doubt, agents would be descending on London to locate Madame Chairman's former favourite to either kill or reacquire him. She sat thinking, as she made her way through London's labyrinthine tube system, of the meetings of nervous, frightened and angry people which would be convening in cities all around the globe. She knew with certainty that not everybody attending those meetings would survive them. How right she'd be proven to be.

***

In an elegant Mayfair mansion only a few miles from the Morozov apartment somebody else had been watching the ten o'clock news on the BBC. She does so every night. It's a habit. She has to have her BBC ten o'clock news fix before she can go to sleep. She presses a button on the side of her hospital-style bed. Her call for attention is responded to by a sentinel, not a nurse.

"Is Lisette awake?"

"I don't know, Madame Chairman. I'll check."

"Tell her she's to come straight away." The sentinel made her way to Lisette's suite which is located on the same floor as Madame Chairman's. Lisette was in a lightly medicated sleep when she was woken. It took her sixteen minutes to get ready, get into her wheelchair and motor her way along the corridor to Madame Chairman's suite.

"Is this what you call straight away? Is it? Hmmm? I told Annie that you were to come straight away. It's important."

"Stop moaning and get on with it. I'm here, aren't I? I came as quickly as I could."

"Lisette darling, prepare yourself for a shock," announced Madame Chairman in her compassionate tone of voice. She'd been practising.

"Well, I'm sitting down at least, so let me have it."

"It's Michael. He's been taken." Lisette shook her head to check reality as she'd been known to hallucinate under the influence of some of her medications.

"Are you sure?"

"It was on the bloody BBC News at Ten programme so I'm pretty bloody confident that he's been taken." Compassionate tone of voice switched off.

"Who by?" asked Lisette ignoring Madame Chairman's obvious irritation with her.

"A group calling itself ISBJ. Ever heard of them?"

"No I haven't. Annie? Annie! Come here, Annie." Annie entered the room at a pace. She's careful not to get involved in arguments between these two increasingly cantankerous old women. "Annie, have you heard of IS… what is it?"

"ISBJ, you old fool."

"Yes, ISBJ."

"They arrived on the scene a few months ago after kidnapping a man in the East End. They said they are going to behead him and six others in the week leading up to Ramadan. Until then nobody had heard of them."

"Marvellous. Well done, Annie. I know that much from watching the bloody news."

"We've never looked into them for obvious reasons."

"Well, Annie, we need to look into them now."

"Yes, Madame Chairman. I'll get on it right away." Annie couldn't wait to leave the room; she practically sprinted out.

Back in compassionate voice mode: "We must be first to find Michael. I'm putting you in charge."

"Are you sure? Do you think I'm up to it? In case you haven't noticed I'm not very well. And neither are you by the way."

"I can't think of anybody else I or Michael would want in charge. You're the most capable person I know, darling."

"You know we should have retired years ago, don't you?"

"It's a good thing we didn't though. Maybe we were meant to stay on… you know, hang on… for this one last job together."

"Don't start with that karma crap again."

"It's not crap. Just look at what we've seen, darling. Look at what we've seen. Look at the evidence." Annie entered the room again.

"We've just intercepted a communiqué. It's astonishing after all this time but… the Mediterranean man has been reactivated. He's in the USA… east coast."

"So it begins. It's only right I suppose that it should be him. Find out if he's with the Irishman. Order my sentinels to drop whatever they're doing and don't stop until they find Michael."

"Sorry, boss; cancel that order, Annie." Lisette paused to look at her tired old boss before continuing. "London will soon be awash with agents looking for Michael. They'll be tripping over one another because they'll all be following the same crumb trail. It'll be mayhem and you'll be vulnerable without your sentinels. Some of those coming to London would love to find you unguarded." Then turning back to Annie: "Assign all but eight sentinels to find Michael. I'll select which ones. You will of course be in charge of them. Okay, Annie, that's it, dismissed." The sentinel looked toward Madame Chairman for a confirmation nod and left the room.

"You wouldn't have done that to me in the old days."

"What? Your memory is playing tricks on you." They both laughed.

"Make sure we find Michael and bring him home safe and sound and in one piece."

"Of course I will. Brandy?"

"Yes please!" exclaimed Madame Chairman with emphasis. "Do you suppose it's okay for us to wash our tablets down with brandy? Apparently with some of them you aren't meant to…"

"In our state what the hell can it matter? What's it going to do? Kill us? You know, Margaret, I often gargle with your best brandy?" They laughed again.

"Annie is a doubler. Did you know?"

"Of course I know. That's precisely why I put her in charge of looking out for your safety. I want her where I can keep an eye on her. I'll clean your favourite chromium-plated Brownings for you. We don't want any misfires at a critical moment. We've had too many of those in the past, haven't we?" Madame Chairman wondered exactly to what Lisette was referring before concluding she was probably alluding to her love life which had been full of misfires. Lisette could always be guaranteed to bring things back to sex.

The two old friends – no, not friends, it's hard to say what they were – reminisced into the small hours.

DARK POOLS

London, 12th May

1120 BST.
London Metropolitan Police's Special Incident Call Centre.

"Have you noticed that since that Russian bloke was snatched those lot showed up?"

"Yeah, and they only seem to be interested in him and none of the others. What's going on do you reckon?"

"I reckon they're Russian spies. You know what they're like. See it all the time on the telly."

"Russian spies? Are you serious? If they're Russian spies they're not very good at keepin' a low profile then, are they?"

"Well… maybe MI6 or MI5 or the other lot, whatever they're called… GQHC, that's it."

"How do you know?"

"It's just suspicious, that's all I'm sayin'."

"We used to have a bit of a laugh comin' to work but not anymore. I'll be glad when this is all over and we can get good old Bernie back runnin' the place."

"I heard he's not comin' back. I heard…" An incoming call breaks up the conversation.

A Special Incident Desk operator answers the call in her clear, concise, clipped telephone-voice English: "Good afternoon, sorry, good morning, you're through to the Police's Special Incident Desk. May I take your name please?"

"There's no need for my name," replied the female caller in a slight foreign accent.

The Special Incident Desk operator put her mic on mute: "'ere, I've got a Russian on the line. You could be right you know, Sharon, they could be Russian spies." Following instructions not to press people too hard for their personal details the Special Incident Desk operator continued, "How can I help you? Do you have any information regarding the recent abductions?"

"I called a couple of days ago and I'm calling again to check if there's any progress in locating one of the men who has been abducted. His name is Mikhail Morozov." On hearing that name the Special Incident Desk operator raised her hand in the air to signal one of the 'new people' to join her. The agent sat down behind her, pushing her hair away from her ear and switching on her Bluetooth headset. "The caller sounds Russian, and she's asking about the Russian who was kidnapped."

The agent hiss-whispered to one of her colleagues, "Trace this call."

"I'm sorry, caller, I'm not at liberty to divulge details of the case over the phone. We're set up to receive information to pass on to officers investigating the abductions. Do you have any information concerning Mr Morozov or any of the other people who've been abducted recently?" There was no response to the question. "Updates regarding this and related matters are given out by the media. May I ask if you are a relative or friend of Mr Morozov?"

"Don't treat me like an idiot, I know you're stalling for time. Tell me please, when the scene of Mikhail's abduction was searched was there any sign of a walking stick… walking aid?"

"I'm afraid I'm not at liberty to divulge details of the case over the phone. If you could…" The line dropped. The agent tracing the call identified it had been made from a public phone box in Covent Garden. CCTV was immediately requested for the call area.

"Funny," said the Special Incident Desk operator to nobody in particular.

"What's funny?"

"She's the second or third person asking that same question. Sammy had a bloke asking the same thing a couple of days ago."

"What question?"

"You know, the one about whether a walking stick had been found at the scene of Mr Morozov's abduction."

"Why didn't you say something sooner? During the daily briefings perhaps?"

"Dunno, didn't seem like it was worthwhile mentioning, I mean, it's only a walking stick. Is it important then?"

"Pull the recordings of those calls and send them to me within the next ten minutes."

Yes, Your Majesty, thought the Special Incident Desk operator.

***

The agent left the call centre and took out a point-to-point mobile phone designed to operate through the dark pools equities trading network. "I think we may have a break. There have been at least three calls concerning a walking stick which Frost may have had with him at the time of his abduction. I'll double check but I don't recall there being any walking stick found at the scene but I'll review CCTV in case somebody lifted it before we got there."

"Who made the calls?"

"I'm looking into that right now but the call two minutes ago was made by a Russian female calling from a public phone box in Covent Garden."

"Really? Covent Garden? There must be dozens of CCTV cameras within a couple of hundred yards of that location. I'll lay you any wager you like that CCTV will come up blank. Being connected with Frost she's bound to be a professional." The dark pools controller wildly overestimated Svetlana's ability to wipe out CCTV coverage of a whole area of London but she had at least disguised herself, entering shops shortly before and immediately after calls to change her look. That was it, that was the extent of her cunning.

"Her call probably indicates Frost wasn't alone while living in London. Do we have an address yet?"

"We're looking into that."

"We seem to be looking into a lot of things, don't we? Keep looking. He must have had a home base somewhere. You do realise the feminine of Morozov is Morozova. Is that name being checked too?"

"Yes of course. There are hundreds of Morozovs and Morozovas in London, it's a common Russian surname. We're about sixty percent of the way through the list."

"I assume you're checking addresses nearest the abduction location followed by those along the Jubilee Line first…? Hello, are you still there?"

"Sorry, I was momentarily distracted. Yes, we are of course checking locations along the Jubilee Line first," she lied. *Damnit… Jubilee Line stations. Of course.* She coughed and then continued, "I'll verify the search pattern regarding the prioritisation of locations and get back to you."

"Call me twice daily with updates." The call dropped. It was impossible to say where the call was picked up from as it was routed through six or more countries and bounced off a number of satellites. The dark pools controller could have been in the same building as her for all she knew.

Shit, she thought, *I knew we should have used our own people on the phones.* The agent made another call, this time on her MI5 mobile: "Hi, it's me. Just a thought. I assume we're checking for Frost's, or rather Morozov's, address starting nearest the abduction location?"

"Of course."

"But you've drawn a blank so far? Yes? So, how about this? How about the next priority is to look for addresses for Morozovs or Morozovas living closest to stations along the Jubilee Line?"

"Morozovas? What's that all about?"

A horrible realisation dawned on the agent. She took her mobile away from her mouth, squeezing it very tightly while mouthing a massive silent scream. Regaining her composure she continued, "Yes, Morozova, it's the feminine form of Morozov. You know, in case he was living with somebody."

"That wasn't in the briefing notes. We've been looking for a Mr Morozov not a Mrs Morozova. I'll start checking out any Morozovas and get back to you." Before the agent could say anything else the line went dead.

***

An Organisation faction conversation

"Ladies and Gentlemen, an interesting development," announced the dark pools controller. "There's a possibility Mr Frost may have taken some help with him into whatever hole he's being held in. Apparently there have been several calls made to the London police's incident room asking whether Mr Morozov had a walking stick with him at the time of his abduction." The dark pools controller let out a snort of derision. The gathered group did likewise.

One of the group called out, "If he does have it with him, he could fight his way out... perhaps getting himself killed in the process or maybe he'll slaughter his captors... and probably the other abductees too. Then we take him after he escapes." Everybody offered an opinion at the same time.

A loud voice emerged from the shout-debate: "He might be so old and infirm, given his advancing years," this snide remark produced sniggers from the group, "that he has no fight left in him and he's just sitting there waiting to receive God's justice. He's no spring chicken after all." After a short pause she continued over the hubbub, "There's something disconcertingly James Bondish about delaying the execution of one's captives which never seems to turn out well in the movies. I say they should just get on with it and kill him rather than discover what he has tucked away in that weird head of his." Mock applause.

"Hmmm. That would be preferable were we not to be the first to find him. On a slightly related topic, do we know who faked the messages authorising the Russian Embassy to issue denials about the émigré status of Morozov?" Shaking of heads from around the group. None had any clue who'd done it. "I'm getting the feeling that somebody is playing games with us. Let us find out who it is and introduce them to the Irishman and his friend. They'll like that."

"What about Madame Chairman?" called out one of the group as some were making to leave the meeting.

"What about her?"

"Is there any news on her hunt for Frost?"

"She's no nearer to finding him than we are, or the French for that matter."

"What about the Americans and the Russians? What are they doing?"

"As you know, the Russians have sided with Madame Chairman. It's obvious they're trying to find him for themselves but she'll realise that too. The Americans on the other hand seem to be playing a rather different game than expected. I'd have thought they'd have wanted him dead but apparently not so. There are several rumours flying round as to why they now want him alive."

"Could you share those rumours with us?"

"Not at the moment, old thing, I don't want to set any hares running. It might all be a bluff and in any case it doesn't change our position."

"If Madame Chairman…"

"Stop going on about Madame Chairman," he screamed. "She's a decrepit old woman and a spent force. She can hardly leave her house for goodness' sake. She was fortunate to survive the…" He stopped and returned to the original topic, "We will stop at nothing to acquire Michael Frost and we'll destroy anybody or anything that gets in our way, including Madame Chairman and her sentinels. That's it, meeting over. Everybody out except Lisette."

A faction conversation

"Well, what's the latest?"

"I love the way you always ask open questions like that, leaving me to decide what it is I think you want to know. Fishing?" He made no reply, leaving Lisette to carry on speaking. "The Americans are asking questions about ISBJ. They're wondering why none of their doublers inside established Islamist groups have heard of them before. They're also wondering why statements of denial about the existence of ISBJ haven't been broadcast. They're thinking ISBJ isn't real. What are you…"

"Don't worry about ISBJ… or the Americans… or anybody else. It'll all soon be over, only a couple of weeks to go."

"Good. I think she's getting suspicious… of me, I mean, not…"

"She's always been suspicious of you but never quite suspicious enough to do anything about you. Lucky you, I say."

"Where's the Irishman?"

"He's still in America, I believe," he lied and Lisette knew it. For a moment she thought she might just end it here. End it now. All she had to do was let slip her .38 from her sleeve. Instinct told her the time was not yet right. She let herself out.

MARGARET'S STORY – HOW SHE BECAME A ROTHERAM

London

1st September 1939

The Noelle-Neumanns welcomed their daughter Alice to the world on the same day as the LeForts welcomed their first set of twins. That same day Hitler invaded Poland, after the Organisation gave him a nudge to get things started.

The Organisation hardly impacts the lives of people such as the Noelle-Neumanns. It doesn't need to because families like theirs are so busy watching over their empires they have little time to look around and notice things they're better off not noticing. Nevertheless, they are its unknowing servants. If any of the Noelle-Neumann clan does happen to look around they will not survive to tell the tale. Though a very wealthy and influential family, the Noelle-Neumanns have never numbered among the four hundred.

What a world of privilege and luxury little Alice had ahead of her. Just as with her elder half-sisters she would want for nothing. Mr Noelle-Neumann had two daughters from a previous marriage and, despite war now being inevitable, he was determined that the new-born would follow their life's path.

As soon as he found out his new wife was pregnant, he set

the family machine in motion. They entered Alice's name onto the rolls of the same schools her elder half-sisters had attended and they even checked for suitable male children born from 1930 onwards for when the time came for her to marry. She'd have some say in the matter, so long as her future husband came from the list.

***

The Noelle-Neumanns had made their fortune, over the past four hundred years, in Germany, Switzerland, Austria, Hungary, Italy and France and this branch took the family business to England in 1933 after the death of Frederik's wife, Anastasia. He set up home in Surrey with his daughters. They weren't great party goers but they enjoyed the culture, society and entertainment London had to offer. It was cleaner and purer than the decadence of Berlin and not gilded like the gaudiness of Paris which somehow managed to pass itself off as chic.

***

Frederik never found out how his first wife died. He wasn't allowed to see the post-mortem report.

Being unable to find out how his wife had met her end ate Frederik up inside. The family decided he needed to leave Berlin for his sanity's sake. They'd wanted to expand into England for some time and the tragic events surrounding Anastasia's demise were the catalyst for them doing so. Also, Frederik needed to get away before he said or did something which might lead to his arrest or worse.

The whole family helped set up the business in London. They found suitable offices and worked tirelessly to recruit staff, set up contracts and generally take the burden off Frederik's shoulders so he could spend time with his daughters.

Things didn't work out as intended though. Instead of taking the time to settle himself and his daughters in their new home, Frederik worked night and day, driven on by self-pity. He simply couldn't forget Anastasia or take his mind off thoughts of what might have happened to her. The family implored him not to neglect his daughters and encouraged him to take some time away from the business with them. He interpreted this as them wanting to take the business away from him. To stay in control, he doubled and redoubled his efforts and saw even less of his daughters. With all he'd been through and all that he was still going through he collapsed and was rushed to hospital where he was diagnosed with extreme physical, mental and emotional exhaustion. He was an empty shell.

A Noelle-Neumann family conversation

"At least he's getting some much needed rest."
"If you can call hospital rest."
"We'll have the girls come and stay with us, they'll like that. They won't have to put up with…"
"What are we going to do about Frederik?"
"What do you mean?"
"You know very well what I mean. He's incapable of running the business."
"Oh, don't take that away from him too, not at a time like this."
"I, for one, will not hear of it," he lied.
"Over my dead body," another lied.
"Have it your way for now but if he…"
"We'll demand he takes a holiday and decide after his return."

***

The family elders visited Frederik in hospital and gave him an ultimatum. He either takes a holiday with his daughters or he'll be removed from the board. He understood they were doing this for his own good and so agreed to take some time away from the business.

They went travelling in Anastasia's Russian homeland. It was more of a pilgrimage than a holiday, recalled the girls, but they had a wonderful family time together despite the Bolsheviks arresting them on four occasions. The girls had their father back and he had his daughters back and to keep the family together he decided to leave the business. He'd all but lost interest in the family firm anyway and so resolved to resign from the board upon their return to England. He planned to go to America where he felt they could make a fresh start.

However, upon his eventual return to the London office, he discovered that the business was thriving thanks to somebody he hadn't noticed before. She was a bright young office manager who'd just been promoted around the time he'd left for Russia a year earlier. Now, after only a comparatively short time, she was running the whole show. She was smart, educated, diplomatic and kind and knew how to get the best out of people. She ran things by consensus so people willingly fell in behind her. Frederik was astonished and enchanted.

Having seen how well everything was being run, Frederik promoted the bright young office manager to the position of financial director. They worked closely together and over the next eighteen months their feelings grew toward one another. In late 1936 he took her to meet his daughters on some pretext, which they both forgot the premise of, each telling them a different story as to why this delightful young woman was walking in the park with them. The twins were not so naïve as to think there was nothing going on between their father and his financial director. They were happy for him. He announced his engagement to the new love in his life in the early spring of 1937 and they were married early the following year. They so wanted a child together to make their lives even more perfect.

A Noelle-Neumann family conversation

"What do you make of Frederik's announcement? I'm very happy for him," he lied.

"Oh, it's wonderful news, isn't it? I hope the girls aren't feeling too put out by it all though," she lied.

"I don't know what you are talking about. It's a disaster. She's not from one of the old families. Her father is a factory worker for goodness' sake."

"Aunty, he's a factory owner, there's a big difference."

"What does it matter if they love one another?"

"What does it matter? Don't you ever go doing anything similar or you'll find yourself cut off. The very idea. Who the hell does she think she is marrying, a Noelle-Neumann? She'll never be one of the family. She'll never be a Noelle-Neumann in my eyes."

"The world is changing, Grandma."

"Grandma? Grandma? Who is this grandma you are referring to? If it's me then I'm your Grandmother. Do you see what's happening? Do you? The whole world is collapsing. There are no standards anymore. Everything is so vulgar."

"Come on, Grandma, get with the times. This is the 1930s. I love you to pieces but you're such an outrageous snob."

"I'm not a snob, ask any of the servants. I am simply unwilling to lower my standards nor will I accept riff-raff such as Frederik's new fiancée. She's only after his money, you know. She'll never get a penny of it if I have any say in the matter. She'll never be a Noelle-Neumann in my eyes."

"She's good for Frederik. And she's very smart too. Look at what she's done with the business. We've all benefitted because of her."

"Rubbish. Total rubbish. How can you believe that a woman, a woman of all things, could do it all by herself, even with a hundred like her? A woman, pah!"

"Women can do all sorts of things you know, Uncle; we can vote, go to university, travel, climb mountains, fly aeroplanes and drive cars; race them even. On top of all that we can have babies. So there."

"Where do you get this from, child?"

"Times are changing and I think Celia is perfect for Uncle Freddie."

"She'll never be a Noelle-Neumann in my eyes."

***

In the early months of 1940 the Noelle-Neumanns faced the possibility of internment despite half their ancestry being French. This was largely due to Frederik's old pals back in Berlin being amongst those who were running the Nazi war machine. It was Frederik himself who, to prove his loyalty and to keep his family out of the internment camps, came up with the idea of him spying for the British. He hated the Nazis and had been glad to leave Berlin when he had, for obvious reasons.

***

On 8th June 1940, under the cover of darkness, Frederik Noelle-Neumann came ashore at Antwerp docks and made his way to a house the family owned in the Berchem district. When he arrived, he was surprised to find a relative living there. This cousin was one of several black sheep of the Noelle-Neumann clan. The cousin was immediately suspicious. *How could Freddie have got out of England?* he asked himself and, more interestingly, *Why did he leave England?* Frederik confided in his errant cousin, telling him that as he'd been under threat of internment he'd escaped England by stealing a small fishing boat and sailing it to Antwerp. His intention, he said, was to make his way to Berlin to assist the Nazis in any way he could. He said he felt certain they could find a use for him. All the cousin was interested in was whether he would be allowed to remain in the house as he had nowhere else to go.

This unexpected turn of events was just the lesson Frederik needed to make him aware of the danger he now faced and how carefully he'd have to tread in future. He'd heard the expression 'expect the unexpected' and thought it a stupid thing to say but now he understood exactly what it meant. He left the house in his cousin's care.

Shortly after Frederik departed for the railway station, the cousin went to the local Gestapo HQ and alerted them to Frederik's presence and his concerns about his story. Frederik Noelle-Neumann was picked up four hours later at Antwerp railway station. A search of him and his belongings turned up false papers. He was taken away by the Gestapo never to be seen again.

The Gestapo allowed the cousin to remain in the house in Berchem. They made clear the price he would have to pay to remain out of their hands. Vigilant locals, ever quick to spot the tell-tale signs of collaborators, made plans to rid themselves of the traitor in their midst.

Eight days after he had sold Frederik out, the cousin was walking between buildings along the quayside of Antwerp docks. As he neared a junction with a side road, four men moved to block his path. His guilty conscience immediately guessed why they were there and what their business was with him. He turned and quickened his pace. Before he made the thirty metres to the opposite end of the road another group of four men appeared and blocked his path. He thought of crying out but in his moment of hesitation the first group had closed in on him with one of the men placing an oily hand across his mouth.

The men didn't speak a word to one another. They just stared at him. He heard the clanking of a metal chain behind him and then felt a crushing blow to the back of his head. When he regained consciousness he found himself lying on the floor of a bonded warehouse, wrapped in chains. He made to speak but only a muffled sound came from his gagged mouth. The oily gag was removed as a priest entered the room.

An interrogation conversation

"We know all about you, Mr Neumann, and what you did to your cousin Frederik. We have our spies too," he confided. "Tell me who you spoke with when you went to see the Gestapo. What did you say to them? What did you hear while you were with them? Who did you see while you were there? Who can you name as a traitor?"

"I don't know what you're talking about. You've made a mistake. I'm no spy."

"Mr Neumann, you're a collaborator. Don't bother denying it. We already know this. You went to the Gestapo of your own free will and told them about your cousin Frederik Noelle-Neumann. Don't bother lying to us. We know everything."

"Then you don't need anything from me," responded the cousin defiantly.

"I want to hear it from you. Tell me what you know. I want you to confess everything, my son. It'll be good for your immortal soul if you cleanse your conscience."

After a minute's consideration Mr Neumann spoke his last words: "Forgive me, Father, for I have sinned, it has been eight weeks since my last confession…"

Once he'd given up all he knew he was tossed, grunting through his oily rag gag, into the freezing waters of the Hansadok. It is impossible to swim wrapped in chains as he was. When he hit the bottom his body twisted and then turned for him to see the sun's light dancing on the surface of the water above. He counted seven head shapes peering through the ripples his body had made entering the water before his life light was extinguished.

***

Word of Frederik Noelle-Neumann's death was passed back to England via a network of brave Belgian and French resistance fighters. Once confirmed, the Ministry of War passed the tragic news on to the family. They didn't even bother telling them personally, which would have been the decent thing to do under the circumstances. They just sent them the usual telegram containing the words 'missing in action, presumed dead'.

The family never found out how Frederik Noelle-Neumann met his end nor did they ever get to know the cousin's part in it. Life for them all would never be the same again. Frederik's widow feared the plans they had for the girls would never be realised.

The thoughts some people have in such tragic circumstances can seem inappropriate. There's nothing wrong with them no matter how practical or pragmatic, rather than grief-stricken, they are. The future is something which figures highly on the list of thoughts of the living for obvious reasons: Where shall we live? How shall we survive? What shall I do with his clothes? Do his debts die with him? Was he having an affair? What if she wants to come to the funeral? What if…? Such thoughts following the death of a loved one shouldn't make the thinker feel guilty. Everybody has them.

Immediately after Celia received the telegram, relatives divided up the family businesses between themselves; piece by piece they took everything from her. "She's in no fit state to run the business," they said in justification of their actions. "We can't let all Freddie's hard work go to waste, can we?"

A Noelle-Neumann family conversation

"She's not even a real Noelle-Neumann, she only married into the name. Frederik was a Noelle-Neumann and so are his children but she is not."

"But Frederik loved her. That's why he married her. If I take your argument to its logical conclusion then I'm not a Noelle-Neumann either."

"Nonsense, you have breeding, darling."

"We cannot allow the children to suffer. I won't hear of it."

"He was going to leave her, you know."

"Rubbish. You're just saying that to…"

"Let's leave Freddie's wanderings out of this. In all conscience we cannot let Celia or the children suffer further. Little Alice is so sweet and she deserves the life she was born to. If nobody has any other suggestions I'll take Alice into my care until things have settled down," suggested the childless Audrey who was a Noelle-Neumann by birth but who was a Rotheram now.

"Oh, you just couldn't wait, could you? Hasn't she suffered enough? Now you want to take her children away from her."

"Not children, sister, child. Alice. The other two are quite grown and will be leaving the family home shortly, which will give Celia a chance to rebuild her life… with no children under her feet. I never liked the name Alice."

"She's drinking, you know. Quite heavily I hear."

"Can't say I blame her. She was so in love with Frederik but he's gone and she's alone."

"No, she's not alone. She has her children. Remember?"

"Yes, but how will they cope with a mother who's an alcoholic? No, it's better this way."

"What way?"

"Haven't you been listening? The two older girls will attend finishing school in Switzerland and young Alice will go and live with Audrey. It's for the best."

"Who mentioned anything about attending a finishing school in Switzerland?" asked the great-aunt who wasn't invited to a previous family conversation.

"Who'll talk to her? Who'll tell her?"

"Me, I'll talk with her. It's best coming from me. I've got to know her quite well. We're practically neighbours so it won't be that much of a wrench when Alice comes to live with me. I'll tell her she can come and visit Alice any time she pleases. She'll be much better off living with me. Imagine the education I can give her."

"What about the authorities?"

"I don't think we'll have any trouble with the authorities with the mother being a drunkard."

"Better to make it official though, I think. Don't you? I'll speak with the company lawyers tomorrow and get the ball rolling on the paperwork."

"Please don't do this."

"Do what, darling? It's for the good of everyone. You'll see. Now where did I leave my sherry?"

***

At the age of ten months, Alice Lavinia Arabella Noelle-Neumann went to live with Mr and Mrs Cyril Rotheram at their family home on the outskirts of Reigate in Surrey. The house was large and surrounded by lawns which were so perfect they resembled bowling greens. Beyond the lawns were shrubs and beyond the shrubs were wooded areas. In all, the house sat in eight acres of fine Surrey countryside.

Having lost everything she loved and held dear, Celia Noelle-Neumann went to live and work in London to help with the war effort.

***

Christmas 1940 was fast approaching and though there wasn't much cheer to be had everybody in the land was determined to celebrate as best they could under wartime conditions.

Churchill was constantly on the radio bolstering the morale of the country with rousing speeches delivered in his growling style. He'd even been out and about among the ordinary people of London and other cities which had been bombed in the Blitz.

In Liverpool he was photographed atop a mound of debris that had recently been the middle four houses in a terraced row. Cigar in hand, he'd shouted defiantly to the gathered crowd, "They shall never defeat us. We can take it." A mother who'd lost all but one of her eleven children in the bombing raid which had demolished her terraced house shouted back, "You might be able to take it, mate, but we're fed up with it." She was removed by bodyguards.

***

Opinions varied between the factions of an increasingly fragmented Organisation. They ranged from jubilation that the war had finally got underway to bewilderment as to how another war could have started so soon after the last one to anger that it had not stopped Hitler when it had the chance to. The world was in turmoil once again but that was just how many in the Organisation liked it.

***

Celia wrote to the Rotherams about her coming to see Alice on Christmas day. They ignored the first letter and, it being wartime, Celia assumed it had got lost so she wrote a second. The reply she received devastated her.

Dearest Celia

Thank you for your letter of the 15th inst.

We are all so proud of what you are doing for the war effort. We all do our bit of course but what you are doing puts the rest of us to shame. You'll be delighted to learn that Alice is in fine health and thriving under our careful supervision.

She spoke for the first time a couple of days ago. She called me Mummy and today she called Cyril Daddy. Now that she's started talking there's no stopping her! She rabbits on and on in a strange language we cannot comprehend one word of. We try to correct her but she doesn't seem to understand. Oh well, early days yet!

Until recently she was crawling on the floor and pulling herself up on furniture, leaving sticky marks all over the place. We put a stop to that by the use of cotton mitts from the local hospital. Apparently they use them on children who might otherwise scratch themselves.

Just took a break from writing as I was interrupted by the nanny. Apparently Alice just took her first unaided steps and she wanted me to see. Only four I understand but it's a start, I suppose. She fell in the end and cried a little but the nanny soothed her. It'll be teeth next, I'm led to believe.

About you coming here for Christmas. I'm not so sure that is such a good idea. Alice is just starting to settle and I feel seeing you will unsettle her. Perhaps we could pencil in Easter? Easter isn't too far away so it should not be any hardship for you.

All my love

Audrey XXX

After reading the letter for a fourth time Celia walked back to her digs in a numb daze. As she neared her lodgings one of many stray bombs dropped by the Luftwaffe that night exploded near her. She wasn't killed outright, she lingered for days before passing. Lying in her hospital bed she drifted in and out of consciousness and as she did so her mind re-read the contents of Audrey's letter. Alice was thriving under careful supervision. But what of love? Was there any love in Alice's life? Alice spoke her first words. Alice took her first steps which were witnessed by a nanny. She was Alice's mother. She should have been there for the things a mother should be there for in her children's lives. How she wanted not to think her thoughts but she couldn't control them or empty them from her head.

Just before passing, Celia suffered the cruellest of her thoughts. Had she failed to notice Audrey's letter sitting on the hallstand that fateful morning she might never have read its cruel contents. She only spotted it after she'd turned to speak to another lodger who'd disturbed a pile of papers there. For a moment she considered not reading the letter until she returned to her digs after work. Instead, she put the letter in her handbag and took it with her. *If only I hadn't turned to complain about the papers being knocked off the hallstand. If only...* A single tear rolled down her cheek followed by a constant stream falling on both. She heard a nurse call to the ward sister, telling her that the patient was crying. "She can't be crying, she's dead."

***

On hearing of the death of Alice's mother, Cyril and Audrey became frantic at the thought of Nazi bombs taking their Margaret away from them. They'd stopped calling her Alice two days after stealing her and set wheels in motion to have her name legally changed. The company's lawyers were handling it. By the time Alice was eighteen months old her name was changed to Margaret Rotheram.

With a little one in the household, they were just like all the other families in East Reigate. They ignored the vicious rumours which had started to circulate about how they'd come to be the guardians of the little baby girl who'd come to live with them.

A limited attendance Noelle-Neumann family conversation

"Shocking, and awful. Just awful."

"Poor Celia. At least it was quick."

"What? Quick? She lingered for very nearly a week."

"I understand she didn't suffer at least."

"How do you know? What do we know? None of us went to see her and don't say you didn't know. She had you down as next of kin for her job with the ministry. We knew. We just didn't go. Guilty consciences, I say. Guilty consciences all."

"What we did was wrong but…"

"But nothing. I'm sure it's occurred to you all, as it has to me, that if we hadn't done what we did then Celia would still be alive today and living with her… living with her daughters."

"They're not all hers."

"I'm not going to argue with you. It's daughters, plural. She was Frederik's wife and the older girls loved her. We killed Celia as surely as if we'd dropped that bomb on her ourselves." All heads bent to the floor.

"What do you propose we do about it? We can't undo what's been done."

"We must look after little Alice. First thing is to have her taken away from Audrey and sent to live with relatives on Celia's side of the family. It's the natural thing to do."

"Audrey will fight it. You know what she's like. Let's leave her there with Audrey but we'll…"

"Are you insane? That poor little girl has been through enough. We must have her taken away from Audrey as quickly as possible. She thinks she's dealing with a dolly not a baby. She's not fit to be a… babysitter let alone a mother."

"It's settled then. We'll have a word with Audrey and…"

"We? Who's this we? I'm not going anywhere near her, you know what she's like."

"I'll go by myself then."

"Good, but leave my name out of it."

"And mine."

"My advice is to leave well enough alone. You know what she's like and what she'll do if we try to take the baby from her. She won't hold back. She'll drop us all in it with the authorities… right across Europe."

"In case you hadn't noticed, there's a war going on; the authorities have got better things to be getting on with."

"But that won't stop them prosecuting criminals otherwise there'd be a free for all. We'll end up in prison for certain and in times of war I dare say some of us will be executed for what we've done… what we've been involved in."

"I'm still going to see her."

The conversation between Audrey and the niece went very badly. Audrey threatened the niece with what she could expect if she did something which might cause her to lose Margaret.

"Who?"

"Margaret. I never liked the name Alice."

The niece started rumours about how the Rotherams had come by their little baby girl. She did so in the hope that they'd be investigated. She wrote to child protection leagues and even met with one of their representatives. That was her biggest mistake. The representative was a Rotheram family acquaintance who contacted them about the activities of their niece. Audrey followed through on her threat. The niece was arrested and charged. On remand she suffered fatal injuries while working on a lathe turning gun parts for the war effort.

***

The war was hotting up. Thoughts of how best to protect and keep little Margaret safe were uppermost in the Rotherams minds. They couldn't bear the thought of sending her away on the evacuation programme. The nightly bombing raids, however, convinced them they must do something.

If she were to be sent away, where should they send her? The Noelle-Neumanns had family and other connections across Europe and beyond. Should they send her to a neutral country? Ireland? Spain? Switzerland? They liked the thought of Switzerland most as that was where she would be finishing her education. Most of all they wanted to remain close to her. They made plans to travel to Switzerland. They'd been guaranteed safe passage but Audrey had a bad premonition about the journey and those plans went up in smoke. What about nearer home? Wales perhaps? They considered time and time again what to do when Cyril, unusually, spoke up. He suggested that they build an air raid shelter in the woods beyond the shrubbery of the garden. They could dig it deep and cover it with tons of concrete and steel mesh. Audrey thought about Cyril's idea for all of ten seconds and told him to stop dithering and get on with it.

Cyril Rotheram acquired thousands of black-market rock-hard engineering bricks along with hundreds of bags of concrete and tons of steel meshing. He paid a local builder to construct a bomb shelter in the woods. It took the builder and eight labourers just over two weeks to complete the work and run an electrical supply to it. When it all was finished the Rotherams held a grand opening party, something which was quite out of character for them. The nanny said it would be a good thing to do because it would introduce Margaret to other children and would help dispel the "horrible rumours" that were flying around once the neighbours met them.

For the grand opening, the bomb shelter was lit with candles for atmosphere. Carrot cake was served with orange juice. All the nanny's idea. Audrey thought the nanny was having a few too many ideas lately. She didn't like the way she looked at Cyril either.

The nanny's ideas worked a treat. The rumours ceased almost completely and local parents even got involved in decorating the bomb shelter to make it as light and bright and homely as they could. They brought along toys, including a massive dolls' house complete with miniature furniture and figures. The bomb shelter became the play HQ of the local children. An unforeseen bonus was, for the first time, as a couple, Cyril and Audrey Rotheram socialised with people who were nothing to do with the family. They recognised the potential and ensured that everything they did for Margaret they too could benefit from.

Few bombs or doodlebugs landed on that part of Surrey during WWII and, of those that did, none landed within a couple of miles of the Rotheram bomb shelter.

***

Throughout the war years, children who'd remained at home instead of being evacuated went around to the Rotherams' house almost daily. They got the builders in again. This time to dig a swimming pool. Margaret fast became the most popular child in the neighbourhood. The children who came to play at the Rotherams' house were a socially diverse lot, from the poorest and ill-educated to the over-privileged and classically educated. The kids just mucked in with one another, oblivious to the pressures their parents felt, especially those who were mixing above their social station. The Rotherams did their best to make their social inferiors feel unwelcome. Eventually they disappeared off the scene as did their socially inferior offspring. Margaret missed the kids who disappeared, preferring most of them to most of those who hadn't disappeared.

Several of the older children had ponies. One of them rode her fourteen-hander to the play HQ one day and an explosion went off in Margaret's head. She'd seen horses and ponies go by in the lane but had never been allowed to get near them. Mum and Dad felt they were dangerous animals, likely to kick out at any moment. Audrey was horrified when she and Cyril paid the play

HQ a visit later that day. She demanded the young gal take her pony away. Margaret, for the first time, answered her mother back. The other children froze. They were more than a little wary of Mr and Mrs Rotheram. They were scared of them truth be told. Some thought the days of the play HQ were over and were surprised when Mr Rotheram relented and told the girl that she and her delightful pony were welcome to stay. He dragged his wife away by her elbow.

"Don't you see?"

"See what?"

"Ponies. Girls and ponies. Perfect for Margaret, socially speaking. And for us too of course. And they'll keep her away from boys."

"But they are so dangerous. One hears all the time of dreadful accidents involving them. They throw their riders. They hate being ridden, you know."

"Nonsense." He hadn't said that to her in a long time. "I see people riding in the lane all the time and never have I seen anybody get thrown or hurt. We should get her a pony."

"But she's too young. She's…"

"She's a Surrey girl and Surrey girls and ponies just go together. How about this: we take her to a riding school and see how she gets on. Who knows, she might hate it. But at least we'll know and she'll be safe in their expert hands." He glanced at his worried-looking wife, "We'll meet so many of the right sort of people. The right type of people. People who can do us good."

Audrey wasn't entirely convinced but agreed that Cyril could take Margaret to a local riding school to see if she liked riding. What neither of them recognised in Margaret answering Audrey back was the start of their precious daughter rebelling against them. It was to become a battle of wills.

***

After the war was over, Margaret attended a local school for a term before Audrey enrolled her in a prestigious private school close to Reigate so she wouldn't have to board. Audrey couldn't have abided Margaret boarding. The school took gals from four to fourteen. Academically the school was middle of the road but socially and sports-wise it was excellent. Margaret was set for the next eight years. Those years were a blissfully uneventful and happy time for her. No broken bones. No bruises. No scabbed knees. No dirty clothes. No scuffed shoes. "Perfect," said Audrey. "Perfect." The one aspect of her daughter which Audrey was disappointed with was her total lack of musical talent.

Margaret socialised with nice children who had nice parents and did very nicely at school, which she represented at most sports, including hockey and netball, also becoming Surrey schools' under-sixteen record holder at cross country, four hundred and forty yards hurdles and the mile. Many of her records lasted well into the 1990s.

At all times she behaved in a civilised and polite manner, which made Audrey and Cyril feel very proud. They couldn't have chosen a better child. Had they witnessed her language and her ways when with her school or pony club friends they would have been shocked and appalled. Margaret was just doing what all the other gals were doing and knew enough to keep it out of the line of sight of Mum and Dad.

Mum and Dad were moulding Margaret into a little Audrey. She'd attended garden parties and dinner parties from an early age. While at dinner parties she entered into intellectual conversations in between courses. *All good foundations for her*, they thought. And they were right but not in ways they could possibly have foreseen. While socialising with the right sort of people, Margaret came to the attention of a local man who would change her life beyond all recognition.

***

For her tenth birthday, Audrey and Cyril bought her a Palomino pony to make her little Surrey girl life complete. Overnight she'd become a southern princess and was in danger of becoming a spoilt brat but she was made of better stuff than that.

MICHAEL'S STORY - STREET KID LIFE

The Organisation relied on the old ways to keep control: the ways of fostering despair, defeat and desperation among the masses through their political and trades union familiars but times were changing. The old ways allowed it to function as it pleased because the people didn't have time to raise their heads and look about them to see what was going on in the world. Which was exactly how the Organisation liked it.

Results-wise, the first quarter of the twentieth century was looking okay, not fantastic but okay, so why change? The Boer War had come to a satisfactory conclusion; troublesome Freddie Ferdinand had been bumped off; the Kaiser had been sent packing; the Great War had been profitable and, with its help, the Bolsheviks had won power in Russia, overthrowing Kerensky and slaughtering the Romanovs, plus there was a new chap starting to look the part in Germany. What a cracking start to the century; the Organisation hadn't had one like it for a long time.

Governors were congratulating each other with slaps on their old fart backs over the recruitment of an operative whose life they'd saved during the Boer War. They had high hopes that Mr Churchill would achieve his potential and have a long and illustrious career in politics. He was tipped for the top and with the Organisation's help he'd get there.

***

At the end of WWII, the Organisation, furious at the cancellation of its wartime aluminium fabrication contracts, adapted its production lines to produce beer barrels and other products essential to post-war Britain. At the time, it suspected the French were behind the sudden cancellation of their MoW contracts. Intelligence indicated the French splinter was making plans to marginalise the Organisation from future prosperity across an open European market. An open market is a dangerous place as far as the Organisation was concerned but it didn't want to miss out on opportunities.

Whether times are good or times are bad, times are always good for the Organisation. Not so for the barrel-coopering industry which, after a millennium of existence, was wiped out overnight by the Organisation's move into aluminium beer barrel production.

***

After meeting in the Grafton Ballrooms and following a courtship lasting a year, Michael Frost's mother, Margaret, and his father, Patrick, married in 1951.

The forebears of both families had migrated to Liverpool from southern Ireland during the potato famine. In the eighty intervening years they'd moved from the starvation line to the poverty line. Patrick was one of sixteen children but he was the only male child to survive beyond 1935. Margaret was one of ten children; her family had identical levels of child mortality to Patrick's.

On 7th October 1952 Michael Frost was born at Margaret's family home in poverty-stricken Everton; he was a bonny baby weighing in at a healthy 9lb 10ozs. Margaret's parents' house was large and as all their other children had left home by then there was plenty of room for the Frosts. They even discussed staying in the house and Michael going to Margaret's old school which was only thirty foot from their front door. But the amateur social engineers of Liverpool's City Council had other ideas. All the houses in Everton were bulldozed flat before Michael reached school age. The amateur social engineers isolated the city centre from the rest of Liverpool. It became an island in a sea of broken bricks. They did a better job of destroying Liverpool than the Luftwaffe had.

***

The little school opposite the house held bad memories for Margaret. Being almost totally deaf from the age of three, after contracting pneumonia, she'd been treated very cruelly by the children at the school in the way only children can be cruel. Fortunately she found a friend in the playground one day who protected her from the children's antics. They remained life-long friends and were maids-of-honour at each other's weddings.

***

At age twenty months Michael contracted whooping cough. He whooped and whooped and whooped for two weeks solid.

After the first week of non-stop whooping, Michael's nana intervened with an old wives' remedy of placing hot tar in an enamel bowl and having Michael breathe in the fumes while holding a damp tea towel over his head. She felt she needed to try something, anything, as Michael was very weak. Nobody realised that he was on the mend and that the hot tar treatment would have long-term consequences for his health. It caused a thinning of the lining of the nasal passages, making him prone to heavy nose bleeds, as well as damaging his developing lungs. In the fighting streets of Liverpool's docklands having a nose that bled easily was a big disadvantage when it came to sorting out differences street kid style.

Relieved at Michael coming through his whooping cough scare, Patrick and Margaret began discussing their concerns about their son. Despite him being nearly two, Michael hadn't spoken a word so far and, what's more, he never laughed or cried. He just went about his life seemingly in his own little world. They didn't think he was deaf. He looked at people when he was being spoken to but through his blank stare nobody could gauge what he was thinking or feeling.

To get to the bottom of what was going on with their son, Patrick and Margaret took him to see a specialist. Nothing was found wrong with Michael that would explain his lack of speech or anything else. Physically, Michael seemed fine, so why wasn't he talking or laughing or crying? He seemed to know what was being said to him as when asked if he was hungry he'd nod his head or shake it if something was said he didn't like. Recalling the dreadful treatment she'd suffered as a child at the hands of cruel children, Margaret didn't want Michael suffering in the same way. To keep him safe Margaret made a recluse of Michael by keeping him indoors for over a year.

***

After Michael was born, Margaret had been told by doctors that he would act as her ears. He'd listen out for the things she couldn't hear. A knock at a door. An oncoming bus. These thoughts pleased her but what did it all mean in light of his lack of speech, especially as she and Patrick were thinking about having another child? Would number two turn out to be the same as their number one son? Little did they realise but Margaret was already pregnant so the question was moot.

***

On 5th December 1954 the Frosts welcomed their second son, Thomas, to the world. By comparison with Michael's birth weight he was scrawny at 6lb 2oz. During the first year of his life Thomas was in and out of hospital a half dozen times. He finally came home to stay on 4th December 1955 just in time for his first birthday the following day.

The whole family were so excited as few had expected Thomas to survive. They gathered at Margaret's parents' house to celebrate a day many thought they would never see. There were ridiculous amounts of presents bought for Thomas, most of which the givers could ill afford, but it was a special birthday for a special little boy and, besides, being poor meant they knew how to suffer through financial sacrifice as a demonstration of their love and devotion.

At the end of a rousing chorus of 'Happy Birthday to You', Michael walked over to his little brother, kissed him on the cheek and said, as clear as a bell, "Happy birthday, Thomas." The whole house fell into a stunned silence. Had Michael really just spoken? Margaret, of course, hadn't heard a thing above the noise of the singing but she was aware something was going on judging by the looks on the faces of the family. Patrick grabbed her by her elbows and, looking straight at her, spoke with exaggerated mouth shapes: "Michael just spoke. He said happy birthday to Thomas." Margaret couldn't believe it. Part of her told her that they were just playing one of their cruel jokes on the deaf girl. Those thoughts were soon washed away as she could see with her own eyes how shocked everybody was. Michael refused to repeat his act of speaking despite the urgings of relatives and by the look in his eyes he showed no sign of recognition of what he'd done. "Leave him alone. Leave him alone," shouted Margaret, scooping Michael up and carrying him off to the cellar kitchen, away from the crowded parlour.

She sat Michael down on one end of an old threadbare burgundy-coloured crushed velvet sofa. The one with the rusty springs poking out through the fabric. It had been a very grand sofa in its day. It was the very sofa from which Michael had first seen the demon; It was the terrifying one with the yellow eyes… he had watched It as It made Its way down the last treads of the stairs… hungry looking… snarling and slavering …. drool dripping from Its maul… rotting flesh hanging from the gaps between Its broken fangs… never taking Its eyes off him for a universal second… always keeping Its head turned to keep him in Its sight… never stopping on Its journey… finally disappearing through the door leading down into the dark, dank, damp cellar. Margaret looked directly at her number one son. "Can you hear me, Michael? Did you just speak, son? Did you just wish Thomas a happy birthday?" Her questions received a blank unknowing stare. There was no look of recognition whatsoever in his eyes; Michael hopped off the sofa and went back into the parlour to get some birthday cake.

For the next eight minutes everybody tried to get Michael to speak again. Each wanted to be the one who Michael talked to. But there was no more speaking from him that day and even though he wasn't looking in the least bit upset by the urgings of his relatives, Margaret decided enough was enough and anyway it was Thomas's special day so she kept Michael by her side for the rest of the party, shooing away anybody who approached him.

***

Two weeks later, Thomas came down with whooping cough and already being weak from months of hospital treatments it nearly saw him off. Mercifully he was spared his nana's old wives' cure. He made a full recovery within two weeks and apart from one minor bout of illness he had a medically incident free childhood.

***

Just before Easter 1958 the Frosts heard of a terraced house which had become available. It was in an appalling state of repair and technically it was a condemned property but due to the housing shortage brought about by the amateur social engineers they had no choice but to move in. Its previous occupants had been moved out by those same amateur social engineers to a new housing estate in Runcorn, a desolate place twenty miles from anybody or anything they knew.

The little terraced house was located just twelve yards from a busy main road called Great Homer Street, known to all as Greaty. During the previous four months, two local children had been run over and killed by buses while riding home-made steering carts across Greaty. Such was the fate of street kids when left to their own devices.

Next door to the Frosts lived a yappy little Jack Russell which took an instant dislike to Thomas. Whenever it was on the doorstep he would call for Michael to come and escort him past it as it never seemed to bark at him. In fact as soon as it caught sight of Michael it would run up to him, lay on the ground, roll over onto its back and invite Michael to tickle its tummy. Once, Thomas tried to join in the tummy tickling but the dog went rigid, bared its teeth and growled until he withdrew his hand.

Being from an enormously large Liverpool Irish family, it was no surprise that four families in the street were related to the Frosts, including their immediate neighbours, the Mulhalls. They had seven children, all of whom were older than Michael.

***

One morning during his walk to school, Michael was confronted by the notorious Sharkey twins. They set on him for no reason he just stared at them while blood flowed from his nose. The flow of blood was exacerbated due to the lining of his nasal passages having been thinned by his nana's old wives' cure for whooping cough. Passers-by intervened in this one-sided battering of a little boy in short trousers and the Sharkey twins took off before they could be collared. On reaching school, Michael's nose continued bleeding; his pullover was absolutely saturated with blood. A teacher took him home straight away.

Upon seeing her number one son covered in blood, Margaret went into a blind panic. She'd never seen so much blood. Michael was looking very pale and so Margaret laid him down on the settee. She grabbed a wet flannel to wipe away the blood from his face and neck. The flannel was soon blood-sodden. She went to the kitchen sink to rinse it out. When she returned to the lounge there was a man sitting on the edge of the settee pinching Michael's nose closed.

"Excuse me, who are you please?" asked the ever polite Margaret.

"I'm Doctor Kerwan, I was next door when I heard about your son's nose bleed. Michael, isn't it?"

"Can you speak up please? I'm a bit hard of hearing." Margaret used this expression throughout her life because, according to her, she wasn't deaf, she was 'hard of hearing'. She could lip read but wasn't anywhere near as good at it as she thought she was because she had so few reference points for grown-up words. Despite her being almost totally deaf, Margaret never sought assistance for her deafness. In her mind she viewed contacting support groups for the deaf as admitting she was deaf which, of course, she wasn't, she was 'hard of hearing'. Doctor Kerwan repeated his words while mouthing them clearly.

Margaret replied, "He's alright, it's just a bit of a nose bleed, that's all. He'll be okay."

"Mrs Frost, this is a very severe nose bleed and could be dangerous for your son."

"Don't be daft." She immediately felt embarrassed at what she'd just said as in those days you didn't disrespect, question or doubt doctors. "I'm so sorry, Doctor Kerwan, I meant to say he'll be okay after he's had a lie down."

"Mrs Frost, Michael needs a little treatment at the hospital. His nose needs cauterising to prevent bad nose bleeds happening in the future. I'll write a note for you to take to the hospital." After writing the note, Dr Kerwan read it out to Margaret, asking her if she understood everything. She replied that she did and thanked him for his help.

A week later Michael had his nose cauterised. After scar tissue built up in his nasal passages he didn't suffer any more bad nose bleeds.

***

The little terraced house off Greaty was a lucky house for the Frosts and they were all very happy while living there. On 1st July 1958 the Frost boys were joined by a little sister, Rose. From the minute she arrived, Patrick was besotted with his daughter and she would want for nothing from him throughout her life. Though the boys were dressed by charities right up until 1963, little Rose 'Queenie' Frost was dressed in new clothes and shoes and given toys that were the envy of the street. Thomas grew up resenting the treatment lavished on Queen Rose by Patrick but Michael was oblivious to it all as he didn't think in those terms.

***

Following his run-in with the Sharkey twins, Timothy 'Timbo' Mulhall, who was one of Michael's cousins living next door, decided to teach Michael to box. Even at the age of nine and a half, Timbo was somebody not to be messed with. Despite his young years, Timbo owned and operated a street reputation.

Timbo was big, fast and mean, could hit hard with both hands and was not averse to throwing in the odd head-butt when the opportunity presented itself. He was a natural boxer and a great street scrapper. When Timbo started instructing Michael on how to box he just didn't get it and was an easy target for Timbo's punches, though he held back on their power. Every morning during the summer holidays Michael showed up at precisely 9.30 a.m. and sparred with Timbo for an hour. At first he showed no signs of having any boxing ability whatsoever. However, over the weeks of the school holidays of 1958, Michael closely observed Timbo's technique and movements and so learned to box by mimicking them, even appearing to improvise punches by the end of August, just in time for the start of the new school year. What impressed Timbo most about Michael's boxing was that he was comfortable in either the southpaw or orthodox stance. Timbo coached Michael to be a busy boxer, switching stance every couple of punches to keep his opponents off balance.

***

It was a month after the start of the new school year before Michael came across the Sharkey twins on his walk to school. This time though he was with cousin Timbo. The Sharkey boys well knew Timbo's reputation and didn't fancy their chances picking on Michael with him around.

A fighting circle conversation

"Hey you, Kevin Sharkey, our Michael wants you out. You too, Colin Sharkey," shouted Timbo to the twins, using the traditional words spoken to start a fight.

"Nah, no thanks, we're on our way to school so we don't want to get into trouble."

"Never mind 'nah', you were on yer way to school last time when you hit our Michael so what's the difference now, eh?" The difference now of course was that Michael was in the company of Timbo Mulhall from whom they'd already taken a couple of hidings both in and out of the ring. They were made even more concerned when a large crowd of kids joined the fighting circle surrounding them.

"Ye scaredy cat chicken ye," shouted a girl from the fighting circle.

"Get lost you, Maureen Dring," yelled Colin Sharkey at his twin's taunter.

"Maureen Dring would burst you easy, Colin Sharkey," yelled another of the crowd. The kids in the fighting circle laughed at that taunt.

"C'mon, Kevin, what are you scared of, mate?" asked Timbo using a friendly tone of voice.

"If we fight your Michael then you'll join in and batter us," replied Kevin.

"Look, youz can fight him one at a time and I promise yez that I won't join in." Everybody knew that promises such as this from Timbo were worthless but you couldn't say that to him.

As Kevin Sharkey removed his overcoat Timbo whispered to Michael, "Go on, our Michael, get in there and burst him. Kick him in the plums if ye get the chance. Remember all the sparring we did? But this time it's for real so burst him." Motivational talk over, Timbo retired to the inner edge of the fighting circle. Kevin Sharkey was two years older than Michael and an experienced street fighter and as soon as he removed his coat he launched himself at Michael with fists and feet flailing.

Michael regarded the oncoming blur that was Kevin Sharkey with total calmness, he simply stepped back out of the way of the initial onslaught and assumed the southpaw stance. Kevin Sharkey stopped dead in his tracks.

"What's all this then?" shouted Kevin to Timbo. "Have you been teaching 'im boxin'? That's not fair."

"Put yer dukes up," shouted Timbo in reply, which Kevin Sharkey immediately did, a stance which Michael recognised as the start of the fight and marched to within punching distance.

One punch was all that Michael threw before the towel was chucked in. As soon as the punch landed Kevin Sharkey backed off and started crying. He put his overcoat back on and walked away with his head down and holding his right cheek. "Okay, Colin Sharkey, it's your turn now," announced Timbo but Colin was already running across the road to shouts of "chicken" and "bock, bock, bock" noises from the fighting circle. This is always the way with bullies; stand up to them and they have nothing.

"Ye did well there, our Michael, but next time try and keep the fight goin' so everybody can see what ye can do… show everyone what yer made of."

Michael continued his boxing lessons with Timbo and joined the school boxing team. With a nose that no longer bled profusely he earned himself a reputation. After the age of eight he won nearly all of his fights both in and out of the ring.

EAST COAST USA

5th May

1900 EST.

The phone rang on the Deputy Director's desk just as he was about to leave the office to attend his daughter's play in forty-five minutes' time. Why was he leaving it so late and what was he doing in work at this hour? It was the same every day.

When somebody isn't very good at their job they compensate by being first in and last to leave the office. Despite his efforts his colleagues had little respect for him. He'd worked hard to get where he was and wasn't going to let them get to him. He had a family to support and had to stay strong for them.

Colleagues wondered how a pencil-necked desk jockey with zero field experience had made Deputy Director. He did in fact have a significant single piece of field experience that none of them was aware of. So, in an effort to look as good as he could, the Deputy Director busied himself for twelve to fourteen hours a day. Doing what? Nobody was entirely sure. He'd thought about bugging the office to listen in on what was being said about him but with all the anti-surveillance equipment around the building that wouldn't be such a good idea.

Truth be told, the Deputy Director was more than a little

paranoid and should really have been receiving specialist help. He often drifted off on Deputy Director Daydreams to pass the time and this was becoming more and more noticeable by all who came into contact with him, including his family.

***

He'd intended visiting a mall on the way home to buy a few jokey gifts to present to his daughter as she triumphantly took her bows at the end of the school play but as he was running late he'd give the mall a miss. He had to get on the road soon otherwise he'd miss the opening act. As a good husband, father and a great dad, he'd never missed a single event in the lives of any of his children; birthdays, sports events, first solo bike rides, you name it he was there. It was no coincidence that agency matters went more smoothly when he was out of the office, so nobody ever brought it up with his superiors or made any complaints to HR.

He said, to himself of course, "What's the point in being the boss if you can't take the time to attend the important events in your children's lives? They grow up so quickly and…" His Deputy Director Daydream was brought to an abrupt halt by the scratchy voice of the PA to the Director of Special Operations.

"Your phone? Didn't you hear it? You're needed downstairs. Now. Pick it up next time and save me a journey."

"I was just on my way out…"

"Right: was. It shouldn't take long. I'll keep you company on your way to the Director's office." She turned on her heels and gestured to him to follow with a crooked finger.

Subtlety was never her strong sui,. he thought. He felt she'd always been against him and had never shown any respect for his position. Still, the Director couldn't have too much longer to go before retirement… and they went back a long way, so maybe… just maybe. He'd fix her little red wagon then. Bitch.

The PA to the Director of Special Operations and the Deputy

Director walked single file to the lift and once inside travelled down in hate-filled silence. He wouldn't deign to lower himself to make eye contact with this glorified secretary. Bitch. He appeared as though he was attending to some urgent business by tapping away at his tablet. Anything not to have this nothingness think he wasn't always busy.

Still, she was very attractive, he could give her that at least. She smelled nice too. Short hair, which was a shame, but great, great, great body and… the lift ended its journey with its customary ding. And so another Deputy Director Daydream came to an end. As they exited the lift he saw a large sign designating, in six-inch block black lettering on a yellow background, the floor number. It read "Basement Level Minus Three". He'd never been beyond basement level minus two before. He didn't know anybody who'd been to basement level minus three.

The PA to the Director of Special Operations pointed the way down the corridor before riding the lift back up.

***

The fluorescent lighting in the hallway was the type that makes white skin translucent and casts no shadows. Typical for installations such as this, the two security guards were dressed as lookie-likie MPs. They wore white-painted metal helmets, button-down regulation light khaki-coloured shirts, knife-creased light khaki-coloured trousers, shiny black belts, shiny black lanyards and high-shine black boots. They were both just over six feet tall and weighed around 225lbs. Their light khaki-coloured button-down shirts clung to their chests like Lycra even though there was no give in the material. The Deputy Director didn't recognise their side arms nor was he confident they were standard issue.

Under these conditions the Deputy Director felt very uncomfortable and started sweating profusely. He couldn't tell whether his sweating was due to the stifling atmosphere of the corridor or if it was him being scared out of his wits. But why was he so scared? What did he have to be afraid of? He was a Deputy Director and the last time he checked this was still America. He started to relax just a little when he noticed there was somebody else in the corridor. Before he could make the acquaintance of the third man a security guard said, "Sir, I need to search you so please assume the position."

What? Did he really say that? 'Assume the Position'; what a dork! The Deputy Director was shocked at this affront and thought of protesting, but then thought it easier to cooperate so he could get out of there as quickly as possible and get on the road to his daughter's play. SoBs. The search by the security guard was conducted very quickly for which the Deputy Director was grateful and was very thorough which made him feel uncomfortable. "Are these guys gay or what?"

Once the security guard moved out of his path he was directed by the other guard toward the only door in the corridor. As he did so the third man rose, stood statue still for a moment and then also moved toward the door. He was quite short at about five foot eight and though his build wasn't as impressive as that of the guards he had a solid physique. *He obviously looks after himself.* The Deputy Director guessed that the third man was sixty to sixty-five years of age and having a trim physique was probably something he was very proud of. *Mind wandering again. Concentrate. Concentrate. Let's get this over with and get on the road to my daughter's play. For God's sake, what time is it now?* he thought while blinking wildly for no apparent reason.

***

The Deputy Director and the other man stepped through the door into a small ante room furnished in comfortable leather seating and lit by four chromium uplighters. There was a large smoked glass and chrome coffee table in the centre of the room; there were no magazines on the table… *or a water cooler come to think of it… mind wandering again… concentrate… concentrate.* A buzzer accompanied by a flashing green light indicated that they should proceed through the large double oak doors at the far end of the ante room.

As the Deputy Director and the other man entered the office of the Director of Special Operations the contrast with the conditions of the hallway could not have been more stark. The Director's office was extremely large and air conditioned. It had subdued lighting. The lighting was not so much subdued as barely lit to the extent that the Deputy Director could only just make out there were two people standing behind a truly massive desk ahead of him. To his right there was a truly massive oval meeting table with at least twenty chairs around it. To his left the wall was entirely taken up by bookshelves. There were few books but there were several silver trophies glinting in the partial light and what looked like the outline of photograph frames. When the Deputy Director closed the large double oak doors he thought by their construction the room was probably sound-proofed.

The Director's desk was twenty feet from the double oak doors. The other man moved off to the Deputy Director's right and sat down on one of the high-backed leather chairs surrounding the oval meeting table. A light went on behind the two men standing behind the Director's desk. They both stood silhouetted against the backlight. One of the silhouettes, with a gesture of his hand, invited the Deputy Director to sit on the chair in front of the Director's desk. The silhouette sat opposite him. The Director's chair was at least ten percent larger than his chair. *Classic upper management meetings psychology*, he thought and had himself a little smile.

The Deputy Director made to speak but was stopped from doing so by a hand gesture, this one directly to his face. *Speak to the hand*, he thought and allowed himself a little internal grin. Big Leather Chair Man spoke to him with a soft Irish accent. This took the Deputy Director by surprise because he'd worked with the Director in the past and there had never been a trace of an Irish accent previously. *Perhaps it's all done with voice-altering electronics? Mind wandering again. Concentrate! Concentrate! Let's get this over and done with, get out of here and get on the road to my daughter's play. What time is it now?* Before the Deputy Director could look down at his watch, Big Leather Chair Man spoke again but this time using a comical Irish accent as though mocking him.

"Oi'll repeat meself as ye don't seem to have heard a word oi said. Oi said, have ye seen de BBC News, today Mr Deputy Director?"

"No, I…"

"Dats what oi taught, udderwoise yer'd be shoittin' yerself roight now." Then in his normal soft Irish accent, "Play the video."

A screen deployed from the ceiling.

On it appeared a scraggy-bearded man who'd obviously been badly beaten. He was kneeling in front of a man holding a huge curved sword. The scene then switched to a BBC News reporter who, according to the caption at the foot of the screen, was standing outside Scotland Yard. *Dah,* thought the Deputy Director, *that's obvious as he's standing right under a revolving sign that has Scotland Yard written on it. Concentrate!* The BBC News reporter was saying something about a man called Mikhail Morozov having been captured by a gang calling itself ISBJ and they had four other hostages and they were going to kidnap a couple more people and cut off their heads in the week leading up to Ramadan… blah, blah, blah. The Deputy Director didn't find it interesting that some homeless-looking Russian person had been so stupid as to get himself grabbed off the street by lunatics. The news clip finished and the screen disappeared back into the ceiling.

What the hell does this have to do with me? This makes no sense, he thought.

"Well?"

"Well, what?"

"Did ye get it?"

"Get what?"

"Mikhail Morozov?"

"Yeah. Poor guy."

"Do ye know what Mikhail Morovoz translates to in English from Russian?"

"Let me Google it."

"Let me save ye the trouble. It translates as Michael Frost. Does that name mean anything to ye, Mr Deputy Director?" Mikhail Morozov translates as Michael Frost; hiding in plain sight, classic Frost. "Does that name ring any bells at all?"

"Sure. I iced a guy called Michael Frost ten years ago in London." The Deputy Director smiled at his word play.

"I see that little pun still amuses ye. I remember when ye gave yer report about Mr Frost's demise to the security oversight committee. Ye used that pun then too." Voice change. "And yer had yerself a noice little smoil den too," said the Irishman while wearing an inane grin.

The Deputy Director flinched at the change in the Irishman's accent. *Mocking me again the SoaB,* he thought. "So, tell me, what does all this mean?"

"Are ye thick or what? Moikel Frost is aloive, ye big eejit," screamed the Irishman in a thick accent.

"That's impossible. I shot him and he fell on the subway tracks in Bond Street station right in front of a train. He took another man onto the tracks with him. They were both smashed to pieces. People don't survive that sort of thing. There was blood and body parts everywhere. It was in all the newspapers. The subway network was closed for over two hours while they recovered the bodies… the body parts at least. Guys, Michael Frost is dead. Dead." In his response the Deputy Director displayed a calmness he really shouldn't have allowed himself to have.

Big Leather Chair Man stood, leaned toward the Deputy Director and from two inches away from his face sputtered a deluge of spittle while screaming, "Den who de hell is dat on de telly? His ghost? He's aloive. D'ye get it? He's bleedin' aloive." After regaining his composure, the Irishman continued in his soft Irish accent, "Michael Frost is alive, Mr Deputy Director. Alive."

"So what? After all these years what can…" The Deputy Director didn't manage to complete what turned out to be his last ever sentence in this life. Unseen and unheard by him the other man had, after removing his fine Italian slip-on shoes, slipped from his chair and silently crossed the luxuriously carpeted office floor of the Director of Special Operations to stand immediately behind the Deputy Director.

From the perspective of the Director all he saw was a slight, if sudden, forward nod of the Deputy Director's head. Then, at the inner corner of the Deputy Director's right eye, a small triangular point of light appeared. A tiny droplet of blood mixed with some oozing opaque fluid hung on the tip of the triangle. It bobbed and grew until it reached a size large enough to break free and dropped onto the Deputy Director's shirt front before another droplet started to form. That droplet did the same thing as the first but a little quicker as it was soon heavy. Before a third droplet could fully form the triangular point of light disappeared back inside the Deputy Director's eye socket.

***

Over the years the Mediterranean man had despatched more than eight dozen souls with his Toledo steel stiletto, the twin of which was in the possession of one Michael Frost. He mainly employed three varieties of kill strike. The kill strike he used to off the Deputy Director was his favourite. The stiletto is located on the right hand side of the little knob of a vertebra at the base of the skull. Then, with little more than a slight push, the shaft travels through the brain to exit in the inner corner of the right eye orbit, as the Mediterranean man is predominantly right handed. Death is instantaneous.

The second kill strike is best deployed from directly in front of the victim. The tip of the stiletto locates just behind the line of the jaw bone and once again all that is needed is a firm push, this time in an upward and slightly forwards direction. Being quite diminutive is an advantage in this kill strike scenario for obvious reasons. As with kill strike one, death is instantaneous. Perhaps this was his favourite, he couldn't quite decide; this kill strike meant he was looking into the eyes of the soon-to-be-deceased and not the back of the head. He'd have to give this some more thought.

The third kill strike leaves the victim alive and semiconscious for a short time. Which is useful if you have some final message you wish to pass on or want something from the victim, especially if he or she doesn't realise they are done for. This third kill strike can be performed from almost any angle but preferably from directly in front of, or directly behind, the victim while he or she is standing, sitting, walking or even having a nice little nap. The stiletto is thrust with considerable force straight through the sternum, or the rib cage, depending on the direction of the attack, to pierce the victim's heart. The victim experiences a massive loss of blood pressure before becoming fully yielding within a few seconds. If necessary one of the other kill strikes can then be employed in the event he needed to move on quickly. Like he'd been discovered… or something.

Occasionally he'd gone temple to temple as a last resort.

***

The Irishman moved round to the front of the Director's desk to stand in between the Mediterranean man and the recently deceased Deputy Director. They spoke in rushed whispers.

"What was the hurry? Ye could have waited. We could've gotten something useful out of him."

The Mediterranean man disagreed. "He's got nothing. He's a moron. He couldn't even tell if somebody was dead or alive."

"It's obvious this eejit was set up, ye know, conned like; but by who? Who did he make contact with to get the lead on Frost in London? Even we didn't know he was there. Doesn't it all seem odd that this eejit does what nobody else managed to? We needed to know all he knew so we could piece it all together to work out who the double crossing shite is who arranged it to look as if Frost ended up looking like he went under a train." The Irishman paused to look at the Director before continuing, "An' not only that, it's clear the Russkies must have been in on it. He said he's a Russkie émigré on the telly, added to which, the Russkie Embassy comes out with a double quick denial of having any knowledge of who this fella is. Don't you think that's just a little bit suspicious now?"

The conversation between the Irishman and the Mediterranean man provided the Director of Special Operations the opportunity to slip into his big leather chair.

He was anxiously regarding the two men whispering together in his office. What did they have to say that needed to be spoken in whispers? Was he next? Were they planning to stick him with the stiletto too? At that moment the Mediterranean man glanced briefly in the Director's direction, wiped the shaft of his eight-inch Toledo steel stiletto before sliding it back into its kid leather scabbard. Simultaneously, the Director's right hand reached under his desk to wrap itself around the handle of his Browning 9mm. The hatching on the Browning's handle felt reassuring. An old and reliable friend. Now he had his friend in his hand he felt much better. Locked inside his sound-proofed bunker he could do anything he wanted with these two old fools. Anything, and nobody would be any the wiser. It wasn't as though they had a signing-in book on this floor.

The Irishman turned toward the Director. "Yer have no need to be fingering yer 9mm under the desk. Yer name's not on the list."

"All the same I'll keep my hand where it is."

"Suit yerself. We'll be going now. We won't meet again for a long time. If ever."

"What about him?" asked the Director of Special Operations pointing at the slumped-over body of the Deputy Director.

"Well, ye know, he's a big lad and I'm sure you wouldn't want two auld fellas like us putting our backs out lifting him. You've a couple of strapping lads out front who can do the job."

"I can't be involved in something like this."

The Mediterranean man moved forward at speed. "You are involved; if it hadn't been for your incompetence none of what needs to happen tonight would be necessary."

"What needs to happen tonight? What? Oh God, there's more?" exclaimed the Director in disbelief.

The Irishman chipped in, "We have a few calls to make and need to be on our way. And if yer thinking of doing something stupid like getting yer two large lads out front to stop us then think again. If we are hindered leaving this place you won't find a hole deep enough to hide yerself in."

Without another word the two men turned and walked toward the large double oak doors. As they did so the Irishman let slip from his hand a small plastic wedge and kicked it toward the doors. On reaching the doors they turned and looked at the Director. He pushed the four-button sequence on the control pad to unlock them. Turning to close the doors behind them the Irishman slid the small plastic wedge against the right hand door to keep it slightly ajar. This action had two purposes. Firstly, in case the Director of Special Operations double crossed them they could gain quick access back into his office and off the SoaB. The second reason would become evident in about eight minutes from... now.

The two men passed through the security door, walked back along the corridor and entered the lift. They rose four floors, exiting the building without a missed step. On passing through the outer doors of the building they turned east and matched their pace with the people on the sidewalk. Move with the speed of the herd if you want to remain unnoticed. Classic counter-surveillance technique. They didn't speak until they were fifty yards from the door of the building.

***

"Do you know what occurs to me?" mumbled the Mediterranean man so he couldn't be overheard by passers-by or have his lips read by CCTV.

"If your performance tonight is anything to go by, I have no idea," replied the Irishman with his back to the wall to minimise surveillance opportunities.

"This denial from the Russkie Embassy means two things. Firstly, all our contacts in Russia are either dead or under arrest and those travelling will go to ground. Secondly, the Russkies want to make the kidnappers suspicious by getting them thinking about why a normally silent Russian Embassy is making a statement of denial."

"Is that all?"

"Yes. No. What if somebody recognised Michael and contacts the kidnappers? I don't want to think what that'll mean if it happens."

"Yer not just a pretty face, are ye? Did all that thinking hurt at all?" The Irishman was in playful mood thinking about what was about to happen thirty metres below ground in two minutes' time, "Now, laddo, get yerself to London, get a team together and get hold of Michael Frost before any of the others get a hold of him. I've a few visits to make, so I'll be on my way. See ye in London." Then he added absentmindedly, "Do you think herself has seen the news about himself?"

"I'm sure she knows by now."

"I wonder how she took it? Do ye think she knew he was alive all this time?"

"I doubt it," he lied.

"Yeah, after what he did she'd have joined in the hunt for him if she thought he was alive. Do ye think she'll want him taken alive?"

"I can't see why. If he's rescued and spills his guts it'll all be over for her."

"I hear she's not too well at the moment."

"Yeah, I heard the same thing."

"Maybe you can pay her a visit while you're over there?"

"Maybe. If I have time. Frost, though, is the primary target."

"Yeah, but if ye get the chance, ye know?"

"Yeah, if I get the chance." He glanced at a couple who seemed to be paying them too much attention. "One more thing. Keep the body count low. We don't want to attract any attention. If you create too much mayhem they'll run or go to the authorities, which is okay as we can get to them then. So, how many do you think?"

"Six, no more. Maybe a couple of others if they're still alive, but ten max. Probably. Thirteen if you count those below us."

"You're a psychopath."

"Takes one to know one."

Actually it doesn't, thought the Mediterranean man, *there's a dictionary definition for a psychopath and...* What the hell, the Irishman was right, the evidence was against them, they were both psychopaths.

***

The two men parted without shaking hands or doing anything recognisable as a farewell. Each turned on their heels with the Irishman continuing east and the Mediterranean man returning back west toward the government building. He counted his steps to estimate how far he was from the Irishman while at the same time waiting for the impact of one of those new Tungsten-tipped hybrid mercury and copper three-stage bullets to come tearing through his ultra-light Kevlar vest and rearranging his internal organs into a mush. Twenty yards. Thirty yards. Forty yards. That should now be enough distance between them on a crowded sidewalk to be safe. Surely? No impact. Walk on. If the Irishman knew what he had become he would surely kill him. Or knowing how they operated maybe he wouldn't, they like to know who their doublers are. When you're walking a tightrope it messes with your head not knowing if you're blown or not. It was all in the timing if you were ever to be offed. Shelf life and all that. Classic Organisation Operations Protocols Manual; friends close, enemies closer.

As he passed by the door to the government building the Mediterranean man felt a sudden thud, or perhaps it was more of a thump, through the soles of his fine Italian slip-on shoes and maybe he heard something too but he couldn't be sure.

***

At the exact moment the Mediterranean man passed by the door to the government building, thirty-three metres below the pavement 8lbs of Composition 4 exploded in the office of the Director of Special Operations. The Irishman had deployed the device from the bottom of his briefcase. It was bound in the same leather as his briefcase so when he walked out of the Director's office it appeared completely intact. The explosion was huge. Its power was amplified by the cone effect of the confined space it had detonated in. The doors to the Director's office were slightly ajar thanks to the Irishman's small plastic wedge. This little gap was all that was needed for the force of the explosion to rip open both oak doors and send the security door between the hallway and the ante room flying through the air. The ensuing blast and fireball blew the three living people and the recently deceased Deputy Director to smithereens. There was now no telling how the Deputy Director had met his end. The Mediterranean man muttered, "Of course your name was on the list. Dumbass."

***

The actual target that night had been the Director of Special Operations. Offing the Director was a relatively simple task if that was all that was required but dealing with all the dirty little secrets he kept locked away in his office bunker presented quite a different challenge.

Hacking the Director's computer systems showed he was extremely careful with his security, data management and communications. Few opportunities there then. An insider identified that the materials the Organisation needed to acquire were kept in a hidden safe. The Director of Special Operations had designed his basement bunker office himself with his own particular needs in mind. His main need being to keep his bargaining chips with the Organisation safe to guarantee his continued existence.

The basement bunker office was located in the third basement level of a highly secure government building which was bristling with surveillance technology as well as dozens of heavily armed guards, plus everybody in the building had access to at least one firearm. Storming the building was not considered a viable option for obvious reasons. A small tactical nuclear strike had not totally been ruled out. The Organisation could blame radical Islamists or a group of anti-government malcontents, dozens of which exist in the USA like budding fifth columnists. The challenge was to get past the building's defences, grab the goods and get back out again in one piece. It was no good whatsoever getting in and then failing to get out with the goods, thus alerting the authorities to things the Organisation didn't want them finding out about. The Organisation had mapped a dozen scenarios whereby, depending upon the exposure threat level, they would act and take the Director out and either acquire or destroy the materials.

Big problem though. Quite apart from the surveillance and security systems and the dozens of guards and the hundreds of armed personnel, the materials were housed in an eight-inch-thick custom-built safe hidden behind the sparsely used bookshelves on the north wall of the office of the Director of Special Operations. The safe was four feet high by four feet wide by four feet deep. Its door was secured by sixteen triple-layer locking bars made up from blends of chromium steel, each separated by sheath bearings made from ceramic splinters, making it virtually impossible to cut into. It was secured, front and back, into the wall by eight hardened steel poles arranged as two tic-tac-toe grids with the safe occupying the centre cell. The wall behind the safe was bedrock.

Once the site for the safe was selected, forty one-inch-diameter holes were drilled into the bedrock to a depth of twelve inches. Each hole housed a one-inch-diameter high-tensile steel rod eighteen inches long, which was hydraulically compressed to secure it using a titanium wedge at its front. The safe, complete with rear tic-tac-toe grid fixed to it, was lifted into position and welded onto the ends of the one-inch steel rods.

Next, sliding shuttering was placed six inches from the bedrock. The space was filled with 120N/mm2 fast-curing concrete. Once the first layer of concrete was cured the process was repeated every six inches, each layer being secured by ten one-inch-diameter steel rods inserted right through all the layers of concrete to a depth of twelve inches into the bedrock.

Finally, a six foot by six foot, two-inch-thick, titanium-hardened steel facia, with locking aperture for the safe door, was welded to the flattened ends of the final set of steel rods. If that wasn't enough, the safe's locking mechanism itself was formidable. It was fitted with two combination dials, each with thirty-six characters, and needed to be turned in the correct sequence and to the correct character to successfully open the safe's door. Built into the safe's door was an electronic clock which only permitted access at certain times, known only to the Director of Special Operations, or so he believed. Errors in accessing the safe would activate self-locking rams behind the sixteen triple concentric locking bars, sealing the door shut on all four sides. To open the safe under those circumstances would necessitate removing it from site or bringing a military grade laser into the bunker office. There were no failsafe devices fitted. The thinking of the Director of Special Operations on this topic was simple. *If somebody has to go to extremes to open the safe then I'm already dead and I want what's in it to get revenge on those who I've been living in fear of for the past twenty years. Especially the Organisation.* This was one of his happy thoughts.

It was therefore a futile exercise to blow the Director of Special Operations and his bunker office to pieces if the contents of the safe couldn't be recovered. The authorities would gain access to it eventually and then the gig would be up. The next part of the plan was the most audacious part, even bearing in mind the audacity with which the Irishman and his Mediterranean associate had gained access to the inner sanctum of the Director of Special Operations, planted a bomb and talked their way out while leaving the still warm body of the Deputy Director slumped over the desk of the Director of Special Operations thus leaving him with the problem of what to do with the corpse. Classic Irishman, cool as a bloody cucumber.

***

As the Mediterranean man passed the end of the government building a leggy female with a great body and short hair emerged from a door to his right, joining the crowd on the sidewalk. She settled in alongside of him, matching his pace.

"We're going to London," he muttered out of the side of his mouth.

"I guessed as much. Where's that Irish maniac?"

"Ask no questions and you'll live longer. Well, that's what I heard anyway."

"Are we travelling together?"

"We are, and congratulations by the way, we're married."

"What about the age gap?"

"To be honest you're a little older than I usually go for but I'm sure we can pull it off." He gave his luscious companion a slant-mouthed smile. She did not look the slightest bit amused.

"Get this straight from the start, mister. We will not be consummating this marriage."

The Mediterranean man loved a challenge.

***

The Organisation had waited years to sort out this rats' nest. The timing was now right as its hand had been forced through the surprise reappearance of Michael Frost. What's more he'd managed to get himself captured by a bunch of radicals. Should ISBJ discover Mikhail Morozov's true identity and obtain the secrets inside his head then the materials in the safe of the Director of Special Operations would take on a whole different level of significance. This could not be allowed to happen. No, no, no, this could not be allowed to happen. The situation necessitated a raid on the bunker office of the Director of Special Operations to keep the balance of power in the right place. With the Organisation that is.

Right on schedule the Organisation's teams arrived. The inside team showed the security guards their standing orders and commandeered the use of two lifts, riding them to the third basement level. They cleared the area around the safe and gained access using their insider information. However, on opening the safe of the Director of Special Operations, it was empty. The cupboard was bare. Had they been made? If so, would they be able to get out of the building in one piece? They were prepared to fight their way out if necessary. Perhaps, like the Russkies, the Director of Special Operations had received advance warning of the re-emergence of Michael Frost and had moved the materials fearing an attack. No, that was paranoid thinking, it made no sense. Why would he remove the materials? He had an impregnable safe in his very own private bunker office. Another possibility filled the leader of the group with total dread. Somebody had the same information as them and had got to the safe before them. There was a timer window to open the safe one hour after the blast. At that very moment however, whatever the answer was made little difference as all they were interested in was getting out of the building in one piece.

This was actually achieved without any incident whatsoever. The inside team rode the elevator to the car parking area on the first underground level and went straight to the waiting vehicles. As planned, two of the inside team exited the building via its main doors to check out the departure point for the convoy and, it being uncompromised, gave it the go ahead to leave. They then went across the street to a coffee bar, exiting it via its rear door and stepping into a waiting sedan. Clearly nobody in the building had any idea what was going on. This was good news. Wasn't it? The teams left the immediate area, split up, as planned, and headed separately to the RVP. To aid their escape, a city-wide failure of the CCTV system occurred which lasted twenty minutes and then, as if by magic, came back on line again, seemingly of its own accord.

MARGARET'S STORY - FIRSTS

Arrangements for the pony club Christmas fair were being finalised. All the proceeds, of course, would, of course, go to charity, of course.

Living the Surrey southern princess life, the teenage Margaret Rotheram filled her time with school and study and ponies and plans for university and conversations with her closest female friends about boys. They each had one boy in particular in mind. Not the same boy in every case.

Margaret's parents wanted her to hold the pony club Christmas fair at their home. Through their stolen daughter they'd socialised so much over the past fifteen years and had loved it. The advantages of having Margaret had been far greater than they'd imagined.

The grounds of their house were extensive enough to hold the pony club Christmas fair. By then the bowling green standard lawns had been destroyed by horse boxes, Land Rovers, paddocks and stables having been built, an outdoor arena installed, jumps erected here and there and all the wear and tear that comes with horsey stuff. They couldn't have been happier though as they'd benefitted enormously from the contacts they'd made through their daughter and her interests. They'd long since cut their ties with the family after a niece had attempted to blackmail them into giving up their longed-for child. Though Margaret had been the cause of their break from the family she'd been the source of them making a new and far better life.

***

Audrey and Cyril were never physically cruel or unkind to Margaret but they weren't exactly loving parents. In the early years of their parenthood they'd been extremely overprotective, treating their daughter as though she were made of sugar glass. Now that they had a child at last they were petrified of losing her. Cyril getting Audrey to agree to riding lessons was a big step for her to take and whenever Margaret had a fall or got hurt around horses she'd give Cyril hell, telling him to tell Margaret there'd be no more riding. Cyril never delivered the messages. How could he? He could see the sheer pleasure Margaret got from being around horses and the delight in her eyes every time he dropped her off at the stables. He knew he'd just have to give Audrey a few days to level out again. He'd give the most implausible excuses imaginable as to why Margaret couldn't stop riding at that precise moment in time. She'd shake her head and scowl at him, her eyes telling him that she didn't believe a word he'd said.

Cruel? No. Unkind? No. Controlling? In the extreme. Their controlling nature suffocated the life out of Margaret and the older she got the more she came to recognise and resent it. Audrey and Cyril couldn't see it though because they were far too concerned with taking advantage of the situations their daughter created for them. Riding was her escape.

***

As much as Audrey and Cyril were determined that the pony club Christmas fair would be held at their home, Margaret was more determined that it wouldn't and so made her own plans.

Plans which included boys. She knew that plans that included boys wouldn't go down at all well with her parents. She was being secretive, cunning and conniving with the arrangements for the Christmas fair and she was determined to have her own way in the matter.

The older she got the more strong willed and rebellious she became. "Gets that from her father", they'd say out of her earshot. They knew they were losing control of Margaret but they didn't know what to do about it. Whenever they were losing a battle, out came the cheque book. One would have thought that they'd have seen the flaw in that approach, but no.

With a good deal of prompting and prodding from Margaret, the local committee decided that the pony club Christmas fair would be held in the field next to the cricket club. Which, in turn, was next to the rugby club. All the boys she knew played both cricket and rugby and she was determined to get them involved in the Christmas fair as she had her eye on one of them. She was besotted with a gangly six-footer called Timothy and being tall herself she felt it was a match made in heaven. There were lots more popular and hunky boys around than Tim but she only had eyes for him.

Everybody said that Tim's father, Rex, was an interesting individual. Nobody was quite sure what he did for a living. When asked, "What line of country are you in, old chap?" he'd simply tap the side of his nose with his forefinger as if to say, "Sorry, can't say, old chap." This side-of-the-nose tapping irritated the hell out of everybody, and he knew it. Inside he was smiling and thinking, *If you only knew.* It was widely rumoured that there were a large number of military intelligence and spook types living in the Reigate area so everybody assumed Rex was 'one of them'. Which he was, just not in the conventional sense.

***

An Organisation conversation

"It's me."

"You're a little early, aren't you?"

"Yes but with the time of year and all that... you know? Got to get away to the slopes and all that. How about you? Going away with the family for the Christmas hols?"

"Yes. We're going on a cruise of all things. It's the wife's idea."

"What about young Timothy? What's his preference? Skiing or cruising?"

"It's girls at the moment actually. Well, a girl actually. Singular. He's smitten with a rather sweet young girl from the village. From what I can tell it's reciprocal."

"Oh, to be that age again."

"Yes. Quite. Shall we get on with it?"

"Indeed. To speed things along can you just give me the highlights rather than going into detail? We can do the full thing at Easter. What do you say?"

"You're the boss. I don't have any concerns presently so I'll go straight to prospects. The young girl who's taken Tim's heart is somebody I'd like to propose for inclusion on the lists. She's about the right age, a little young perhaps, right background and as bright as a button. Interesting thing about her is that her parents are not her biological parents."

"She's adopted?"

"After a fashion. It's all rather sordid actually. I won't go into detail just yet but suffice it to say she's a Noelle-Neumann."

"Really? Now that is interesting. Are there any familial connections?"

"None currently, I understand. Two generations back there was one but that should be okay, shouldn't it?"

"Perfectly fine, old love. Write your recommendation on her... list A, would you say?"

"Yes, she's perfect for list A."

"Well, if there's nothing more?"
"No, nothing. Have a lovely Christmas, old thing."
"Same to you, old love."

And so Margaret Rotheram had come to the attention of the Organisation. Hers was a more usual route than Michael Frost's would be.

***

Her first alone time with a boy was in the cricket equipment storage room after the pony club Christmas fair. It was very disappointing after the build-up he'd given it. Was kissing meant to be like that? She didn't give up. There were a couple of local boys but nothing serious. Going all the way was out of the question. There'd been no men so far, though she came close at a national horse trials. She was involved in the behind-the-scenes organisation of a three-day event. He was in his mid-thirties and married but she wasn't bothered by that as she didn't want anything serious, just a bit of fun with someone who knew their way around a woman. In her lust she wasn't thinking straight: "If his wife is interested in her husband then why isn't she here with him?" Afterwards she couldn't imagine how such thoughts had even entered her head. Nothing came of the closeness she felt they shared and this knocked her confidence, making her wonder if she was unattractive. It was nothing of the sort; she was beautiful, well, very handsome at least. It was simply that the man in question wasn't that sort of person. He was in love with his wife and adored his children and having an affair, even one with no strings attached, was the last thing on his mind. He hadn't even noticed her.

After this, what she felt was, rejection, Margaret focused on her studies, much to her parents' delight. They'd become concerned that she wasn't going to do well enough academically to get a place at a top university. She'd previously done well at school; the private tutors helped as had the educational holidays they'd taken as a family to Greece, Egypt and Italy in particular. Mr and Mrs Rotheram had great ambitions for their daughter and it now looked as though she was back on track to fulfil them.

***

As part of her school's community outreach programme, Margaret became involved with various charities working with underprivileged children. Her contribution was to teach riding and all that came with it, including mucking out stables. Her charity work took up more and more of her time, much to the chagrin of Audrey and Cyril. They could see their social life going up in smoke after all the hard work they'd put into it. To restore things more to their own liking, they bought their daughter a top quality eventer in an effort to rekindle her horsey passion. It didn't work as well as they'd hoped but at least she was spending more time with her new horse than she had with her old pony. They didn't notice that it was time with them she was sacrificing as her charity work continued undiminished. All they saw was her riding and winning and socialising with the right sort of people. Meaning they too socialised with the right sort of people, which was especially important as the family had completely abandoned them over what they'd done to poor Celia.

***

How fickle families can be. None of the Noelle-Neumann clan stepped in when they had the chance to stop Audrey stealing Alice. If they hadn't done what they did, Celia wouldn't have moved to London and wouldn't have been killed that night by a stray bomb. She'd have been tucked up safe and sound with her children. Instead, the two older girls were living abroad and Alice was living a life for the benefit of the Rotherams. Guilt laid heavy on their consciences as each blamed themselves and one another for Celia's death. The family salved their guilty consciences by ostracising Audrey and Cyril. Out of sight, out of mind.

***

Involved as she was in charity work and being extremely successful at eventing, the local newspapers always seemed to have articles about Margaret Rotheram in them. Her photograph regularly adorned the front and back pages of local rags. With her long honey blonde hair and strong facial features she was extremely photogenic. Friends suggested that as she was so strikingly good looking she should do some modelling work. Then a school friend who was a photographic model told her, quite bluntly, that she was too athletically built to be a model. Afterwards, when she looked at herself naked in a full-length mirror, she had to agree with her. She was a fine figure of a young woman, well seated as they say in horsey circles. She hoped the puppy fat would burn off one day. It did.

***

Final exams came around and, as expected, Margaret did extremely well in them. With her results, and with the institutional contacts her parents had, she secured interviews at Oxford and Cambridge.

While waiting to hear back from the colleges she decided to go on vacation with a couple of gals from her old pony club days. Picking up with somebody when you've moved on yourself can be difficult, or even a disaster, but as they had horses in common they each felt it should go well.

Audrey and Cyril were horrified at the news of their only daughter going on holiday alone.

"I'm not going on holiday alone, Mummy, I'm going with some of my old pony club friends. You remember Zuzhana? You always liked her and her family. Her father and you are great friends, Daddy."

"I wouldn't go so far as to say we're great friends," he lied to keep the truth away from Audrey, "I like Tom and Alice but they're…"

"They're… well… they're…" Interrupted Audrey, "We've moved on, haven't we, Cyril dear? I mean to say, they're rather… common. Don't you agree, Cyril dear?" Cyril hesitated in supporting his wife which earned him a scowl.

"It's not that we don't want you enjoying yourself, because we do. Don't we, Audrey dear? It's just that this is a trip abroad and…"

"I've been abroad dozens of time so it's nothing new."

"That's not what we mean and you know it. It's not safe for young girls to go…"

"I'm not a young girl, I'm a young woman in case you hadn't noticed. Which you obviously haven't. What's more I'm off to university after the summer hols and I'll be living in Cambridge. You know, where the spies came from."

"Now, Margaret, no need to go upsetting your mother. Please reconsider this ill-thought-through idea of a holiday abroad… why don't you come with us, darling? We'll go anywhere you like. How about America? You always love it there."

"Daddy, I'm too old to be going on holiday with my parents."

"Nonsense. All your little friends still go on holiday with their parents."

"Little friends? How old do you think I am? Two of my friends are already married and two are engaged to be married. Some have children already."

"Well, we know why that is, don't we, so we won't be going down that avenue."

"What avenue is that, Audrey?" She'd never called her Audrey before. The mention of her name in those circumstances created a deathly silence in the room.

"Please don't call me that, darling. Call me Mummy. Please."

"Sorry, Mummy, but I'm going on holiday with Zuzu."

"I won't sign for you at the bank so you can't get any money."

"Mummy, I've been signing for my own money for ages. Daddy signed at the bank so I could do it whenever I liked." Audrey tossed Cyril his second scowl of the conversation.

The argument went on for four more hours.

"It seems you're not going to change your mind but let's not let this come between us."

"You're too soft on that girl. She's always been able to wrap you around her little finger."

"Nonsense, dear, that's not true is it, darling?"

"Of course not, Daddy," she replied casting a sly grin in Audrey's direction, "you do what you do for me out of love. And if you genuinely love me you won't stand in the way of my going on holiday with the girls."

"Look. See? She's doing it now, you fool."

"Audrey darling, we're just going to have to accept that Margaret is a young woman now, able to make her own decisions and live her own life. She's going away to university after the summer for goodness' sake." Audrey stormed out of the room. "I'll go to her later. You tell your friends that everything is alright and you'll be going on holiday with them."

"I know. I love you, Daddy."

***

"Get out. Leave me alone."

"Are you a fool? Well, are you? If we alienate her we'll lose her. She's growing up so we'll have to play things differently from now on. After university, she'll get a job in London and she'll probably want to live there and…"

"Surely not."

"Surely so. Then she'll meet some man and get married. Have children. That will open up a whole new world for us so please don't do anything to mess it up."

"I'm not sure I can bear it. You don't know how a mother feels."

Neither do you, he thought. "I know this is hard on you but it's hard on me too. I was hoping we'd get introduced to a lot more people on the eventing scene but that doesn't look like it's going to happen now. We must support her through university and afterwards too. No matter what she does. We must visit her regularly while she's in Cambridge. We'll be the type of parents other students will envy her for having. We'll make contacts of her friends' parents. It'll be a new direction for us. You can see that, can't you, dear?"

"I suppose you're right. But I'm right too. That girl wraps you around her little finger. She grinned a sly grin at me when we were arguing."

"It's only natural in the circumstances. She wants to show…"

"There you go again, always taking her side. There'll be men all around her while she's on holiday and you know what that means, or don't you care?"

***

The atmosphere in the Rotheram household in the days leading up to the holiday were frosty. Margaret was doling out her best silent treatment for maximum effect. She knew what effect it would have on Cyril in particular. She'd learned that the best way to get something out of him was to keep silent and let him do all the talking. She knew that sooner or later he'd say something to her advantage rather than endure her silence. He asked her about her hotel, what it was like and how many stars it had. She said she thought it had one star, "perhaps none, I really don't recall".

He begged her to reconsider. When she said she wouldn't he said, "At least let me give you some money so you can have better accommodation. There's no telling what will happen to you in a one star hotel." She thanked him, saying that an extra hundred and fifty should do the trick. She knew Audrey was listening and when she passed her in the hallway she threw her one of her now trademark sly grins. Cyril got it in the neck for that one.

***

Margaret and her friends had a great time on holiday: relaxing, drinking, staying out all night, sleeping late, taking it easy. Meeting men. She was determined to do all the things she hadn't done while on so-called holidays with her parents. An added bonus was a holiday romance with a handsome waiter. All three girls had hooked up with waiters from the same bistro-bar.

For their last night on holiday they made a pact, or perhaps it was more of a dare, to each have sex with their handsome waiters. After a night out drinking and dancing, followed by lots of kissing on the beach, the girls were in the mood to take things further. Margaret felt exhilarated at the thought of sex with her very muscular waiter, though a little nervous as she'd heard so many stories about sex which left her feeling nauseated. Did they really do that? Pictures in magazines left her in no doubt but she wasn't keen on the things she saw the pornomodels doing.

The girls split up, each going their separate ways along the beach for privacy's sake. The evening was warm, the breeze gentle and the surf was softly rolling in along the tidal margins. The atmosphere was perfect. Margaret knew the time was right for her.

She wasn't sure how he'd managed it but after only a few minutes' kissing and groping she found herself naked and lying on her back with only an upturned boat atop a small sand dune for cover. Where her clothes were she had no idea. Her pants, at least, hadn't gone far, they were caught on a toe. Her handsome waiter's muscular hairy chest was bare and he was trouserless. He stood to remove his underpants. She felt his eyes wandering over her nakedness. The thought of what must have been going through his mind turned her on. As he slid his tight underpants down his thick thighs she noticed their elasticated waistband straining against the bulge of his penis. As they passed over the end of his cock it sprang violently erect, slapping his stomach then waving in the air as though a victory had already been had.

She'd never seen a real-live erect penis before. She was surprised at the size of it and how it had behaved after being released from the underpants. Having now seen it, she was feeling apprehensive as she'd heard so many horror stories of first time sex from the girls at her school, involving pain, tearing and bleeding. Looking at the size of his penis she could easily believe the stories.

He laid on top of her, roughly prising her legs apart with his knees. She loved his raw strength. She reached down and grabbed his penis to guide it inside her. She'd been told by the girls at school that was the thing to do.

"Margaret? Margaret? Where are you?" She ignored the shouting voice. Was it in her head? No, it was definitely Zuzhana shouting.

"What the hell do you want?" she shout-replied using a voice she didn't recognise.

"Where are you?"

"We're over here." Zuzhana followed Margaret's voice, coming upon them naked and entwined.

"Oh God, put some clothes on. Get dressed, will you."

Refusing to move Margaret replied, "Why? So you can have him?" still using the voice she didn't recognise and wondering why she'd asked her friend such an obviously irrational and stupid question.

"Eeeeue, no thank you." She squirmed. "You'll thank me after you've heard what I have to tell you."

"Tell me what?"

"These bastards have made arrangements to meet up with some other girls after seeing us. What do you think of that?"

"Zuzu, we're on holiday and they're waiters and they probably meet dozens or perhaps hundreds of girls during the summer. You weren't thinking of marrying yours, were you?"

"What are you saying?"

"I'm telling you to get lost and leave us alone. I'll see you back at the hotel." Zuzhana thought for a moment before walking back along the beach toward the spot where she'd left her waiter in the hope that he was still there.

Her handsome waiter assured her that he had no plans to meet any other girls that night. The night was hers.

Margaret's only reservation about her handsome muscular waiter was that he was very much shorter than her and while they were making love she pictured him as a mountain climber. No matter how hard she tried, she could not shake that image from her head. That image became the first thing that entered her head whenever short men came onto her. Though she went on to have lovers who were shorter than her, she shuddered inside whenever diminutive men approached her in hope.

Outside the bistro-bar where the waiters worked a sad-looking forty-something woman sat alone at a table waiting and wondering where her handsome young waiter was.

***

After they returned to England the girls stayed close, meeting regularly throughout the summer. They often reminisced about that warm night on the beach with their handsome waiters. Such talk made them flush-faced and giggly. Often, after a few glasses of bubbly on girls' nights out, they'd swap lurid stories as though in some sex-poker game; "I'll see your anal and raise you a threesome."

"Are you, erm, writing to yours?"

"Oh God no. Why, are you?" Zuzhana's blush was her reply.

"What about you, Margaret?"

"Too busy getting myself ready for uni. I have a lot to do before I go up to Cambridge."

"No time for men?"

"I've enough on my mind at the moment, thank you. I've had some… never mind."

"Don't forget to invite us to the wedding, Zuzu."

"Ha, ha, ha, very funny." Not so funny as Zuzhana married her handsome waiter eighteen months later. They went on to have four children and lived in Surrey all of their married life. When Zuzu died from cancer, at only fifty-five years of age, Margaret attended the funeral though she didn't make herself known to any of the mourners for obvious reasons.

***

An Organisation conversation

"Well, that all sounds very interesting, well done. Now let us proceed to the prospects lists and see where we are with them."

"Indeed, Madame Governor, firstly I'd like to discuss the Margaret Rotheram case."

"Ah yes, I remember you mentioning her. Odd that you refer to it as a case. I hope she and Timothy are no longer seeing one another?"

"You will be pleased to hear that they are not. I too am pleased as she's showing extraordinary promise. She's at Cambridge, you know."

"Jolly good. Much better than that complete dump Oxford."

"I'm an Oxford man."

"Yes I know, I was teasing you. What's she studying?"

"Politics and economics."

"Excellent. Things have changed since I was a young gal; they have so much more choice today. I can't say that I find either of those subjects of interest personally; but for an operative? Perfect, wouldn't you say? How will you trap her?"

"Rather cruelly, I'm afraid. Do you remember when I told you that there was something sordid involving the family?"

"Of course I do, I'm not very likely to forget something like that. I was waiting for you to bring it up."

"I'm slightly concerned that when she finds out the truth about her so-called parents her reaction to it might send her over the edge but it's the only plan I can come up with to recruit her."

"Tell me more. But not until I've poured myself a drink, this all sounds rather juicy."

Rex told his governor the Frederik Noelle-Neumann story and how the Rotherams had taken the family's youngest daughter, Alice, away from their mother who died shortly afterwards in the Blitz.

"Are you certain there is no other way? I mean to say, this could send her off the deep end. We usually go in for a nice line in blackmail or corruption to trap recruits, but this? I'm not so sure that your plan is such a good one, I'm afraid."

"It's too late. I tracked down Alice's sisters and told them where they could find her. They'd been told she had died in the Blitz alongside her mother. Their reaction to the news that Alice was alive was rather mixed – shock, disbelief, scepticism and so on – but after they spoke with relatives, and had it confirmed by some, they accepted it. 'Imagine', the relatives said to them, 'what might have happened had we not taken charge of the situation?' But they would say that, wouldn't they?"

"Well, as you say, it's too late now. When will they meet?"

"In four days' time."

"Let me know how it goes. I'm not sure I want to finish my drink, I've a rather nasty taste in my mouth."

MICHAEL'S STORY - GOODBYE OLLER

While waiting to be rehoused the Frost kids were busy going about their childhoods.

Right facing the Frosts' house was an open area called Oller which was formed when a German bomb landed on Christ Church, completely flattening it. No damage whatsoever was done to any of the surrounding houses. Everybody said it was a miracle. The Oller was covered with black cinders and had a tubular monkey-bar playground at its northern end. Its southern end was fringed by three advertising hoardings configured as a single hoarding running parallel with Greaty and two smaller hoardings, one at either end, like ears. The hoardings, or 'tins' as they were known locally, were twenty feet high and supported by two inch-wide angle iron, the ends of which were concreted into the ground to brace the whole structure. It was solid enough to carry the weight of the tins and that of over thirty kids while playing their favourite game of Vampires and Victims.

The rules of Vampires and Victims were simple, following other tag-type games. The big rule was once the game started, Victims weren't allowed to touch the ground; anybody doing so became a Vampire. The game began when one kid was chosen to be a Vampire. The chosen child would chase after the other kids to turn them into Vampires by touching them. The tins were a sight to behold on summers' evenings with over thirty kids swinging on them. They were just like little monkeys. Some kids would run flat out along the top of the tins; they'd do anything to avoid being turned into a Vampire! This game was not without its casualties though nobody broke any bones.

The same could not be said for the game of shimmying up the walls of the entry ways, known as jiggers, between the terraced houses. This wasn't so much a game as a test of nerve as well as a feat of strength, daring and bravery, or possibly just plain old street kid stupidity.

Jigger Shimmyers would compress their hands and feet against the walls of a jigger and shimmy up toward the roof to reach as high as they could before descending again.

Some kids, including Michael, scamper-raced up the jigger walls to touch the roof guttering and race back down again. The really 'brave' kids went one step further. This often turned out to be a climb too far. Instead of lining up to touch the guttering at the lowest part of the roof they'd line themselves up to touch chimney pots at the highest part of the roof. This added more than a dozen feet to the shimmy. The chimney stacks themselves had been subjected to repeated heating up and cooling down for over a century making the mortar between the bricks crumbly. When the mortar was disturbed it formed a dusty, talcum powder-like lubricant on the bricks. Also, at that height, the chimneys were covered in a slippery, slimy residue making them doubly treacherous to climb. Once you lost your grip you were done for unless you were really strong or lucky and managed to slow your descent before you hit the ground, or your observers, over thirty feet below. Nobody died but if you went home crying to your parents and told them what had happened you'd get your backside dusted for being so stupid.

***

July 1961 was the start of Michael's last summer on the Oller before moving house to the leafy suburbs. He had no idea where these leafy suburbs were. "I'll miss ye, Michael. Promise me that you'll keep yer boxing up after ye move away. You're a good little boxer and, who knows, maybe you might be able to beat me one day." Timbo passed a muffled laugh at the idea of little Michael Frost ever beating him at boxing, but he felt he had to give his protégé something to shoot for.

After three years under Timbo's tutelage, and being a veteran of a dozen boxing tournaments, Michael was already good enough to give cousin Timbo a run for his money. He'd TKO'd an American lad called Victor Christian a year previous during a Golden Gloves exhibition tour. What was impressive was that after being chased around the ring for two and a half rounds, Michael switched stances and landed a single punch which brought his opponent literally to his knees. None of the kids had ever seen anybody hit so hard. A one-punch TKO is not easy for anybody to produce and especially not a boy of Michael's build.

"Oh, by the way, I'm going to live with me Aunty May soon so we won't be that far from one another after ye move. That's good news, isn't it?" Michael nodded.

***

One hot summer's day the kids of the Crete Street Gang attacked the Oller kids, probably out of boredom more than anything. Leading the attack was an older kid, a teenager known locally as Buckhead, King of the Kids. The Oller kids were quickly surrounded and wondered what was in store for them.

Buckhead had heard about Timbo's reputation and so goaded him into a fight. Timbo couldn't back down in front of everybody so agreed to fight the older, and much bigger, Buckhead. As he was removing his jumper Buckhead head-butted Timbo hard in the face. He fell to the floor with blood streaming from what turned out to be a broken nose. Buckhead was about to send the boot in when Michael pushed him away.

"Go away, you, and leave my cousin alone."

"Piss off you… you… you… you." The Crete Street gang started laughing at Buckhead's inability to finish a sentence. "Shurrup or I'll burst youz lot as well."

"Go away. Leave my cousin alone."

"Fancy yerself do ye, mong boy?"

"Leave our Michael alone, you, he's not even ten yet and he's… well, you know… he's not right in the 'ead like."

"What do you mean?"

"Nothin', Michael… nothin', it's just tha'… well, you know… you're a bit slow in the 'ead like, aren't ye?" Michael had no idea what his cousin was talking about.

"C'mon then, big mouth, fancy yer chances, do ye?" screeched Buckhead challenging little Michael.

In response to Buckhead's challenge Michael raised his hands into his favourite southpaw stance. Buckhead laughed, comically miming rolling up his sleeves, not unlike Popeye when getting into a street scrap with Bluto. He bent down as if to scratch his leg and from his crouching position rushed full speed onto Michael. Learning from his bout with Victor Christian, Michael, this time from a southpaw stance, took a big step to his left and sent a lightning fast punch across Buckhead's jaw with a precise eighty percent travel and twenty percent impact. Buckhead was out cold before he hit the deck.

Those who'd witnessed the Frost/Christian fight swore the left which floored Buckhead was an even sweeter shot than the right which had floored Victor Christian. As the street kids of the Oller were cheering a great victory Margaret emerged from her front door. "Have you been fighting again, Michael? What have I told you about your fighting? What are we going to do with you, eh son? Come inside, now." As ever, Margaret was quick in dishing out punishment, slapping Michael hard four times across his bare little stick legs. As with every other occurrence of this punishment, Michael didn't cry and Margaret was sorry five minutes later. This wouldn't be the last time Buckhead and Michael would meet and cross swords.

"You're going to have to learn not to fight, son, especially when we move house. We don't want our new neighbours thinking we're common."

***

The big day finally came; the Frosts were on the move to their new house and just as their old house had been a lucky and loving house their shiny new home would turn out to be the opposite.

***

The fresh air of the leafy suburbs was good for Michael's lungs though the house move unsettled him as he found it difficult to meet new people. Thankfully though, as Thomas made friends easily, Michael hung out with a group of local lads he got to know through his little brother.

***

They were all just sitting kicking their heels on a wall one day when they noticed the notorious Sparrow Hall Gang heading their way. If they ran there was no guarantee they'd outrun them. Michael hopped off the wall and walked toward the Sparra boys.

"Alright, Timbo?"

"Awright, our Michael. What you up to?"

"Sitting on the wall."

"Do you like living here? I think it's great. Are ye doin' any boxing at yer new school?"

"They don't do boxing."

"What? Are they fruits or wha'?"

"They do cricket and football and sometimes dancing."

"Yeah, thought so, fruits. Tell ye what, come with me to my new boxing club next week. I'll come for ye at five next Tuesday and we'll set off."

"Okay."

"Are you serious, Timbo, takin' that little fruit boxin'?" sneered Baz, who'd taken a dislike to the new boy.

"I tell you wha', Baz, he'd burst you," replied Timbo in defence of his cousin.

"Get lost," snorted Baz, highly sceptical of Timbo's claim.

"Listen. When I was gettin' me head kicked in by some big turd called Buckhead it was our Michael who KO'd him. One punch was all it took. An' in a boxing match with some big American lads he put their best fighter on the deck, with one punch."

"D'you think I'm soft in the 'ead? 'Im? Get out of it. If he's so good then I'll take him on."

"I'm warning ye, Baz, don't do it, mate." But Baz was in no mood to listen. He saw the chance to hammer one of Timbo's rellies.

"Michael, you don't have to fight this fella if you don't want to."

"Let him speak for himself," interrupted Baz.

"Leave the lad alone, Baz," chorused the Sparra boys.

"Piss off, youz lot. Who are yez? His ma?"

"Leave him alone, he's not all there in the head if you know what I mean," said Timbo.

"What do you mean?" asked Michael.

"Michael, you're different to the rest of us… you know… different like. A bit, erm… slow like," sputtered Timbo using the words he'd heard the grown-ups use when describing Michael. Michael had no idea what he was talking about.

"Look, Baz, he's only ten so leave him alone."

"But accordin' to you he's the next bleedin' Cassius Clay." Without warning Baz punched Michael on the nose which started it trickling with blood.

"You sneaky rat, Baz. Are you alright, our Michael?" asked a concerned Timbo.

"My nose is bleeding."

"C'mon then, Micky, put yer dukes up or are ye chicken?" taunted Baz, up on his toes.

"My name is Michael. I promised Mum I wouldn't fight anymore."

"See, Timbo, he's just a chicken."

Ignoring Baz, Michael turned to his mates. "Let's go Bridge Dropping."

Walking away from the Sparrow Hall Gang, they kept looking over their shoulders until they were certain they were safe.

"See you at five next Tuesday, our Michael?" yelled Timbo.

"Okay."

"Christ, Michael, are you alright?" asked Stevie Newcombe.

"Yeah, it didn't hurt."

"Ye did the right thing not to get into a fight with that Baz Grogan, he's a right bastard."

"I'm not scared of him. I promised Mum I wouldn't fight anymore."

***

As with most street games, the rules of Bridge Dropping are straightforward and simple. The Bridge Dropper works his way – no girls seemed overly interested in this game – along the girder supporting the bridge, hangs there for a short time to attract the attention of passers-by and then drops to the pavement nineteen feet below. If you wish to receive the admiration of your peers you must add style to the drop. For example, synchronised dropping with a buddy or two and/or rolling, paratrooper style, on landing. Points were deducted for blood or ends of tongues being bitten off.

***

As arranged, Timbo turned up at Michael's house at five o'clock on Tuesday and again on every Tuesday and boxing tournament day for the next five years.

They hardly ever had any money so they either walked to the boxing club or they'd sneak a free bus ride, especially if it was raining. Some bus conductors threw fare dodgers off the bus but most didn't and the same could be said for the crews on the Mersey ferries and the ticket checkers working on the barriers at the train stations, but not railway inspectors for their trips to Southport. For a couple of kids with no money they became very well travelled around Merseyside.

***

The time came for Michael to sit the eleven plus exam for grammar school selection. The parents of the local kids didn't get involved in their children's education. They said that was the teachers' job. Homework was seldom checked by parents. Kids were left to get on with things by themselves.

Of all the local kids only Michael passed the eleven plus and won a place at a grammar school. When the kids heard he'd passed the exam they taunted him. Things were just as they were in Margaret and Patrick's day: don't let them advance; keep them here with us so we don't get left behind.

To set Michael up for grammar school Margaret and Patrick made a lot of sacrifices, but they made them willingly as they were so very proud of their number one son.

This sense of pride didn't stop Michael's parents splitting up and divorcing shortly after he entered grammar school.

Henceforth, Michael and his siblings qualified for free school meals and he for free bus travel. Margaret used to say to them, "Fill up on your school dinners as much as you can and see if you can bring some pudding home if there's any going spare."

***

After Patrick deserted the family home, neighbours, so-say concerned about the Frost children, contacted Social Services, claiming Margaret was neglecting them as they were left home alone while she went out to work. The way Margaret saw things was simple enough: they were her kids and she was going to pay her way and didn't need charity. She could do it. She knew she could do it. She hoped she could do it.

It was an almighty fight but Margaret managed to keep the children living with her despite the best efforts of the amateur social engineers to split the family up.

PARIS

6th May

0110 CET.

The evening's corporate hospitality event was drawing to a close. It was very well attended and had been a great overall success, despite a drunken scuffle between two females over a gluten-free vol-au-vent. The specially selected guest speakers delivered witty after-dinner speeches crammed with humour, colourful anecdotes and raconteuring of the highest calibre. *Well worth their enormous fees,* thought Hugo. His father's chateau provided an elegant backdrop to the evening's happenings and entertainments.

What would make the whole night perfect depended on whether he could slip away with Nicole, his secretary-cum-mistress. He caught her eye and indicated with a slight nod of his head that she should go to the Napoleonic gate which led to a maze in the ornamental gardens. He'd found the perfect spot for this evening's liaison while he was planning his latest corporate hospitality extravaganza. It was nicely secluded but not too hidden away thus conjuring up their flight of fancy of somebody coming upon them while they were in the act.

Though they both found the thought of discovery very exciting, for her modesty's sake the chosen spot was behind bushes two metres tall and beginning at ground level. They didn't want to attract a crowd after all. Thoughts of what they were going to be doing in a few minutes' time came flooding into Hugo's brain like a bursting dam, making him flushed from his tightening collar to the top of his balding head and causing a massive diversion of blood, preventing him from thinking straight. Sexual tunnel vision made him completely oblivious to all those around him.

Adopting a casual demeanour, he started toward the gate; all he could concentrate on was… a hand came to rest on his shoulder from behind. He turned to look at its owner.

"Father."

"You're not thinking of disappearing, are you?"

"What can I do for you, Father?"

"You can stop shagging your secretary and pay some attention to your wife and my grandchildren for a change. How about that?"

"Is that what you've come over here to say? Left your important business discussions to tell me to go home to my wife?"

The Count wasn't going to get into another argument with his son tonight, there was important business to attend to. "Hugo, you've done a great job in arranging this evening but it's not over yet, there's more to be done. Tell Miss Slutbunny to go home and then join me in my study in five minutes."

***

Hugo was beside himself with anger and frustration. He'd been looking forward to having an *al fresco* post-corporate-event session with Nicole. He ran to explain to her that tonight was off but she was nowhere to be found. She'd observed the conversation between Hugo and his father and got the message that the night's liaison was off, if the animated father/son conversation was anything to go by, so she decided to take her leave.

By the time Hugo located her she was waiting in the queue to exit the car park of the chateau. He gazed for a whole minute in her direction but she didn't look around, she just continued looking straight ahead not wanting to risk seeing Hugo's annoying face. She was angry with him for being so pathetic, weak and… no, not annoying face, she was sorry that she'd thought of him in that way. Hugo was kind, passionate, gentle and loving and she knew that he loved her as much as she loved him. From what Hugo had told her, his father was a bully and had dominated her poor little Hugo ever since his childhood. She was Hugo's salvation, or so she believed. She felt much better now her head was full once again with loving thoughts of her Hugo. She'd give it an hour before sending a message to their secure email account assuring him that all was still okay between them. Yes, an hour. That should be enough torture time.

"Shit," he muttered as he walked like a foot-dragging hormonal teenager toward his father's study. *Shall I put a book inside my pants in case the headmaster wants to cane me?* he thought and recalled visits to the headmaster's study at his English public school where he'd received a classical education while simultaneously being introduced to its archaic, and somewhat questionable, practices and traditions.

***

"Sit down but don't get too comfortable, this isn't going to be a long meeting."

"I wished you'd told me that before."

"Why? So you could put that tart on ice?"

"Father, has it ever occurred to you that I'm deeply unhappy with my life? And that I want to make a new life away from you and the cosy little family you decided was for me?"

"Right now, Hugo, I really don't care what is going on in that head of yours, so shut up and listen to what I have to say. It's very important. There's been an interesting development that will require your fullest attention. Apparently, earlier this evening, there was a BBC News broadcast about a man claiming to be a Russian émigré who's been abducted by ISBJ."

"I've heard of them. Tragic. Poor fellow," Hugo said with mocking insincerity in his voice.

"Yes. Shortly after the news broadcast, I was sent a video of it which I was told to watch straight away. You probably noticed I left the party for a while?"

"No, not at all."

The Count gave his son a sideways look. "The clip was sent by one of my associates."

"Ah, one of your 'associates'. I see. Well, that makes all the difference."

"Yes it does. After seeing the clip I was about to call back and ask what it was I was supposed to be looking at but then something stirred in my memory and as soon as I recognised who it was I was looking at it felt like a bolt of lightning had hit me. I was looking at the face of Michael Frost. After all these years of believing him to be dead there he was on the TV for all the world to see. Can you imagine what's going to happen now that he's back in the world of the living?"

"No, not really."

"Are you trying to be an arsehole? You know Michael Frost so stop acting like an idiot. Secret Service organisations from around the world are making their way to London. The Organisation is vulnerable and we must act to rescue Michael Frost so he doesn't fall into the wrong hands."

"And who is the wrong hands, Father? You think I don't know who your associates are?" Hugo had long known who his father's associates really were and who and what they represented.

The old man looked down, gathering his patience and said, "Son, we must find Michael Frost before anybody else does. He's the key to our return to our rightful place in the order of things." He hadn't called Hugo 'son' in a very long time.

"So, why are you telling me this, Father? Why are you involving me now?"

"Because, Hugo, I'm old, frail and very ill. I've tried to protect you since Albert's…" He couldn't say the word. "But now it's time for you to play your part. I don't have the strength to do what must be done. It should be me who goes to London and lead our search for Michael Frost but I simply can't do it. Despite everything that's passed between us, Hugo, I love you as my son and I need you to do this for me. It's your time to take over from me. You shall go to London in my place to search for Michael Frost. You'll need to be extremely careful, there will be a lot of dangerous people there, desperate to find him. It'll be hard to tell whether they will want to kill or capture Frost especially as some will undoubtedly be doublers working for the Organisation. You won't be able to tell who is friend or who is foe, so trust nobody, Hugo. Please, Hugo, my son, find Michael Frost and bring him back to us here in France, alive."

Hugo had lived in hope that the day would come when he'd take over his father's empire but he could hardly believe what he'd just heard. The day was today. Maybe he could use this opportunity to start to live his own life?

"When do I leave?"

"Right now. There's no time to lose. People from across the globe will be descending on London as we speak. You must leave right now."

Within thirty minutes Hugo was on the road to the airport, his coded instructions safely hidden away. He wouldn't be able to read them until they were matched with a counterpart which was in the possession of the woman he was to meet in London. He had deep misgivings about what he was getting into but for the chance of having a future with Nicole he'd do whatever was necessary. How he hated, loathed, despised and detested his father.

***

A splinter conversation

"Hugo's on his way to the airport. He should be on the ground in London in about two and a half hours. The rendezvous has been arranged."

"Does he suspect anything?"

"I don't think so but if he acts in any way suspicious he'll be eliminated."

"But he's your son, Maurice."

"And what greater sacrifice can any man make? We absolutely must get to Michael Frost before anybody else does. We cannot afford to miss this opportunity of destroying the Organisation once and for all."

"We were a brotherhood once, funny how things work out, isn't it?"

"Like all families, we have our disagreements but we'll sort things out and put ourselves back where we belong."

"Just so you know, she's ordered her sentinels to find Frost."

"I could have guessed as much. They won't be the only obstacle for us to overcome. Do you think she knew he was alive? Maybe she's been hunting him herself all these years."

"Or running him? No, we'd have known if she was hunting him, her organisation leaks like a sieve."

"Yes, but the information is not always reliable. Now that she has no protection around her should I arrange to…"

"If you have time but Michael Frost is our primary target. Besides, she's not totally unguarded, Lisette kept back a unit of sentinels to protect her." The caller thought a while. "Though I'm confident Hugo will do a fine job, you'll be needed in London to keep an eye on things."

"Of course, that was always my intention. My car's here. I must be on my way. Goodbye."

"Good luck."

MARGARET'S STORY - NOT ALONE

Margaret was in a hurry to get back to her student house in time to change her clothes and get to her bar job when she heard somebody call out, "Alice?" She paid no attention but something inside her made her slow her pace. "Alice? Alice?" Louder this time. She turned toward the direction of the caller. An elegant-looking, well-dressed woman was standing next to another similarly elegant, well-dressed woman. They were looking straight at her. "Alice." Though strangers, they both looked familiar. With their strikingly handsome features they both looked like her.

"Excuse me, ladies, are you referring to me?"

"Yes, yes we are. She looks so like Father, doesn't she, Lilly? It's the hair… and the eyes too of course."

"She does, Hen. Alice, please don't be frightened. We're… please let us go somewhere where we can talk in privacy."

"I'm sorry, ladies, but I think you've mistaken me for somebody else, my name is Margaret and I'm in a hurry, so please, if you don't mind?" She turned to walk away.

"I think you will want to hear what it is we have to say to you."

"Look, I've told you, my name is Margaret and I don't know who this Alice is you are referring to." Even as she spoke she knew she should listen to the two familiar-looking strangers.

"Okay, have it your own way. There's something we need

to tell you and we can do it right here if you're in so much of a hurry."

"Don't be so heartless, Hen, she doesn't know. How could she, she was just a baby when… your name isn't Margaret, your name is Alice, Alice Lavinia Arabella Noelle-Neumann, and you're our little sister." As the woman spoke, teardrops spilled over the lower lids of her eyes and flowed down her cheeks to her neck.

Those words made Margaret's head spin and put her chest in a vice. She instinctively knew Lilly was telling the truth. "Look, let's go somewhere. We have a car here. Come with us… please. Come with us."

Margaret walked trance-like through the crowded pavement toward the car door opened for her by Hen.

***

Cars are the perfect places to hold conversations. They offer a confined, secluded, private space in which you can talk freely and, as they are often on the move, it's hard to get away from difficult topics.

***

The sisters began by introducing themselves: Henrietta, Hen, and Lilia, Lilly. Twins, not identical but very nearly so. They were obviously a good deal older than her. Hen explained that their father, Frederik, married Alice's mother in 1938 after he'd come to England in 1933 following the death of their mother, Anastasia. The family decided he needed to make a new start and so set up the family business in London to help him get away from the memories of Berlin.

The move to England didn't work out as planned. He simply couldn't forget their mother. He spent all his time at the office, wallowing in self-pity and neglecting his daughters. It all became too much. He collapsed at work one day and was rushed to hospital where he was diagnosed with extreme physical and emotional exhaustion.

To recover his health, he took some time away from the business which they spent travelling together in Anastasia's Russian homeland. It was more of a pilgrimage than a holiday. Away from the business, they had a wonderful time together. He talked with them about leaving the business to make a new start in America.

When he returned to the London office, he discovered the business was flourishing thanks to somebody called Celia. Over time, they fell in love.

He brought her to meet them in Regent's Park for lunch one day. They were not so naïve as to think there was nothing going on between their father and his new financial director, as she became, but they were happy for him. The most difficult thing, he told them, was going to be telling the family he intended to marry her.

Then came the part of the story concerning Alice. The twins asked if she wanted them to go on. She said she did.

They told her that after war broke out the authorities were going to put them all in an internment camp. To stop this happening their father volunteered to spy for Britain. The plan was for him to travel to Berlin, join his old friends and pass information back to London. They said Celia told them that they were held hostage in case their father double crossed the authorities. "Which he never would have done of course." Hen paused in silent recollection of past events. Lilly took over telling the story.

"Something happened. We don't know what, but Father got captured. We got a telegram telling us he'd been killed. As you can imagine, Celia was devastated. The family rallied round and it was decided that it would be for the best if we went away to Switzerland and you remained in England with Celia."

"We actually ended up in Lincolnshire as members of the women's land army for a while and then Lilly got a job intercepting

Nazi signals and passing them on to a place called Bletchley. Do you know it?"

"No." Though she did. She didn't know why she said she didn't.

"It wasn't long after we arrived in Lincolnshire that Aunt Eugenie came to see us with the news about you and Celia being killed by a bomb. I don't know how she can have been mistaken."

"What if she wasn't mistaken?"

"What do you mean?"

"Nothing. Carry on."

Hen and Lilly continued their tale which involved a finishing school in Switzerland before going on to work in the family business in Italy and then France before finally moving back to Germany. They told Margaret they were both married, with each having a daughter named Alice.

"Who told you where to find me?" Margaret's senses were on high alert.

"It was all very peculiar. We were contacted by a lawyer from Bern in Switzerland who said that he had information about a relative living in England who we thought had perished in the war. We wanted to meet him to discuss this but he refused, saying it was a trifling matter which didn't require a meeting. Over the next two months he contacted us four or five times before finally confirming your identity and giving us your address here in Cambridge."

"My address in Cambridge? Not Reigate?"

"No, Cambridge. Why Reigate?"

"Because that's where I live with my… parents."

"Who are your parents?"

"Go on with your story please."

"That's it really. There's nothing more to add except we are wondering what your story is."

"I'm wondering that myself."

"Who are your parents, Alice?"

"It seems odd but when you call me Alice… it seems right."

She thought for a few seconds before continuing, "My name now is Margaret Rotheram. My parents are Audrey and Cyril Rotheram. We… they live in Reigate."

"We lived in Reigate with Father and… oh dear. What's going on, Alice?" The twins were visibly upset and shaken. Holding back her tears Hen said, "The Rotherams are relatives. Audrey was a Noelle-Neumann." She started to sob.

"Take me back to Cambridge please," ordered Margaret flatly with no trace of sisterly compassion in her voice.

The sisters didn't talk much on the drive back to Cambridge, opting to stare out of the car's windows. When they arrived at Margaret's student house Hen asked if they could meet later that evening for a meal, a family meal, to get to know one another. Though she wasn't in the mood for socialising, Margaret agreed to meet up with her half-sisters because, as she thought, they'd done nothing wrong and she needed more information to piece the puzzle together. There was another reason though. She had sisters. She wasn't alone in this world if she had sisters. And they had children. Margaret was not alone in the world. She wanted so much to call her mother, no, not her mother, Audrey, and find out what the hell was going on. *No, not yet. I need to find out who is behind my sisters' coming here. There's something terribly wrong with all this.*

***

That evening the sisters met for dinner and had a tearful but pleasant time together. Diners sitting close to them felt uncomfortable with some of the things they were overhearing and so asked to be moved.

A sisters' conversation

>"What will you do now?"
>"I don't know," she lied.

"It must have been as big a shock for you as it was for us. At first we didn't believe it. When we decided to travel to England to check if the story was true we weren't sure what we'd do if we found you. How should we approach you? Through a lawyer as we'd been approached? Write a letter? We weren't sure. But when we saw you walking along the street we knew. It had to be you. It had to be, so we shouted your name and then there was no going back."

"Yes, we were very concerned why we'd been told you'd died along with Celia in the Blitz and now, suddenly, you're there, right in front of us. We knew it had to be you because we share our father's looks. His hair… his eyes. He was such a handsome man. We're so alike we three, even though we have different mothers."

"Did you like my mother?"

"We adored her."

"Did you love her?" The two sisters looked at one another before Hen answered.

"Your mother was a wonderful woman and Father was very much in love with her. If anybody was to replace our mother we were glad it was Celia."

"What will you say to your… to Aunt Audrey and Uncle Cyril? Will you mention anything? It might be best not to mention it."

"How can you say that, Lilly?"

"Digging up the past might lead to… who knows where it might lead but nowhere good, that's for certain."

"I don't know what I'll say to them," she lied.

The twins reminisced about their lives in Germany before the war and what she was like as a baby. Then it struck her. Audrey and Cyril had hardly mentioned anything about her as a baby. She hadn't thought it odd up until then but it was now crystal clear why that was so.

As the sisters parted that night they held each other close before making arrangements for the following day. Margaret returned to the hotel four minutes later to leave a note at reception for her sisters to pick up in the morning, informing them that she had to go away.

***

As soon as Margaret left the hotel she practically bumped into Rex, Timothy's father. Had she been in a less fragile state she would have thought it too much of a coincidence but she wasn't thinking straight. They greeted one another with the now mandatory kissy kissy face dance, ensuring not to touch cheek with lips. Rex asked her what she was doing out so late. "Shouldn't you be studying?" He laughed to show her that he wasn't being entirely serious. She made up a lie on the spot, as to tell him she'd been to dinner with her sisters would require lengthy explanation. He asked how her studies were going and casually mentioned that he had a new job which involved him awarding funding to students of underprivileged families attending Cambridge and handed her his card. He said he had an early start the next day and, at his age, he needed to get to his bed. After they parted he shouted from the door of the hotel, "Give my best to your parents when you next speak with them."

***

Margaret travelled to London early the next day to stay with friends. They knew there must be something amiss as she had exams coming up but they didn't want to pry. Zuzu was shacked up with her handsome waiter and her housemates all had boyfriends so they had no time for Margaret, but what should she say if they asked? They'd assume it was man troubles so she concocted a suitably sad story of infidelity and rehearsed it so as not to get caught out. She couldn't possibly tell them the truth. She supposed the news of her going missing would soon get back to Reigate and that her overprotective parents would panic. She didn't want the police involved. She decided to meet with her so-called parents face to face and have it out with them. No, she didn't ever want to see them again. She'd call instead. She'd call that very evening.

"Hello, Reigate 655…"

"It's me."

"Oh darling, we were so worried about you. Lorraine called to say you weren't at your lectures today and you'd been seen getting on a train for London. Where are you?"

"In London."

"Are you alright, my darling? Is anything the matter?"

"No, I'm not alright as it happens. Who are my parents?"

"What do you mean, darling? What's this all about?"

"Stop lying, Audrey, I know the truth." There was a long silence on the other end of the call.

"Come home, my angel. We can talk about it when you get here. I'll make you your favourite…"

"I'm never coming home again. I never want to see either of you ever again. If you try and contact me I'll go to the police as I'm fairly certain that what you did was illegal." She wasn't sure if any crime had been committed but mentioning the police couldn't hurt in her view.

"Please don't so this, Margaret darling. We love you. We… come home please. Don't do this to us. It'll kill your father."

"My father is already dead. He was executed by the Nazis. But you already know that. Goodbye, Audrey. Remember what I said about not contacting me. I mean it. Never ever try to get in touch with me. If you do you'll regret it. By the way, my name is Alice. Alice."

Having finished the call she felt a great sense of relief, satisfaction almost, but she also felt empty inside. Having no reason to remain in London she caught the train back to Cambridge the next morning. When she arrived, she went straight to the hotel to see her sisters. They were still there, though they were making to leave as she'd disappeared. She told them about her call to Audrey and asked them not to mention anything of their visit to other family members. They told her that they'd told various relatives about their trip before they'd left Germany. She begged them to lie when they returned home, saying that the information from the lawyer was incorrect and the person he'd traced wasn't her. To help sell the lie, they should return to Germany early. She promised she'd contact them after the dust had settled in a few months' time. Now that she had sisters she didn't want to lose them. They unconditionally agreed to keep the truth a secret. The three of them spent the rest of the day and evening together. Before they left to return to Germany the twins gave Alice photographs of her namesakes. They said they'd write regularly to tell her how they were doing at school and send frequent photographs as "they change so quickly". They each instinctively knew they'd probably never meet again.

***

As Margaret was waving goodbye to her sisters – she couldn't believe it when that thought entered her head; saying goodbye to her sisters! She had sisters… and nieces…! – Rex appeared standing next to her at the hotel entrance. He waved too.

"Who are we waving to?"

"Oh, just some German tourists I got friendly with. They came into the bar where I work and we got talking. My German isn't half bad and I'm always looking for somebody to practise with."

"I hope you don't mind me saying so but you bear a remarkable resemblance to them. Remarkable."

"Do you think so? I don't see it."

"Really? Well, I never was much good at things like that… you know, faces, names, ages. But you do look alike. Will you keep in touch with them, they seem rather nice. I had a chat with them yesterday. They seemed concerned that you'd gone missing."

"I wasn't missing. Why does everybody keep saying that? I went to London on urgent business."

"Well, they thought you had. They seemed quite… no, they seemed very upset. Strange behaviour wouldn't you say for people you'd only just met? And you were here with them rather late the night before. You must have got on like a house on fire to have had dinner with them after so short an acquaintance."

"What do you want, Rex?"

"You and I need to talk. But not here. I know your secret. I've an interesting proposition to put to you." She looked at him in a knowing way that only a woman can look. "No, not that. This is business. This is your future."

"I'm not sure I know what you're talking about."

"Oh yes you do. You called your… you called Audrey last night."

"Enough. What the hell do you want, Rex?"

"I told you, I've an interesting proposition for you. You know I have a new job and I have it in my gift to finance your education… as your sponsor if you will. What do you say, Alice, will you listen to what it is I have to say?"

"Alice? Who is Alice? My name…"

"Stop it, Alice. Do you think I pulled that name out of thin air. I told you, I know your secret. I know you'll never go back to Reigate ever again. You can't complete your studies on what a part-time bar job pays so let me do a favour for an old family friend."

"If you think this will get Tim and me back together again, you're mistaken."

"This has nothing to do with you and my son. In fact a condition of my sponsorship will be you never have anything to do with my son ever again… except on a social level that is. You look confused. Let me be frank with you. You're an exceptional, a very exceptional, young lady and I think I may have a suitable career for you once you leave this place."

"People say you're a spy. Are you a spy, Rex?"

"No, Alice, I'm not a spy. Have a think about what we've talked about and call me on the number on the card I gave you when you decide you want to hear what it is I have to say to you."

"Oh, can I have another please, I seem to have misplaced the one you gave me." She smiled.

An Organisation conversation

"It's me."

"I'm supposed to say that. This is highly irregular."

"You wanted to know how things worked out with Margaret Rotheram."

"Well?"

"I spoke with her after she met with her sisters. I told her that I knew that she knew that her mother wasn't her real mother. If you get my meaning?"

"Go on."

"Yes. She didn't go over the edge as you feared she might. Quite the opposite in fact. She seems to have developed a steely determination. I suggested she consider my offer and to give me a call when she's ready to have a meeting. She called me not two minutes ago and we're meeting tomorrow afternoon."

"Be careful, Rex old love, she may be more fragile than you think. What are you going to offer her?"

"I'll offer her a grant to complete her education with the proviso that she does some work for me. I'll make it sound cloak and daggery to feed her suspicions. She'll believe she's being recruited by MI6."

"What about her parents?"

"Sadly, her father doesn't have long to live."

"Does he not? Is he ill?"

"No, not that I'm aware of."

***

The following afternoon Rex and Margaret met up at a pub in Milton, just outside Cambridge. Rex looked different to her somehow and then she realised what he'd done. He'd dyed his hair a slightly different colour and was wearing different spectacles; he'd parted his hair on the opposite side and was wearing gloves and holding a trilby hat.

"You're looking very smart today, Rex," she lied.

"Thank you. I've come straight from… the… erm… office," he replied, laying it on thick.

"What is it you want to talk about?"

"Drinks first, we can't sit in a pub and not get a drink. That would look suspicious." After the drinks arrived he continued, "Have you had time to consider our conversation?"

"I have."

"Well?"

"I'd like to know more. I'll start by asking if you're behind all this?"

"All this what?"

"My sisters showing up in Cambridge… and Audrey and Cyril… you must have known…"

"Things come to our attention but that doesn't mean we're behind everything. No, I learned of your circumstances second hand."

"From whom?"

"Sorry, I can't say. Security and all that," he replied followed by his customary, and very annoying, tapping the side of his nose.

"Fine. This meeting is over. If you can't tell me what I want to know then…"

"Alice. Please. Sit down. There are things I can tell you today and things you will learn over time. I just can't go round telling people what is in my head. I've signed certain covenants and if I break them I could go to jail," he lied for effect. "Please, Alice, listen to what I have to say and be assured there will be more tomorrow."

"But tomorrow never comes, Rex, does it?"

"Young lady, I'm not here for a philosophical discussion, I simply want to talk with you about funding your education and, if you pass muster, there could be a rather interesting job after you graduate."

"I have no intentions of becoming a spy."

"There are more jobs than spying, Alice. Look, for the time being just accept the funding I'm offering you as a family favour. There are no strings attached, I promise. You need the money and I need to show that I'm doing my job by funding impoverished students. I assume you are impoverished now that you've broken ties with your family?"

"They are not my family. My parents are dead."

"So, Alice, do we have a deal? There's nothing to sign, all I need are your bank details and we're all set to go. Simple. What do you say?"

"Give me some time to think about it."

"Certainly. You can have twenty-four hours from… now."

***

Even before the bus arrived back in Cambridge she'd made up her mind to accept Rex's offer but she'd be extremely cautious and the minute she saw something she didn't like then she'd… what? What would she do? She needed money to complete her course and graduate. Yes, graduate. Then she'd make her own choices in life. Take up a career of her choosing. In politics. In economics. She already knew she didn't want a career in either of those paths.

As soon as she got back to her student house she called Rex to tell him that she was prepared to accept his offer, but with certain conditions. Rex replied that there were no conditions on his offer and he expected likewise from her. He told her that if at some future time she wanted to walk away then she could but in the meantime he required her to attend certain functions to demonstrate that his choice of candidate was appropriate. She argued that, contrary to what he'd said, he was imposing conditions on her, to which he replied he certainly was not as what he required of her was normal for any academic grant. "Besides," he said, "you might enjoy it. By the by, there's a little departmental get together next weekend which you should find interesting and not a little fun. It'll be perfect for you for building up your network of contacts." It was as though he'd read her thoughts.

She saw the sense in what Rex was saying. She was brought up knowing there really was no such thing as a free lunch and so agreed to attend Rex's little departmental get together. She wouldn't enjoy it though. She was determined not to enjoy it. Before the call ended, Rex asked for her bank details.

"We haven't actually talked about money yet."

"You're right, we haven't. What would you like to know?"

"Well, for starters, I'd like to know the size of the grant and how much I'll be getting annually and what date the money will hit my account. I'm behind with the rent, you see."

"We can't have that. We can't have our little star out on the streets."

"Are you mocking me, Rex?" she said in the tone of voice she would soon become famous for. A tone that could reduce the temperature of any room in an instant.

"You're very firm, aren't you?... Strict even... I can see why Tim liked you. No, Alice, I'm not mocking you. I'm just trying to be a bit jovial. I'm not all about work you know? I do have a sense of humour."

"I see," she replied with a smirk. "Rex, in future, please promise me you'll let me know when you're being humorous," she said using her Madame Chairman tone of voice to mock him. Rex liked her ways.

"I will, and thank you for the advice," he replied sarcastically. "You'll receive enough to cover your rent and your studies plus an allowance of £2,500 a year for your personal use – clothes, entertaining yourself and the like. No need for receipts."

"That's very generous. My rent is…"

"We know how much your rent is, it's pretty standard in Cambridge. Oh yes, you'll be reimbursed any expenses incurred while on little departmental get togethers and the like."

"I see. Where is the next one, by the way?"

"Paris. You have a passport, I believe?"

"I do but it's at Reigate and I have no intention of ever going there again."

"Not to worry. I'll arrange a nice fresh new one for you. You'll pick up your flight tickets at Heathrow. Catch a taxi Frogside to the get together. An itinerary and your new passport will arrive in the post tomorrow."

"Tomorrow? That's quick. Are you a spy, Rex?"

"Please, Alice, this isn't a secure line." He thought he'd better stop laying it on thick otherwise she might catch on. "This is the last time I will refer to you as Alice."

"Why? I'm going to use my proper name in future. Alice Noelle-Neumann."

"Ah, about that, your passport will be issued in the name of Margaret Rotheram. We can talk about changing your name later but for now it will complicate things with the funding and all that. Is that okay, Margaret?" She hung up the call not answering his question.

***

This is how it begins for the vast majority of the Organisation's recruits. Margaret Rotheram would be sucked down deeper and deeper. Every act would be recorded, every indiscretion and worse filed away to ensure her obedience, compliance, submission. She was a fly stuck on their web and she may just as well stop struggling as it only attracts the attention of the spider at its centre.

She was one of the few who would become a willing recruit. She was predestined to rise rapidly through the ranks of the Organisation. On her upward trajectory she attracted the attention of the Mandarins. But that was always Rex's plan. The Mandarins were looking for somebody like her to lead the Organisation into a new era. Somebody with fresh, new ideas. Somebody with imagination. Somebody who would change it because it needed to change.

Her promotions would come quickly, one after the other. Those around her had a choice. Hang onto the coat-tails of her rising star and go where she goes or languish and wait for her judgement.

MICHAEL'S STORY – TROUBLE IN PARADISE

Unexpectedly, Michael settled into his all-boys grammar school from day one. There were a few fist fights at first to establish the pecking order but he didn't get involved in them, he just went along to watch and learn. Apart from football, rugby and cricket, the school sports curriculum included archery, fencing and boxing. Not being keen on team sports, Michael applied to join the sports clubs.

Michael went along to the fencing club at the start of his second week. As it was oversubscribed, the teacher asked if any of them had any experience with swords.

"I was in a pantomime once as Peter Pan," shouted Spike, who had already established himself as the class clown. All the kids laughed.

"Yeah, very funny." The teacher said he'd give them all a try out to see who was best at fencing.

One at a time they donned fencing gear, picked up a foil and did the exercises shown them so the teacher could see what they had. He was looking for balance, speed, strength and not a little aggression. Things were not looking good. Then came Michael's turn. When he took up a foil for the first time the teacher said, "Oh good, you're cack-handed, we need some lefties. You're in if you can do the exercises." Michael completed the exercises and repeated them using his right hand. "Ace, you're an ambi. Brilliant. You're in." None of the pupils had any idea what an ambi was but if it got you on the team they wanted to be one. None of them noticed that Michael had switched hands and repeated the exercises, they just thought he was showing off and anything he could do…

"No, no, no. Just do what I tell ye to do, you divvies. None of this fancy stuff, you're not Errol bleedin' Flynn. What's up with you lot?" shouted the teacher.

"You picked Michael after he did fancy stuff so we're doin' it," came Spike's voice from the back of the group as usual.

"Frost didn't do any fancy stuff, as you call it. He did the exercises using his left hand and then repeated them with his right hand. He's an ambi. Ambidextrous? Have any of you lot heard that word before? It means he's as good with his left hand as he is with his right."

"Our kid's like that when he plays with himself," grunted Spike trying to disguise his voice. The kids in the fencing class doubled up with laughter.

"I know that was you, Spikey boy. Come on down, let's see if you can fence as good as you talk." Spike, it turned out, was already pretty good with a foil as he'd previously had fencing lessons with his scout troop. He was definitely on the team.

The following day Michael went along for boxing club selection. His reputation preceded him. The boxing coach was excited at the prospect of having 'the' Michael Frost on his team.

***

The first school year flew by. Michael was like a sponge when it came to mathematics and languages but languished in the second from bottom set in all other subjects except metalwork and woodwork because, "He's good with his hands", as Margaret always said.

At the end of each school year there were streaming exams for the following year. In the second and third years, pupils could choose to drop some subjects with others added to their curriculum. It became a straight choice for Michael between Geography and History. He chose to continue with History as he was very good at remembering dates. Goodbye Geography, hello French.

***

The passing of school time for Michael was neither boring nor enjoyable. It just was. He continued to do well in Mathematics, German and French and, uniquely at the time, in his third senior school he was one of only eight pupils invited to join a specially sponsored Russian language class. As with his German and French lessons, he was the best of the school's pupils with Russian too.

Outside school, Michael spent most of his spare time in libraries, studying alone and reading books on languages and mathematics. It was impossible for him to study properly at home. One day, he came across a book on military strategy which had been left in the languages section. He was on his way to take it to the librarian's desk when some words on the back cover caught his eye; they fired his imagination. In future he included military books in his readings.

Apart from spending much of his time in the library, Michael kept up with going to the boxing club every Tuesday with Timbo. This routine continued until the autumn of 1967 when Timbo, along with four other members of the Sparrow Hall Gang, were sentenced to between three and five years in prison for a series of robberies. During one of the robberies a bystander had been stabbed by one of the gang and there being a strict code of 'no grassing' they each received stiffer sentences than they would otherwise have got had they pointed out Baz as the knife man.

***

Feeling out of sorts at having no cousin Timbo to go to boxing club with, Michael's head became seriously out of kilter. His visions became more frequent and terrible and produced feelings of despair in him as he couldn't share his torment with anybody. He was boiling up inside and it wouldn't take much to set him off. It was only a matter of time.

***

Thomas was playing in the street outside the house when he attracted the attention of a local thug who set upon him for no reason.

While he was being attacked by this much larger and older kid, Thomas shouted, "I'm gonna get our kid onto you."

"Go and get him then. I'll burst that college puddin' if he comes out 'ere." Michael heard what was said while staring out of the single-glazed, uncurtained lounge window and needed no other invitation.

Without uttering a syllable, Michael set about Thomas's assailant with a ferocity he had never shown before. Within seconds, kids ran to form a fighting circle. As they approached the fight they slowed, with some even stopping dead in their tracks at the sight that greeted them. The teenager who'd attacked little Thomas had a big reputation and what they were seeing was Michael making mincemeat out of this notorious local thug. Some of the kids were quietly enjoying seeing this bully getting his just desserts. One of the crowd, however, was the teenager's BFF and he jumped on Michael's back causing a separation between him and the thug. *We'll do this div now*, thought the joiner-inner until he saw thug boy legging it down the street and leaving him alone to face Michael.

The joiner-inner jumped off Michael's back. "Sorry, mate. I was just tryin' to break up the fight in case you got hurt," said the quick-thinking joiner-inner.

"Yer a liar you are, John Divine. You were joinin' in the fight to make it two onto one, ye lyin' chicken ye," shouted one of the girls in the fighting circle which then started making bock, bock, bock noises.

"No, honest, mate, I wasn't. I just didn't want ye gettin' hurt sort of thing. An' you, Daisy O'Dwyer, you shut yer gob an' stop stirrin' it." With that the joiner-inner went to attack Daisy O'Dwyer which was his biggest mistake that afternoon. With the joiner-inner running toward Daisy O'Dwyer, Michael reached out and grabbed him by the hair, dragging him backwards and causing his head to hit the ground with such force that blood streamed from a gash wound.

"Somebody dial 999 and ask for an ambulance."

Margaret emerged from the house having just seen what had happened from the lounge window. When she pushed through the tightly knotted group she saw a lad laying on the ground with his head resting in a pool of blood. It was all too much for her. She immediately started crying and ran back inside the house, dragging Michael by his shirt collar behind her.

"Are you going to hit my legs, Mum?" asked Michael.

"No, son, I'm not. I think you're in real trouble this time with your fighting. What have I told you? Eh? What have I told you? I've told you a thousan' times not to fight." Through lip reading, Margaret couldn't tell that the word thousand ended with the letter d. There were many misspoken words in Margaret's vocabulary. When speaking with her, some relatives used her misspoken words to make fun out of her but she didn't catch on to what they were doing. But Michael did. He knew what shits some of his relatives were to his mum.

***

After the ambulance medic patched up the head of the joiner-inner kid, who was nowhere near as broken as at first feared, the ambulance crew sent him home to lie down. But that wasn't the end of the matter. Answering a knock on the front door, Michael came face to face with Police Sergeant Bill Huggard.

"Are you Michael? Is yer mum home please, son?"

"Yes, I'm Michael. I'll get her for you."

"Oh good Jesus, who called the police?" exclaimed Margaret when she saw the uniform.

"Now don't panic, luv, I'm here to have a little chat with you and Michael about what happened this afternoon. I've already spoken with some of the kids in the street and though what Michael did was wrong he's a bit of a hero for what he did to those bullies."

The Police Sergeant and Margaret had a long chat about Michael and what had gone on, after Margaret had said to him, "You'll have to speak up please, I'm a little hard of hearing."

"Now then, Michael, yer mum's told me you've been going to boxing for the past few years and yer pretty good."

"I used to go with Timbo until he went to jail."

"Yeah, yer mum said. Tell yer what, though we don't have a boxing club here we do have a karate club. It's run by the Police Association and I'd be glad to take you along if you like? We even have lessons in Japanese sword fighting, ye know, like Samurais and stuff; I hear you're on the school fencing team so that might be interesting for ye. They use wooden swords, mind you, not the metal ones. Ye wouldn't want the kids round here getting their hands on real Samurai swords," joked Sergeant Huggard. "And once a week I run a minibus full of cadets down to Bootle for the Royal Tank Regiment. How do ye fancy givin' that a go? They do all sorts of stuff and they go away to Altcar out by Southport for weekends. It'll be fun goin' away with lads yer own age."

"I like fencing."

"Okay then, we'll start you off at the dojo and see where we go from there, eh? I've left the address with yer mum. There's no subs so it doesn't cost anything. I'll see you tomorrow night then, young man?"

***

During his first visit to the dojo, Michael kept glancing over at a kenjutsu class practising with wooden swords. "You can have a go at that some other time," said Sergeant Huggard having noticed he'd become preoccupied. One of the swords wasn't wooden though. One of the swords was a beautifully decorated katana held by the sensei.

"Nice sword," whispered Michael. Karate lesson over Michael was introduced by Sergeant Huggard to the sensei taking the kenjutsu class.

"Sensei, this is Michael, the lad I told you about."

"Hello Michael, Sergeant Huggard told me you're quite the boxer and that you are on your school's fencing team. Is that wood fencing or metal fencing?" joked the sensei.

Not getting the joke Michael replied, "Foil," which the sensei took to be an even better joke until he registered the blank expression on Michael's face.

"Yeah, I was just making a little joke there, Michael. Never mind."

"Is that what ye call it," laughed Sergeant Huggard. "That was rubbish, no wonder the lad didn't laugh."

"I like your sword."

"Here, hold it." Michael took hold of the sensei's katana and immediately felt at one with it. A fire took hold of him. His eyes shone silver reflected from the blade. He posed with the katana as he'd seen the sensei doing and performed a couple of exercises from memory.

"Wow, he really likes my katana. Would you like to join my kenjutsu class next time you're here, Michael?"

"Hey you, not so fast you, I need him for my karate group."

"Yes p… pl… please." This was the first time in his life that

Michael had ever spoken the p word. He found it hard to say as it stuck in his throat. No matter how many times friends, relatives, teachers and family tried to get Michael to say please he'd never spoken that word until then.

"Okay, Michael, we'll get you in early next week so you can do both classes. Karate first and then some Japanese swordplay," suggested Sergeant Huggard. Another first for Michael was he was looking forward to something without it occupying all of his mind. Instead, he had a warm feeling of contentment in his stomach.

***

Michael practised with the katana at every opportunity, blending Japanese swordplay with traditional fencing techniques; the combination producing an interesting, devastating and unique style of sword fighting.

***

The following evening Michael went with a whole minibus load of kids for his first evening with the cadets of the Royal Tank Regiment. They started off with some square bashing. He took to the routineness of it like a duck to water. He loved doing things that quieted the voices in his head even if only momentarily.

The cadet NCO screamed, "Squaaaaaaaaaaaaad… aboooooout… face," while the cadets were on the march.

"Check. T. L. V. Check," shouted the cadets in unison while carrying out their about-face manoeuvre.

"Squaaaaaaaaaaaaad… Halt!" Thump, thump.

"Squaaaaaaaaaaaaad… stand aaaaat… ease!" Thump. "Stand easy." Shuffle. While the two ranks of cadets stood at ease, one cadet's shoulders were going up and down like pistons and tears were streaming from his eyes.

"Corpwal. Who is that cadet and why is he waffing?" On

hearing the officer's speech impediment both ranks of cadets stifled their laughter.

"That's Cadet Munroe, sir."

"Why is Cadet Munwoe waffing, Corpwal?"

"I don't know, sir."

"Munwoe?"

"Sir?" answered Tommy Munroe.

"Why are you waffing Munwoe?"

"I don't know sir. I think it's because of the name of the cadet next to me."

"What's so funny about his name, Munwoe?"

"I can't remember, sir."

"Well, Munwoe, I think that Munwoe is an even funnier name, don't you, Munwoe?"

"Yes sir." By this time all the cadets were almost peeing their pants holding in the laughter building up inside of them listening to the Captain's speech impediment. "Please, no more, please," they silently begged.

"This cadet doesn't appear to be waffing, Corpwal. What's this cadet's name?"

"I don't know, sir, he's new tonight. What's your name for the officer, Cadet?"

"Some of the cadets said his name is Captain Rupert, Corporal," replied Michael misunderstanding the request. There was a gasp followed by an expectant hush from all the cadets until one of them snorted out a huge snot bubble at what Michael had said. They tried their best to continue standing at ease but rocked on the balls of their feet unable to fully control themselves.

"Captain Wupert, eh?" echoed Captain Hywel-Jones. "What's your name, Cadet?"

"My name is Michael Frost, Captain."

"Say sir when addressing an officer, Cadet Frost," interjected the Cadet Corporal.

"Michael Fwost, eh. I'll wemember that name. Cawwy on,

Corpwal." At that the Captain left the drill yard. The Cadet Corporal spun round to face the ranks of the cadets, his face beetroot red through holding in his laughter.

"Stone me, Frosty, I thought I was gonna piss myself there. You're a case you are." The Cadet Corporal had a strong Brummie accent which Michael couldn't decipher. He had no idea what the Corporal was talking about but everybody seemed to be having a good time so he went along with it. He didn't appreciate being called Frosty though.

***

Every week became blissfully routine for Michael. He lived for the dojo and the Royal Tank Regiment. During his fourth week at Cadets he got to use a Lee Enfield .22. Shooting relaxed him. Unlike the other cadets he didn't mind cleaning his rifle afterwards.

As he left the barracks that evening he recognised someone standing in a group of TA soldiers. It was Buckhead. He hadn't noticed Michael but it could only be a matter of time before the two of them would come face to face.

BACK IN HIS OLD KREMLIN OFFICE

Moscow, 6th May

0330 MSK.

There he was, back in his old office. He hadn't been there since his retirement party fifteen years previous. What a great party that was. At least that's what he'd been told.

He'd got so drunk he couldn't remember ninety-nine percent of it but by all accounts he was on fine form and despite being very drunk he was his usual charming self and had danced and sung like it was 1969. That was the year he'd been approached by the CIA and for the next thirty years he willingly betrayed his country. No, not his country, he loved his country, his Russia; he wasn't betraying his country, he willingly betrayed the Soviet Union.

Now, looking out of the office window onto a deserted Red Square, he recalled how hard he'd worked to get this view. It was rumoured that Stalin himself had worked in that very office. During his time he'd fooled his Soviet comrades and his deceptions continued throughout the era of glasnost but the late night call told him that the game was up and maybe he hadn't been fooling anybody at all.

The morning's events started at 0105 after a call from somebody describing herself as "a friend" and advising him to "switch on your TV to the International News channel". She hung up before he could ask any questions but he knew from the old days that one ignored such calls at your peril. He got out of his lovely warm bed and switched on the International News channel. When the TV flashed into life there was a news item on loop concerning a Russian émigré living in London who'd been taken hostage by the notorious ISBJ. He reached for his glasses as his failing sight couldn't make out what was going on behind the head of the Russian news anchor. As soon as he recognised the face staring back at him from the TV screen he vomited with fear. He immediately reached for the phone and called his daughter, Svetlana. What a relief it was to hear her sweet voice. His darling little Svetochka. She sounded like she was in a hurry. He advised her to get out of London as quickly as possible and make her way back home by one of the old routes. They, at least, could still be relied upon if you needed to stay below the radar. He finished the call by telling her how much he loved her and how much he missed her and how she needed to be careful.

He made many calls during the next hour, right up until the call he received ordering him to return to his old office. The caller advised him that a staff car was waiting outside his apartment building and he had two minutes to get dressed.

***

Now, sitting alone in his office, albeit with four square-shouldered FSB agents guarding the corridor, he went to his secret stash of the good stuff. Would it still be there? To his delight it had remained untouched. Eight bottles. He wondered how he was going to get through them in the time he had left. What should he do with the bottles he couldn't finish? Smash them? Now, that would be a crime. Whisky of this vintage deserved better than that, but better smashed than warming the throats of the new political elite. Gone were the long hard vodka drinking days habitual to the elite of the Soviet ruling party. In the new Russia only the best whisky was good enough for those who bled dry the country he loved so dearly.

***

Born Sergei Sergeyevich Kozlov in Leningrad in 1939, just twenty-four months before the sneak attack by the Nazis on his beloved motherland, he and his family were evacuated to Omsk as hostilities began.

"Such a pity that Zhukov didn't seize power when he had the opportunity, when all the Soviet Union worshipped him," he muttered as he poured his first glass.

While under evacuation he witnessed the shooting of his elderly uncle, Dyadya Vasya. Dyadya Vasya wasn't a blood relative uncle, he was an honorary uncle. A title given him by Sergei's mother's family whom he had helped years before Sergei was born. Such a lovely man. Such a good Russian man. Good Russian people were being slaughtered for committing the most minor of misdemeanours or even for doing nothing at all; they were often simply the victims of vendettas or greedy local Soviets.

The stories his mother told him about Russia before the Bolsheviks and the things he witnessed in Omsk turned Sergei against the Soviet Union. He was schooled to keep his mouth shut and so never voiced the things he felt in his heart or spoke the thoughts in his head.

***

At his first opportunity Sergei became a spy for the Americans. He wasn't in it for the money and declined most inducements. He was the hardest type of spy to root out: an ideologically motivated spy. Had he been caught he knew what his fate would have been along with that of his entire family and probably his friends too. When the good old Bolsheviks cut out a cancer they didn't just remove the lump they took the whole lung.

***

Now, as to Sergei's present predicament; in the old days he would have simply been left in a room with a bottle of vodka and a revolver to save the inconvenience of a trial. Khrushchev was a great enthusiast of this form of self-administered justice. But these days? It was anybody's guess. Popular during the winter months was the white death. Rather than go to all the expense of using a bullet, victims would simply have snow forced into their mouths until they choked to death.

Footsteps in the corridor followed by low, muffled talking. The sound of boots walking away from the door of his former office. Had his FSB guard been dismissed? A knock at the door.

"Come in." The door opened cutting a V-shaped yellow slice of light into the carpet.

"Good morning, Sergei, I see you've started early, or is it a nightcap?"

"Good morning, Sacha, will you join me in one last toast? For old times' sake."

"One last toast? Why? Are you going somewhere?"

"Let's not play games, Sacha. We've known each other for far too long to play games. I'd just like to be allowed to finish this glass of fine malt whisky and then we can get on with it. Will you join me? No? All that I ask is that you spare my sweet Svetochka. She didn't know that she wasn't working for you. She's always been loyal. She just did what I told her to do. I acted alone at all times." Sergei knew his pleas were useless as his fate was already sealed, as was the fate of all those he knew, but he had to play the game.

"We both know that's untrue, now don't we, Serge? I can still call you Serge?"

"Of course you can, my old friend, I'm glad they chose you to do it." Sergei was attempting to flatter his old friend even though he knew his old friend wouldn't buy it. Keep playing the game at all times.

"Please, Serge, we are not Americans. You're living in the past. We no longer dispose of those who make, shall we say, errors of judgement when they have so much more to offer us alive. We are your salvation. I am your Father Confessor. We already know a lot of what's been going on but now it's time for you to fill in the blanks. And please, Serge, no lies. Time is short and if I don't achieve results quickly then I'll be replaced. And you know what that means. It's all up to you, everything is in your hands. We have both seen the BBC News broadcast. Michael Frost, or as you made him, Mikhail Morozov, is alive. The Boss is actually impressed with what you managed to achieve right under the noses of professionals who should have been more vigilant. They will have time to consider the error of their ways in an environment commensurate with their incompetence. So, Serge, my old friend, over to you."

"Where to start?"

"Please start with how Frost became a Russian citizen. How you kept him and his identity hidden from us for so long. How he came to marry your daughter and how he managed to return with her to England unnoticed by anybody. What has he been doing for the past ten years? We must find Frost before the Americans, the British, the Jews, the Islamists or the French… especially the French. Time is very short. Our monitoring services have picked up communiqués from across the globe ordering the capture or the killing of Michael Frost. Some want him dead and others want him alive for obvious reasons."

"Then why the hell did our Embassy issue a statement of denial about Mikhail Morozov? That's bound to grab the interest of his captors and reduce the time left to find him. Permission for a denial of that sort could have only have come from Vladimir Vladimirovich himself."

"You'd think so, wouldn't you? I'm going to tell you something, Serge, and I swear to God that if you tell another living soul I will put you and Svetlana in a room with the Irishman and his friend."

"Why mention the Irishman and his friend? Surely they're both long dead."

"It appears not. We intercepted signals reactivating them both. It turns out they are alive and living in America. So, worse than being dead." Sacha chuckled at his jibe. "It's going to be bad news for somebody with those two back in business." Sergei nodded his head slowly in agreement. "It appears our ciphers were hacked and our London Embassy received a pre-prepared statement for them to pass to the BBC. The statement was nothing to do with us." Sergei contemplated the magnitude of what he'd just heard without commenting on it. Sacha continued, "Vladimir Vladimirovich has been fully briefed and a thorough investigation is underway."

Sergei knew that to be code speak for unleashing the most brutal and thuggish people imaginable on Russia's Secret Service communities and right now many people would be being picked up or had already been spirited away never to be seen again. *Sacha is right,* thought Sergei, *this is not America.*

"The Boss wants regular updates so let's get on with it."

Sergei poured himself a generous measure of his thousand-dollar-a-bottle malt whisky and made himself comfortable on the deep button-backed English Chesterfield sofa under the window of his former office.

"I think I will join you but let's make it our last until we're done," said Sacha pouring himself a large measure. He leaned forward and chinked glasses with Sergei. "*Nasdrovia.*"

"*Na Zdarovye,*" replied Sergei. Each downed half the contents of their broad, deep facet cut crystal glasses. "What's happened to you, Sacha? One glass? It used to be one bottle. Before lunch!" Sergei laughed loud but laughed alone. "Okay, I assume there are others listening and this conversation is being recorded so no need for notes?"

"Yes, of course," he lied.

Sergei took a sip of his whisky followed by a couple of deep breaths and started. "Forty-six years ago I was recruited by…"

"I thought we'd agreed on recent history?" interrupted an impatient Sacha.

Sergei gave Sacha the stink eye and carried on. "… the CIA. I had been waiting and hoping that I would be recruited. It happened exactly as I had thought: a bit of small talk while attending government functions. The people I was introduced to were 'Agricultural Equipment Research Attachés' and others with similarly ridiculous job titles. You know the drill. In those days we all knew who was a spy and who wasn't. It was the big game in town. I was invited to gatherings such as 'International Cultural Development Councils' and I went to cocktail parties in the knowledge that I was being watched and reported on by the KGB. I, of course, declined all approaches and reported each of them to my superiors, making it clear that I wasn't interested in spy games. But eventually I got what I needed. A contact. As she didn't appear on any lists I was confident she was clean and clear and not a double agent. Perfect."

"Make sure you provide all names in your written report."

"I was a bit old to be entering the spy game for the first time. My career hadn't been meteoric so nobody was really aware of my existence. I hadn't come to the attention of anybody." Sergei laughed to himself and then carried on. "I started off doing small errand boy jobs, taking packages to dead letter drops etcetera. The packages had nothing in them for the early drops in case you got caught, before you learned how to be careful. I made it clear from the start what I would and what I would not do. I told them I would not do any physical harm to anybody and that I wouldn't provide information relating to the defence of the Soviet Union, Russia really; I didn't care about places like Ukraine, Poland or Kazakhstan and especially not that shithole Stalin was born in. I told the CIA they could bomb the shit out of Georgia for all I cared."

"Yes, yes, yes, Serge, but please, only forty minutes before I have to report back and if there isn't enough then… they only gave me first crack at you because we go way back, so can we please get on with the Michael Frost story? You can be fully debriefed at a later time."

"I want to put things in context so that you and the people listening cannot make me out to be something I am not. I know how good we are at twisting the truth out of all recognition."

"Serge, please trust me, I promise you that you'll get your opportunity to make a full confession in your own words but for now time is of the essence. Foreign agents are already descending on London and we are sitting here drinking whisky and reminiscing. If you love Russia as much as you say you do then get to the point. Please, Serge, please."

After a pause for careful thought, Sergei resumed.

"One day I received a request which seemed odd to me. I was asked to set up a meeting between my CIA handler and somebody I knew to be a KGB double agent. The two people concerned already knew one another very well and could easily have set up the meeting themselves, so why was I needed? But I didn't ask any questions. When I came into the office the next day I was called into a room along with several colleagues. We were all sworn to secrecy. We were told by a KGB officer that two agents, one foreign and one Russian, had been murdered right outside the walls of the Kremlin the previous evening and they believed somebody in one of our departments was involved and they wanted us to think about who this might be.

"Of course I understood this to be the classic KGB 'putting the fox among the chickens' tactic. I remained calm. I understood that these events throw up all sorts of surprises, leaving the KGB to pick up those reported. It was just like being back in the old days of the denunciations. Lazy KGB. Later that morning I picked up a message at a dead letter drop. It ordered me to report in ill at work and go to my apartment straight away. When I got there two men followed me through the outer security door and into the lift. I didn't recognise either of them but they didn't look KGB to me. One turned out to be the assassin of the two agents who'd been murdered by the Kremlin walls, a crazy Irishman, and the other was Michael Frost. This was 1989. Unlike the Irishman, Michael Frost spoke excellent Russian. Even after only a few minutes I noticed there was something strange about Michael Frost. No matter what was going on he remained impassive and emotionless, speaking matter-of-factly without any intonation in his voice. Though he made me feel uncomfortable I didn't think he would do me any harm."

Sergei took a long sip before continuing, "The Irishman told me I was not to tell the CIA about the arrangements I had made for the previous day's meeting. Then, astonishingly, he told me that the orders I'd carried out over the years were not from the CIA but were from an organisation he worked for. Why he was telling me this soon became clear. He said in future they would be running me directly. I realise it sounds farfetched but it's all true."

Sacha indicated that he wanted Sergei to speed up by making a rolling motion of his right hand as if to say, "Get on with it."

"Over the next ten years, right up until the time of my retirement, I carried on doing what I had always done but not knowing who it was I was working for. It gave me an ulcer. I knew I couldn't get out of whatever it was I was in because I believed the Irishman when he'd told me that some of our own KGB worked for this Organisation.

"I wished I had never started what I had willingly started. What a fool I had been. I was so relieved when my retirement came around. The night of my retirement party I danced and sang myself hoarse. I was free at last. Why would they want me now that I didn't have access to anything anymore? What use could I be to them? I was free! I didn't remember much about the party but I did remember wandering outside onto the balcony for some fresh air and coming across a man." Sacha flicked his head to one side, he'd long known Sergei's preferences.

"We stood close as we talked. I felt something against the underside of my chin; it turned out to be a stiletto dagger. He motioned for me to be quiet by putting a finger to his lips. He told me that some people were hunting Michael Frost and if he turned up in Moscow I was to contact him immediately. I was to inform him and only him. He said that any deviation from this instruction would be very bad for me. He spoke this in a tone I will never forget. I believed every word he said." Sergei drew breath after reliving that vivid moment. He felt drained just speaking about it. "I need a piss. I'm used to pissing three or four times a night." He smiled a straight-mouthed smile.

"Yes, we know," said Sacha pointing to the door, following up with, "And come straight back. We're both too old to go running around this place at our time of life." Then as an afterthought, "And leave your mobile phone here with me."

***

Sergei used his lavatory break to get a few things in perspective. He decided to speed up his so-called confession and get out of there as quickly as he could. Assuming he was really going to be allowed to leave, which he had serious doubts about.

When he returned to his former office he said to Sacha, "You'll have to report to the Boss soon. Do you have enough for him to let you continue?"

"I spoke with him while you were taking a piss and he's okay for us to carry on but we need to pick up the pace."

Snap, thought Sergei as that played nicely into his plan.

Sergei began, "Rolling forward to early in 2005."

Thank God, thought Sacha.

"I was living alone as my wife had passed away in 2002 and

my sweet Svetochka was living in St Petersburg. How happy I was when the name of the city of my birth was changed back to St Petersburg. I celebrated by getting very drunk. I decided to stay in Moscow. If I moved I would miss all that Moscow life has to offer to somebody like me."

Sergei looked sideways at Sacha waiting for some comment but as none was forthcoming he continued on. "I was returning home after an evening at the theatre with friends, when I was pushed through the security doors of my apartment block. I lay face down on the floor pretending to be unconscious. 'Stop messing about, I didn't push you that hard,' said my assailant. I recognised his voice and his perfect Russian, it was Michael Frost. I asked him what he wanted. 'We're going to your apartment,' he said. I'd gathered that much at least. When we entered the apartment he pushed me to the floor again and I told him I was getting fed up with this rough treatment. He ignored me, tying my hands and ankles with cable ties and searching the place before allowing me up again. Of course he found nothing because I had retired from the business.

"He started telling me about the workings of the organisation he worked for and that there wasn't just one Organisation, there were many. He called them splinters. He said the Irishman who'd visited me all those years before was heading up death squads and that he was top of their hit list because of what he knew. The way he described it was, 'because of the things I have locked away in my head'." Sergei looked toward Sacha to prompt him to ask questions but he was contemplating his navel and turned to simply nod for Sergei to continue.

"'Why have you come to me?' I asked. His answer was, 'Nobody is interested in you and you have the contacts I need.' I asked him why he thought I wasn't under surveillance. His reply cut me to the core. 'Because your file says you're a delusional fantasist who believed he could overthrow the Communist state by being a messenger boy for the CIA. Your file says that you're a Walter

Mitty character and should be treated as such.' Is it so, Sacha? Was I simply regarded as a delusional crackpot?"

Sacha put a finger into the dregs of his whisky, wiping it around the inside of his glass before putting it in his mouth. "Waste not want not. Serge, I put that note on your file to keep you safe after your retirement. I never thought for one minute that somebody like Michael Frost would contact you. I'd known for a long time that you were working for the CIA and, to be honest, it served my purposes."

"But did you think me delusional, Sacha?" Sergei felt deeply wounded by Sacha's unspoken confirmation. The realisation dawned on him that perhaps he had been delusional after all and that he had made little contribution to the overthrow of the Communists in his beloved Russia, but he was satisfied that he'd kept Michael Frost out of the hands of the enemies of his Russia.

"Serge, we all do what we can but we need to recognise our limitations. Was what you were doing ever really going to change anything? Of course not, but I didn't think you should be shot for doing the bidding of the organisations who were pulling your strings. Besides I didn't want to alert anybody to the existence of the Organisation. That's one of the big no-nos. It was suggested that we simply just kill you immediately after your retirement party but I said we should keep you on ice in case we needed a package delivered. You know, low level stuff you're good at." Sergei noticed that Sacha mentioned the Organisation without batting an eyelid.

"Are you one of them?"

"Please, Serge, carry on. Time is even shorter. Get on with your story," he said, impatiently tapping the face of his watch.

Sergei couldn't gather himself for half a minute after Sacha mentioned the Organisation. Who was this man sitting in front of him who he'd known for more than half his life? Godfather to his beloved Svetochka. He cleared his throat, poured himself another whisky and continued, "Over the next couple of days

Frost told me about the Organisation and the things it was involved in. He knew so much, and in very great detail, so I could easily understand why they were hunting him. He had the dirt on so many governments and prominent people and he talked about a group called the Four Hundred. I didn't get to the bottom of that one."

"Did you write any of this down?"

"No, certainly not, I didn't want a record of anything Frost said as it would be useful to the wrong people and dangerous for me, and why did I need a record? I had Frost. He was speaking from first-hand experience so it was clear that he was involved in all the things he was telling me about. I recognised this information as being extremely valuable but I also recognised the danger in turning Frost in. If I did turn him in, how could I do so without its consequences ending up on my doorstep? I would be killed for sure. Nobody could take the risk that he hadn't told me about the Organisation. Also, what was in it for me if I handed him in? What was in it for this delusional Walter Mitty character if I turned him in? Nothing good, that's for sure.

"We made a plan. I used my old contacts to create a Russian identity for him. As I said, he speaks perfect Russian so he fitted right in. He has quite a sharp sense of irony and humour, if you could call it that; he said he wanted an identity in the name of Mikhail Morozov. I was against it at first for obvious reasons but he wouldn't be dissuaded. Mikhail Morozov it was. We decided he should hide out in St Petersburg. After a few calls an apartment was arranged for Mikhail Morozov."

"Through Svetlana?" Sacha interrupted.

"Svetochka had nothing to do with arranging Frost's apartment and indeed she did not even meet him during his first two years in St Petersburg. Anyway. I discovered he was coming and going in and out of the country. To do what? I had no idea. I needed to find out as my safety depended on his safety. So, in an effort to find out about Frost's comings and goings I contrived a meeting between him and Svetochka. She's a pretty girl and alone, in the way that so many Russian women are, so I thought Frost wouldn't be suspicious of her. I told her I was representing my old employers," he lied, "and they had a job for her. In order to get close to Frost she got a job waitressing at a little restaurant he liked to frequent and after a few weeks they were on speaking terms.

"Frost though was always very, very careful. He's suspicious about everybody and everything so we had to move slowly and let him make the running. Nothing was happening between them and as we couldn't make anything happen, without arousing his suspicions, we were beginning to despair when one evening, after her work was done for the day, we got a break. Svetochka was walking home along the same street where Frost was living when she caught the attention of a couple of men. They were well-known local thugs. They shouted something disgusting to my daughter and she shouted something disgusting back at them. They got into a shouting match and one of the men hit out at her. Nothing serious, just a small back-hand swipe which hardly made contact. Frost suddenly emerged from the door to his apartment block and walked toward the men. He asked what was going on. Svetochka said nothing was going on but one of the men told Frost to 'go away or there will be some trouble for you, old man.' She told me how Frost moved with incredible speed, grabbing the arm of the man who had hit her and breaking it in several places. Svetochka told me later that Frost said he broke the arm of the hand which had struck her.

"The other man carried his companion back to their car and sped away. Svetochka asked Frost why he'd got involved. He simply said, in his usual way, that he cannot abide bad behaviour toward women. From my conversations with him I could understand what Svetochka was telling me. He seems to operate on an old-fashioned, chivalrous level. I believe, from my conversations with him, that his dispensing of this form of moral justice comes from the time when his parents' marriage was breaking up and he saw his father strike his mother. Frost cares for his mother very much and she doted on him and spoiled him; perhaps because of his strangeness. But that is another story."

Thank goodness, thought Sacha.

Sergei continued, "This incident brought Frost and Svetochka close and they started dating, if you could call it that. I'm not really sure what was going on between them but they seemed to enjoy each other's company. It would take another year before they moved in together and during that time she drip fed him the details of her past, most of which were specially designed to play on his emotions regarding his closeness with his mother. The past we constructed for her included a dead father. This meant we could manipulate Frost by…"

Sacha interrupted. "It's just as well there is no family resemblance between you and Svetochka otherwise Frost might have become suspicious, which is doubly fortunate as you're no oil painting." Sergei winced at these remarks. "Oh Serge, I see I've hurt your feelings. I apologise, it was just a joke." But the so-called joke had hit its mark. Sergei had long suspected that Sacha had figured out he couldn't be Svetlana's biological father.

Drawing a calming breath Sergei continued. "We constructed a past where her father had died from alcoholism when she was eight. Her cover story proceeded through the normal stages of a child growing up in St Petersburg which she borrowed from her own life's path so she wouldn't trip herself up on details as Frost has a truly remarkable memory. During her conversations with Frost, Svetochka embellished the details of the breakup of her marriage to make it similar to the breakup of his parents' marriage. We threw in extra bits of cruelty for good measure to really tug at his heart strings. Over time, they settled into the normal routines of life and I think they actually grew close. After a couple of years they got married and, completely without warning, they moved to

London. I was angry when they did that and I've never received a satisfactory explanation about why they moved. They were safe in St Petersburg, where I could keep an eye on Frost. Svetochka told me, no matter how hard she tried, she couldn't find out what he did when he travelled abroad." He always knew when she was lying. "She said he was very secretive about his trips. I suspected he was still involved in his old ways and we both know what that means. I tried several times to…"

"Okay," interrupted Sacha. "You write down all the names of the people who knew Frost while he was living in St Petersburg and what their involvement was with him. I want the addresses where he lived, places he frequented and so on and the same for London. I have to go and meet the Boss to give him an update."

As he sat alone in his former office, Sergei contemplated his next move. Above all else he wanted to keep his daughter safe. During his talk with his old friend, he'd used the familiar form of Svetlana as Svetochka as many times as he could in the hope Sacha would humanise her in his mind as her godfather and not just think of her as an object. He knew it was a long shot but he had to give it a try.

***

A splinter conversation

"It's clear the old fool has nothing important to tell us about Michael Frost."

"What shall we do with dear old Serge now?" asked the Boss.

"I'll go back into the room and tell him he's free to return to his life of retirement as though this night had never happened. There will be a little surprise waiting for him when he gets home."

"Good. Is the little surprise going to look like another tragic, but nowadays all too common, bungled burglary?"

"Of course. It's so commonplace in Moscow these days, isn't

it? Gone are the days of people accidentally falling out of tenth-storey windows. We overdid that one, didn't we?" Sacha let out a little chuckle which was met with an approving grin from the Boss.

"Get hold of Svetlana and bring her back home as soon as possible. By as soon as possible, I mean preferably today. We don't want her on the loose."

"What about Madame Chairman?"

"What about her?"

"Do you think she'll be looking for Frost?"

"Of course and so will everybody else. We just need to make sure we find him before anybody else does."

"It's those French I am worried about. They've always been one step ahead of everybody else. I wouldn't be surprised if they'd staged the whole thing to bring him out into the open."

"Maybe or maybe not. Who cares? Michael Frost is the prize. This is our chance."

"Do we want him dead or alive?"

"Alive of course, he's no use to us dead. The Americans will want him dead and that's another good reason to get to him first."

"We'll be in Madame Chairman's back yard. It'll be dangerous operating there without coming to some arrangement."

"Correct. Make sure you contact her first thing in the morning to give her the news of Michael Frost's re-emergence. She will of course already know but she will thank you. You can use that as your opportunity to arrange a meeting to discuss how we can be of service. Make it appear as though we're not interested in looking for Frost."

"She'll never fall for it."

"I know but she'll try to use you for her own benefit. You know what she's like."

"You keep on saying the word 'you' as though it'll be me who will go to London."

"It has to be you, Sacha. Who else can I trust?"

"But what if she has me killed? You know how she and the crazy Lisette woman feel about me."

"Oh, I dare say that's all water under the bridge as the British say. She has bigger fish to fry than her vendetta against you. After all, you'll be there to help. She'll see it as a conciliatory move on the part of the Russian splinter. She won't turn down the offer of help if it means getting to Frost first."

"I'm nervous about…"

"Sacha, trust me. After your call to her I'll call her and thank her for giving us this opportunity to work together again after all these years. I'll tell her that I'll send her a peace offering. If she sounds insincere I'll let you know and we'll make an excuse for sending somebody else in your place," he lied. "Now go back and finish your business with Sergei."

***

Before returning to the office, Sacha took a long shower and hung around drinking coffee and talking with the Kremlin's FSB security guards. When he re-entered the office Sergei wasn't writing. Had he finished or was there another reason? He didn't really care. "Good news, Serge, we're finished here."

"Really? Finished? You haven't read my report."

"I'll read it later, I'm a bit tired, as I'm sure you are, and I'd like to get back to my bed. I've arranged for a car to drop you off at your apartment."

"There's no need," replied Sergei.

"Nonsense, it's past seven o'clock and we've had a long night so the least we can do is to drive you home. Besides, public transport is so unreliable, not to mention the people who use it. Serge, it's the least we can do as you've been so co-operative."

Sergei was worried that the trip home would turn out to be a trip to the forest for a meeting with his maker but he knew there was no point arguing. He left the office accompanied by Sacha, shaking hands goodbye with him at a service door leading onto a courtyard inside the Kremlin complex. Parked in the courtyard was a black Mercedes limousine, sitting with its engine idling. "For me?" asked Sergei.

"Only the best for you, Serge," replied Sacha. "We'll speak again soon, my old friend, but for now go home and catch up on your sleep."

Sergei walked toward the rear of the car. As he did so its engine revved slightly, which made him jump. As he sat in the back seat, he was relieved to see his driver was a very pleasant-looking young woman and nobody else was with them. *Maybe I'll survive this day after all*, he thought.

"I have your address. We should be there in minutes. Sit back and enjoy the ride. There's hot coffee in the thermos."

Sergei was feeling mightily relieved. He poured a black coffee into a stylish Russian gold-rimmed glass, loading it with more sugar than was good for him. The journey was smooth and uneventful. They arrived at Sergei's apartment after twelve minutes.

***

Meanwhile, back in the Kremlin, Sacha glanced at Sergei's report. He expected to tear it up as he doubted it would contain anything useful. He looked down the list of contacts Sergei had produced, all of whom he was aware of, then, at the bottom of the list, there was a section that made his head spin. He reached for his mobile phone to call off the hit on Sergei but then stopped himself. *No, let things play out as planned,*" he thought. *I'll keep this to myself.* Just then the door to the office opened and in walked the Boss.

"Anything interesting?"

"No, just as we thought, Sergei's information is useless, we know everybody on his pathetic little list."

"Okay. Now go home and get some rest. You're going to be very busy until we find Michael Frost." On leaving the room, the

Boss left the door ajar as a hint for Sacha to make tracks. He didn't need telling twice.

Sitting in the back of a black Mercedes limousine waiting for his driver, Sacha read Sergei's note again. It detailed how Michael Frost had supposedly died in London in 2005 in what was a botched attempt to fake his death but things worked out better than he could ever have hoped.

The hit on Michael Frost was bungled due to the ambitions of an area controller in the CIA's London field office. Sergei had used his old contacts to identify a gullible young agent on assignment. Through intermediaries the gullible young agent was advised how he could advance his career if he followed instructions to rendezvous with one of the world's most hunted men, Michael Frost, and bring him in. "I guess Frost wants to come in from the cold." He smiled at his little word play. Unsure as to how he should proceed, the gullible young agent went to his CIA Controller and was advised to keep the rendezvous and apprehend Michael Frost. The CIA Controller immediately contacted his Counsellor and told him the gullible young agent's story. His Counsellor ordered him to sit tight, he would send somebody to the rendezvous and eliminate Michael Frost, along with the gullible young agent, so there would be no loose ends.

The gullible young agent went to the rendezvous at Bond Street tube station armed with a .38 Smith & Wesson in chrome. How he loved that gun. As he approached Michael on the platform at Bond Street tube station, the would-be assassin showed his hand too early and he and Michael Frost ended up in a tussle. The gullible young agent drew his .38 and fired it in the general direction of the grappling men. He hit neither Michael nor the would-be assassin and, upon seeing an approaching tube train, Michael grabbed hold of the would-be assassin before throwing them both onto the tracks. Michael landed with his back hitting the centre rail, he then slid down into the space below while holding the would-be assassin on the track for the train to run over him. As the train came screeching to an emergency stop, Michael crawled toward its rear, emerging into the tunnel behind it. Sergei wrote that this wasn't how things were meant to play out but it achieved what they wanted to achieve. They wanted people to stop hunting Michael Frost.

Sacha could hardly believe what he was reading. *That old fool Sergei did this? Perhaps we underestimated him.*

In the ensuing commotion Michael calmly walked out of the tunnel, disappearing into the crowd. The gullible young agent went on to claim that he had shot Michael Frost because he had no other choice and that he and "some other guy" ended up under an oncoming train and were both killed.

After reading Sergei's note for a third time Sacha relaxed back in the rear seat of the black Mercedes limousine smiling the smile of a man who could see his own star rising while holding an ace-in-the-hole which guaranteed his longevity. Sacha recognised the names of the men mentioned in Sergei's note and knew the CIA Controller to now be the Director of Special Operations and the gullible young agent was now a Deputy Director. He had them by the balls. He owned them and all those who had screwed up the 'Michael Frost Affair' as he thought he would name it. Classic old-fashioned KGB thinking, not fit for purpose in today's intelligence-led world.

"Take me home." Exiting Red Square in the direction of Tagansky Distrikt, Sacha continued with his marathon self-satisfied-smug-smiling session oblivious to the events which had unfolded on the American east coast while he was listening to Sergei's story, not knowing that his aces-in-the-hole were in-a-hole themselves.

***

"I'll see you to your door," said the pleasant-looking young woman in an insistent tone of voice.

"It's not necessary but I suspect you have your orders."

"I do."

They took the elevator to the sixth floor in silence and when the doors opened the ever gentlemanly Sergei gestured for the young woman to step first out of the elevator. She knew the way to Sergei's front door. He took out his keys and opened the apartment door. He turned to thank the young woman but never got the chance. He was pushed through the open door with considerable force and was lying, once again, face down on the apartment floor. He lay there, just about on the same spot where Michael Frost had pushed him, pretending to be unconscious.

"Get up," said a male voice. Sergei knew it was pointless pretending to be knocked out so he got on all fours and then to his knees before finally standing upright. He looked around at the devastation in his apartment. Everything was smashed and broken. Nobody had come to investigate the noise, which was normal in these times.

Of course, he thought, a *bungled burglary*. He asked, "What now?"

There was no reply from either of the two men or the pleasant-looking young woman. The man who'd told him to get to his feet walked four paces, drew his suppressed 9mm and shot Sergei between the eyes, execution style. Old habits die hard.

"Idiot. It looks like a hit. Shoot him a few more times in the body. In the arse too," choke-laughed the other man. The first man shot Sergei seven more times but not in the arse.

In the nine hundred and eighty milliseconds it took for the assassin to raise his pistol, squeeze its trigger and send a standard 9mm round toward his brain, Sergei existed outside of time. His memory flashback continued even as his skull was splintering from the impact of the bullet. He felt comforted in the knowledge that his wife had loved him deeply despite everything. Things hadn't always been easy for her with him being the way he was. But she had stood by him despite everything as they carried on the charade of living a married life, even having children for them to dote upon. Ah, sweet Svetochka. Svetlana's biological father never knew of her existence. In his stateless vacuum, Sergei pictured his mother standing next to the fireplace in the family home in Leningrad, no not Leningrad, St Petersburg, with his sisters but he couldn't see the image of his father standing there with them for some reason. He saw the happy smiling faces of his childhood friends from school number 41 on Nevsky Prospekt. Summer Pioneer camps where he first met Alexei… a final darkness signalled the end of the movie running in Sergei's head.

"Get out," ordered the pleasant-looking young woman. Both men complied with the barked order without hesitation. She glanced over the devastation before reaching into her jacket pocket to retrieve a mobile phone and punching in a number.

A splinter faction conversation

"It's done. Sergei is no longer with us."
"Did Sacha go to the apartment too?"
"No. He decided to stay in the Kremlin."
"Pity. We could have squashed that bug at the same time without raising too much suspicion. Why didn't you save Sergei? He might have been useful to us."

Without hesitating she replied, "He was too old to run." After another brief glance around the apartment she continued, "There's nothing of interest here. Have the team pick up Dumb and Dumber and let's see what they have to offer."

"What are you going to do next?"
"Go to London of course."
"That means you'll break your cover and it's taken us years to establish it. Many people have been sacrificed to maintain your cover. Think carefully if that is what you really want to do."

"Michael Frost is alive and he must stay that way. We must reach him before the others do. I have no other choice. I must leave before Sacha realises what's going on. He's in for a shock." She let out a little laugh at the thought of Sacha being on the receiving end of a grilling or worse by the Boss. *With any luck he won't survive*, she thought.

"It's a race then, comrade. Be first! Good luck." The phone line went dead.

Before leaving the apartment the pleasant-looking young woman deleted the number she'd just dialled from the phone's memory and broke the SIM into four pieces.

MARGARET'S STORY – RISING STAR

Following her graduation in 1961, where she achieved a double first and was awarded a coveted economics prize, Margaret joined a firm in the West End after a friend of a friend recommended her for the job of PA to a partner there.

The firm was a typical do-very-little-for-enormous-fees advertising/PR consultancy. The job was approved by Rex and the Organisation but she needed to rise to a position where she could be useful to it. In those times it wasn't easy for a young woman to carve out a career in such a firm especially as she'd been hired more for her looks than her qualifications. She'd have to work at least twice as hard as the men to get anywhere plus she had her duties to fulfil for the Organisation.

The Organisation doesn't like operatives moving around too much as it invests enormous resources in combining their outputs to those of other operatives to achieve synergy for efficiency's sake. Few were really certain what it meant by that but that's the way things were and always had been. You stay put in your role and little by little you make small, almost imperceptible, changes at the direction of the massive machine that is the Organisation. That way, over time, nobody questions your actions and that's just the way the Organisation likes it.

***

Thanks to circumstances orchestrated by Rex, it didn't take Margaret Rotheram very long to commence her climb up the greasy pole.

***

A Mandarins and specially invited guests conversation

"It's all taking too long. Far too long."

"If we rush things we'll get found out."

"What about you? What are you doing about it?"

"I'm doing my bit, thank you."

"Ladies and Gentlemen, let's not fight among ourselves. We knew the road would be long when we started our endeavour."

"When will we see some action… some results? We're doing a lot of talking and spending vast amounts of money but…"

"I will not see our plans go up in smoke for the want of a little patience. Look at the progress we've made over the past five years, let alone the previous thirty. We are on the brink and if it takes a few extra years to achieve our goal then so be it. We're about to destroy seven hundred years of history. We nearly succeeded with Bonaparte but we were betrayed. We will not make the same mistake this time. So, I implore you…"

"It's okay for you, you have time on your side. What about me and Sophia and Angelique? We're worried that we won't be around for the big day if things go on as they are. Please, I implore you, get things started…"

"I can assure you all, we are entering the final phase, the players are in place and we just need to let time do our work for us as it always does. We can't just go about changing the Chair with the click of our fingers."

"Why do we need to change the Chair at all? He's in our pocket, isn't he?"

"He's an incompetent fool who…"

"Didn't you put him where he is?"

"He doesn't have the confidence of controllers, let alone governors. If he attempted to carry out our plans we'd have wasted the last five years."

"Then what do you propose we do about him?"

"Isn't it a bit late to be having these arguments now? Allow me to…"

"Quiet, all of you. You're like children. I am not concerned with whether you or you or you will be alive to see the great day. Others too have worked to achieve our goal and have passed along the way without complaint. We will only make our move when the time is right for us to do so and not a minute or even a second before. We all want the same thing, don't we?" There were no dissenters. "Good, then let us continue with our meeting. Recorder, please continue reading the agenda."

There was only one more item of business for the Recorder to read out. It was the latest report on how the candidates for the post of Chair were progressing. Two had recently been killed in a road accident. The circumstances had been fully investigated but nothing suspicious had been found. They should have looked deeper. They were down to four candidates plus an outsider introduced recently by Rex.

"Your outsider should be withdrawn. She's a distraction. The four remaining are all strong candidates, any of whom would make an acceptable Chair, capable of executing the plan."

"You call her an outsider but I see her coming up on the inside rail to become the favourite."

"Your horse racing analogy is pathetic, just like your candidate."

"You've only introduced her into the mix so that you can run things yourself in the background."

"I assure you all, she's no patsy of mine. Unlike the four

remaining, she was a willing recruit. She has a tragic personal history, which works in our favour. She's full of self-doubt and is ambitious and foolish enough to believe she can achieve self-validation through success. She will see her rise as just reward for all her hard work and we will ensure that she rises. She believes change is necessary for survival. We can manipulate her because she will do whatever is necessary to bring about change as she believes the Organisation is run by a corrupt and moribund old boys' club. She's already undermined her counsellor on a couple of occasions and he's threatened to have her officially reprimanded. He's got a tigress by the tail with that one." Rex laughed. "She's the one. Believe me, she's the one."

"Yes, hmmm. Thank you for that, Rex. I believe the meeting is now over. Thank you, Recorder, for a job well done. I will make arrangements to meet with each of you individually over the coming six months."

Several around the table thought, *Who put him in charge?*

"Six months is good timing for our next meeting."

"Yes I know it is, that's why I suggested it." Not everybody would survive their one-to-ones with Max.

***

From the very beginning she was an exemplar for change in the quarters in which it mattered. As an operative she established her own cell of blind operatives in key political positions right under the nose of her Counsellor. He was a member of the old farts club and wasn't controlling his units as he should have in an era of social change driven by the music of the young. It was the swinging sixties and Beethoven was playing in his head.

A blind operative is one who is unknowingly directed to do the bidding of the Organisation while never having been recruited by it. For obvious reasons, some potentials become blind operatives after they fall off the lists. This is normal practice as having invested so much time and effort in them it would be a waste to simply let go those who didn't make the grade. Better to somehow use them for the benefit of the Organisation.

Once off the lists, potentials are largely left to get on with their lives. The thing that originally brought them to the attention of the Organisation is probably still there inside of them and it's the job of counsellors to find it and use it. Blind operatives are not on the payroll of the Organisation which makes them doubly valuable.

***

Her view had always been: in the absence of control you must assume control. Do what you need to do to get the job done. Classic Machiavellian principle, though in his day it was: in the absence of power you must assume power. It's the same thing… in principle. This is where Margaret's background, education and upbringing came into play. People like her are used to taking control. They feel they are born to it and in many ways they are. She'd led others all her life, even before her pony club days when the eleven-year-old Margaret assumed control of the local gymkhanas. Whenever she was with children from the poorer part of town she was the organiser, the leader, the one in charge, the one they listened to, the one they obeyed. They willingly fell in behind her. She was her mother's daughter in that regard.

***

Having been reported by her Counsellor to his Controller for the unsanctioned recruiting of blind operatives, she'd been summoned to Half Moon Street for a reprimand, or worse. In her Counsellor's opinion she'd overstepped the mark and needed a good carpeting. She waited nervously for her turn to be admitted to the Controller's office. There were a lot of people in to see the Controller that day. *Surely they can't all be in for a reprimand?* she thought. Though she had eight people ahead of her she was called in next.

No names were used. "Follow me," was all the PA said. Turning, he walked on ahead of her, knocking on the Controller's office door and opening it before being invited to enter. He obviously knew the ropes.

"Sit down please. No, not there; there," said the PA pointing, "Miss Rotheram, sir."

"Miss Rotheram? Good. I've been looking forward to this. You've been making quite a name for yourself. Please don't talk," he said in anticipation of her attempting to get her defence in early. "You seem to be, what some might call, a loose cannon. Would you agree? I told you not to talk," he said at her slight motion to do so.

"If I can't talk then how can I answer your questions?" she replied in her soon-to-become-Madame-Chairman voice while holding him in the icy grip of her pale blue eyes. He felt the temperature of the room go down a few degrees.

He cleared his throat. "Now I see what they mean. It's clear to me that you're in need of something more to do. A challenge if you will. So here it comes. Are you ready, young lady? Effective immediately you are promoted to Counsellor and you'll take over the units of your erstwhile Counsellor."

"May I ask why?"

"You tell me. Why do you think you're being given this opportunity?"

"In my opinion my Counsellor is…" She hesitated as he entered the room, sidling along the wall just beyond her peripheral vision.

"Go on, Miss Rotheram, you were saying about your Counsellor."

"In my opinion my Counsellor is lazy and incompetent and should be put out to pasture."

"Is that it?"

"Isn't that enough?" She turned to stare at her former Counsellor before continuing, "He's not doing the job that needs to be done. The job of Counsellor is a very important one as it controls frontline operatives and I don't feel… no, I don't believe… no, I know… that he has neither their respect nor their confidence; he certainly doesn't have mine. He needs to go and the sooner the better." She crossed her arms and turned to face the Controller again.

"What do you say to that, old thing?"

"A bit harsh I'd say. I've done my bit and I try my best and…"

"Stop blithering for God's sake, Leo. Yes, I agree with you, he's all those things and more besides but he's got more contacts than any other of my counsellors. He's worth his weight in gold which is why I'm creating a special position for him and moving you into his shoes. Everybody knows exactly what he is and would probably have said the same thing about him as you've just said. The answer to my question though was simple and has nothing to do with your rationale. You displayed initiative and we applaud the use of initiative, when correctly exercised of course. Do you feel you have an apology to make?"

"No, I don't. I stand by what I said and, what's more, if there are any more like him wandering around this place then you need to create special positions for them too and move people into the post of Counsellor who can do the job."

"I'll take your opinion under advisement. Now you two need to get together for a handover of responsibilities. I hope that's not awkward for you after what you've just said about your former boss. He'll tell you everything you'll need to know for now, including when I want my reports and how I like them. And if you find you don't like the way I run things then, who knows, you might well find yourself sitting in my seat one day."

Next stop controller, she mused and smiled.

***

After only two days with her former Counsellor she'd extracted the information she needed to take over from him. She now had a hundred and twenty operatives under her plus thirty-two blind operatives. Hers was a large unit as most of those times usually only had around a hundred personnel in total.

***

As the boss, she was willing to listen to her operatives but she left them under no illusion that there were no guarantees that she'd implement their suggestions. Any suggestions she did implement she gave full credit for them coming from an operative, though for obvious reasons they were never named. This policy of anonymity proved useful when she implemented changes which were her own ideas but to ensure acceptance she gave credit to them as coming from an operative. Not that her ideas were draconian or punitive but some were to do with tightening up administration and nobody wants tighter admin as it means less wriggle room. She wasn't scared of putting controversial policies in place but like most people she wanted to be more loved than feared or disliked. She'd always felt that way instinctively and was less than delighted to discover that Machiavelli disagreed with her. It is better to be feared than loved; those around you must understand that their prince knows how to be the opposite of kind.

Her moves were being closely monitored by Mr Chairman. He was reporting on her activities to the Mandarins. Only one mandarin nowadays actually as the others seemed to be less involved lately for some reason. Rex too was watching but from the sidelines, waiting for his moment.

***

Her reign as Counsellor was short lived by anyone's standards. It seemed that no sooner had she been promoted to Counsellor she was promoted to Controller. She, in turn, promoted one of her operatives, Lisette, to take over the role of Counsellor of what had rapidly become the best-performing unit across the entire Organisation. She saw a good deal of herself in Lisette with the exception of the sex side of her life which Lizzie was reputed to take to extremes at times. Also, in her opinion, she took far too many recreational drugs, but that might work to her advantage, if ever she needed a favour doing, for example.

Not many controllers die in the job but hers had. Generally speaking, once they get to a certain age or they lose their edge, they are usually put out to pasture in some role glad-handing bigwigs or making deals for the benefit of the Organisation. At that level, retirement from the Organisation usually comes in the form of semi-retirement, seldom death.

Rumours spread like wildfire that the extremely young, and not unattractive, new girl had killed her Controller and as she had something on Mr Chairman he had no alternative but to promote her into her dead boss's shoes. She heard the rumours but did nothing to dispel them. She liked the notoriety. The Mandarins liked it too as it meant everybody was watching Margaret Rotheram and not noticing the things going on around them.

Yes, she'd been fast-tracked but she was outperforming everybody so why shouldn't she be given the opportunity to show what she really could do? *Next stop Governor,* she mused and smiled.

***

Under normal circumstances, controllers do not hold down external jobs. The Organisation is their employer. Margaret, however, wasn't used to not working ultra-hard and so kept the

PR/ad agency job she'd fought so hard for a partnership in. She was one of those people who, it seemed, the more she did the more she was able to do. Besides, her husband was the MD of the firm so she could come and go pretty much as she pleased. This didn't please her Governor though and he demanded she quit her job as he particularly didn't want her working with her husband. He counselled that she might find herself in a conflict of interests which might cause him to 'act to protect the Organisation,' he threatened.

After six months in the job, she asked herself out aloud, "Am I doing the job wrong? Am I not doing the job right?"

"Sorry? What?"

"What the hell do these people do all day?" She found she could do her Controller's job standing on her head and so was bored; bored people quickly become mischievous.

"Madame Controller, you have to keep yourself ready for when something happens. Don't you worry, something will happen and when it does then you'll be rushed off your feet."

I need a new PA, she thought. *Where's Lisette?*

"Let me check her diary. Ah yes, she's reviewing the lists of potentials with her teams."

"Call her and get her to come in immediately. Is it unusual for controllers to have two PAs?"

"Why do you ask?"

"I'm going to light a fire under this place to get things moving and to do that I'm going to need another PA."

"You're getting rid of me, aren't you?" asked the aged PA, her voice tinged with resignation.

"Not at all," she lied. "Lisette is more used to my ways and with what I have in mind my PAs are going to be more like a council of war than bookers of restaurant tables." As it turned out, the aged PA was perfect in her new role as a war council PA having served in SOE during WWII. She'd operated behind enemy lines for over two years before being captured and tortured. She'd been due to face a Gestapo firing squad but was liberated just in the nick of time by advancing American soldiers.

***

Perhaps her success was due to her having put the effort into her new role in the early days, forcing her counsellors to follow her policies; her results were astonishing. Her region ran like clockwork on greased wheels, making money like it was going out of fashion and building new networks of blind operatives. The work she did in advancing the mission of the Organisation was second to none as she micro-adjusted events to overachieve on all her targets. She made it all look so easy.

Her success caused consternation and disquiet in the other controllers because she was making them all look bad. They weren't achieving similar results despite often having more resources than her nor were they making as much money for the Organisation. She was the golden girl and each recognised the danger for them in that.

***

A Mandarins and guest conversation

"I told you, she's everything I predicted she would be and more. She has them looking over their shoulders so they don't have time to notice what is really going on." Classic Mandarins, using the Organisation's own methods against it.

"What makes you think she'll cooperate when the time comes?"

"That's the beauty of it, we won't require her cooperation. She'll do all the hard work and then we'll make our move. By the time she realises what's going on it will be too late."

"I'm still not convinced she's right for us. She's too headstrong, too arrogant and…"

"And ambitious. Don't forget ambitious. She's ambitious and power hungry. She'll do whatever it takes to become Madame Chairman once we dangle the carrot under her nose." He checked reaction around the room. "We need to get her promoted to the Chair and soon."

"It'll be dangerous if we…"

"Time is of the essence. If we don't act quickly we'll lose our advantage."

"What about the others? They will be against what we're doing. They have their own plans for the Organisation. They want to see a new structure at the top. One that isn't autocratic."

"I agree with them on that point. It'll enable us to place people around her to restrict her and report everything she does back to… back to us."

"What if she refuses and decides to run things her own way?"

"We'll make it a condition of her appointment. After all, we are responsible for selecting the Chair."

"There are only four of us… we're in the minority. We'll be outvoted."

"I only need to change the mind of one of them and then we'll be the majority. I'm sure that even I can change one little mind."

"We must be careful. We mustn't alert the others to what we're doing." Then, "I know for a fact that Allegra will be against our plans," she added to seal the fate of the woman she'd hated for years. She'd been looking for an excuse to eradicate Allegra and saw this as her opportunity to do so without any repercussions.

"You let me worry about Allegra."

MICHAEL'S STORY - ALTCAR

Early one Sunday morning in May 1968 Sergeant Huggard called at the Frosts' house to ask Margaret if Michael would be attending the summer camps at Altcar with the Royal Tank Regiment. She shouted to ask him if he knew anything about this and why hadn't he told her anything about it if he did.

"It costs a lot of money and we don't have any money."

"Well, son, I'm sure we can do something if we try. I've been doing a bit of overtime lately so I'm sure we can get you to Altcar with your mates." The reason Margaret could afford to send Michael to Altcar was Patrick had been sending her money for the children but she diverted it to buy groceries and pay bills. Though she herself wouldn't accept money from Patrick she was happy to run the household using money meant for the children. Classic Margaret: independent, defiant and with her own unique logic.

***

The tank cadets congregated outside the barracks waiting for their coach to Altcar. Walking toward them was a group of TA soldiers who were going to Altcar for the inter-regimental exercises. As the two groups jostled with one another to get the best seats Michael looked behind him and standing right there was Buckhead. They both recognised one another instantly.

"Awright, gobshite. Look who it isn't, fancy seein' you 'ere. Bet ye never thought y'd be seein' me again, eh?"

"Do you know him?" asked Tommy Munroe.

"His name is Buckhead. I had a fight with him once."

"Jesus, he's massive. He must have battered ye."

"I knocked him out."

"Yeah, right. Anyway, he doesn't seem to be too happy with you so I'd watch me back if I was you, he looks a nasty bastard."

***

When they arrived at Altcar the cadets were separated from the soldiers and sent to a different area of the camp for orientation.

The first exercise for the cadets was de-tanking. This involved groups of four cadets at a time loading themselves into a tank before simulating it being hit and rendering it inoperable. This was to be their first experience using Thunderflashes. The cadets de-tanked and took up defence positions, moving as a unit away from the tank to find cover without engaging with the enemy.

Sod this, thought Tommy Munroe. *I'm gonna shoot something.* As he and his crew went to take up initial defence positions he leapt on top of the tank making "pyoo, pyoo, pyoo" shooting noises with his mouth and spraying his wooden SSMG like a hose pipe. Everybody fell about laughing.

"Munwoe, is that you, Munwoe? Come here, Munwoe. Put that cadet on a charge, Corpwal."

"Oh shit, it's Captain Hywel-Jones. He's such a divvy," mumbled Cadet Munroe more or less to himself.

"Listen to me," said an observer dressed in a uniform the cadets didn't recognise, "Captain Hywel-Jones is a great soldier and a highly decorated officer and he's as tough as you're going to find anywhere. Just because he talks funny doesn't mean he is funny. He's a former Royal Marines officer and he's seen proper action." Cadet Munroe shook his head in surprise. "So show some respect, mon amie, okay?"

"Oui, mon amie," replied Tommy Munroe, saluting the stranger in the unfamiliar uniform to laughter of the cadets.

***

Later that day, during shooting practice on the rifle range, Buckhead snuck up on Michael while he was shooting from the prone position and stood on his ankles. He screamed in agony.

"What are you doing, Lance Corporal? Are you trying to hurt that cadet?" shouted the soldier in the strange uniform.

"No sir. I'm making sure he learns to lay his feet flat when shooting so he doesn't get shot in the heels. He'll thank me for it someday."

"Well, Lance Corporal, that won't be today. Are you alright, Cadet?"

"Yes sir."

"Are you okay to carry on?"

"Yes sir."

"Carry on then, cadet." As an aside the soldier whispered to Buckhead, "If you do anything like that again I will kick you in the bollocks. Do we understand one another?"... "Now, Cadet," said the soldier to Michael, "I noticed you're not a bad shot but this time control your breathing. Take a few deep breaths and when you're ready to shoot breathe out completely, giving the trigger a gentle squeeze and see how that works for you."

After giving his legs a good loosening shake to sort his knees out, Michael laid back down, this time with his feet flat to the ground. He breathed in and breathed out and then rapidly fired his ten rounds. "What's the hurry, cadet?" asked the soldier.

"I ran out of breath and had to shoot off all the rounds," the soldier laughed. He wasn't to know about Michael's breathing problems from his nana's old wives' tar treatment for whooping cough.

"I should have mentioned that you can still breathe in between shots; so, take a deep breath in then breathe completely out for each shot. Okay? Let's see how you've done and if you haven't done that well then you can have another ten rounds as I didn't explain myself properly." The target sighter reported all ten rounds had hit centre with less than a three-inch spread. "I don't think you need repeat that again. By the way, what is your name, Cadet?"

"My name is Michael Frost, sir."

"Okay, Cadet Frost, I'll see you later. Dismissed."

***

After shooting practice, the cadets sat around talking and generally messing about while waiting for their evening meal.

"You lot, come with me," ordered a TA soldier.

"What for?" asked a cadet.

"Are you questioning a superior soldier, Cadet?"

"No, Corporal." The cadets were taken on a hike over the sand dunes in the direction of some noisy chatter and stinking cigarette smoke.

"Well, if it isn't Annie Oakley and her girlfriends," sneered Buckhead when the cadets arrived at some old huts by the sea shore.

"What's goin' on, Buckhead?" asked one of the TA soldiers.

"I owe this little turd a hiding."

"Get lost, Buckhead, he's only a kid, leave him alone. I thought we were just goin' to get them wet in the sea or somethin'. I'm not havin' anythin' to do with givin' a kid a hidin'."

"Well, piss off then and don't forget to pick yer jam rags up on yer way." Most of the TA soldiers laughed at Buckhead's taunt to fit in with the Buckhead TA gang. Then, pointing to the other cadets, "Youz lot can piss off back to the barracks and keep yer gobs shut or I'll burst yez."

"Michael told me he knocked you out once and I didn't believe him but I do now, ye big chicken ye," shouted Tommy Munroe from the front of the group of cadets. "If you touch him you'll have to take us all on. C'mon lads let's burst him." The rest of the cadets looked very unsure but they knew they had to back Tommy and Michael up.

"Yeah!" they all screamed in their squeaky voices.

"No need for anything like that," spoke the soldier in the unfamiliar uniform appearing from out of the dunes. "If Lance Corporal Buckhead is so keen for a fight then he can fight me. But the proper way. You and I will meet in the boxing ring at 0700 hours tomorrow. Any problem with that, Lance Corporal Buckhead?"

"I've got no argument with you, sir," grovelled Buckhead.

"Are you declining my invitation, Lance Corporal?"

"Yes sir." All the TA soldiers looked away, some in disgust and some in laughter.

"Did you really knock Lance Corporal Buckhead out, Cadet Frost?"

"Yes sir."

"Do you think you can do it again?"

"Yes sir."

After regarding Michael for a few moments the Soldier in the strange uniform said, "I'm sure you could but not here and not now. There's a boxing tournament the day after tomorrow and, who knows, you two might be able to sort your differences out then. Everybody return to the encampment. Now."

***

After they got back to their bivouac the tank cadets were so agitated they couldn't sleep. "Nobody told us about no boxing tournament," was the general sentiment as tank cadets, unlike most cadets, don't ordinarily box. They had a bad feeling about the 'day after tomorrow'. What they didn't realise was that boxing wasn't compulsory and they were in little danger of an angry infantry cadet rearranging their beautiful faces unless they volunteered to fight.

"Do you really think you can knock that big turd Buckhead out?" asked one of the cadets.

"Yes, I do."

"He's really big though. How long ago was it that you knocked him out?"

"Years ago."

"Was he big then?"

"Not very."

"Well, anyway, I doubt they'll let a cadet fight a soldier so you'll be alright."

***

The following day was taken up with Red on Blue exercises with the tank cadets not doing too well as they weren't allowed to use tanks. "Are you looking forward to the boxing tournament tomorrow, Cadet Frost?" asked the soldier in the unfamiliar uniform.

"What's that uniform?" asked Michael.

"It's a French uniform which I prefer to wear when I take part in camps such as this. I'm kind of an observer. I have no authority but I'm tolerated." There were no come-back questions from Michael, he simply accepted the explanation he'd been given.

***

The final day started with all ranks taking on the obstacle course. It was a bit of fun as well as being fiercely competitive. The tank cadets didn't cover themselves in glory.

"Before we break camp this afternoon there will be the

traditional end of camp boxing tournament," announced the camp commander. "Any cadet who does not wish to take part please raise your hand now. Good, that's everybody in then. Well done, chaps." None of the tank cadets felt they could raise their hand with everybody looking on for obvious reasons.

"Right, if you've boxed before, put your hand up. Those of you who've boxed before go to rings A and B, all others go to rings C and D." Michael was the only tank cadet who made his way toward rings A and B.

"Where the hell are you goin', Michael?" asked Tommy Munroe.

"I've boxed before so…"

"Yeah, I get it. Why don't ye come with us, it'll be a laugh and ye won't lose yer good looks," joked Tommy Munroe to Michael's back.

***

After the first four rounds of competition all the remaining names were put into a hat for a pot-luck draw. Everybody left in wanted to get drawn against the only cadet left.

"You have an interesting style of boxing," commented the soldier in the French uniform.

"I like to box that way."

"How long have you been boxing?"

"My cousin Timbo trained me when I was five."

"Five! And you've kept up with your boxing? Do you box for a club?"

"I boxed for Penrhyn Street School and for Timbo's boxing club until he went to jail. I box for my grammar school and when we moved to Huyton I learnt karate and kenjutsu. I like swords. I fence for the school team but I like Japanese swords best." This was a lot of unsolicited information for Michael to give all in one go.

"Does anybody else here know you've done so much boxing?"

"Sergeant Huggard does. He's the policeman who takes me to Cadets."

Okay, thought the soldier in the French uniform, and then smiling to himself, *perhaps Lance Corporal Buckhead deserves his opportunity for satisfaction after all.*

***

"Allow me to assist," said the soldier in the French uniform stepping forward to stand in front of the upturned camp commander's hat. "First out of the hat is Lance Corporal Buckhead and he will be fighting… Cadet Frost of the Royal Tank Regiment." After the announcement of the contenders for the first bout the tank cadets thought it was all just too much of a coincidence. There is an unspoken rule that when soldiers come up against cadets they take it easy on them. Soldiers must not lose to cadets for face-saving purposes, but it's frowned upon if allowances aren't made, particularly when soldiers come up against cadets in certain situations, such as boxing for example.

Both boxers having received their instructions retired to their corners to await the bell. As soon as the bell sounded Buckhead flew out of his corner and straight at Michael in a way redolent of the final round of the Victor Christian fight and as in that fight Michael back-pedalled twice around the ring. Buckhead stopped in frustration as he hadn't managed to lay a glove on Michael. "C'mon, you chicken bastard, come here where I can hit you," Mumbled Buckhead, his annunciation being greatly improved by his gum shield. Michael was unmoved by this invitation and simply stayed in his southpaw stance. Buckhead came forward behind a pretty solid-looking jab but he wasn't much of a boxer and Michael stepped inside his lead and let rip with a left hook to the ribs. A few steps backwards and Michael changed to orthodox stance and did the same to the other side of Buckhead's ribs.

Both shots were delivered with a ferocity that caused the crowd to wince. Buckhead came swinging at Michael with everything he had. If he'd have connected with any one of the shots it would have been all over. He put everything into round one and had run out of steam.

When the bell went for the second round Buckhead stayed sitting on his stool making it look like he'd thrown in the towel. Everybody was cheering but the referee had said to the boxers, "Defend yourself at all times", and as soon as Michael was distracted Buckhead pounced on him, hitting him with good straight left jabs and a solid right cross. Michael found himself on the seat of his pants looking up at Buckhead who was triumphantly jumping around the ring whooping wildly despite the boos of the crowd. "Four, Five, Six, Se…" Michael was back up on his feet before the referee could count to seven; he clapped his gloves together and did a little hop, Timbo style, and moved with a sense of purpose towards Buckhead who, without Michael laying a glove on him, went down on one knee and took a count, again to the boos of the crowd.

Michael waited for Buckhead to get up; he wasn't going to take his eyes off him again. When he got up at the count of eight Buckhead reached out in an attempt to entice Michael into a glove touch to show there were no hard feelings. Michael declined the glove touch. With electrifying speed Michael set about delivering an overwhelming series of combination punches which rained in on Buckhead from all angles. Once again Buckhead went down on one knee and took a count which the referee decided was enough when he flattened the palms of his hands towards the canvas and crossed them over each other three times to indicate the fight was over.

Buckhead went back to his corner and sat on his stool. As soon as Michael turned his back he leapt up and ran towards him. A scream of "Look out, Michael!" was all there was time to shout before Buckhead had closed the distance on him.

Hearing the warning shout, Michael rolled paratrooper style to his right and settled himself in a karate stance before delivering a perfectly executed mawashi geri roundhouse kick to the left side of Buckhead's jaw. Once again, Buckhead, after receiving a single blow from Michael, was out cold before he hit the deck. The only sound from the crowd was "Oooooooooh." Most of them had no idea what they'd just seen but the soldier in the French uniform knew exactly what he'd just seen. *A future recruit perhaps?* he thought.

Outside the marquee, the soldier in the French uniform sidled up to Michael. "That was very impressive, Cadet Frost, I can see that you're a special fighter. A very special fighter indeed. But do not fight anymore today. Tell them you're under my orders not to continue in case you damage anybody else. It's a joke, Michael. But seriously, no more fighting today. Okay? I'll see you again."

***

Robert Buckhead never amounted to much; he lived an ordinary life; worked hard; got married; had three children, who turned out okay; was faithful to his wife; was a good dad; started reading books when he was forty-five and realised what he'd been missing out on all his life. A late developer, he took and passed an OU degree course in philosophy; saw the BBC News report about the abduction of Mikhail Morozov and felt sorry for him and thought about what his family must be going through. He didn't recognise the face, which was lucky.

***

An Organisation conversation

"How good of you to be on time for once. How did things go? Do you have your report to hand?"

"My train was on time for once. Things went very well and I do have my report with me, thank you."

"Okay, you can start with the potentials."

"Okay, list A. Most are making satisfactory progress, they're doing the right things and showing the right signs. A few are falling behind academically which, from experience, usually means they've plateaued and I doubt they will pass the next stage. I estimate we'll get ten to fifteen percent yield, which is normal."

"Are there any potential doublers in list A, do you think? There usually are, you know, either one way or the other; which is fine by us but probably not so fine for some others."

"I have my suspicions about a Major in the Royal Tank Regiment."

"A Major you say? Not a Captain?"

"No, a Major. I'll cover that later. I'm proposing to strike off over fifty percent from lists B and C." The French Captain waited for a comment and there being none he continued, "There was an unexpected bonus. A cadet from the Royal Tank Regiment."

"Interesting. The last recruit we had from that Regiment did very well for us. A cadet, you say? He must be young, too young for us surely? Are you proposing to add him to a list? What's so special about him?"

"I'm thinking he may be suitable for list B, depending on how well he does academically. He has a tremendous gift for languages, so who knows where he might end up? The Foreign Office? A desk in MI6? Other than that he's an absolute fighting machine, so, potentially, he could end up on list D as a sentinel."

"What's his background?"

"Nothing spectacular. Very ordinary really. He lives in a small council house on an estate in Liverpool. He passed the eleven plus and attends a very good grammar school. He represents his school in boxing and fencing."

"He sounds quite ordinary to me. My instincts tell me not to allow this, but go ahead, convince me."

He read from his report. "Name is Michael Frost. He's a grammar school pupil and he does extremely well in languages. He's practically fluent in German, French and, get this, Russian too. He's been boxing since the age of five. In a tournament at Altcar last week I rigged a draw for him to fight an old adversary who was big, aggressive and muscular and until he cheated he never laid a glove on the boy. After the fight was over this TA soldier went to attack Frost from behind. Instinctively he rolled out of the way, regained his balance and put himself in the perfect stance to deliver mawashi geri with such perfection that he KO'd the TA soldier. It was beautiful to watch. I spoke with him after the fight."

"You did what!! That's against protocol. I can't emphasise how risky behaviour like that is to us. You never know who is watching at places like Altcar. It's a recruitment ground for all sorts of organisations, including mine and yours."

"I do know that but as we had this meeting scheduled time was short. I've done some investigation into Frost's background and while he's not a typical prospect for recruitment he has some remarkable talents. During my time I've recruited dozens of agents and I feel it in my bones that Frost will be a top recruit. I doubt he'll ever make it to Intelligence Officer but he'll make a damn good operative or a deadly sentinel. I'm convinced of it. I'd stake my reputation on it."

"Okay, it's your funeral. I hope you don't live to regret this decision of yours. He's your responsibility. Understand? I want six-monthly reports on him in standard format and if things don't look right at any time he'll be dropped. Don't get so close to him again. Place him on list B for now. Next?"

The report went on for two hours. "Well done, LeFort, you're a good man. It's a pity you're on the other side so to speak. Do you think you'll ever convince the French splinter to heal the wounds?"

"I genuinely hope so, sir. Do you think you'll ever convince your High Council to play their part?"

The Field Marshall looked at the French officer and grinned. "Touché, Monsieur LeFort."

***

An Organisation conversation

"It's me. Have you reported to your MI6 paymasters yet?"

"Yes I have, thank you very much."

"Where's my copy?"

"A little patience, if you please. MI6 isn't a lending library, you know."

"An operative's already seen your report and she tells me there's a new recruit. Tell me about him."

"At present he's a potential on list B. His name is Michael Frost."

"How old is he?"

"As you've had a briefing you already know how old he is."

"What's so special about this boy? He beat up a thug, so what."

"It was the way he did it. He destroyed him. His style is unique… he has such strength and speed. Phenomenal. Very impressive. He's an A student in mathematics and just about fluent, I believe, in German, French and Russian. With his language skills, I'm fairly certain I can get him inside MI6 on the Russian desk. I doubt he'll ever make Intelligence Officer, he's not made from the right sort of stuff."

"What's next for him?"

"I'll start planting the idea in his head of him joining up."

"Where to? Not the guards I hope?"

"Of course not, I'll want him where I can keep an eye on him."

"So, the Royal Tank Regiment then?"

"Of course, where else? He'll do…"

"Are there any familial connections?"

"None. But talking about familial connections, what news

about the Count bringing his son Albert into the French splinter?"

"Sad news about Albert. He was found floating in a lake at his Father's chateau."

"Drowned?"

"No, crossbow bolt through his right temple."

"How did the Count take it?"

"Very badly, I hear. But, he ignored the rules, which makes him an idiot." He carefully considered his next words before speaking. "The French splinter has always thought it can just do as it pleases. What it does affects us all. We regularly turn a blind eye to their acts of nepotism but we cannot afford to do so when it comes to dynasty building. He still has little Hugo and presumably he wouldn't be so stupid as to ignore our warning. I mean, he'll want to keep Hugo safe, he's fast running out of heirs to hand his little Froggy empire onto. No doubt he'll retaliate by starting up a little war. They do come in handy from time to time though, don't they?"

"Is little Hugo going to be taken care of?"

"Oh goodness me no. If we take care of little Hugo then the Count will be a man who has nothing to lose and a man who has nothing to lose is a very dangerous man. In trying to protect little Hugo he will suffocate him and then things will get interesting. Are you going back to your day job at MI6 any time soon?"

"I am. By the by, who's the operative there that you mentioned? I'm not familiar with any female operatives who would have ready access to reports at my level."

"You know the rules. One day you may rise high enough to see the curvature of the Earth itself but until then keep you head down and your arse up and don't ask stupid questions. Report on time in future. Goodbye."

PAKISTAN

N.W. Pakistan, 12th May

1226 PKT.

At a fraction under 40°C the midday heat in the open market was unbearable so Zulfiqar Ali slipped inside his fourth favourite café, the Al-Madina Tea Stall, for a refreshing glass of hot sweet tea.

He searched through the collection of coins in his pocket and discovered he could afford some meat, vegetables and bread too. Happy day. An old fourteen-inch TV behind the serving counter was tuned into the local news channel. The reception was terrible due, some say, to interference of the TV signal by the CIA or local military transmitters or something like that. This was nonsense; the poor TV reception was simply due to the quality of picture that can expected from a thirty-year-old analogue TV in a digital world.

Due to the small size of its screen and its flickering lines, if anything interesting appeared one had to crawl onto the serving counter to get a closer look at what was going on. Zuf, as he'd been known during his military service, sat down in time for his favourite programme – *The 1230 Global News Report*. The news was heavily censored, as were all TV programmes, as it needed to be approved by a half a dozen government departments, religious leaders and military authorities. The editing of news items was amateurish, as much of what was broadcast was smattered with continuity errors. This was usually disguised by overlaying the anchorman's face in front of items running in the background.

Keen to get on with things, Zuf shouted at the TV schedule announcer who had just appeared on the screen, "Get out of the way, get out of the way. Get on with the news." The other customers in the Al-Madina Tea Stall café thought it was them he was shouting at so they quickly moved away so as not to agitate this heap of rags further. Zuf was widely regarded as a colourful local character. This is quite something in a town that has more than its fair share of what most Westerners would regard as being colourful local characters.

All the news items that were to be broadcast were at least a week old.

"It is 1230 and here is the news." The preview of the news items was looking dog-eared as it had been cut up and sewn back together by the various censors. Nevertheless, Zuf was happy to sit and drink his tea and eat his meat, vegetables and bread and relax out of the heat of the sun.

The very first news item caught his attention as it concerned ISBJ. *What have they been up to now?* he thought to himself. A glance over the shoulder of the news anchorman at the item running in the background caused him to rise to his feet and move closer to the TV. He was now only paying attention to the grainy picture of a man appearing to be kneeling on the shoulder of the news anchorman. Not listening to a word of what was being broadcast, Zuf climbed onto the serving counter and grabbed the TV by its edges. After four or five seconds he tuned back into the news item. The scruffy man on the screen was claiming to be a Russian émigré but when Zuf had met him in 1991, when he was a part of an international expeditionary force taking part in the Gulf War, he knew the man to be English. He'd heard the man speak perfect English to his compatriots. Zuf removed his hands from the TV's sides and slid away backwards without taking his eyes off the image now sitting once more on the news anchor's shoulder.

News item over, Zuf left the Al-Madina Tea Stall café in a daze, stepping into the street and almost ending up under the wheels of a forty-year-old truck which, had it been newer, might have been going fast enough to hit him. He'd seen that face before. It was one of a group of faces belonging to a military unit he'd encountered in the desert regions of southern Iraq in 1991. He had good reason to remember these men. He had to find an elder, tell him his story and ask his advice.

Having had a few minutes to think about his next move, Zuf made his way to the outskirts of the town where he knew there to be recruiters operating. Or so he'd heard. These recruiters had been variously described by local elders as propagandists, extremists, bandits and radicalisers but they were mostly just local men and boys trying to relieve the daily tedium of living in a one-horse town by playing at being warlords and running around with guns. Guns, everybody had guns, it was no big deal really. All the same, it was a risky strategy as these people were partial to summary trial and execution and Zuf's past wasn't exactly unblemished. In fact if he were to show his face outside of his home town area he ran the risk of becoming a victim of summary trial and execution. How should he make contact? What should he say? He decided to play it by ear and hope he could walk away with them both still attached to his head and his head likewise attached to his neck.

This, he hoped, was his opportunity to be seen in a different light by the townsfolk and possibly get him some respect and maybe even secure him a little safety so he didn't always have to go around looking over his shoulder.

***

He walked for over a kilometre. There was a distinct change in the behaviour of the men milling around the ramshackle buildings. As he proceeded he was approached on three sides by armed militia.

"What are you doing here? What's your business? Where is your ID? Show me your ID." They clearly weren't police so no need to get the bribe money ready. Not that he had any anyway.

"I'm a believer who has news of interest for those fighting the forces of the evil West."

"And who might they be?" asked an armed man.

All Zuf could think to say was, "The enemies of Islam," hoping that would be enough to get their interest. The men looked bemused. What did this old fool think he was doing just walking in there like that? He was known in the locality for being a bit of a nuisance but this was totally out of character even for him.

One of the men had known Zulfiqar since his own childhood. His parents were friendly with Zuf's family before his wife died. "This place isn't for you. Say exactly what you want, speak clearly and quickly."

Zuf decided to take a chance. "I saw the face of a man on the 1230 Global News programme that I've seen before but his details weren't the same as when I knew him."

"So what?"

"When I knew him he was a Special Forces soldier, but not really a soldier, but he now says he's Russian and I know him to be English… and he's been taken by ISBJ in London." The local commander was standing at the back of the group of men so as not to attract the attention of snipers. He whispered in the ear of one of his Lieutenants.

The Lieutenant approached Zuf. "Come with me. We're going to search you and if you're armed you're a dead man. Do you understand?"

"I'm not armed."

The Lieutenant and Zuf made their way via crude holes knocked through the walls of several buildings, emerging at the entrance to an underground bunker. They entered the bunker and followed a maze of makeshift corrugated iron-clad tunnels. At the end of the tunnels was a heavy metal door guarding a small room beyond. When they entered the inner sanctum, the commander was sitting cross-legged at the head of a low table upon an ancient hand-woven rug. The man nodded in Zuf's direction indicating to him where he should sit.

"Tell me your story," he said while staring intently at Zuf.

"There are parts of my story of which I am now ashamed and I ask you to forgive me and take me into your protection so that I may be cleansed of my past indiscretions."

"Tell me your story and then I'll decide your fate." The man placed his AK47 underneath the table.

Zuf had a bad feeling but there was no going back now. "In 1991 I was in southern Iraq working as an interpreter for the coalition forces. At the time I was a Sergeant. I had no choice, believe me, I had no choice." Zuf stopped speaking and looked around the faces in the small room to check reaction to what he'd just said. There was shouting and somebody called for his death but the commander just held up his hand to demand silence. Zuf tentatively carried on with his story. "While I was there I became part of an international group processing people to determine their true identities and investigate their past." More yelling and shouting. "One day I was working alone in one of the offices catching up with some paperwork."

"More like sleeping if I know you, you old fart." The group of men laughed until the commander raised his hand for them to cease. The man who'd spoken out was the same one whose family had been friendly with Zuf's and he was breaking the tension to help Zuf out.

"OK, I was sleeping. I was making no noise. Not even snoring. I was woken by some loud talking coming from one of the other offices. When I became fully awake I realised Iraqi soldiers were being questioned and then beaten if their interrogators didn't like their answers." The commander held up his hand in advance of the group commencing their next round of yelling. "Some of the prisoners were from the elite Republican Guard but they didn't seem so tough in the hands of these men. Those doing the questioning spoke English between themselves but their Arabic was quite good when questioning the prisoners. One of them spoke perfect Arabic but he was definitely English. Some called him Frosty which he ignored until they called him by his proper name, which wasn't so very different, it was simply Frost. I didn't want to get discovered by these men so I made my way out through the door at the end of the corridor but was grabbed by a sentry and taken back into the offices."

"How many men were there?"

"I saw eight but I had a feeling there were more. I was interrogated. One of the men came straight toward me and without warning he hit me to the ground. I'd never been hit so hard in all my life. I was very surprised by the power of his punch as this man was quite small especially when compared with a couple of the others. He was told to stop hitting me by a man who I took to be their leader. Then they talked amongst themselves in German and must have decided I wasn't important enough to worry about so I was left to sit in the corner and told not to move. While I was sitting, my eyes met the eyes of the man I saw on the TV news report this afternoon at the Al-Madina Tea Stall café. One of the men spoke to him calling him Frosty, asking him to pass him the IDs of the soldiers they'd captured. He ignored the man, simply turning his head to stare at him until he called him Frost. After he passed the man the IDs he stood very still with only his eyes moving to watch me. He was holding a black sword with a dragon etched into its blade. The sword wasn't like anything I'd ever seen before. Apart from passing the man the IDs Frost never moved a muscle all the time I was sitting on the floor."

"What happened to their prisoners?"

"I don't know. I never saw them again. I didn't even see them being taken from the camp."

"Carry on with your story."

"I saw the men again when I was assigned to a group of international observers. We were returning to base camp near a local village and walked straight into an ambush. It was dusk and we were walking into the setting sun and were blinded by its glare. There was lots of gunfire and people were running everywhere. I saw two men making a break for it as it was clear that the ambush had been foiled. As these two men rounded a broken concrete column of a nearby building I saw an extraordinary thing. From behind the column, hidden from view by what could only have been a few centimetres, a man emerged. His face was covered by a shemagh. He came out of nowhere it seemed to me. The two men stopped dead in their tracks and changed direction but it was too late for them. The man was on them in a split second, felling them with kicks and punches. He then removed a sword from a scabbard strapped to his back and threatened that if they moved even an eyebrow he'd disembowel them both. Despite the shemagh I could tell it was Frost by his sword. After the two men were secured he slid the sword back into its scabbard and went to join the observers I'd been escorting, standing directly in front of one of them, not moving at all. He was like a statue."

"One minute you say you were working as an interpreter and the next you say you were a military escort for international observers. What is the truth?"

"I was in the army and so had to do as I was ordered. On this occasion I was part of an escort, other times I acted as an interpreter; a translator. Nothing unusual."

"Carry on."

Zuf was becoming increasingly worried that his story wasn't going down well. "I was glad to be alive. One of the men drew two large circles in the sand with his heel. We were told to sit down in one of the circles while the soldiers they'd captured sat in the other circle. The man who I took to be the leader made his way into our group and touched three men on their shoulders. They were removed from our circle, as was the man Frost had gone to stand in front of. I never saw them again."

The Commander could tell this was turning into a very interesting story. "Everybody leave us," he ordered and the men piled out of the small room without even so much as a backward glance. "Do you want some tea?" the Commander asked Zuf.

This is more like it, thought Zuf. "That would be most welcome." Zuf didn't know whether to chance his luck by asking the Commander what he thought of his story but ultimately decided against it. He was hopeful that the Commander was interested in what he had said so far and that his story would convince him to offer him protection. The tea arrived and they took their refreshments in silence as the Commander was deep in thought over Zuf's story.

***

Tea finished. "Continue, Mr Zuf," ordered the Commander.

"Some from my group were taken to an encampment in the dunes by a couple of soldiers. The Iraqi soldiers were made to kneel down. They had their wrists and ankles secured by plastic cable ties. Some of the international observers objected to this treatment and they were moved half a kilometre to the west along with two soldiers to guard them. It was obviously easier moving the observers because…"

"Yes, yes, yes, that makes sense. Carry on," shouted the Commander, clearly getting irritated with Zuf.

He got the message so decided to get to the meat of the story. "I was kept in the encampment as I was in uniform and, looking back, I think they wanted a scapegoat if things went wrong. The leader gathered his remaining soldiers and spoke quietly to them while pointing at a map. They dispersed to stand behind the

Iraqi soldiers. The leader bent down and whispered something to one the Iraqi soldiers; after he shook his head the soldier standing behind him just seemed to touch the back of his head and he fell forward, his face burying itself into the sand. He was dead. I couldn't figure out what was happening. I was now very, very frightened. These men could do exactly as they pleased and nobody was going to come and rescue me. Frost moved forward and drew his sword. The silver dragon cut into its blade seemed to dance in the light of the setting sun. The Iraqi soldiers started praying."

Zuf took a few deep breaths before carrying on after reliving that moment in the desert. He was crying. Tears streamed down his cheeks. "Frost then went to stand right in front of one of the kneeling soldiers, sword at the ready. He raised his head to look into Frost's eyes and then looked at the silver dragon dancing on the sword and wet himself. He threw himself on the sand and begged for mercy. The leader of the men came up to the soldier and whispered something in his ear to which he nodded. He was led away. The remaining Iraqi soldiers had words whispered into their ears by the leader, some of them nodded and were also taken away. Four soldiers did not nod agreement and were left kneeling in a line. All but one of the soldiers went to the other camp where the international observers were being guarded; or maybe I should now say, being held. All that remained in the encampment were four Iraqi soldiers, myself and the soldier the leader spoke to before departing for the other camp.

"The Iraqi soldiers kept looking at one another. The remaining soldier was similar in size to the one who'd killed the first soldier but he had very light skin colour and hair. He stood behind the line of kneeling soldiers and after five minutes he drew his pistol and attached a silencer to it. I could see what he was doing but the Iraqi soldiers couldn't otherwise they'd have panicked. I was about to ask if I could go to the other camp to be with the observers as I was supposed to be their guide. Before

I could speak, the soldier shot one of the Iraqis at the base of his skull and he toppled forward into the sand, dead. The other soldiers started wailing, praying and crying and begging for mercy. He shot another Iraqi soldier. The two remaining Iraqis got to their feet and hopped away in opposite directions. The soldier was totally calm; he went after one of them and shot him in what he called 'a good old-fashioned Belfast kneecapping'. He then went after the second Iraqi and did the same thing to him. Shot him behind both knees. They were writhing in agony. In the moonlight, their blood looked black like oil spilling into the desert sand. I could only think, 'When is it my turn?' I thought there was no way he'd let me live after witnessing this. I'd seen all their faces. I prayed to Allah in what I thought was my last prayer. The soldier went back to the first Iraqi soldier, put his boot on his neck and placed the end of the silencer against his ear and pulled the trigger." He repeated the same thing with the other Iraqi soldier.

***

In the early days of his career the Irishman didn't like getting close to the action, invariably opting to carry out his work at distance. Which meant, as a minimum, being out of range of the arc of an arterial spray after impact.

His preference for distancing himself from his work was for several reasons; firstly, and most importantly, was economy. He'd grown up in abject poverty and his parents had driven into him that wastefulness wasn't acceptable. So when he did his work he always did it as cost effectively as possible and this included keeping cleaning costs to a minimum. This approach to his work did sometimes create an additional cost because accuracy suffers with distance which meant that sometimes he'd had to use two bullets instead of one, but a bullet was cheaper than having to buy new clothes or having to clean his work clothes. Also, this cost was acceptable as he usually didn't have to pay for his own bullets.

Second was vanity. When the Irishman was growing up he noticed how the young men who were clean, well presented and smartly dressed got the prettiest girls. "The peacocks get the prizes," as his elder brother would say in the time before he shot him. It simply wouldn't do for the Irishman to go around spattered in blood, would it now? Putting all those lovely young girls off and all because of the type of work he did. It wasn't fair. He had to look smart at all times, and especially so his shoes. They had to shine and reflect better than anybody else's.

Third was hygiene. The Irishman wasn't an overly hygienic person; he washed and all but he wasn't what one would call OCD clean. He thought the hygiene point spoke for itself. "Who the hell wants to get spattered in somebody else's blood and guts?" was his simple view. Most other people in the Irishman's line of work were paid considerably better than he was but he wasn't in it for the money. Time and circumstances, though, change everybody and now the nearer he got to the action the better he liked it. He was better paid too nowadays.

***

"The soldier looked toward the other camp. After a few more minutes I heard gunfire coming from the other camp. The observers had been shot by the soldiers guarding them. The man turned to me and shouted, 'Come here, ye filthy raghead ye.' I walked shivering with fright towards him. When I drew close he raised his gun to shoulder height and shouted 'Bang!' and laughed. I almost passed out with fear. My knees gave way and I fell to the ground where he pushed the silencer against my ear. It was hot. 'Bang!' he shouted, even louder this time and laughed even louder but the effect on me was much less as I had resigned myself to die in the desert.

"He then said, 'Just so ye know. I'm not goin' to shoot ye so ye can relax.' I wondered if this was just part of his cruel game. 'We need ye to do something for us. You'll be well paid for yer troubles. What d'ye say?' 'What do you want me to do?' I asked. 'You'll be told in good time and until then keep that hole in the front of yer face shut in case I change me mind.' He walked away in the direction of the other camp. He turned and pointed to the other camp and gave me a sign to follow him."

"Where was the man Frost?"

"He was at the other camp. When we got there, the bodies of the observers were sprawled on the ground; their blood had run into the sand next to them. The soldier said to the leader, 'Our rag-headed friend is in.' He then went off to join the others. The leader came over to me and said, 'We're going to be leaving soon. You're going to stay here and when the coalition forces turn up you're going to give them the story which we're going to give to you. Don't worry about being questioned over your story, that won't happen. One day soon we'll come for you. Now go and join the other men and have something to eat, it's been a long day.'

"I studied the story I was given very carefully. When the coalition forces turned up I told it to the investigators, signed my statement and that was that. After I was discharged from the Army I returned home. They promised they'd come for me but they never did."

"Are you sure the man you saw on the TV was the same man you saw all those years ago; Frost?"

"I'm positive, you don't forget people like that one. Even though he'd been badly beaten and has a beard now, there was still that same coldness in his eyes. What do we do now? What happens next for me?"

"I need to think about what you've told me and then I'll decide what to do with you. In the meantime you'll remain here with us." The Commander called for two of his henchmen to take Zuf away.

MARGARET'S STORY - THE ROVING AMBASSADOR

Margaret Rotheram's life appeared as though it couldn't get any better. She was on the crest of a tsunami wave of success and her reputation in the Organisation was going from strength to strength.

But it wasn't enough for her. Yes, she was ambitious, but she was beginning to think that her ambition was misdirected. The top half of the greasy pole of the Organisation wasn't turning out to be what she thought it would be. She'd relished her work as a knowing operative because it was exciting, often dangerous, and filled with intrigue. When she'd been promoted to Counsellor it was more like being a nurse maid than anything else. Now that she was a Controller, well, life was positively dull. Maybe she was too young for the job, but not for the reasons her peers might think. She felt she was too young for the job because it was an administrative job and she was an action girl. Now, with everything set up, there was very little for her to do. Her new job was even more mundane than her Counsellor job had been.

***

As Rex passed the open door to her office he slowed his pace, glancing in at her before walking on. He then walked backwards past her door and glanced at her again, but this time with his eyes crossed. He walked to and fro, forwards and backwards, three more times. Every time he passed he pulled a different face at her. He looked so ridiculous. It made her laugh.

Since Rex moved in down the hall they'd seen very little of one another. She didn't trust him anymore and had purposely avoided him. But he was always such wonderful fun to be around. He was very witty and humorous, so she couldn't help but like him in an odd sort of way.

"Now, Margaret, I'm no trick-cyclist but you look depressed to me."

"Is it that obvious?"

"I keep on telling her to buck up."

"Yes, thank you, Lisette."

"What's wrong old girl?"

"Old girl?"

"Just a figure of speech. Tell Uncle Rex what's wrong."

"No matter what I do here it doesn't seem to make much difference. Lisette, can you leave us for a moment and close the door behind you please."

After Lisette had left the office Rex continued, "You're making a huge difference. Just look at what you've achieved."

"What have I achieved? I got promoted, so what."

"It's nothing to do with getting promoted, you silly sod, it's what's happened to this place since you arrived. Look at them, they're like rabbits caught in headlights. You're the tonic we've needed for some time now."

"Am I? I don't feel much like a tonic."

"We'd become inward-looking… stagnant. We'd made no progress with the splinters and our numbers had plateaued; fallen actually in some regions. Since you arrived on the scene people are looking over their shoulders. They're making the efforts they should have been making for years. You've shown them it can be done and how to do it. They're all copying you, Margaret."

"So what if they are? That just means they'll catch me up and then what? Eh?"

"They'll never catch you up because you're an innovator. They'll play catch-up forever while you lead them on to new heights."

"I want to go back to being an operative. Is that possible?"

"It's been done before but I have another idea."

"Another one of your great ideas like the one that got me here in the first place?" she replied caustically.

"Precisely, old girl," he replied disregarding her tone of voice. "I have an idea for a role for you that will challenge you like never before. I'll need to talk it over with Mr Chairman first and, if he's agreeable, then we'll have you in for a nice little chat."

"Shouldn't you discuss it with me first?"

"No." Rex left her office whistling a tune she'd never heard before.

***

When Lisette re-entered Margaret's office she asked what Rex and she had talked about. She told her they'd talked about her quitting her job as a controller and going back to being an operative. Lisette asked why she wanted to do that and Margaret told her she was bored. Lisette said she knew what she was talking about as she too was bored. She added, though, that if she did go back to being an operative would she please put in a good word for her for the vacant controller position. Margaret gave her a straight-mouth smile accompanied by a wide-eyed look that said it all. Lisette said she thought it unlikely that they'd just let her quit. She insisted that she wasn't quitting, she was just going down another path; a reassignment. Margaret thought Lisette seemed to know a lot about the Organisation's higher policies.

As it was nearing lunch they went to sit in Green Park to check out the talent. They lay down on the grass and stared at the rare blue sky. It'd been grey for months.

While walking back to the office Margaret told Lisette that she'd made up her mind. She was going to move away from London and take up an operative role in… she couldn't quite think where at the time but she thought it best to leave London; leave England perhaps. Lisette jokingly asked if her dark mood might be due to the miserable weather they'd had lately. Margaret tutted and shook her head but smiled as she knew Lisette was trying to lift her spirits. They weren't friends exactly but they were as close as anybody could be to being friends in the friendless Organisation. They held hands as they crossed over Piccadilly from Green Park, each giving reassuring squeezes to the other. Back in the office Margaret typed her resignation/reassignment letter.

As soon as the letter was finished she walked down the corridor, straight past Mr Chairman's PA and into his office. She didn't want to think about it in case she changed her mind, she just wanted to slap the envelope on his desk and stand there while he read it.

"He's not in," screamed the PA at Margaret's back.

"Where is he?"

"Out."

"When will he be back?"

"I have no idea. Whatever it is it wasn't in his diary. Mr Chairman and Rex took off after he told him about his conversation with you." The PA thought he'd finished speaking but his anger got the better of him. "Look, you might think you're the best thing since sliced bread but you need to show some respect and consideration for others. You think you can do exactly as you please and everybody has to lap it up. Well, I think you're a shit. A selfish shit. You've been handed everything on a silver platter but that's not good enough for you, is it? You've created mayhem here this past couple of years and now you want to walk away from the steaming pile of shit you created. You have no idea what Mr Chairman has had to put up with because of you. Nobody likes you and they want you out but Rex thinks you're the next coming or something. To be honest, love, I don't see it."

"Thank you for sharing your opinion but I am not to blame for the decades of neglect and mismanagement that has brought about the appalling state of affairs which…"

"Oh, shut up. You need to take a good look at yourself in the mirror, love. You don't know these people. You don't know what they've contributed. You don't know the sacrifices they've made."

"We all make sacrifices just to be here. I've left a letter on Mr Chairman's desk. Please bring it to his attention as soon as he returns. I'll be in my office." The PA had got to her.

When Margaret returned to her office she asked Lisette to hold her calls and admit no one but Mr Chairman's PA. She closed the door and sat facing out of the window at the people in the street below and at those in the offices of the building opposite. She wished she could turn back the clock on Rex's offer. She pondered on the life she might have had.

***

A mandarin and guests conversation

"Let her go back to being an operative. She's far too much trouble."

"People like her don't grow on trees, you know."

"There are others."

"But they're not with us."

"Neither is she."

"She's young and an idealist and she's driven by ambition, all of which makes her perfect for our purposes. She's also very insecure. She'll jump at the opportunity to become Madame Chairman when it's dangled in front of her. With the strings that will come with the job we'll have exactly what we want."

"Couldn't I just do it? There's no need to go through all this palaver."

"If you do it, it'll raise everybody's suspicions and the splinters will rally round to help them. The governors have to be removed before we can proceed, but not by you. It has to be by somebody else's hand and hers is perfect."

"But she wants to go back to being an operative."

"Nonsense. She just needs a challenge, that's all. What's your plan, Rex?"

"As you know, she has a vision for the Organisation which she can't fulfil in her present role so I suggest we provide her a steppingstone to achieve that vision."

"Which is?"

"Haven't you been listening?" tsk tsked the mandarin. "She wants to bring the splinters back into the fold. Which of course we do not want for a minute. How do you suggest we go about it?"

"We create a roving ambassadorial role for her. She can meet with the splinters to sound them out for a reconciliation. That should keep her busy until we're ready to make our move."

"Isn't that rather risky?"

"Granted, it doesn't come without its risks but knowing the conflicting ambitions of the splinter leaders she'll have her work cut out to get them round the table. None of them will see it coming."

"Then what?"

"We let time do our work for us as it always seems to. After a suitable period you'll resign and she'll win the vote to make her Madame Chairman. She will see it as recognition for her efforts as roving ambassador. You'll need to set things up in order to…"

"Going straight to the Chair without being a governor? Impossible. They'll suspect something. Can't we…"

"It's always problems with you, isn't it? Glass is always half empty. We'll create a situation whereby she will be proposed and seconded to be entered into the race for the Chair."

"A race? There hasn't been a race for hundreds of years. It always caused problems in the past. Those who were unsuccessful were often killed and candidates slaughtered those who hadn't voted for them. No, we…"

"No? What do you mean 'no', Mr Chairman?" The threat in the tone of voice was clear.

"Well, what I'm saying is that it might cause problems if there's a race, that's why the Mandarins always choose somebody preordained for the Chair."

"In order for everybody to accept her she has to be seen to win a race. It's the only way."

"What will happen to the unsuccessful candidates?"

"You need not concern yourself about that, they will be well looked after. They'll get their just rewards." Mr Chairman failed to grasp the meaning behind those words.

"What about our present predicament? Do you think you can talk her into it?"

"I won't need to, I guarantee she'll jump at anything we put in front of her so long as it speaks to her ambitions and panders to her ego."

"What about her PA? The young one, not the crabby old one."

"I think there's a certain amount of resentment and jealousy between her and her boss," he lied, "so I suggest we promote her to Controller once Margaret is off doing her new job."

"That should be okay. It won't be for very long. Yes, let's do that."

"Never mind her. What about me?"

"I understand there will soon be a couple of vacancies on the Mandarin council." He paused to let those words hang in the air and allow their full effect to take hold before continuing, "I always thought you'd make a good mandarin," he lied.

Mr Chairman's head was in a spin. He felt much better about the plan now he'd practically been told he was getting a seat on the Mandarin council. He'd go along with anything they wanted now.

***

On returning to the Half Moon Street building, Rex approached Margaret's door despite Lisette telling him that she didn't want to be disturbed. Not for the first time, Lisette asked him what he did, what his job was, and for the same amount of times he tapped the side of his nose with his forefinger and whispered, "It's a secret." Like everybody else, she found his side-of-nose tapping infuriating.

He didn't wait to be invited in, he simply popped his head around the door and told her that she should come immediately to see Mr Chairman. She asked him if it was about her note. He asked, "What note?" but then said it didn't matter and suggested they first have a chat before going in to see Mr Chairman.

He said he thought very highly of her and that she shouldn't sacrifice all her good work by throwing away her career. He told her she needed to give serious consideration to a job offer Mr Chairman was about to make her. She wanted to know what the job was and he told her that a position was being created that would totally occupy her. She was interested to know more. He added that the role would help her in her desire to see the Organisation reunited. He knew she'd be intrigued. He knew her as well as she knew herself.

When they entered Mr Chairman's office the PA left the room immediately, having confessed all to his boss about his earlier outburst. He nodded an apology to Margaret on his way past her. Rex apologised to Mr Chairman for spoiling the party by having outlined the offer he was about to make to Margaret but he said he did so out of pure excitement. The liar. Mr Chairman sat swivelling in his chair fifteen degrees left and right from centre. He was fanning himself with the envelope containing her letter. He asked her if he should read her letter first or wait until after he'd told her about an exciting new opportunity he'd thought up for her. Rex smiled a grimacing smile at that one. She said she'd prefer to wait until after he'd told her what was on his mind. He smiled at the way she put it. He liked her turn of phrase.

After he told her about the new role he had in mind for her he asked if she needed some time to think about it. She said she did not. As she accepted the job, she moved confidently from her chair to snatch her letter from his hand saying that there was no need for him to open it now. She looked at Rex and smiled. Rex look at her and smiled. She asked who'd be taking over from her. They said they hadn't had a chance to consider that question yet. The liars. She suggested that Lisette might be considered. They looked at one another and both said, in unison, "That's a good idea" but she shouldn't say anything to Lisette 'for obvious reasons'. They wanted to ensure Lisette knew who she was beholden to for her promotion.

The words that stuck most in her mind were 'the international dimension of the role'. *That means a lot of travelling*, she thought. A lot of time out of the office. That would suit her fine at that precise moment. The way things were going with her marriage she imagined that would suit her husband too. She still loved him and he loved her as far as she could tell but them marrying was a big mistake.

***

When she returned to her office, Lisette was tidying up her desk, which was very unusual for her. She asked Margaret if she was still her boss. She suggested they go to a bar in the Ritz for a chat. The Ritz is just across Piccadilly from Half Moon Street. Lisette looked apprehensive. She asked if it was a farewell drink or a celebration to which she replied that it could be considered a bit of both.

As they approached the entrance to the Ritz they nodded to the doorman. They'd bumped into him some months earlier in a bar in Soho. He had a fascinating past and they both thought he was just the right type of person to be an operative. They concluded it was a pity he was past his prime. He admitted them to the hotel's lobby and they made their way to the upper bar as there were usually more tables available there at that time of the day.

"C'mon then. Give me the worst."

"I put in my letter of resignation today. Well, not so much resignation, more a reassignment request."

"If you go I want to go with you."

"I'll see what I can do. I'll probably need a PA for my new role." She smiled smugly.

"What? You've got a new job? It's not Madame Chairman, is it?"

"Better. I'm going to be a roving ambassador with responsibility for bringing the splinters back into the fold."

"I didn't know there was such a role."

"There wasn't until today."

"Be careful, Margaret, it sounds too good to be true. No disrespect, but why you? You don't know any of the splinters."

"That's not entirely true. I've met lots of people from the splinters…"

"Yes but this is different, this will be dealing with the heads of the splinters and if stories about them are to be believed they're a pretty ruthless lot."

"I know. Fantastic, isn't it? What a great opportunity."

"Aren't you scared? They could be setting you up."

"Why would they do that?"

"A thousand reasons, for example…"

"Lizzie, I could probably think up as many reasons as you for why this could be a setup but I'm going into this with my eyes wide open. This is something I've wanted to do for a long time. I can do it. I know I can. I'll need a PA of course. Would you like to apply for the role?"

"Apply for the role? Why you cheeky so and so." They laughed and toasted their future successes.

***

The next day when she entered her office Rex and Mr Chairman were already sitting waiting for her. She hadn't ever known them to be so early. They explained that as her new role would soon become common knowledge it was best if she left her post as Controller immediately. She asked who would be taking over from her. She was more than slightly surprised when they said they'd already offered the role to Lisette. She said she was pleased and that Lisette would make a good Controller, adding she had her in mind for her PA. She was told by Mr Chairman that one PA wouldn't be sufficient in her new role and that four IOs would be assigned to her as PAs. *They'll be there to keep an eye on me and report back,* she thought.

Lisette entered the office with a sheepish expression on her face. She explained to Margaret that she'd been asked not to discuss the job offer until after Mr Chairman and Rex had spoken with her. She said she understood. She asked when she'd been offered the job to which she replied that Rex and Mr Chairman were waiting for her when she arrived at her flat the previous evening. Rex and Mr Chairman made their excuses to leave the room, saying that Lisette and Margaret probably had a lot to talk about as the handover should begin immediately. It was a very uncomfortable morning with neither apologising to the other for any misunderstandings or whatever they were. They both went their separate ways for lunch and continued the handover in a professional, if frosty, atmosphere in the afternoon.

***

Rex made a short phone call to let the mandarin know that everything was in place and that Margaret would be out of the office and on the road within days. He was a little alarmed when the mandarin told him that he intended to make contact with her when she visited the Italian splinter. He wanted to ask why that was necessary but he didn't have the guts.

MICHAEL'S STORY – THE OLD HUT BY THE SEA

Right on the heels of Michael's 'O' level exams were the 1969 Altcar summer camps and, as ever, money was tight in the Frost household. Margaret was bracing herself to tell Michael she couldn't afford to send him away to Altcar.

As with the previous year, Sergeant Huggard turned up to talk with Margaret about Altcar, but this time he arrived with some particularly good news.

"Hi Margaret, it's that time of year again. Altcar."

"Come on in, Sergeant Huggard, I'll put the kettle on and make us a cup of tea. Biscuits? Sandwich?"

"Yes to both thanks, luv." He was on earlies and had missed his breakfast after sleeping past his alarm.

Margaret spoke first. "Sergeant Huggard, I'm afraid that I don't have the money for Michael to go to Altcar. The other kids need…"

"Margaret," butted in the Sergeant, "can I just stop you there, luv? I've had a message from Altcar saying that Michael's subs have been paid by some foundation. I've been told they do this sort of thing for kids they think deserve some help." Poor deluded Sergeant Huggard. He wasn't to know that Michael's subs were being paid through a government budget assigned to the Organisation, masquerading, in this instance, as a charitable foundation. As part of his continuing observation of Michael, the soldier in the French uniform arranged for the so-called charitable foundation to pay his Altcar subs. Classic Organisation, spending other people's money for its own purposes.

"That's very kind of them, but who are they? I know we haven't got much money but I pay my way thank you very much," said Margaret defiantly.

"Please don't get upset, Marg, everybody knows you pay your way but this is different. It's like drawing out a lucky ticket. Y'know, like a raffle and Michael won. It's not charity, it's something this foundation does week in week out for loads of kids. The details are in the post. The final decision is yours but it's a great opportunity for Michael. You have a think about it and when the letter arrives you can give your answer then. Okay? C'mon now, Margaret, that tea won't make itself y'know," said Sergeant Huggard trying to break the tension with humour. He was pushing against an open door as Margaret had already decided Michael should go to Altcar, she just wanted to put on a show of independence.

***

At the end of every school year there's a limbo time after exams when pupils ask the question, "Why am I still here when there's nothing to do?" To address this situation, teachers occupy small children with doing lots of finger painting, middling children listen to music that some teacher brought in which isn't to anybody else's taste and the big kids are expected to entertain themselves. Very dangerous. It's a time bomb waiting to go off.

"How about we stage a boxing tournament?" suggested the school's boxing club coach in a pre-planned brainwave which had been suggested to him in a pub a few weeks earlier by a stranger. He thanked him and adopted the idea as his own.

"Yeah, why not," replied an unenthusiastic student body.

"Good, I'll get in touch with a couple of boxing coach mates and get it sorted. C'mon, youz lot, show a bit of enthusiasm, it'll be fun."

"Look, sir, we just want to get out of here and get on with earning some money for the summer holidays. Who's with me?" All the students raised their hands except Michael. "What's wrong, Michael, aren't ye interested in earnin' a few bob?"

"I'm going to Altcar again this summer with the Royal Tank Regiment."

"Are you still doing that? Give it a miss and come with me and Jacko and the rest of the lads and we'll earn a few bob doing gardenin' and cleaning cars and stuff. It'll be a laugh. C'mon."

"All in good time, youz lot. First we'll get you boxing and then you can go and earn some money for the summer holidays." He made to leave the gym. "You lot do a bit of sparring while I get on the phone and don't kill one another while I'm out of the room. Okay?" What the boxing coach really meant by arranging a tournament was that it would be a great skive for the teachers. Classic PE teacher end of term stuff.

The idea of an inter-school boxing tournament was leapt upon by all the boxing coaches. It turned into a big event, likely to spread over three or four days. *Why haven't we done this sort of thing before?* thought the teacher body. *What a great skive.*

***

The outer doors of the gymnasium were opened up to allow students to peer in from the paved areas surrounding the building. All the real interest was in the big-boys card, not least from an observer who'd come to check on Michael's progress. The observer sidled up to Michael and introduced himself as a boxing coach from London. He said he'd heard a lot about Michael and had come to watch him fight. He suggested that he try to win on points so he could check out his form.

"Are you okay with that?"

"Yes," was all Michael said in reply. When his first fight was called everybody went to the ringside.

"C'mon, Michael. Show him what ye can do," shouted the school coach. The fight started slowly with a few range finders before Michael started throwing sets of combination punches. He was doing as he'd been requested by boxing to win the fight on points. In the middle of the second round though, his opponent went down on one knee and took a TKO.

"What was that all about, Frost, you div?" asked the boxing coach. "You were love tapping him. What's going on? Is he your boyfriend or something?"

"I fought to win on points." Something happened to Michael during that fight. Boxing that way gave him a warm feeling in his stomach. He enjoyed testing himself to see what was possible. It was as though he was standing outside his body and observing the fighting. It gave him a tremendous sense of power.

"Well, don't arse around like that in yer next fight, a boxing ring isn't the place to go arsing around in because if you do arse around in the ring you're going to get hit and nobody likes to get hit. Am I right?" After the school boxing coach left Michael's side, the London schools boxing coach appeared next to him.

"Well done, Michael," said the London schools boxing coach, "that was excellent but next time try to keep the fight going to the end so we can all see what you're capable of. Show off your technique, use your skills, but don't go for power."

"But the coach told me not to arse around in case I get hit."

"Look, nobody doubts your ability, you're probably the best boxer here, but power isn't everything. Lead your opponents into traps, bring them in and let them out like they're on a string. Control yourself, control your opponent and control the fight. You can do it, Michael, I know you can. Now go and shadow box your next fight from start to finish in your head. Imagine how the fight will go in your mind. Win the fight in your head and then win it for real." Michael understood exactly what the London schools boxing coach meant.

An hour and a half later it was time for Michael's second match. His opponent this time was a regional ABA champ instead of one of the Liverpool boxers. He was a few years older than Michael and had been hand-picked to fight him by the London schools boxing coach. He was a very elegant and technical opponent. Michael admired much about his style and technique, mimicking in real time what he was observing of his movements. Then blam. After a period of close, in fighting, Michael's opponent stepped back and caught him with a sweet right hook followed by a left uppercut to the jaw. One two. He didn't hit the canvas but he was groggy from the punches. His opponent didn't move in for the kill though, he stood off him, throwing daisy drops over his shoulders until he'd regained his senses. The bell ended the second round.

"What the hell did I tell ye about arsing around, eh? You took two big punches there; are ye okay to carry on, son? It's not a real tournament, ye know, so it's okay to throw in the towel."

"I will not throw the towel in. I haven't lost a fight for over four years and I'm not going to lose this one."

"Michael, son. He's a regional ABA champ and he's probably going to turn pro within the next eighteen months so do yourself a big favour and give it a miss. You've got nothing to prove here, lad." Michael wasn't listening to the school boxing coach. At the bell he jumped up off his stool, slapped his gloves together and did a little hop, Timbo style, pumping the air with a dozen uppercuts before touching gloves with his opponent for the start of the last round.

"Good luck," mumbled Michael's opponent through his gum shield.

"Same to you," mumbled Michael while thinking, *Defend yourself at all times.*

What Michael hadn't realised was that his opponent had been going easy on him but now it was totally on. The ABA champ set about his business with combinations of body and head shots but all from distance. Michael took up his favoured southpaw stance, then quickly switching to orthodox and throwing his opponent off balance, forcing him to cover up from an onslaught. Both boxers regarded each other from behind high guards. Michael then dropped his gloves to his waist and started body swerving the punches being served up to him, Muhammad Ali style. Using his speed he closed the distance to his opponent and sent a sickening uppercut into his solar plexus. The ABA champion immediately put a knee on the canvas to take a count. After a count of seven he got back to his feet and offered Michael a glove to slap which he accepted as a sign of mutual respect. Recalling what the London schools boxing coach said to him, Michael finished the third round by moving and controlling his opponent around the ring. At the bell both fighters held up each other's hands, declaring the fight a draw themselves.

"You had me in the second. Why did you back off?"

"I've heard a lot about you and I wanted the fight to go on. Y'know, see what happens. You learn more by stepping back than going in for the kill. I learned a lot today which will help me in the future."

"Well done, lads," said the school boxing coach wrapping his arms around each boxer's shoulders.

"Excuse me," said the London schools boxing coach to the school boxing coach, "do you mind if I have a minute with the boys?"

"Not at all, be my guest. Who are you by the way?"

"I'm a boxing coach from London here to see how my protégé is getting on." He didn't indicate which of the boxers he was referring to.

"Hey, you're not nicking our lads to take them off down to that London, are ye? They're better off staying here in Liverpool an' not swanning off down to that London."

"I doubt they're better off staying in Liverpool but I have

no intention of nicking your lads as you put it. Now excuse us please?" replied the London schools boxing coach firmly if not a little rudely.

"That was the perfect way to demonstrate your talents, Michael. I think you could be a real prospect. What do you think of our Roberto here?"

"He's a great boxer. The best I've ever fought by a mile. His hair is very black."

The London schools boxing coach choke-laughed at the non-sequitur. "You'll be seeing some more of him at Altcar."

"Which regiment are you with, Roberto?"

"He's not in a regiment, he's going to Altcar to run some hand-to-hand combat classes for the grunts."

"Your hair is very black, Roberto. My dad's hair is very black. His family are from South West Ireland. Are you from there too, Roberto?"

"No, I'm from London but my parents are from Sicily."

"I've heard of it."

"Yeah, it's an island in the Mediterranean near Italy. I've never been there but I hope to go one day. Maybe even box there, who knows. See you at Altcar, Michael." Roberto and the London schools boxing coach left the tournament. They'd seen enough.

***

"What do you reckon then, Roberto? Is he as good as he looks?"

"Better than good. He's got fantastic technique and he hits like a sledgehammer. My ribs are killing me. If he can do the business at Altcar I reckon he's a real prospect. Now I'm off back to my hotel room for a long hot bath. See you later for a big steak and it's on you. By the way, stop calling me Roberto you make me sound like a spiv."

"You know the rules. No real names, so as far as I'm concerned, you're Roberto."

"Yeah, but call me that name again and you'll be eating your steak through a straw. You need to think of a less spivy name or you and me are going to fall out."

***

The coach trip to Altcar was more enjoyable than the previous year probably because there was no Buckhead on board. Strangely, they were no other cadets on board.

Once they arrived at Altcar they were bivouacked in a newly erected wooden barracks. There were bunk beds everywhere. They went to the far end to be the bad boys at the back of the room.

"I'm not sure about this setup. Why haven't we got our own bivvy like last year?"

"Would you like your own suite or perhaps a room in the West Wing, your lordship?" asked a Sergeant sarcastically. "Right, you lot, put your kit bags on your bunks and be out on the parade ground in one minute; 59, 58, 57…" Once assembled on the parade ground the Sergeant barked out his orders for everyone to fall in. "Atteeeeeen'hun. Stand aaaat… ease. Stand easy. Sir, soldiers and cadets are fell in, sir."

"Thank you, Sergeant. Now listen up, all of you. In an effort to keep at the cutting edge of warfare we are going to be conducting several exercises which will be new to some of you and if that's the case, consider yourselves guinea pigs. Her Majesty's Government has a concern over our state of preparedness for nuclear and biological warfare. The exercises you'll be undertaking will concentrate on potential future Armageddon scenarios. Though the exercises will primarily focus on defence there will naturally be some offensive content. There will be three scenarios staged as Red on Blue with Blue being the defence of the realm. In all scenarios the Cadet forces will play the part of the general public or other such non-combatant roles as assigned and will be permanently attached to Blue teams. That is all except Cadet Frost." The tank cadets looked at one another in surprise but with enormous pride that not all of them were going to be playing the part of corpses.

Major Finn continued with the briefing.

***

The tank cadets weren't involved in the first exercise so they went to the assembly point for the Red team to see what Michael was up to. As they approached the briefing zone to get a closer look a couple of Royal Marines commandos came out of nowhere.

"Passes?"

"What passes?"

"Okay, on the floor, you lot. Now! Hands behind your heads and keep them there. Got some spies here, sir." The commando guards kicked the cadets behind their knees sending them crashing to the ground to let them know they weren't joking. "I told you lot, hands behind your heads and keep them there, I won't tell you again."

"Spies eh, Corpwal. Is that you, Munwoe?"

"Yes Captain Hywel-Jones, sir, it's Cadet Munwoe here having his neck stood on by a commando." The tank cadets didn't know whether to laugh but thought it best not to.

"Let them up, Corporal Roberts, I'll deal with them. Follow me, cadets." The cadets knew it was all a big game but nevertheless it was very frightening having commandos come at you from out of nowhere, pointing guns in your faces. "You do realise that technically I could have you shot as spies? It would mean the end of the games for you and that would be a shame as we'd have no injured civilians to look after or any corpses littering the streets. You cadets play a vital role in all this. You might not think so but you do. If we don't make it real then we'll make mistakes when it comes to the real thing. Understand? Understand, Munroe?" The tank cadets couldn't help but notice that Captain Hywel-Jones's speech impediment had disappeared.

"Sir, your speech impediment has gone, sir. Are you cured, sir?" asked Munroe cheekily. The tank cadets laughed.

"Gone? Weally, Munwoe? Whatever do you mean? Now stay here and wait until you're called by your team leader and keep your noses out of things that don't concern you."

"Yes sir. Sorry sir and sorry for taking the piss out of your speech impediment… if you ever had one in the first place, sir." Tommy Munroe had more balls than sense at times.

***

For their first exercise the tank cadets went to assembly point four. En route, they passed Michael and some TA soldiers in a debriefing session with an officer who was using a stick to point at a blackboard. *Just like being back in bleedin' school,* thought the Cadets.

The last exercise went according to the script and everybody assembled in the debriefing zone afterwards. This was the first time they'd had the chance to properly check out what was going on with Michael. They sat at the back of the debriefing zone and picked out Michael amongst the soldiers. He was just sitting and taking notice of what was being said about what had gone well and what needed working on and receiving instructions of what he needed to improve on. Funny thing was, they thought, Michael looked like he fitted right in. In his bio-suit he didn't look like a boy amongst men, he looked like a soldier.

***

By the time the tank cadets got back to the barracks, the whole place was full of proper big rufty tufty soldiers. They made their way to the far end of the barracks wishing they'd chosen bunks near the door. "Hey, Cadet Frost. Well done today, lad. If you sign up then make sure it's for the Marines and not those cloak and dagger merchants," said a Corporal pointing to some SAS soldiers who'd been on exercises with them.

"If the lad wants to try for selection then that's up to him. Don't let anybody pressurise you, Frosty."

"I'm in the Royal Tank Regiment and I want to stay there."

"Just saying though, if you do sign up then for Christ's sake don't be a grunt."

"Looking forward to tomorrow, lads?" an SAS NCO asked the tank cadets.

"Yeah!" they all said, trying to sound enthusiastic, then asking, "What's on for tomorrow?"

"Unarmed combat. They've got some kind of expert coming in."

Shiiiiiiiit, unarmed combat. They won't want us to do that, will they? thought the tank cadets, before recalling the previous year when the camp commander asked publicly if anybody wanted to back out of the boxing tournament, then realising they couldn't back out as they'd look like chickens in front of everybody. *At least,* they thought, *we'll go down swinging.*

***

A cadets' conversation

"How come d'ye reckon that we're the only cadets at camp?" Jamesey Hill asked of no cadet in particular.

"I know, weird isn't it?"

"I reckon they just needed a few of us to make the numbers up for the nuclear stuff. Y'know, bodies and injured people and tha'."

"Then why wasn't Michael with us then?"

"Yeah Michael, why wasn't ye with us, eh? Just askin' like. No offence and all tha'."

"I don't know. They just picked me out and told me what to do and I did it."

"Yeah, but why you do ye reckon they chose you and not somebody else?"

"Don't be so bleedin' thick, Jamesey. Michael's different to us and if ye can't see that then you're thicker than I already think ye are."

"Are you lookin' for a fight, Munwoe?" joked Jamesey bobbing around on his toes, sparring like a boxer. The cadets fell about laughing.

"Seriously though, Michael, I'd watch me back if I waz you. There's somethin' goin' on. I'll be watchin' yer back for ye, don't you worry, mate."

"Thanks, Tommy, I'll be careful."

"Yeah, dead right, Michael. Any funny stuff and we'll burst them." Whoever them was.

***

The next morning as the cadets were getting ready for their mud bath run they heard a soldier shout, "Oh bloody hell; no."

"What's up, Simmo?

"Some dirty bugger's pissed in me boots."

"Oh, that'll be the phantom slasher. Nobody knows who it is but he sneaks around the barracks in the middle of the night and pisses in boots. He's been doin' it for years."

"If I get me hands on 'im I'll cut 'is nuts off."

"He doesn't piss in anybody's boots," said Michael.

"What do ye mean?"

"He takes a piss in a cup and then pours it into boots."

"'Ow the bloody hell do you know that, eh? Are you 'im?"

"Don't be stupid, Simmo, he hasn't been here when the phantom slasher's struck so it can't be 'im, can it? That's not a bad thought though, Frosty. When did ye figure out that he pisses into a cup and then pours it into somebody's boots?"

"It's obvious. Nobody would risk pissing into a soldier's boots in the middle of the night in case he gets caught."

"The lad's a bleedin' genius. Well done, Frosty. Now all we've got to do is find out who's been pissing in his cup."

"He's not pissing in his own cup, he pisses in somebody else's cup."

"I wish ye hadn't said that, Frosty."

"Is there no end to your talents, Michael?" asked Tommy Munroe. "Ye couldn't figure out the winner of the 4.45 at Haydock for me, could ye?"

"No," said Michael missing the joke as usual.

***

Before breaking camp the soldiers were given a demonstration of hand-to-hand combat.

"Hello Roberto, you said you'd be coming here."

"Hi Michael, my name's not Roberto, that was just him over there messing about," he replied pointing at the man Michael knew as the London schools boxing coach.

"What's your real name?"

"I'm here incognito so call me Roberto for now. Okay? But only you. And not too loud."

The camp commander asked the soldiers and cadets to gather close on the parade ground as he didn't want to have to shout. "This is the final morning of camp and it's been a tremendous success. You can all be proud of what you've achieved here this week. What we have for you before we break camp is a demonstration of hand-to-hand combat. The instructor has advised me that once each demonstration starts it'll be realistic to the point where maximum force will be used to subdue anybody who acts up. You all know what I mean by 'acts up'? Good. Enjoy the demonstration and afterwards we'll all assemble on the parade ground for a speech by a very special guest speaker. Dismissed."

In the marquee there were several rows of benches surrounding a single canvas fighting mat. Standing in front of the mat was the person Michael knew as Roberto.

"Come in, all of you. C'mon, quick as you like and take a seat. C'mon get a move on, I said," shouted Roberto. The soldiers wondered who this punk was who was talking to them like they were children. "Right then, now that we're all sitting comfortably we can begin. Can I have a bit of hush?" he shouted. "I'm going to be doing a demonstration of hand-to-hand combat and I'll need some volunteers to lend a hand. You'll have everything explained to you when you come to the mat and I warn you that if you try anything off your own bat you will get hurt. Understand me?"

"Excuse me," said a soldier raising his hand, "who are you please? I don't know your rank or anything so I don't know whether to call you sir or salute you?"

"It's not important who I am and as far as you lot are concerned Army protocol is suspended for this session. Okay? So no saluting or calling people sir or using rank or any of that usual Army bollocks. By the way, keep irrelevant questions to yourselves. Now, let's see who we have on the list." Roberto paused to peruse the list. "I understand that those on here have been specially selected by their COs because they are the best of the best. Let's see how you get on with me and then I'll decide how good you are." Roberto read out a list of six names.

Each of the soldiers on hearing his name called out had the same thing in mind: *I'm going to flatten this cocky little sod when I get to the mat. Who the hell does he think he is?*

"First off though I'd like to invite Cadet Frost to come and join me on the mat." Michael heard his name called out but stayed in his seat. "Michael, please?" spoke Roberto indicating that he should leave the audience to join him on the mat. "Now, Cadet Frost, I believe you've been on exercises with this lot. How did they do? Any good?" The soldiers were becoming more furious with Roberto by the second.

"We worked well together and we learned a lot from the exercises. They are good soldiers and they look after one another."

"Any favourites, Michael?"

"I like Corporal Enis. He's a great shot. He won the shooting competition."

"Before we get to the main event I'd like to introduce you to the finest bladed weapon ever invented. It's called a katana. It was originally used by Samurai warriors in Japan. I'm not sure if any of you is aware of it but Cadet Frost has been using one of these things for a few years now." Everybody stared at Michael in disbelief as though he was something from another planet. "Cadet Frost, please would you demonstrate what you can do with one of these." Without answering, Michael stepped forward, taking the katana from Roberto and withdrawing it with a flourish from its saya. The blade reflected silver in his eyes. "Now, Cadet Frost, I'd like you to go through some warm-up exercises for about a minute. After you've warmed up I'd like you to strike the straw and canvas body you see in the middle of the mat. Strike it right across its centre... across its stomach if it had one. Do you understand, Michael?"

"Of course."

"Okay, off you go."

Removing his shoes, Michael took the katana up in his right hand and strode to the edge of the canvas mat. Raising the katana slightly, he took hold of the handle in both hands and performed a series of exercises for precisely one minute. Hardly a sound was heard. At the end of the warm-up, Michael brought the katana over his right shoulder and ran at the straw and canvas body and with a single stroke he cleaved it in half. The crowd sat stunned and were left in no doubt that they'd seen a killer katana strike.

"Well done, Cadet Frost, please take a bow." Michael returned the katana to its saya before handing it back but didn't bow; he just stood stock still until Roberto told him to return to his place in the audience but using a softer tone of voice: "Well done, Michael. Sit down and join the others please."

After Michael took his seat Roberto inspected the cut on the canvas and straw body. It was perfectly flat, indicating excellent striking technique. When Michael joined the ranks of the tank cadets they all gave him the customary 'well done' slap on the back. They were all very proud of Michael and not a little amazed by what they'd just seen him do.

"Well now, which of you lucky ladies is first to come to school? Oh yes, it's Corporal Enis. Lucky your Christian name isn't Phil or Peter, eh?"

"Yeah, dead lucky that. I've never heard that one before; yeah, good one," replied Corporal Enis sarcastically. His blood was just about boiling as he walked towards his figure of loathing.

"Now, pal, listen carefully. I'll speak slowly 'cause I know you northerners aren't too quick off the mark. We're going to start with the basics. This is a commando dagger," he said to the Commando, "and it's sheathed so you shouldn't come to any harm when you handle it. Now I understand you're a bit of a judo expert so you should easily be able to handle a little chap like me even when I'm holding a knife. Okay. Come and take the knife." Corporal Enis was already like a coiled spring and leapt the four feet between himself and Roberto in the blink of an eye but didn't manage to grab anything but thin air. Roberto used Corporal Enis's momentum to throw him onto the mat. He then put him in an agonising arm lock which he immediately released and sprang to his feet. "Now then, Phil, it's your turn with the knife." Corporal Enis was up for this. He took up his start position. A soldier in the crowd shouted, "Take the sheath off, Enno, and stick the little gobshite."

Corporal Enis ignored the shout. He crouched in the middle of the mat, beckoning Roberto to come to him. Roberto casually sauntered up close to Corporal Enis and when the Corporal thought he was close enough he struck out at Roberto with the sheathed dagger. The result was exactly the same as previously with Corporal Enis ending up in exactly the same agonising arm lock which was, once again, immediately released.

"What was Corporal Enis's mistake?" Roberto asked the crowded marquee.

"He left the bleedin' sheath on the knife instead of stickin' it in you, yer gobshite," shouted the same shouter-outer. The crowd roared its approval.

"No. Wrong. Corporal Enis wasn't thinking straight when we fought. I messed with his head with the things I said to him. I messed with all your heads. Remove the head and the body dies. Remember that if you don't remember anything else from today; remove the head and the body dies. Remember that, okay? Apologies for the disrespect and rudeness but I'm not here to be your mate. I'm here to teach you to be better at hand-to-hand combat which just might keep you alive one day. You're already good but if I started off by saying that you're already good then you'd have coasted this session. When it comes to the real thing you have to be in control and the first thing you need to control is your emotions, then you can control your adversary. Never ever ever get mad at anybody. It should never be personal." He held the crowd in his gaze before continuing. "Now what I'm going to do is go through a half dozen exercises where we'll swap positions; so, first I'm the defender and then you're the defender. Okay, chaps? Enjoy and let's get to it." They got to it with a vengeance.

***

After the hand-to-hand combat exercises were over, the soldiers came and spoke with Roberto to discuss what training was available to them. Michael was hoping to speak with him too but after the Q&A session ended he walked briskly away in the direction of the exit to the camp.

Outside the marquee, Roberto was joined by the shouter-outer. "You were a bit rude back there," he said to the man known as the London schools boxing coach.

"It needed to be realistic. Anyway, I got that lot right wound up, didn't I?" he said to Roberto, smiling a cheesy smile.

"You certainly did. Did you see the colour of that Corporal's face when he had the dagger in his hand? I thought he was going to bust a gut. Anyway, where are we going to meet with the others for the lists review session?"

"There's an old hut down by the sea. The PPS to the Minister of Defence is waiting there for us. C'mon, let's get a move on, I want to be out of here before the camp spills out. I need to get back to London PDQ." The two men made their way over the dunes and toward the sea. The old hut was one of a group of signals huts which, in the recent past, had been used for buildings entry exercises in hostage rescue scenarios. The huts each had three interconnecting rooms which made them extremely difficult to enter without being detected.

Stealthily tip-toeing behind the two men at a distance of thirty or so yards was Tommy Munroe. He made his way using the peaks and troughs of the sand dunes for cover, occasionally traversing along their tops to keep the men in sight. After a couple of minutes the men entered an old signals hut. Tommy Munroe crept up to the west wall of the hut adjacent to the sea so he couldn't be spotted from the sand dunes. He pressed his ear against the wall. He could hear the voices of those talking inside the hut surprisingly well. He picked out three distinct voices, two male and one female. It was clear from the conversation that the female was in charge. Apparently, she was very unhappy about some things that'd gone on during the camp.

"You're complacent and sloppy. You're talking openly to the people we're here to monitor. The last thing we want is to attract attention."

"Relax, nobody has a clue who we are. Why would they?

The problem with you is you're paranoid. People don't question authority, it's not what they do. They follow orders."

"There are SAS, paras and commandos on the base and they can't be relied on to follow orders. They might already be suspicious of who we are. The brief I provided called for you to come here as an observer," she said pointing at the London schools boxing coach, "and for you to do a demonstration of hand-to-hand combat, not run a circus. You're encouraged to use your initiative but not in circumstances where it is inappropriate, such as here." She paused to light a cigarette. "In case it's escaped your attention, we're on an MoD facility. We might be being watched. Might we not? I'm reporting these events as a serious breach of protocol and then it's up to others to decide your fates. Now, gentlemen, give me your updates on the candidates including your recommendations. Compile everything into a report and have it with me within two weeks. Let's start with list D and work up to list A." The two men went over the names in their lists.

At this camp were four A list potentials plus four others from the B, C and D lists. Tommy Munroe could hardly believe his ears especially when they started talking about Michael. "Michael Frost continues to impress. He's going from strength to strength, honing his skills in self-defence and he's developed a steely determination when going about his work. He's maturing nicely. Academically there are still question marks over him but he's extraordinary with foreign languages, which is useful for obvious reasons. Something else: he's freakishly good with numbers. He's been top of the entire school in mathematics since the end of his third year. I recommend he remains on list B. There's something I'd like to add at this point."

"Go on."

"I'm not sure about his Captain, Hywel-Jones. There's something about him that's not right. Something's eating away at me but I can't put my finger on it."

"Well, if you come across anything concrete then bring it up at the next review or sooner if it's urgent. You know what I mean by urgent, right? Anyway, let's proceed with the review. We're all agreed about Michael Frost, he stays on list B for now but he may prove more suitable for list D. From what you've previously said about him he might make a deadly sentinel. Pity about his academic side but we can't all be intelligence officers, can we?" The PPS to the Minister of Defence smiled a self-satisfied smile.

Outside, Tommy Munroe couldn't believe what he was hearing. Instinctively he knew this was not the place to be caught with his ear up against a wall. He looked around the northern corner of the hut to check if the coast was clear. He thought he spied the top of a balaclava bobbing above the furthest sand dune but convinced himself that it was just his imagination. To be on the safe side, instead of heading north he headed south to make his getaway. He had to get back to the camp to tell Michael and Captain Hywel-Jones what he'd overheard. He made it to the cover of the first sand dune, turning to check he wasn't being followed. All clear. Next, he approached a massive sand dune. He made his way to its top to survey the surrounding area. His heart was racing. Then he thought, *What are they going to do to me on a military base surrounded by hundreds of soldiers?* He really shouldn't have allowed himself this thought. He relaxed. Tommy rolled down to the bottom of the massive sand dune and as he was dusting himself off he was knocked face first into the gritty sand from behind. A black bag was pulled tight over his head and a couple of heavy blows to his kidneys removed any fight he might have had in him.

***

The door to the hut opened with a crash and a man wearing a black balaclava entered the room, pushing Cadet Munroe in front of him. "Saw him outside with his ear pressed up against the wall. I'm not sure how much he's heard."

"Hello. You're one of Cadet Frost's friends, aren't you? Cadet Munroe?" said the London school's boxing coach.

"Yeah, that's right. What are youz lot doin' with Michael, eh?" asked a frightened Tommy Monroe to the people in the hut.

"Tell me, Cadet Munroe, what did your piggy little ears pick up while they were pressed against the wall listening to things that don't concern you? What did you hear us talking about, Cadet Munroe?"

"Nothin'. Nothin' at all. The walls are really thick, I didn't hear anythin', honest."

"Really? Then why did you ask what we're doing with Michael Frost?"

"How long do you reckon he was out there?"

"Dunno. Maybe he followed you two here. That would make sense, wouldn't it?"

"Did you follow me and my friend here, Cadet Munroe?"

"I thought ye might be doin' somethin' interestin' so I followed ye but I was only listen' at the wall for about ten seconds. I didn't 'ear much, honest. Swear on me brother's grave, I didn't 'ear much. In fact ye can't hear anythin' through these walls. Try it. You go outside and we'll talk in 'ere and I bet ye won't 'ear a thing."

"I watched him for a good five minutes. He was at the wall all that time."

"Now, Cadet Munroe, you started off by saying you didn't hear much, then you said you didn't hear a thing. You say you were listening for ten seconds and he says he watched you listening for five whole minutes. What's the truth, Cadet Munroe? Don't worry, young man, you'll be okay if you just tell us the truth."

"What are youz lot doin' with Michael, eh? I 'eard yez saying 'ow yer watchin' 'im and 'ow it's a pity he can't be an intelligence officer but he's okay at bein' a grunt an' stuff. And what about the other blokes yer watchin', eh? Captain Hywel-Jones. Why are yez watchin' 'im, eh? What's goin' on 'ere, eh?"

"Cadet Munroe," spoke a voice in a whisper. Tommy turned

ninety degrees to his right to face the man who'd whispered. As he did so an eight-inch stiletto dagger was plunged with considerable force straight through his sternum and into his heart. Instinctively Tommy grabbed hold of the hand that had pushed the dagger into his chest and tried to remove it so he could pull the dagger out. He didn't want to look down but he had to. He didn't want to see that thing sticking in his chest. He couldn't help it. He had to look. After seeing the end of handle of the dagger he went into a state of shock. He looked around at the faces of the people in the room. They were looking back at him.

There was actually very little pain and virtually no blood so he wondered if he was going to be okay.

He tried again to grab hold of the handle of the dagger. With that, the stabber pushed him hard, backwards, against the hut wall, placing his free hand over Tommy's mouth. Tommy removed his hands from trying to grab the dagger and went to trying to pull the hand off his mouth.

Now standing on tip-toe and with his back pressed hard against the wall, Tommy stared at the four pairs of eyes staring at him. Nobody was speaking. There was only silence and staring. His breathing became more and more difficult as mucus built up in his nasal passages. After the hand was removed from his mouth, his breathing became more like rapid panting than breathing. He felt hot, he was pale and sweating. Tommy's rapid panting was exactly like that which relatives witness while standing around the deathbed of a loved one who is about to pass from this life. He was soon fully yielding and didn't need restraining any longer. Once he felt Tommy go limp the Mediterranean-looking man let go his hold on him. Tommy's legs couldn't support his weight so he fell to the ground, now holding onto the black ebonised handle of the dagger he'd so desperately been trying to get at. After he hit the ground, the Mediterranean-looking man knelt down beside him, cradling his head and looking into his eyes while removing the dagger in one slow continuous movement.

Once the stiletto was removed from Tommy's heart, blood leaked faster into his chest cavity. The colour had now completely drained from Tommy's normally rosy, apple-cheek face. All was silent in the hut, nobody was making any noise, not even Tommy. The Mediterranean-looking man moved his face close to his victim's. From only a few inches away he gazed intently into the dipping crescents of the irises of the sparkling blue Liverpool Irish eyes as they turned milky and lifeless.

"Are you out of your bloody mind? Are you? The boy probably had to die but why do it here? Why do it now with the Minister still on site? We could have had him away and drowned him in the sea or something. A post-mortem will show that he's been stabbed. Statistically, not many people get stabbed with a stiletto and as you're rather prolific with that thing the police might start noticing a pattern. Arghhhhhhhh!!!" the London schools boxing coach screamed in anger and frustration straight into the face of his associate. He continued more calmly, "Right... let's assess the situation. The boy will be missed at the final parade, which is in about ten minutes' time. The Minister of Defence is going to make a speech thanking everybody for all their efforts in improving the country's preparedness for a nuclear attack. What a load of crap, we'll all be blown to pieces if that happens."

"What the hell are you talking about nuclear attacks for? Why bring that up now? We're standing in a hut with the dead body of a child and you're just waffling on," screamed the PPS to the Minister of Defence while glaring at Roberto. She stopped speaking to consider whether she should kill him but concluded that could make a bad situation even worse. After the moment had passed, she continued, "I need to leave with the Minister before a search is mounted for the boy so you need to hide the body to buy us some time."

"Keep your pants on, I'll take care of it. Immediately after his speech make an excuse for the Minister to leave quickly. Say he's got an emergency to attend to back in London or something. Then get him into his car and drive straight through the guard post. The guards won't stop you, they'll just salute and wave you through. Nobody will stop the Minister of Defence on important business. Is he one of us by the way?"

"And what exactly are you going to do? Blow the whole place up?" asked the Minister's PPS. "And you should know better than to ask questions like that."

"No I'm not going to blow the place up, I'm going to take care of this like I said I would." With that Roberto picked up Tommy Munroe's limp body and asked the guard to lend a hand carrying him to the sand dunes. *She doesn't know if the Minister is one of us or not. She's not as important as she likes to make out. She's a gofer just like me,* mused Roberto to himself.

The two men carried Tommy's body away into the sand dunes while most everybody else on the base was occupied with finalising arrangements for the speech by the Minister of Defence.

Roberto ordered the guard to "Go and get me a Thunderflash." Minutes later he returned with two Thunderflashes. "Now go back to the hut and make sure it's empty and anything that shouldn't be there isn't there and that includes the PPS." Once the guard was out of sight Roberto placed a Thunderflash in the breast pocket of Cadet Munroe's jacket. He waited until after the Minister's speech was over before priming it to explode. A few seconds later, the Thunderflash exploded right over the stab entry wound in Cadet Munroe's chest. The explosion attracted attention as Roberto knew it would. He cunningly left the second Thunderflash lying on the ground right next to the body before making his way from the scene.

The sound of the explosion expedited the Minister of Defence's exit from the camp.

***

It took the search teams twenty minutes to find the site of the explosion. The scene that greeted them was shocking. Ahead of them was a body which was obviously that of a cadet and lying next to him was an unexploded Thunderflash. "You there, go and tell the Major and the camp commander what we've found, I'll stay and guard the body. There may be other explosives lying around so check if we've got anybody from Bomb Disposal on site."

The camp commander called for the area to be cordoned off. He gave the order that the body was only to be approached after Bomb Disposal had given the all clear.

"How the hell did a cadet get hold of a Thunderflash?" asked the camp commander.

"We're looking into that, sir. It appears the store wasn't broken into so perhaps the cadet obtained them earlier and intended removing them from camp. It wouldn't be the first time somebody like him has stolen Thunderflashes or other items even," sneered Major Finn.

"Somebody like him, Major? Would you care to explain that remark?"

"Yes, sir. Somebody like him with his background. It probably seemed a good idea to steal a couple of Thunderflashes for a joke or perhaps he thought they were of value and he could sell them. I mean to say, sir, it wouldn't be the first time that one of these light-fingered cadets has stolen military equipment. Many of them come from troubled homes and are prone to certain temptations. He even had an unexploded Thunderflash next to him when he was found. It's pretty clear what happened. He was obviously putting the Thunderflashes into his jacket pockets, primed one by accident and paid the price."

"I think you're jumping pretty quickly to conclusions but I have to say I'm finding it difficult to put a different interpretation on things. Please keep close to developments and give me your written report by this time tomorrow. Everybody dismissed."

***

"Did ye hear what happened to Tommy?" sobbed Jacko.

"I know it's terrible, isn't it? How d'ye reckon it happened?"

"They're sayin' he was stealin' Thunderflashes an' one accidentally went off in his pocket."

"That sounds like a load of rubbish to me. What d'ye reckon, Michael? Do you think it was an accident or wha'? Do you think Tommy was nickin' Thunderflashes? Why would he do tha'? What would he do with them if he was nickin' them?"

"It's hard to set off a Thunderflash by accident," replied Michael. Everybody was openly sobbing except Michael.

"Why aren't ye cryin', Michael? Why aren't ye cryin' like the rest of us, eh? Are you happy Tommy's dead, eh? What's up with you?"

"Give it a rest, youz lot," shouted Jamesey, "Tommy and Michael were best mates so don't anybody go sayin' anything different. He's as sad as the rest of us so shut yer gobs and let's get out of here. I wanna go home. I tell yez wha' I'm never comin' back to this place again." In fact Jamesey, and most of the others, never went to Cadets Club ever again. In some cases it was the parents' decision to stop them going but in other cases it was their own decision. Michael, though, continued going to Cadets, even attending the remaining camps that summer after Altcar was reopened.

***

Investigations concluded that Tommy Munroe stole the Thunderflashes and one of them had accidentally exploded in his breast pocket. Give a street kid a bad name and it sticks. As intended by Roberto the site of the explosion of the Thunderflash covered up the stab entry wound made by his stiletto dagger and as there were no suspicious circumstances the coroner recorded a verdict of accidental death. Stab wound marks on the victims of the Mediterranean man often went undetected during post-mortems for a whole variety of reasons. R.I.P. our friend Tommy Munroe.

***

Tommy Munroe's funeral was attended by school mates and his cadet mates. His coffin was white as was the hearse that carried it, which was unusual in those days. The hearse was crammed full of wreathes. One spelled his name and sat against the back window so everybody could see it. Tommy's family were very poor but knew how to demonstrate their love and devotion by buying costly wreaths they could ill afford. They travelled in a black funeral car and behind them was a procession of cars of the day all decked out with white ribbons. It was more like a wedding than a funeral, but the family were determined there should be no more sadness. There'd been too much sadness already as far as they were concerned. Two of Tommy's brothers joined the Army because there were no jobs on Merseyside in the early 1970s. On a day which was to prove significant in Michael's life, both were blown up in a Republican ambush. One survived and one didn't.

***

Within an hour of the discovery of Tommy Munroe's body the Minister of Defence, his PPS, his driver and another man were making good time on the motorway on their way back to London. "I wonder what all that commotion was back at the camp?" asked the Minister.

"I really have no idea, Minister, but I'll contact the camp commander to find out and let you know," replied the PPS. She never contacted the camp commander or mentioned the incident ever again to him. She couldn't possibly know if the Minister was one of them or not and to ask could prove embarrassing or even fatal.

***

Just before the end of the autumn term of 1969, the school boxing coach approached Michael to sound him out about taking his boxing to the next level, hopefully with him as his coach. Then Michael dropped what the boxing coach considered to be a bombshell.

"I'm leaving school."

"When?"

"At the end of term."

"You can't do that."

"Mum needs me to earn some money. I'm going to join the Royal Tank Regiment."

"But Michael, what about your boxing?" implored the boxing coach. "And your education too of course. We need to see the Headmaster about this right now to put a stop to this nonsense."

The Headmaster wrote Michael a letter for him to hand to his mother, inviting her to come to the school to discuss matters. Margaret, being rather deaf and not liking confrontation or speaking with people she considered to be in authority, didn't go to the grammar school to discuss Michael's future with the Headmaster. Instead, she told Michael that money was more important than school.

Money was always tight in the Frost household plus Margaret didn't value education, as she had none herself to speak of. In her mind it was more important for Michael to bring money into the household to make life easier for everybody which is exactly what happened in her childhood home. Classic Margaret self-perpetuating behaviour.

***

Four days after Michael told the school he was leaving, an Army recruiting officer came to the house to go over his options with him and Margaret. "I'm interested in joining the Royal Tank Regiment," said Michael to the recruiting officer.

"I understand that, son, but I'll have to check to see where we're accepting new recruits." Michael hadn't even considered the possibility that he couldn't join the regiment of his choice. "The important thing is to get you in the Army and then you can apply to transfer to whatever regiment you want afterwards." Not understanding the way things work, Margaret and Michael both signed the pre-enlistment documents.

A few days later Michael received a letter asking him to report to the recruiting office in London Road. When he got there the recruiting Sergeant said to him, "Good news, son, there's a place for you straight away in the Royal Regiment of Fusiliers. If you pass the medical you can be in within a fortnight."

"I want to join the Royal Tank Regiment."

"They're not recruiting right now but if you join the Fusiliers you can apply to transfer to the Royal Tank Regiment when they are recruiting. The important thing is to get in and get the basic training out of the way."

"I've been a cadet in the Royal Tank Regiment for five years and I've been to Altcar twice so basic training isn't necessary for me."

"Son, everybody has to do basic training, even I had to do it and I was in the Cadets for five years just like you were. As I say, the important thing is to get you in and you can transfer to the Royal Tank Regiment when they're recruiting and I bet you'll have no trouble getting in as you know the ropes already. Take these papers to your mum and get them signed and we can get things started." Michael took the papers but had no intention of joining the Royal Regiment of Fusiliers. He didn't have a warm feeling in his stomach about the recruiting Sergeant.

The following evening Michael spoke with Captain Hywel-Jones about his predicament. He was interested to hear Michael was keen to enlist and as he was on the lists he thought he might be useful to him in building up his fifth column inside the Organisation. *Michael might be its fifth member,* he thought.

"You know, Cadet Frost, I think you'd make good tank crew. I might be able to pull a few strings. I'll speak to a few people I know and get back to you. Don't worry, everything will be okay, I'm sure of it."

The next day there was a knock on the Frosts' front door and a motorcycle messenger delivered a recruitment letter offering Michael a posting with the Royal Tank Regiment. He showed the letter to Margaret.

"Oh Michael son, this is just what you wanted. Now are you sure you want to go? If you say yes I'll sign the forms and that'll be that."

"I want to join the Royal Tank Regiment. P… p… please sign the forms, Mum, and I can go after Christmas." Michael always had trouble with the p word. Margaret signed the forms and handed them back to the messenger. There was no going back now.

***

The days leading up to Michael joining the Army were filled with more laughter and tears than usual. Thomas in particular was going to miss his big brother and protector. Things between he and Rose were never great but now that Michael was leaving home to join the Army there was a definite change in her attitude as she became even more conspiratorial and confrontational.

Queen Rose had made Thomas's life hell in the past and the signs were that it was going to get worse in the future. Being the little queen, she was believed when she lied about whatever was going on and got away with everything in contrast with Thomas who'd got away with nothing all his young life. Because of Queen Rose's lies, poor little Thomas was often punished for things he didn't do which made him extremely resentful towards her and his parents. In later life Queen Rose was described by all those who really knew her as a pathological, compulsive and congenital liar. Like all outstandingly good liars she lived her lies so that they became true in her mind, making her convincing in the telling of her lies. She could never get to Michael though; no matter how hard she tried she could never get to him as he operated on a different level.

MARGARET'S STORY - MANDARIN KISSES

In the middle months of 1969, Margaret's shuttle diplomacy between the splinters wasn't going well. She came to realise she'd taken on an impossible task. It was just like herding a flock of cats. Whichever direction one wanted to go in the others didn't.

A change of tack was needed. Instead of trying to resolve differences through individual treaties, she spoke firmly, making it clear that the only way to move forward was through a reunification conference. This idea took hold with the Italians and if they could be persuaded to attend such a conference then she felt confident the other splinters would do so too.

***

While scribbling down the agenda for her next meeting with the leader of the Italian splinter, a distinguished-looking man joined her at her table in the hotel's restaurant. He didn't ask if she minded if he joined her, he just sat down and joined her. She said to him that he'd probably mistaken her for somebody else and would he mind finding another table as she was expecting guests. His reply was simply to say that he knew she wasn't expecting anybody that evening. His assassin stare frightened her. She waited in anticipation of being murdered in some unimaginable way. Where were her bodyguards? On closer inspection he didn't much resemble an assassin so she dismissed that thought. If they were in her room she'd at least have a gun for protection. Then she thought about what circumstances could possibly lead to them being in her room together. He then asked if they could go to her room to talk. She was struck dumb for a moment and then told the distinguished-looking gentleman that there was no way they were going to her room for a talk. *The cheek of it!* she thought. *He hasn't even offered to buy me a drink.* He didn't seem to be put off in the slightest. He wrote something on a napkin and passed it across the table to her. On it he'd written the word 'Alice'.

Realising this was not a random act, she asked how he knew her name. He said she'd find out everything in her room. He stood and offered her his hand which, in her state of shock, she took.

The moment they entered her room she went straight for her 9 mm while he sat single-cheeked on the corner of her bed. He wasn't fazed in the slightest at having a gun pointed at him. He remarked that he knew her to be a deadly shot, as documented in her mission reports, but the noise from the gun would only attract attention. She asked him what he wanted. He got straight to the point.

"I know why you're here. It's a very laudable thing you're trying to do. I applaud your efforts. I think the French are very totally charmed by you, especially the Count. You may have won a heart there."

"Who are you? I'm not afraid of using this," she said while putting a pillow over the gun's muzzle. "You know my real name. Was it you who got the lawyer to write to my sisters in Germany telling them of my existence?"

"No."

"But that means you know about them otherwise your reply would have been different."

"I do know about Lilia and Henrietta, of course I do. But they are not why I'm here. Please, I mean you no harm, there's no need to keep holding such a heavy pistol. Please, put it down. I'll move over there if it will make you feel more comfortable."

"I'll keep it where it is if it's all the same to you."

"I've followed your career with interest, Margaret."

"Do you know Rex?"

"Not very well," he lied, "though what I have to discuss with you may involve him." He glanced about the room before continuing, "I represent a group with special interest in the Organisation. Tell me, Margaret, how do you think the Chair of the Organisation is chosen?"

"I've never given it much thought," she lied. "I imagine a board of governors meet to…"

"I don't mean to be rude but I must stop you there." She noticed a slight twang of a German accent and a cadence in his voice which she recognised as typically German. "If governors elected the Chair it would be disastrous as the Chair would be beholden to those who voted in favour and it would root out those who hadn't." He paused to pour himself a sparkling water. "No, we elect the Chair."

"And who exactly is 'we'?"

"The Mandarins. We've been in existence for almost as long as the Brotherhood itself." She felt in real danger, why was he telling her this?

"Why are you telling me this?"

"Because for some time now we've been of the opinion that the Organisation has lost its way and it needs somebody to put it back on the right road again. We believe that somebody could be you."

"Could be me? But what if you decide it's not me? Will you kill me as you've told me things I shouldn't know?"

He laughed. "Of course not," he lied. "There are many in the Organisation who know of our existence, it's just your turn to find out, that's all. Nothing to be concerned about. Promise," he ended by using his best snake smile.

"You know my name but I don't know yours or anything about you."

"That's easily rectified, my name is Maximillian Grodt, Max, and…"

Max spoke for the next hour and a half with hardly a break or interruption, pausing occasionally to sip from a glass of sparkling water. He told her about the Brotherhood, the Organisation, the Mandarins and, if she was agreeable, he would mentor her for her to rise to be the Chair. He'd be her sponsor. She wanted to know why she'd been selected. He replied that from what they knew about her and her qualities the Mandarins believe she could be the next Madame Chairman. He went on to say that the main characteristics that had attracted their attention were her integrity, leadership and her passion for change and that, more than anything, the Organisation needed to change. He said he believed the Organisation needed to change to meet the challenges of the modern world. Max captured her imagination; it was as though he was wired directly to her. He'd researched Margaret well and knew all the right buttons to push. He knew she craved validation in a world run by men and he could put her where she needed to be to bring about change. He deduced from her responses that everything in her world was all about her and she lusted for power.

Max set out some of his thoughts on how the Organisation might be run in the future. The main one being that it could no longer continue as an autocracy. It needed a leader but not an emperor. He cited Hitler and Stalin as two reasons against having an all-powerful autocrat run the Organisation. Adding that she would be all-powerful in matters relating to the Organisation achieving its mission. As she already knew of the Organisation's mission, that needed no further explanation. In future, Max said, the Organisation would be run by an inner council. Initially it would need to be a secret inner council because changes in how it was to be run could incite revolution. He didn't explain why he thought this might be.

"As soon as the necessary changes have been made there will no longer be the need to keep your inner council a secret. You will of course chair the inner council and choose half its membership. We know most of those in the higher echelons of the Organisation and so are best placed to appoint the other half." She understood exactly why the Mandarins were going to appoint half her council. If she proved incapable then the transition to a new leader would be much easier to effect but her second thought worried her more; it meant they could place people close to her who were loyal to the Mandarins and not her.

"What are the necessary changes you mentioned?"

"I'd have thought it would have been obvious to somebody like you." She felt she'd already managed to disappoint her mentor. "Change can only truly take effect if it's made at the very top. Hence your appointment. The reason why the Organisation has stagnated is obvious. Its leadership is incompetent and corrupt and it needs to go and go quickly. You'll need to get rid of most of them."

"Get rid of most them?"

"Yes, get rid of them. Don't worry, we've already got suitable replacements in mind for eighty percent of them. You'll need to identify the other twenty percent. I suggest that the structure of the regions remains unchanged for now with just their leadership being swapped out. It will need to happen virtually overnight for obvious reasons."

"When you say 'the leadership', which groups are you referring to? Governors? Their IOs? Controllers? Their IOs?"

"You'll be provided with a list but, to set expectations, it's most governors and perhaps some controllers. There are no IOs or sentinels on the list."

"That's more than a thousand people. Why isn't Mr Chairman doing this?"

"You must realise the answer to that question. He's part of the problem. He's the main reason we're being forced to act in the way we are. You were born to do this, Margaret. I have the greatest faith and confidence in you and your abilities. You'll make an outstanding Madame Chairman and with my help you'll be running the Organisation within months, perhaps weeks."

They talked for another hour, agreeing to meet over the following several days and continuing at her next destination, Israel. She felt more than a little disappointed after Max informed her that she wouldn't be a candidate for the presidency of a reunited Organisation. The Mandarins felt a natural choice for President was somebody from the French splinter called Christian LeFort. He promised to introduce him to her at the earliest opportunity at which time he felt certain she would agree with the choice he'd made. *He'd made?* she thought.

***

The Mandarins have been in existence for almost as long as the Brotherhood itself. During their time they masterminded the early Brotherhood's first European expansion, they then became its Mafia-style rulers and then its junior partners following a revolt. Since the last decade of the nineteenth century they had wanted to play a more pivotal role in the Organisation and each started building up their followers. They grew exactly as the Brotherhood had grown, right under the noses of those they sought to destroy. They modelled themselves on the Organisation, right down to IOs and PAs being secret sentinels.

Throughout the centuries there had been many attempts by both the aristocracy and the Church to destroy the Brotherhood but efforts seldom went beyond a single lifetime because subsequent generations are rarely committed to the causes of their forebears.

Such crusaders were usually rich and their children wanted to enjoy life rather than waste it by chasing shadows. Aristocratic progeny simply didn't have the same energy or commitment as the Brotherhood so it outlasted them all. The Church built up a head of steam in the Brotherhood's early centuries but during the times of the Renaissance and Henry it had other matters to attend to and so lost sight of what they mistakenly believed was a ragged group of malcontents. By the end of the seventeenth century the Church had all but forgotten about them. From time to time afterwards, rumour of its existence arose but by then it was untouchable. Untouchable, that is, until Bonaparte. The Mandarins backed him but he and they failed to gain control of the Brotherhood. Defeated, they slunk away. It was fortunate for them that Bonaparte kept their secret safe. They tried time and again to conjure some plot to gain control of the Brotherhood but each attempt ended in abject failure.

Accepting their machinations were getting them nowhere the Mandarins decided on a more direct route. They needed time to build up their numbers to match those of the Organisation and by the 1930s they were ready. They were convinced another world war would tip the balance in their favour but they were mistaken. The man they thought would lead them to victory was exposed as a traitor by the Organisation and, given his position in society, he had to step down or be destroyed.

They now had the numbers but lacked a leader. Then, after one of them died unexpectedly, her son, Max, took her place. He was too outspoken for most of the Mandarins and there being only nine of them he sought to increase their membership to gain a majority of support and enact his plans. This was a step too far for the Mandarins as they had no desire to see their power diluted by increasing their number so Max bided his time until he was ready to make his move. Over the years he gathered information on his fellow Mandarins until he had three of them under his control and two others who he knew he could influence.

At a council of Mandarins, Max set out his plans for the future of the Organisation and the roles they would play in it. Only two of the Mandarins were opposed to Max's plans but most wanted their own favourites to be the Chair. This was a major sticking point. When Max backed Rex's alternate candidate, some of them laughed. What was he thinking putting this young woman forward? She wasn't even thirty. He was accused of keeping her as his mistress. He was furious at this accusation. The meeting broke up without agreement but this didn't bother Max as he now knew with total certainty what the thoughts were of the other Mandarins and who he could rely on for support. He gathered his supporters close around him and made his plans. He had no intention of returning to the discussion with the other Mandarins, he was simply going to go ahead with his own plan.

***

Max had known Rex and Mr Chairman for some years before he decided the time was right to share his plans with them. They knew him well enough by then to know that if they disagreed with him on such matters they were as good as dead. As with the vast majority of humanity, they were more interested in knowing what was in it for them than any moral dilemma they might face. They liked what they heard and were promised they'd be told more when the time was right. They discussed Margaret Rotheram and set about shaping her career. Max instinctively knew Rex had found the right person for what he had in mind.

Soon, the Organisation would need a new Chair, a Madame Chairman, one with new ideas. Max's ideas. It was inconceivable that the post of Chair could be filled by anybody below Governor level but Max had a plan to overcome any objections to Margaret Rotheram being nominated for the Chair. He'd keep it simple. He'd say she had been added to the list by popular demand. But she is not yet thirty, they'd say; she's untutored in the ways of the Organisation, they'd say. They'd all fall silent after she was elected.

Margaret was an idealist who hadn't yet had time to see the Organisation for what it really is, further convincing Max she was the ideal candidate to replace Mr Chairman. There's risk in everything that people do and to combat risks contingency plans are put in place. Max's contingency plan was one of last resort. He hoped he wouldn't have to use it because its fallout would be unpredictable and that state was the last thing anybody wants for organisations whose natural habitat is the shadows.

***

As soon as the first round of meetings with the splinters was concluded Margaret returned to London. Among the first people she bumped into in Half Moon Street was Lisette. Their previous differences were put to one side as they'd both missed each other enormously. They went for a coffee in the Ritz to catch up on events. Margaret asked her how the job was going. She replied that she was bored out of her mind. Margaret said that didn't surprise her as it was a very boring job but with what might happen shortly all that might change. Lisette wanted to know what she meant but was told that everything would become clear in the near future and that she should sit tight for the time being. Lisette knew better than to press for an answer but felt confident that if something good was going to happen then it might work out well for her too.

***

Mr Chairman announced his retirement two weeks after Margaret returned from Europe.

He recalled Max's words; he'd said something like there would soon be some vacancies for Mandarins, or something like that. People only ever hear the words they want to hear, especially when they're blinded by greed or ambition. He assumed Max's words to mean that some of the nine were about to be killed off. He didn't care because he felt sure that if he unwaveringly supported Max then he'd be safe. He'd watch his back though, just in case. He'd be vulnerable with no sentinels to protect him but he'd have Max for that. He wasn't aware that the Mandarins had been building up their forces since Bonaparte. Max said he'd be given half a dozen PAs. What for, he had no real idea.

He kept saying the word over and over in his head: 'Mandarin'. He couldn't believe his luck. He'd no longer have responsibility for all those whingers in the Organisation. He hoped his new PAs weren't whingers but what could they possibly have to whinge about?

***

A Mandarin pre-ceremony conclave

"Are we agreed on the candidates?"

"We are, but why are there three of them?"

"Normally there's usually only one, pre-ordained, candidate but as we can't agree on a single candidate we have three nominees. Whichever of them gets the most votes will become the new Chair."

"We don't have a recent precedent but I see no reason why we can't proceed."

"In that case, are we agreed to proceed with the vote?" There were no dissenters.

"Then let's put it to a vote. The normal rules apply. Each of us has a single vote. Abstentions for the appointment of Chair are not permitted. In the event that the vote isn't unanimous the winner will be the candidate who has the most votes. Brother and Sister Mandarins, please take your place in front of the…"

"Wait, what will happen to the two unsuccessful candidates?"

"They shall be removed from the Tabernacle by the Recorder and placed in the ante-chamber of the Inner Temple to await the decision of the High Council."

"What sort of decision? We haven't been in this situation before and I want to know what will happen to the unsuccessful candidates."

"I have studied the ancient texts and they say, 'Whosoever shall fail in his attempt to become an elder brother shall be taken from the Tabernacle to a chamber where he shall find a sphairai and open his veins'," spoke the Recorder.

"That's from the old Brotherhood days, surely we don't deal with unsuccessful candidates in that way nowadays? Do we?"

"No, of course not," he lied. "There being no recent precedent, the High Council will decide the futures of the unsuccessful candidates. Rest assured there will be no leaving of people in dark chambers with a sphairai for company." Max very badly wanted the two other candidates out of the way permanently. He himself had handpicked them for the purposes of removing them.

"I saw several sentinels enter the temple. What are they doing here? Since when have we invited sentinels to these gatherings?"

"Allegra, nowadays we each of us have our own forces for protection and some of them are sentinels, for obvious reasons."

"The sentinels I saw are from the Italian splinter."

"They are here to ensure that everything is carried out according to our laws; now please, unless there is anything further we should take the vote." Pausing to take a deep breath Max continued, "As I was saying, we each enter the Tabernacle one at a time. Inside you will find three booths separated by curtains. At the sides of the booths is open access to the cheeks of the candidates. With your piece of warmed wax, leave a rite mark on the left cheek for nay or the right cheek for aye on each candidate. You must give each candidate one rite mark."

"They used to be called kisses in the old days," added the Recorder for no good reason.

"Couldn't we just raise our hands to vote?" The other eight mandarins looked in headshaking disbelief at de Heer, the Dutch mandarin.

"After the rites have been checked and counted the result will be announced by the Recorder. The candidate with the most marks of Rite will be the new Chair. If there is a tie the Rites will be rerun until we have a result."

Inside the Tabernacle were three latticework booths that resembled confessionals. Each was separated from the others by a heavy curtain. The mandarins were hooded as they entered the Tabernacle which was lit by single candles placed in front of the booth of each candidate. Adjacent to the cheeks of the candidates were apertures through which marks of rite would be made by the mandarins. The Recorder was in silent attendance to ensure each rite was carried out properly. Each mandarin made their mark on each candidate and left the Tabernacle before the next was called in by the Recorder. Margaret was in the left hand booth when viewed from the entrance and was last to receive a mark of rite before each mandarin exited.

The candidates were blindfolded. Their names were written in ancient script on a plaque above them. They had no idea of the significance of the votes, they just felt their cheeks being touched by what seemed like a warm waxy crayon.

Preparing her for the ceremony, Rex had told Margaret that she'd be sitting naked in the Tabernacle which made her think of murderous cults and whether or not he was telling the truth. It was a half-truth, as all she was wearing was a thin black shroud while sitting in the near total darkness of the Tabernacle. As she sensed each shadowy figure passing in front of her she felt something touch either her left or right cheek.

***

The origins of the rites ceremony date back to the earliest times of the Brotherhood.

In those days the rites were not carried out in a dimly lit tabernacle but in a forest glade at dawn. Following the passing of the founding Esquire brothers the elders decided that the Brotherhood would be governed by a High Council of Elders. As with the Romans, the High Council could opt to be governed by a dictator in times of great need.

The number of ruling elders changed with time. Originally they had been thirteen but more commonly they were nine. Always an odd number so votes could not be tied as abstentions were seldom permitted.

When a seat on the High Council became empty, brethren would be proposed to stand for it. It there was an even number of voting elders the eldest common brother would join the High Council for the rites ceremony. Elders, plus the oldest common brother, then donned hooded cloaks and one at a time approached the line of candidates, kissing each once on either the left or the right cheek. The kissing was observed by the Recorder. Unsuccessful candidates usually took defeat honourably and well, however, some did not. Even though the kissers were hooded it wasn't difficult to identify who was who and on several occasions vendettas were undertaken by unsuccessful candidates, sometimes resulting in the murder of those who hadn't voted for them. It was chaos as this led to several rounds of brethren being proposed for the High Council, rites being held, cheeks kissed and unsuccessful candidates raising vendettas. This situation sometimes lasted for decades at a time.

***

People slighted by defeat may seek revenge in any number of ways, including confessing all to the Church who, being familiars of the aristocracy, passed them the secrets of the confessional. Such was the aristocracy's main source of information concerning the Brotherhood for nearly two centuries. It all changed when an elder called Daniel Smythe was declared Dictator after four brethren confessed all to the Church which led to the slaughter of over eight hundred brethren. He changed the rules on the rites to what they are today. Thereafter, rites were carried out in secret with only one elder at a time admitted to the Tabernacle to vote. A recorder would be present to make sure that the rites were carried out properly and would only see the back of the elders' hooded gowns. It was Daniel Smythe who decided that unsuccessful candidates would be killed, for obvious reasons. They were led from the Tabernacle to a chamber where they found a sphairai waiting for them. The chamber door would be locked as would the door at the top of the stone stairs leading to it.

***

Following the rites ceremony, the Recorder came to stand in front of the mandarins. From beneath his hood he announced the numbers of rite marks for each candidate. When he finished he announced that Margaret Rotheram, being the only candidate to receive five marks, was declared Madame Chairman.

Afterwards, nobody asked about the unsuccessful candidates, they seemed to be instantly forgotten about. Max turned them over to the sentinels from the Italian splinter. Before they were taken away he made the sign of the cross over each of them while whispering the Trinitarian. Each sentinel did likewise but for themselves.

The ceremony of the Chair which followed the rites lasted nearly two hours. Margaret thought it more akin to the coronation of a monarch than the election of a leader of a shadowy organisation. When it was all over she handed back the ceremonial robes and the black shroud. She wanted to keep the shroud as a memento but the Recorder said it wasn't allowed, 'not even for an all-powerful Madame Chairman'. "All-powerful Madame Chairman," she whispered. She liked the way that sounded. An all-powerful Madame Chairman? Yes, she'd work on that one.

***

It was a beautiful sunny morning. As soon as he woke it hit him: today was his last day at the office in Half Moon Street. His only duty would be to announce the Mandarins' decision of who'd be replacing him. He was confident it would be Margaret and so couldn't wait to see their faces when he made the announcement. Then he'd pop a few champagne corks; down a few glasses of the bubbly stuff; eat some canapés; do some glad-handing around the room; make his farewell speech, in which he'd wish his replacement all the very best of luck in the world, and then wave goodbye to everybody as he left the building. Hopefully for the last time.

It all went according to plan. He especially loved the look on everybody's faces when he announced that Margaret Rotheram had been selected by the Mandarins to be their Madame Chairman. Sir Toby almost had a heart attack on the spot as he'd loudly been touting his friend, Lord Fitzroy, for the post. Fortunately for him, old Fitzroy hadn't made the final three. He couldn't have been happier with the announcement of Margaret Rotheram as Madame Chairman because he was one of those who believed the Organisation urgently needed of good shake-up. Besides, at seventy-two, he felt he'd had his day. He shook Margaret's hand firmly while earnestly congratulating her and swearing to do everything in his power to support her.

"Well done, old chap. You certainly fooled her."

"What the hell are you talking about, Toby?"

"What you just said to… I'll shudder when I say it… Madame Chairman."

"Whatever do you mean, you bloody fool, I meant every word of it. Damn fine girl. I'll back her all the way. I'd be proud to have a daughter like her. We need more like her because this place is fast becoming a morgue. A word to the wise, Toby. She might look like she wouldn't harm a fly but I wouldn't be so sure if I were you. Be careful. Take my advice. Retire before you're retired." He left Sir Toby as Sir Geoffrey Hamilton-Cross joined them.

"What was that all about?"

"He's lost his marbles. He thinks she's... oh, I can't be bothered. I'm going to my club for a few. Care to join me, old man?"

"I certainly would. Perhaps we might discuss the opportunities which always seem to come about with change."

"Quite. She won't last, mark my words. She will not last a year."

***

Two weeks later, Mr Chairman was walking along Rue Phillippe-Plantamour in Geneva on his way to his swearing-in ceremony as a mandarin. He hadn't given a moment's thought to the possibility that in order for him to become a mandarin somebody had to die. They might have been retired but he hadn't considered that either.

As he neared the address he noticed a man crossing the road just ahead of him. He thought he recognised the gait more than anything as he wasn't wearing his glasses. As the man approached closer he saw it was Rex.

"Hello Rex old boy. What a coincidence seeing you here."

"Hello Charles old boy, nice to see you again."

"What are you doing here? Business? I'm afraid I don't keep in touch with events so..."

"Yes business. The same business as you as a matter of fact."

"What do you mean?"

"I too am being made today."

"Made?"

"Yes, that's the term we use. I am becoming a mandarin today. Being made. Get it?"

"Oh, I see. So we're both being made today?"

"So it would appear."

"How are things back at the…"

"Like you, I don't go there anymore. No, I decided the atmosphere in the office was just too claustrophobic."

"I couldn't agree more." They reached their destination. "After you, old man," said Charles opening the door to allow Rex to enter the building first.

"I wouldn't dream of it. After you, old man." Charles went into the building first.

Charles's first impression of the inside of the building was not very favourable. He thought it looked rather dated, old-fashioned and shabby like faded glory. The lift wasn't even working and according to the information board at the foot of the stairs their destination was the fourth floor. By the time they arrived at the office door marked MMD Inc Charles was totally out of breath.

"Let me catch my breath for a moment before we go in. I don't want them seeing me wheezing like an old boiler."

"Of course. Take your time."

As they stood waiting for Charles to catch his breath two younger men came along the corridor and entered the room ahead of them.

"Do you think we're in the right place?"

"Oh yes, this is it. Definitely. I was here only last week."

"I don't wish to be picky but the whole place looks a bit of a dump."

"Don't let appearances fool you. The whole idea is to maintain a low profile."

"Ah, yes. Well now, I've caught my breath so let us proceed inside." Charles opened the door and walked into the room ahead of Rex. Once inside he couldn't make out what was going on. The two men who'd entered the room earlier were sitting on a desk in its centre. It was the only piece of furniture in the room. "What's going on…"

"I have no idea," he lied.

"Mr Cavendish?" said one of the men in a soft Irish accent. He hadn't been called by that name in a very long time.

"Erm, yes?"

"I'd like to introduce you to my associate here."

Ah, thought Charles, *this must be the start of the ceremony.* He made to shake the Irishman's hand. "Hello, it appears you know my name but I don't know yours."

"Mr Cavendish?" He turned ninety degrees to face the Mediterranean-looking man who'd just spoken his name.

As he faced him, an eight-inch stiletto dagger was pushed with considerable force through his sternum and into his heart. He looked down in shock. Despite the fact he'd just been stabbed, there was no noise or fuss or commotion in the room and he felt very little pain. There was no blood apart from a small red dot near the middle of his white shirt. The name Ferdinand came to mind for some reason.

When he tried to grab the handle of the stiletto the Mediterranean-looking man pushed him hard backwards, smashing him into the wall. He started to feel light headed. He looked down at the handle of the dagger and then to the three pairs of eyes staring in silence at him. He opened his mouth to scream prompting the Mediterranean-looking man to put his free hand over his mouth. He felt his knees go weak before crumpling. He dropped to the floor. The Mediterranean-looking man knelt beside him and raised his head in the crook of his arm. He brought his face close to Charles's while slowly sliding the stiletto from his chest. His body became fully yielding as his blood pressure plummeted. His heart was pumping blood into his chest cavity. His vision became tunnel-like and sepia before going to grey and finally black. He wasn't dead yet. He could hear noises. His head hit the bare floorboards as the Mediterranean-looking man shoved it off the crook of his arm. It hurt more than the…

"You're gettin' really good with that thing."

"Who was he?"

"Don't ask any questions and ye might live longer. Well, that's what I heard anyway."

"I need to be going now. You'll take care of this?"

"Wait one moment, auld fruit," answered the Irishman in a mocking old Etonian accent. "Our orders don't include cleaning up here, auld fruit."

"Surely you don't expect me to…"

"Will you stop pissing around? Look, fella, get lost, he's just having you on."

"C'mon, I was just havin' a laugh with yer man. Did ye see the look on his face though." The Irishman was in playful mood. "I was just kiddin', ye mate. Go on, get off outta here. Leave this to us. We don't mind gettin' a tip for a job well done though." Rex took out his wallet and gave the men a generous tip so he could get out of the room and be on his way to meet Max for his making.

"What's five hundred francs in real money?"

"Who cares. I was just havin' a bit of the craic with him like."

"We shouldn't really be doing things like that."

"What's wrong with ye? It was just a joke I was havin' with him. Anyway you grab the heavy end and let's get this fella on top of the desk and do the necessary with him."

MARGARET'S STORY – SITUATIONAL DETERMINISM

Madame Chairman was admitted to the Half Moon Street building by a security guard who informed her she was the only one in the office so far though more were expected later.

She was returning to her duties early following the Yuletide holiday. Not that it had been much of a holiday. Her inaugural AGM had been a disaster. She'd hated looking out onto the sea of blank faces staring back at her. She could see in their eyes and hear in their voices what they thought of her. She'd smiled at them from the rostrum knowing that the old farts club had seen its last days; it would soon all be over for them.

The timing of Mr Chairman's resignation meant she hardly had time to prepare for the AGM. The results were so lacklustre that it was impossible to generate any excitement. She had few allies to help her get through the gruelling two and a half days of the AGM. They just sat there like stunned mullets.

She'd wanted to delay the AGM but Max was against the idea; he said it was traditional to hold it around mid-December as most governors had holiday arrangements involving travel. The AGM was the starting pistol for the festive season to commence. It was a time for celebration, glad-handing and back-slapping, especially as most senior governors were men and they'd been brought up on that sort of thing. But not this year.

Throughout the holiday she'd been totally preoccupied thinking about how badly she was doing in her new job. Getting one's feet under the table in any new job can be challenging but getting one's feet under the Organisation's top table was proving much more difficult than she'd imagined. There were a couple of factors making this so, the main one being her age. She was very young for the job, which most governors felt uncomfortable with. She was very attractive which many men found distracting. Very handsome. Very striking features. And smart, very smart. Men particularly felt intimidated in her presence. Or maybe it was her defensive barriers they were sensing.

At the time, the Organisation was run by a bunch of geriatric old farts who were the last remnant relics of the classes of WWs I and II. The old farts club had run the Organisation, and the Brotherhood before it, for nigh on three hundred and fifty years. They were resistant to change but it was high time for a change and those who'd put Madame Chairman where she was wanted to see her bring about change. And quickly.

***

Madame Chairman was not a fan of smoking or smokers and had banned all smoking, particularly cigar and pipe smoking, from the conference rooms during the AGM. This didn't go down well with the majority of the old farts club. One foolish fellow decided that he wasn't going to be told what to do, especially at Christmas time, by a slip of a girl and lit up in the corner of an ante room. Heads were raised like meerkat sentries to see where the smell of cigar smoke was coming from. The rich aroma was too much for many and they reached inside their jacket pockets to pull out leather, silver and even gold cigar cases. Some had cheap cigars in cardboard packs but they were adept at making them appear, magician-like, from their jacket pockets. Before a second cigar could be lit an "Ahem!" came from the direction of the double-doored entrance to the main auditorium. At the "Ahem!" the gathered knots of old farts parted like the Red Sea, leaving Madame Chairman a clear line of sight to the smoker.

She stood over six foot tall in her heels – how she hated heels – and the smoker was a rotund five foot five. She'd swivelled her head owl-like from the shoulders to stare straight at him with her icy pale blue eyes. "Put… that… out." Each clearly enunciated word was spoken with a one second gap and the t at the end of each word was spat. The old fart stubbed out the cigar on a nearby saucer and threw its remains into an ornamental fireplace. "Sorry, old thing," sputtered Sir Geoffrey Hamilton-Cross in apology.

That was the first time they witnessed how Madame Chairman could bring down the temperature of any room by the tone of her voice and a glare from her icy pale blue eyes.

***

To say the AGM hadn't been a great success was an understatement. Madame Chairman blamed herself for its failure by getting off on the wrong foot. It had been her opportunity to announce her arrival on the scene but she'd blown it by her actions against the smoker. *Couldn't I just have let it go? For once? No. I couldn't. Oh well, I have a year before the next one. Yippee. That is if I'm still around in a year's time.* She needed a big win.

There was an event at the AGM that troubled her and she still didn't know what to make of it. Shortly after she'd reprimanded Sir Geoffrey she bumped into a woman, who apologised immediately while pressing a piece of paper into her hand. She knew better than to read it out in the open and so went to the ladies' toilet. As she stood in front of the mirrors over the wash basins the same woman emerged from out of one of the cubicles behind her. Their eyes met in the mirror. She reached inside her handbag for her .38.

"I knew you'd come in here to read it. Wait a mo, I'll lock the door. There's nobody else in here so we can talk without being disturbed. They haven't bugged this place yet so it should be okay." Before Madame Chairman could speak the woman introduced herself. "I'm the new Control."

"I'm…"

"Don't be silly, I know who you are."

"The note makes no sense," she said after glancing at it.

"It wasn't meant to. It was meant to bring you in here."

"What do you want?" She cocked the .38. The click was audible.

"As I said, I'm the new Control…"

"I didn't know we had a new Control."

"I was promoted by Charles just before he retired."

"Charles?"

"Mr Chairman."

"Oh, I see. Why did he promote you? Was he leaving me a surprise or was he simply looking after an old… acquaintance?"

"There was nothing like that going on between Charles and me. We'd known each other for years and over that time we confided in one another… probably more than was wise. He wasn't all bad. He just wasn't a very good chairman. He knew his limitations though and when the Mandarins began pressurising him he confided in me." There was a knock on the door. "Look, we don't want to be discovered together in a locked loo for obvious reasons. I just wanted to let you know that Charles did what he did to protect you. You can always rely on me…" Hammering replaced polite door knocking. "Yes, alright," she shouted, "the latch must have slipped… one minute please." She handed Madame Chairman a key. "You might need this one day. Remember, you can always rely on me." Control departed the toilet, admonishing the persistent door knocker on her way out.

"What was that all about?" asked Madame Chairman emerging from a cubicle.

"I have no idea, Madame Chairman, I became concerned when you were all alone in here with her," replied her ever vigilant sentinel.

"Thank you, Awhah. I know I can always rely on you to protect me."

***

It's odd how some things work out. It seems as though there's some kind of cosmic karma at play behind particular events which shape destinies. Some refer to such occurrences as situational determinism. Others call it conspiracy in action.

Situational determinism is the unseen force which creates opportunities which would not have existed or otherwise arisen had you not been in the market for them. For example, you start a double glazing company and the next thing you know you're surrounded by double glazing conversations, situations and opportunities which weren't there before you started your double glazing enterprise. Situational determinism at work.

***

A Mandarins and invited guest conversation

"Update me."

"Everything is in place. I just need to make the call and hopefully she'll agree to meet with me, that is if she doesn't still bear me a grudge."

"If she doesn't agree to a meeting then I'll get involved but it's better if it comes from you for obvious reasons."

"The CIA and the American splinter are both on board."

"Excellent. When the time is right I'll leak the details to the Russians and the French."

"The French will go crazy."

"That's what I'm relying on. They'll never agree to a deal involving the Americans or the Russians so both being involved will send the Count into a blind rage."

"You should tell the Russians immediately as they'll get to know something is going on as they have eyes and ears all over the Kremlin."

"I intend to tell them in good time to keep her occupied. I'll tell the Frogs at the last minute so they don't have time to think or smell a rat."

"I don't trust LeFort. I think he'll squeal to his Frog boss."

"He won't after he finds out he's being touted as the President of a reunified Organisation. He's barely capable of tying his own shoe laces but he's well liked and won't seem such a crazy nomination. Everybody'll buy it."

"I hope so. I'll have somebody stay close to him, just in case he decides to blab."

"What about the General? How's he holding up?"

"Not too good. He's extremely panicky but with the right medication I'm sure he'll be okay. By the way, will he really be allowed to go to the USA?"

"That's not my concern, you do what you wish with him after the goods have been delivered."

"He knows too much. We don't want him writing his memoirs. You know what they're like as soon as they think they're safe… they write a book… and folks everywhere love that sort of stuff."

"Let me think a while on that one but be prepared to deal with him stateside. We can't afford to have him wandering around Russia after the KGB start their investigations. He'll crack for sure."

***

A tripler who Madame Chairman had got to know while on assignment was passing through London. She called her on the pretext of being interested in knowing how she was getting on in her new job. She'd been as surprised as many at her appointment. No, not surprised, stunned actually, though she'd been impressed by her during their assignment together and thought it natural that others might have been similarly impressed. She didn't know that Margaret Rotheram had been marked out for greatness long before her appointment to the top job. A top job which came with conditions. Despite many of the conditions being onerous she'd accepted it without a moment's hesitation.

The tripler suggested they meet on neutral ground for obvious reasons.

"Hi, thanks for seeing me. Congrats on the new job." The two women greeted one another with the popular kissy kissy face dance making sure not to touch cheek with lips.

"It's so great to see you again," she lied. "How are things in Moscow?"

"Oh, the usual."

"The usual? Can't we be open with one another?"

"Well, you're Madame Chairman and I'm an operative with the American splinter so what can I say?"

"I wonder why you're here then? Coffee?" She wanted to get on with it as she was a busy woman now that she was Madame Chairman. Well, that's the image she wanted to portray.

"Yes please. I want to sound you out on… a… an… opportunity."

"Why me, why not your CIA or splinter bosses? Isn't the American splinter interested in opportunities?"

"I have both of them on board already but this opportunity can be so much more. So much more than they can do with it. You know how hard it is to get some people to listen?" she said pointing a finger toward the ceiling before realising her erstwhile co-assignmentee was now one of those her index finger was alluding to. She smiled in recognition of her faux pas.

"Black? No sugar? Right? You speak, I'll pour."

"You know I've been running a Russian general for some years now."

"Old Vladimir? How is he these days?"

"The very same and he's fine, next time I see him I'll tell him you were asking after him." She took a sip of coffee. "You remember how it is when we want to shake the tree in Moscow. We wind up the clockwork KGB and they go off and pick up somebody to either settle an old score or make it look like they actually know what they are doing. It always ends up the same way. Somebody dies. Usually by being so unfortunate as to fall from the tenth floor of some desolate Soviet tower block. Amazing how often that happens."

"They have no imagination."

"Well, we shook the tree just before Christmas…"

"Cruel timing."

"It was. We wanted the KGB to arrest Illya Vakhnenko. He's been a P in the A for a while. Instead they arrested a whole bunch of people. Slaughtered them all, including Lyudmila Mikhailovich. Shame. That's when old Vladimir came a-running. He thought the KGB might be on to him or one of the arrestees might squeal under torture and finger him. He begged me to get him to the US as soon as possible. He wants to go to California as he's tired of cold weather. I told him I'd have to check with the boys in the office. On my way to make the call it hit me like a bolt of lightning." The tripler paused to see if Madame Chairman was going to ask the obvious question, which she didn't. "When I got to the office I called home and told them my plan. It involved hanging old Vladimir out to dry by telling him that my bosses didn't think he'd done enough to warrant us giving him asylum and he'd have to do one more job if he wanted a ticket to the US. Want to hear what the job is?"

"What would you do if I said no?"

"I'd tell you anyway because I know you'll want to hear it. I told old Vladimir that if he wanted to leave the workers' paradise of the Soviet Union he'd have to help us expropriate some Soviet military hardware. Specifically, Soviet missiles. Not the old stuff but the brand new stuff that they've only just deployed," said the tripler being somewhat economical with the truth about who'd instigated what. The two former co-assignmentees discussed the outline of a plan which called for war games to be staged in West Germany in less than a year.

"That seems a very short timescale to make the necessary arrangements for an operation of this size."

"That's the beauty of it. My bosses at the CIA convinced the President that advancements in Soviet missile technology mean that NATO must be capable of deploying quickly and war games is just the thing to test our preparedness. The order came straight from the White House. The President, of course, is unaware of the true purpose of the games."

"It all sounds terrific but why are you telling me all this?"

"There's always a chance that things could go wrong and so I need to play the CIA game. If it goes bad my head would be on the block with the CIA… and probably the US splinter too. My career would be over and I'm not prepared for that to happen."

"It might be me but I'm not following you."

"I'll tell you about my second brainwave. I went to my splinter boss and convinced her that the best thing for the missiles is that they end up in your hands. You could then sell them and neither the CIA nor the US splinter could be accused of being involved… we'd want a cut. Obviously."

Madame Chairman laughed. "Obviously. You want me to steal Soviet missiles? What makes you think I could carry off something like that?"

"Because they're going to be delivered right to you by the Russkies. All you need to do is drive them away. I haven't got all the pieces worked out yet but we've got about nine months to come up with a final plan and if the worst comes to the worst we let the CIA take them. It would be a shame though to let hundreds of millions of dollars slip through your fingers. It might even be billions if there are any long-range ICBMs." The two former co-assignmentees went into a huddle until one had to go catch a flight and the other had a meeting to go to.

Madame Chairman immediately recognised what this opportunity meant for her and her standing within the Organisation. A bagful of Soviet missiles to trade would certainly make the coffers look a lot healthier and the kudos of pulling off such a heist would cement her place in the Organisation. Success would snap everybody into line and she'd become an overnight legend.

She called Lisette and told her to come to her home that evening for a confidential chat. Though she didn't trust Lisette completely, Madame Chairman had liked her from the very beginning but knew her to be the type of woman who'd be happier if the Organisation were run by a man. One man in particular, but she wasn't aware of that yet.

***

It had started six months previous. General V.V. Grigorovich of the Soviet Army HQ staff working in the Kremlin, who'd been a CIA informant for nearly all his military career, went into meltdown after several associates were arrested, tortured and executed.

He wasn't certain whether any of his erstwhile associates were traitors, but he certainly was. The fact was they were dead and he didn't fancy joining them. He guessed it was just the lazy old KGB putting the cat among the pigeons knowing something was bound to fly out. It always did. Were they spies? Were they traitors? Nobody will ever really know but what was clear was the KGB were on the hunt. When things like this started off it was usually because somebody high up the greasy pole had been given a kick in the arse and was passing it down the line.

The old, old story. Nevertheless, VVG was of the opinion that it was high time for him to get out of town. He was confident he'd done enough to feather his Western nest over the years and that as soon as he requested to leave the USSR the CIA would jump at the opportunity of such a coup. He was in for a shock though. His CIA handler told him bluntly that he simply hadn't done enough to warrant the diplomatic storm his defection would create. But he'd be relieved to know, she said, that there was a way for him to get to the USA. The CIA had known for some time what it wanted from the Soviet Union and what it wanted could be provided by VVG. His handler had been farsighted enough to see the opportunity his defection presented. The timing of VVG's defection to the West could not have been better for the Mandarins either.

What neither the CIA nor VVG knew at the time was that it was the Russian splinter who'd instigated that particular KGB investigation for its own purposes. Seizing upon the opportunity a terrified VVG presented her, the tripler put him under pressure to commit one more act of treason to pay for his ticket to America. When the tripler told her CIA bosses about the plan, which she attributed completely to VVG himself, they loved it. She would get credit no matter what the outcome. Classic doubler/tripler action; heads I win tails you lose. For obvious reasons, the Russian splinter couldn't be involved, or even implicated, in stealing the property of the people of the Soviet Union, but it was happy to benefit financially. Things were about to get complicated.

The Russian splinter let Madame Chairman know that it would not interfere with her plan to snatch the missiles. Now it was her plan? But they would need a cut of the proceeds, "to bribe crooked officials from within the Soviet government," they claimed. As things turned out there was a bonus sweetener at the end which nobody could have foreseen.

***

It was no secret that Soviet missiles of the late 1960s and early 1970s were far superior to anything the West had at the time. The USA in particular was extremely nervous about the capability gap of being able to launch a successful pre-emptive strike with insufficient minimal retaliation time. This is where VVG and the timing of the upcoming war games, which were to be held right next to the East German border, came into the picture.

***

VVG created a great fuss inside the Kremlin about some intelligence he'd received concerning a very large NATO war games exercise planned to be staged right next to their border with West Germany. He feigned outrage at the idea of NATO provoking his beloved USSR in this way. VVG would insist on this being a great opportunity to eavesdrop on the West, understand their capabilities and test the preparedness of their own troops and equipment by staging their own counter-war-games-exercises at the same time. The counter-war-games exercises would necessarily involve tens of thousands of Soviet troops, thousands of tanks and hundreds of their lovely, sparkly, shiny new missiles. The missiles in question were the latest generation of mobile SAMs and short- and medium-range ICBMs. Even the launch vehicles were streets ahead of anything the West had.

The plan was to steal at least a dozen vehicles loaded with the latest Soviet missiles. Simple. The CIA thought it was their plan but nobody could quite remember how it had originally come about but it had traction at the highest levels of government. The plan was a go as far as Washington was concerned.

It was all a game but a game worth playing as it was worth

hundreds of millions of dollars and it would level the balance-of-power playing field. The stage was set.

***

It later seemed suspect to some governments of the time that the Americans suddenly caught up with the Soviet Union's missile technology as they made a giant technological leap forward in 1972.

***

A Mandarin council conversation

"She's managed to alienate just about everybody."

"I told you, she's a mistake. Let's remove her before she can do any more damage. Let's just recognise that we made a mistake and if we move quickly to rectify it…"

"Nobody will be moving or rectifying anything. She's only been in the job a couple of months."

"Why didn't she postpone the AGM until Easter? It wouldn't have mattered just this once surely."

"I suggested that to her but she's so strong willed she insisted she wanted to go ahead with the AGM so she could stamp her authority," he lied.

"Stamp her authority? I thought we were moving away from autocracy."

"We are but the secret inner council isn't fully convened yet. Let us review the situation every three months and rather than replace her we should mentor her more closely. Each of us has something to offer in that regard. Have we not?"

The council meeting ran its course and as soon as it was over Max went straight into another meeting. He told them it was a business meeting with his day-job board of directors.

***

A mandarin and guest conversation

"She must not be allowed to fail. If the others start moving against her they must be eliminated. Each of them. Do you understand?"

"They're well-guarded so I might need a little help."

"Do you have anybody in mind?"

"There's this little Italian fella who's not bad. Not as good as me mind but good enough."

"Is he from the Italian splinter?"

"Nah. He's one of the Organisation's boys."

"A sentinel?"

"He is but best you don't know too much. Knowin' what ye shouldn't might get ye into trouble if things go wrong. Just leave it to me and himself to do the business and you just sit back an' relax."

"I won't forget you if you…"

"Ye bet yer loife ye won't ferget me," he said in a put-on heavy Irish accent and meaning every word of his implied threat.

"Keep close to her. Make yourself indispensable. Do as she says without question. Then when the time is right you'll get your revenge on all of them."

"I just want the one, that's all. Just the one will do for me."

MICHAEL'S STORY – MOVING ON

After basic training was over, Michael travelled to the Bootle barracks where he reported to Captain Hywel-Jones.

"So, Private Frost, how did basic training go?"

"It went…"

"Pretty boring stuff eh, but I imagine you made some good mates."

"I…"

"I have some good news, as you're not part of a regular intake your tank training will be conducted at Altcar, starting with what most young men like: driving tanks. You'll learn to drive a Chieftain and a Saracen APC; then you'll go on to loading and firing then Tank Commander duties then tactical exercises including some of the things you're already familiar with such as de-tanking and holding a defensive position. Any questions, Private Frost?"

"No sir."

"Good. Then let's get you started"

"Thank you for helping me get into the regiment, sir."

"You helped yourself enormously. You created a good impression both at the barracks and at Altcar. The Royal Tank Regiment will make a soldier out of you. After all, we did wonders for Monty, didn't we?" grinned Captain Hywel-Jones. "I think you'll be an asset to the regiment but don't rule out applying for selection to other regiments in due course. I, myself, passed officer selection for the Royal Marines and saw action overseas."

"I'm just glad to be in the Royal Tank Regiment."

"Excellent. The Army's a great life and you have your whole life ahead of you. Now go and pick up your kit and meet me in the parade yard in ten minutes and we'll get off to Altcar."

***

On their arrival, Captain Hywel-Jones introduced Michael to Sergeant Morgan who showed him where he'd be eating, sleeping and assembling for exercises. All of which was unnecessary as he was familiar with the layout at Altcar but this is the Army and they do things by the book.

The discipline within the Royal Tank Regiment is just the same as it is with the rest of the Army but being part of a tank crew is different. It's a brotherhood. A close bond quickly builds between members of a tank crew.

***

When delivering his regular progress report, Captain Hywel-Jones spoke highly of Michael particularly as, according to Sergeant Morgan, he was very capable and self-reliant but he felt there was something missing which he couldn't put his finger on.

An Organisation conversation

"He has limited communication skills. Maybe he's just shy?" Adding, "He's clearly not a simpleton."

"Maybe he's on drugs or something and that's why he's a bit strange. Young people are on drugs all the time, aren't they?" suggested the man known as the London schools boxing coach.

After a deep sigh the Mediterranean-looking man spoke. "Look, just because he's a little different doesn't mean any of that. I think Michael is a bit locked up in his own head and doesn't work like the rest of us 'up here'," pointing to his head, "but he's got talent and we mustn't lose sight of that. People like him don't grow on trees. Consider how few make it. Think about what we ask of people. Look at his strengths. He possesses incredible fighting and shooting skills. I've fought him and I can tell you there's a terrible strength inside of Michael Frost and we've all been in situations where that sort of thing has been the difference between living and dying. I say we keep him on list B. Let's get him through his tank training, and Gareth, see if you can persuade him to go for commando selection ASAP. I think he looks up to you as a bit of a father figure so if anybody can persuade him you can."

"I'm in agreement with our friend here. Frost stays on list B for now but he needs to be removed from Altcar as soon as possible as there are things I have in mind for him," said the Counsellor. "Keep me informed."

The meeting broke up in agreement regarding the direction of those on the lists, including Michael and his immediate future. As they made to leave the old signals hut Captain Hywel-Jones held the Mediterranean-looking man back by the arm and asked, "Is this where you stabbed Cadet Munroe? I understand it might have been necessary to silence him somehow but he was only a child. Who would have believed him if he'd spoken out? He was a good lad and he loved the Cadets. It was his escape from terrible troubles at home. He had a real cheeky way about him, a shining innocence. Couldn't you have convinced him that what he'd heard was a joke of some kind? As a young lad he'd have forgotten about it all soon enough. Was it really necessary to kill him?"

"I don't know who you think you are talking to but I suggest you keep your nose out of things that don't concern you. Never question me like this ever again." It was hard to accept being spoken to that way but he kept his temper and left the Mediterranean-looking man standing alone as he walked hunch-shouldered back to the main barracks.

***

Sergeant Morgan was spending an inordinate amount of time coaching Michael. They'd replicate famous tank battles, then debate what could have been done differently to affect the outcome. He was extremely impressed by Michael's knowledge of military strategy and wondered how he could have come by it.

***

"Sir, we need to talk about Private Frost. I've had tank strategy conversations with him which is way beyond anything I've come across before. He's some kind of… I'm not sure what he is." After their discussion, Sergeant Morgan and Captain Hywel-Jones concluded that a visit to Michael's home was in order to get some background. In the meantime he was placed on light duties involving the organisation of Altcar's summer camps, which translates to basic administrative duties. Performing mindless repetitive mundane administrative tasks didn't seem to faze Michael in the slightest. He just got on with things and was very efficient at everything he did which earned him the nickname 'Robbie the Robot'. This type of work quelled the voices in his head.

***

While on administrative duties Michael bumped into Major Finn. He still had an axe to grind over the day he'd been forced by the French Captain to allow the cadets to target shoot using sniper rifles.

"Do you remember me, Private Frost, because I certainly remember you and your cadet chums? One of your lot proved to be a bit light fingered which cost him his life. He got what he deserved if you ask me…"

"Tommy Munroe was his name and it's not possible for a Thunderflash to go off in the way it was described."

"What do you mean, 'in the way it was described'?"

"The report said that Tommy must have primed the Thunderflash accidentally when placing it in his pocket. Have you tried priming a Thunderflash in that way, Major Finn, sir?" Michael went on to use the exact words Major Finn used in his report regarding the death of Cadet Munroe.

"How did you get a copy of my report, Private Frost?"

"I've never had a copy of your report, sir."

"Then how do you know what it says?"

"I saw a copy on Captain Hywel-Jones's desk, sir. It was upside down but I could still read what it said."

"You're just a little sneak, aren't you? I'm going to speak with Captain Hywel-Jones about his lapse in security and suggest a suitable punishment for you while I'm about it."

"But that doesn't answer the question, sir. How did Cadet Monroe prime a Thunderflash while placing it in his pocket? It doesn't make sense as it can't be done that way."

"Then he must have primed it before placing it in his pocket."

"Tommy wasn't stupid. If that Thunderflash was primed before it was placed in Tommy's jacket then somebody else must have primed it."

"What are you suggesting, Private Frost? Cadet Munroe was murdered? On a secure MoD site while there were over a thousand people here, including the Minister of Defence? Why would anybody want to murder Cadet Munroe? No, Private Frost, Munroe was a thief and got exactly what he deserved. I'll be speaking to Captain Hywel-Jones about you this evening so be prepared for whatever might come your way."

An Organisation conversation

"I've just had an extraordinary conversation with a Private on list B."

"Extraordinary in what way?"

"He's convinced Cadet Munroe's death couldn't have been an accident."

"He can't prove anything. Just keep an eye on him and report back if…"

"Keep an eye on him? He should be removed."

"Negative, Major, do not remove the Private."

Michael would have to tread very carefully around Major Finn in the future.

***

Captain Hywel-Jones took a call at his desk from a Counsellor. This was highly irregular as such calls were passed through a switchboard and could be listened in on. During the call the Counsellor intimated that Major Finn wanted Private Frost to receive more than the reprimand he was scheduled to give to him. To keep him safe, Michael had to be fast-tracked. "Sergeant, we need to bring our visit to Private Frost's home forward. Make some excuse to be off base tomorrow and we'll drive to Liverpool together."

***

The following morning Sergeant Morgan and Captain Hywel-Jones set off for the Huyton district of Liverpool. They hadn't contacted Margaret Frost in advance because they didn't want to alert her. They wanted her responses to their questions to be unrehearsed. They planned to make it appear as though they just happened to be in the neighbourhood and being interested in the welfare of regimental personnel they were taking the opportunity to drop in on her for an informal chat.

Before the Captain reached the Frosts' front door Margaret opened it. Her face was pale. She looked terrified.

"What's happened to our Michael? Is he alright? Where…"

"Please, Mrs Frost, there's nothing to worry about," interrupted the Captain. "Let me introduce myself." Captain Hywel-Jones introduced himself and Sergeant Morgan and mentioned that they were in the area and thought it a good idea to take the opportunity to drop in on Margaret as they would with the parents of any new recruit.

That's nice, she thought. Once the soldiers were across the threshold Margaret offered tea and biscuits. "I'll make us all a nice cup of tea." Then adding her standard expression, "I'm a bit hard of hearing so you'll have to speak up." This drove Thomas and Queen Rose crazy. They told Margaret to tell people she was deaf and not 'a bit hard of hearing' as guests invariably ended up repeating themselves because they'd underestimate the extent of her 'hard of hearingness'.

"Mrs Frost," began Captain Hywel-Jones.

"Call me Margaret."

"Margaret, you have nothing to worry about with Michael. He's getting on extremely well and already proving himself to be a good soldier. I thought we'd take this opportunity to find out a little more about your son, so…"

"I know what you're going to say. He's a bit… strange… no, that's not the word for it, but you know what I mean. He's a good boy and there's nothing wrong with him. He wouldn't hurt a fly." Which wasn't the best compliment Margaret could've paid Michael, he was in the Army after all.

"I wouldn't say Michael was strange, I would say that he has some special talents and I was wondering where he might have acquired them. I understand from his file that he was a very good student and passed his exams in foreign languages with very high marks."

"Oh, you're not going to send him to some foreign place just because he can speak foreign languages, are you?"

"Mrs Frost, Margaret, I can't tell you one way or the other where your son will be posted during his Army service but I can tell you that speaking a foreign language might mean he could be selected for special duties. For example, in one of the Army's intelligence units. He'd be tucked up nice and safe behind a desk so nothing to worry about there," said the Captain wanting to calm Margaret's concerns even if it meant bending the truth.

Margaret liked the idea of Michael having a desk job. Nobody from the family had ever had a desk job before. *This is real progress,* she thought.

The Captain continued, "So, Margaret, what was Michael like as a child? Did he read much, for example?" Margaret went on to speak for nearly two hours non-stop about Michael's childhood giving them an insight into his upbringing and the challenges they both faced. They were very interested in hearing that he didn't speak until he was over three years old and how ill he'd been with whooping cough and how 'his nana saved his life by getting him to breathe in the hot tar fumes'.

At the mention of Michael being subjected to this old wives' cure treatment the two soldiers looked at one another thinking the same thing: "Poor sod, but that explains why he runs out of oomph during physical exercise." Margaret mentioned Michael's boxing, fencing, karate and 'stuff' and that she didn't like him fighting and that she'd told Sergeant Huggard that he wasn't to speak with Michael about him becoming a boxer.

From what his mother told them, nothing jumped out as to how Michael had acquired his knowledge of military strategy. "Did your son read much when he was at home? Did he have any hobbies?"

"He was too busy to have hobbies. He was always studying for exams or doing homework or reading books from the library. I didn't understand half of what he read but some of his books are in the cabinet over there," said Margaret pointing to a classic 1960's drop-front brown faux-wood bureaux with cupboards beneath.

"May I see your son's books?"

"Help yourself, I'll go and make us another pot of tea. Sandwiches?" With Margaret out of the room the Captain opened the cupboard doors to find both sets of shelves crammed full of books plus pads of notes on lined paper. There were a great many foreign language books and magazines, all well annotated. At the back of the shelves were books on fencing, boxing and… bingo… military strategy.

There weren't actually a great many books on military strategy there but it was clear from Michael's notes that he'd borrowed many books from lending libraries and there were foot and margin notes in the books he did have. In front of them was the proof they were looking for but how had he absorbed all this information and then applied it? One book was particularly heavily annotated: *The Art of War* by Sun Tzu, a high-ranking Chinese general. Another book of interest was the *Book of Five Rings* by Miyamoto Musashi, a Japanese sword master and ultimate deadly duellist with both the longsword and the katana. It was evident from his notes that Michael had heavily researched matters relating to things he had no experience of but he was then able to apply his research in the real world.

Captain Hywel-Jones had been right to make the call he'd made and now he had to secure agreement on Michael's future path. "I've just noticed the time and I'm afraid we'll have to be making our way back to Altcar now. Do you have any message for your son that you'd like to give us for him?"

"Thanks, that would be great." After waiting while Margaret wrote out a four-line message the two soldiers made ready to leave.

"There's one other thing before we go," said Sergeant Morgan. "It's hard to explain but does Michael have trouble with… waiting for things to happen, like Christmas?"

"I know what you're talking about. He's always been the same. As soon as one thing arrives then he's fidgety and looking forward to the next thing. We got used to his behaviour and so we wouldn't talk about what was going to happen. That seemed to calm him down. He's a lot better now but he still gets ahead of himself sometimes and doesn't understand when people aren't looking forward with him. Sorry, it's hard to explain, you have to see it to understand."

"I think I know what you're talking about, he was a bit like that the other day while taking part in a tank exercise where he had to coordinate with other tanks in the battle group and found it difficult."

"Exactly, exactly," exclaimed Margaret without really knowing what the Sergeant was talking about, "that's why he's no good at football or rugby. His head's in the bloody clouds at times." She knew what she meant but nobody else did.

***

Back at Altcar, Captain Hywel-Jones gave Michael the letter from his mum. It didn't say much, just the usual "I hope you are alright and you are keeping well and you are having a good time and you are making some nice friends…" etcetera. The normal stuff mums write to the Army sons they're missing. It's hard to write what you really want to say because you don't want to upset the recipient by pouring out your heart and telling them what's really on your mind and how much you want them to leave the Army and come home, which is exactly what Margaret wanted to write and why she could only write four lines. Oh how she missed her ears; the other two children weren't as conscientious as Michael at being Margaret's ears.

After handing the note to Michael, Captain Hywel-Jones told him to report to him after lunch the following day for his officer's review. In the meantime he contacted his Counsellor to get approval to fast track him.

***

The following morning Michael felt as though he had a worm in his brain while waiting for his officer's review.

"What's up with you, Private Frost?" asked an NCO reviewing the tank skirmish exercises Michael and thirty-five others were participating in, "You're separated from the rest of the battle group again. I'm going to have to write you up for this one, it's just too much. It beats me how you can be so good at some things and, quite honestly, so shit at other things. Are you feeling okay?"

"Sorry, Corporal. I can't get my mind off seeing the Captain after lunch. I wish I could have seen him yesterday after he'd been to see my mum."

"Been to see your mum? How did that come about?"

"I don't know. I didn't know he was going." The Corporal put two and two together and got five. He surmised that Michael was getting booted out of the regiment and the Captain had been to his home to prepare his mum. He felt sorry for him as the early days in the Army can be difficult for recruits away from home for the first time.

"I see, well, no need to mention this morning's... what shall we call it?... misunderstandings to the Captain. Eh? I'm sure it'll all be okay." Then thinking, *He's got enough on his plate and doesn't need me to drop him in it. Pity really, he's a nice lad and a great little boxer. Fingers crossed he'll be okay.*

His officer's review with Captain Hywel-Jones only lasted ten minutes. During it, his only concern was when Michael was involved in team exercises. Then, as an aside, the Captain mentioned he was going to be in charge of cadet exercises over the summer and a briefer mention that he was putting him forward for Royal Marines commandos selection the following January, but he had to keep that confidential. This meant he'd have January's RMC selection on his mind for the next six months and in the interim he'd have to perform as a soldier in charge of cadets over the six weeks of Altcar summer camps and then deal with a four-month posting prior to selection. It was make or break time for Private Frost as far as the Captain was concerned. He couldn't risk recruiting him into his little renegade band of fifth columnists to fight the Organisation from within if he was mentally unreliable. If he made it then he would enter the next phase of induction. If he didn't, he would be cut loose and left to his own devices, remaining unaware of the Organisation and how close he'd come to a life-changing event.

"How'd you get on with the Captain?" asked the Corporal.

"I'm going to be in charge of the cadets over the summer camps."

I know what their game is, thought the Corporal. In his mind he wrongly assumed Michael was being set up to fail so his discharge from the Army wouldn't reflect badly on those who'd recruited him. "Well done Private Frost, that shows the Captain has confidence in you," he lied, "I'll act as your observer and be the responsible NCO for reviews and live firing exercises."

"Thank you, Corporal Welsh, that would be great." This interaction was observed and overheard by Sergeant Morgan who reported it to Captain Hywel-Jones.

"Keep an eye on things, Sergeant. I don't know why Corporal Welsh is involving himself in this but we need to find out. Be careful not to do anything to arouse suspicion. A dead cadet playing with Thunderflashes is one thing but the death of a soldier in the same camp will be an altogether different matter. Look into Welsh's background, discretely of course, and if anything suspicious turns up we'll deal with him."

Henceforth, anybody getting close, or even trying to get close, to Michael would come under scrutiny. If he passed the challenges he was to be set over the coming months he would be advanced onto the next stage of the register. From now on, just being around Michael was going to be a very dangerous place to be.

***

Overhearing things, as Sergeant Morgan had, can be very useful. Imagine, though, a world where you never, or seldom, overhear anything. How much poorer your understanding of just about everything would be if that were the case. Now imagine a world where talking manifests itself as an indistinct cacophony and the louder the talking the less is heard. Add to all this an absence of alternate communication channels, a lack of education because your schooling was interrupted by the war, abject poverty preventing you from accessing help and an attitude of denial, defiance and independence. There you have Margaret and there you have the environment Michael Frost grew up in. Communication was limited in the Frost household and was the main reason behind Michael's unexpansive conversation style. Giving talks, such as Red on Blue stratagems, however, is an entirely different matter and Michael becomes totally uninhibited in sharing the knowledge he has inside his head. He'd learned to be careful with his sharing over the years. Regurgitating information, uncensored and uncontrolled, had pushed some people away from him. From his earliest times he'd learned that sharing information, especially about his visions, resulted in legs slapped red. As far as Michael was concerned, communicating just for the sake of it was a bad thing.

Though overhearing is an everyday part of communication it's important not to solely rely on it or place disproportionate emphasis on it, which was Sergeant Morgan's mistake. Looking into the background of Corporal Welsh while observing the interactions between him and Private Frost took up a lot of his time during the Altcar summer camps of 1970. But it wasn't a total waste of time as Sergeant Morgan got a front row seat to observe the developing talents of Michael Frost and he got to see what an asset to the Royal Tank Regiment Corporal Welsh was, which was a good outcome for him.

***

In four days' time the first of the Altcar summer camps would commence. As usual, most of the soldiers stationed at Altcar were either temporarily posted elsewhere or assigned Cadet camp duties.

In the lead-up to the first camp Michael was noticeably agitated which was exactly what Captain Hywel-Jones thought might be the case. Also, an inexperienced, newly commissioned Lieutenant who was unsure about his future in the Army was assigned to oversee the exercises Michael would be running.

The first meeting between Lieutenant Hunt and Private Frost was awkward because one of them didn't want to be there and the other had things on his mind.

***

Not understanding what was required of him, Lieutenant Hunt asked Corporal Welsh to assemble the cadets and ordered Michael to fall in with them. Classic military: when in doubt, fall back on your training to pull yourself out of a hole. Consequently the Lieutenant assumed control and started giving out orders left, right and centre in an effort to demonstrate that he was in charge.

"Excuse me, Lieutenant Hunt, sir," whispered Corporal Welsh, "Private Frost is in charge of running the exercise, I'm the observer and my role is to report on the outcome of the exercise and you're responsible for providing guidance should it be requested… Sir."

"Of course, Corporal, I was just setting things up," stuttered the Lieutenant. "Erm… carry on, Private Frost."

"Thank you, sir," said Michael as he moved from the ranks to stand facing the two ranks of cadets. "Squad!" Thump of feet. "Squaaaaad… 'shun." Thump, thump. "Squaaaaad… stand aaaat… ease." Thump. "Stand easy." Shuffling sounds. "This morning's exercise is a group de-tank into holding a defensive position as described on the blackboard behind you. Don't look, you'll be told when to look," shouted Michael. "I'll go over the exercise with you and then you'll take up your positions. This is a Blue only exercise so no vests are required. Right, everybody gather round the blackboard."

Michael went over the basics of de-tanking and the taking up of defensive positions. A simple exercise and one he'd done dozens of times before. He was focusing on the job in hand with all his thoughts and anxieties about the future pushed from his mind. This didn't go unnoticed by Sergeant Morgan.

After the exercise the cadets got together for a review, identifying what went well and what needed working on. Usual stuff. They got the basics right which was the important thing. However, they got into a bit of disarray when certain scenarios were played out; for example, cadets being removed from the exercise to play dead thus leaving gaps on flanks. Overall the Corporal gave a favourable review but warned them that things were going to get tougher. Classic Army behaviour so you don't get complacent and to get you geed up for what lies ahead

To the surprise of Corporal Welsh, the Lieutenant wanted 'hands-on' involvement in the exercises but he obviously couldn't take orders from subordinates. This was risky for the Lieutenant as the Army frowns on such arrangements. It regards them as symptomatic of weak leadership. In the Army's view the Lieutenant had been stuffed full of leadership at Sandhurst and he should be exercising it.

Between them, they agreed Lieutenant Hunt would act as an additional observer and provide feedback direct to cadets. To make things interesting, Lieutenant Hunt and Michael held separate briefings to the Red and Blue teams and then switched over after each exercise and re-ran it using alternate strategies. This proved to be fun for the cadets and stimulating for the Lieutenant, the Corporal and Michael. By the end of the Altcar summer camps they were working together as a close-knit team, holding twice-daily sessions where they decided how they were next going to stretch the eager cadets who especially loved the interregimental competitive elements of the exercises. Happily, the Lieutenant was actually enjoying being in the Army and thought he might have found his niche.

***

Time flies by and in a blink of an eye for people who are busy. The Altcar summer camps were over. Sergeant Morgan delivered his report to Captain Hywel-Jones in which he concluded there were no security risks in the relationships around Private Frost.

"It appears Private Frost brings out the best in people according to your report, Sergeant. Your early comments about Lieutenant Hunt were quite disturbing but it seems he undertook a proper leadership role toward the end of camp."

"Yes sir, and it seems he was impressed with Private Frost's knowledge of military strategies. I believe he found his company quite stimulating. He's certainly a very different character to the one who walked in here six weeks ago."

"Yes, quite, his father was concerned that he wasn't really fitting into the Army way of life and so pulled a few strings to get him here so I could have a good look at him. I think he's turned a corner and I've told his father that there's now a good chance his son will make a decent officer. As for Private Frost, I don't want to put the mockers on it but I think we've cracked it. He absolutely thrives on pressure and being fully occupied. Could it be that simple? It seems that when he doesn't have a second to think about future events he focuses on the here and now. I wonder how he'll get on during the next four months before RMC selection?" The Captain paused to retrieve some documents. "I've decided to send him to Germany to join the Seventh Armoured Division. We have some of our people there to keep an eye on his development. I don't intend telling them about Private Frost's interesting way of dealing with events and see if they notice anything unusual about him. For him, this posting will be a mixture of being bored out of his mind to being stretched every which way during the upcoming war games. There's a big exercise being run in November by our American cousins which will, no doubt, be the usual cock-up. Tell Private Frost I want to see him please, Sergeant."

"Sir, Sergeant Morgan said you wanted to see me?"

"Yes, Private Frost, come in, stand to attention. You did quite well during the summer camps though I got the impression you were coasting towards the end. That simply won't do, Private Frost. The Army has high expectations of you, as do I, and any slacking off is frowned upon. Do I make myself clear?"

"Yes sir," replied a confused Private Frost.

"You relied too heavily on involving others in things you were responsible for. Do you know what I'm referring to, Private Frost?"

"No sir."

"You formed a cosy little triumvirate with Corporal Welsh and Lieutenant Hunt. Didn't you?"

"Sir, I can't give orders to a superior rank and the Lieutenant wanted greater involvement and I... I... I don't know, sir, I didn't know what to do so I went along with it. I didn't see the harm."

"You went along with it. You didn't see the harm. Exactly. Private Frost, you were under my direct orders to run the exercises with the cadets. You were to be the soldier responsible so I could assess your leadership capabilities. Do you understand?" Before Michael could answer the Captain held up his hand to silence him. "You were not ordered to form a cosy little mothers' club and have nice little tea parties with Lieutenant Hunt and Corporal Welsh. How am I to assess your progress if you abdicate your responsibilities? You've wasted six weeks of my time as far as I'm concerned so now I'm left with no other choice than to have you transferred to the Seventh Armoured Division of the British Army of the Rhine. You'll remain on duty there until RMC selection in January. In future, Private Frost, when an officer gives you an order and that order is countermanded by another officer you're to report that to the original officer. Do you understand? You may answer."

"Yes sir."

"You know, Private Frost, you need to appreciate what a tremendous opportunity you're being handed here. Grasp your opportunities with both hands, Private Frost. You leave for Germany in three days' time and until then you'll remain on camp. Dismissed."

Interesting, thought Captain Hywel-Jones, *no reaction whatsoever, no matter how I spoke to him there was no outward sign of the impact of anything I said. It's as though it's all just words to him. Interesting.* Sergeant Morgan returned to the room.

"Sir."

"Sergeant, have you noticed how Private Frost is a man of very few words unless he's… lecturing? That's the only word I can think for it. He's a totally different person when relying on whatever is inside his head and not inside his heart. Another thing for me to consider in the world of Michael Frost, I suppose. I hope he turns out to be worth all the effort I'm making for him."

"If you don't mind me saying so, sir, you're putting your head well and truly on the block for that boy."

"Sergeant, you have to take some risks in life and the bigger the risks then often the bigger the rewards. But thank you for your concern. Carry on."

THE TRIPLER

The war games were only a couple of months away. Madame Chairman had finalised the plan for the heist and the tripler was acting as go-between with the American and Russian splinters. Knowledge of her connection with the latter being a surprise to her. She knew her erstwhile co-assignmentee to be a doubler but now suspected her of being a tripler.

The tripler reported on the respective positions of the Russian and American splinters. She told Madame Chairman they'd offered to lend a hand with the heist, if requested, but only on the basis of 'utilisation of disposable assets'. Madame Chairman found the tripler's use of English grating at times.

The money part of the plan was straightforward. The Americans and the Soviets originally wanted twenty percent of the proceeds each in consideration of their non-interference. Their percentage was negotiated down to fifteen percent on the basis that the Organisation would cut them both in as partners on future revenue streams, which there always were when dealing with the Organisation or its splinters because that was how they operated. Once a government body or large corporation was involved with the Organisation, or its splinters, it would be colonised by more and more of its people, often as consultants, especially during the early stages of the relationship. Classic Organisation: parasite and host, but mostly parasite.

***

VVG was holding up quite well, especially so after his CIA handler had told him that he wasn't on the KGB's list. She 'knew about these things' according to her. She was in fact invariably right about such matters as she had doubler insiders just about everywhere, including the Organisation, all the way up to a seat on Madame Chairman's secret inner council. Third hand, not direct.

A splinter conversation

"It's decided. The heist is set for the penultimate day of the war games as there'll be a great deal of military traffic on the roads to mix with to conceal them during the inevitable search."

"Who will be involved?"

"A list is to be provided at the next meeting. She plans to use all British personnel. She says that it's not that she doesn't trust their German brothers and sisters, it was just the way the team was chosen."

"I'll leak that to my German contacts in case they don't know already."

"I suggest you don't do that. If the German operation knows already then it'll blow up in your face and if they don't then Madame Chairman will know she has a leak at the top table."

"Then why are you telling me this?"

"I'm keeping you informed, that's the way things work. Something that you might be able to help with though is the British listening post. If they stumble across anything concerning theeee… erm… job… it might prove useful to you. You might be able intercept the missiles before they are spirited out of the country."

"Okay, I'll see what we can do. Let me know if anything changes. I'll assign LeFort to the British, just in case."

"LeFort? Really? Are you sure about that? He's got fingers in too many pies and is only interested in himself."

"Do you know anybody else like that?"

"Very funny. I'll keep in touch."

***

The missile heist team had been chosen months earlier and was already ensconced in Germany. Madame Chairman had no intention of keeping the Germans away from the party. It would be rude not to invite them as it was being held in their back yard. She was keeping the timing of the heist flexible and spreading disinformation to see where it turned up as she was convinced she had a leak in her secret inner council; perhaps two. The German and UK operational units of the Organisation traditionally got on particularly well together. Historically, the only thing they disagreed about was the 1966 World Cup final and the ball that either did or did not cross the line.

***

In the final weeks, the tripler kept especially close to VVG in case he got the jitters. Which he did of course just about every other day. He flip-flopped between confessing all to his bosses and hope for mercy to running away to Israel. With a surname ending in vich he was certain he'd be given a warm welcome in Tel Aviv. Mostly she just rode the storm of his panic attacks until they blew themselves out. Occasionally she'd say to him that if he didn't stop his whining she'd send an easy-to-intercept message back home naming him as her property. This threat usually kept VVG quiet, for a few days at least.

She was keeping a watchful eye on more than just VVG. She was constantly monitoring progress of the plan, wanting to know how it was coming along and whether there'd been any changes.

Madame Chairman was puzzled to understand what was in it for her to run the risks she was running. She'd posed her this question in several different ways and had always got the same response. She said she was an American patriot doing the best she could for her country. She thought the Russians to be dangerous, unpredictable gangsters who had the upper hand in the arms race and she wanted to level the playing field.

"And you're doing yourself some good at the same time, right?"

"Right. There's no such thing as altruism, if it ever existed in the first place." Madame Chairman weighed the risks and decided to trust her and go ahead with the heist.

Madame Chairman did not totally swallow the tripler's story, though she knew of other Americans who felt the same way as the tripler felt. Being snared by the Organisation's methods is not the only way of instilling loyalty. She'd keep a close watch on events as they unfolded and if she saw something she didn't like she'd press the red button, stop everything and bring her people home. How prepared she was to do that she wasn't sure as more than anything she wanted the heist to be a success to prove her worth in the Organisation and show everybody she deserved to be Madame Chairman. She still wasn't comfortable in the role. Perhaps her inner voice was right, perhaps she was being set up to fail as some kind of plot by… whom? By whom? Why put her where she is in order for her to fail? If that were the case then it could only be the Mandarins. *But what if they…* She had to stop thinking this way and get on with the job.

By late September the pieces were in place and all everybody had to do was wait for time to take care of everything as it always seems to. Let things alone and don't attract attention. Just wait. The trap was set and the key was to spring it at the right time. The one thing they were short of was fluent Russian speakers. The Russian splinter offered to help out and were put on standby. It would be difficult sneaking Russians into the listening post or relaying them information, with the danger that if you were caught doing either you'd go to jail for a very long time. The immediate answer was to get Russian-speaking operatives seconded to MI3, and quickly.

***

As Michael waited to make his way to BAOR HQ at Bielefeld, the storm clouds of fate were gathering above him.

WAR GAMES

The military transport landed at Bielefeld Flughafen with Michael's final destination being the HQ of the First Division of the British Army of the Rhine [BAOR] Bielefeld. A long way from Soltau where the Seventh Armoured Brigade were based. At the last minute, Captain Hywel-Jones decided to post Michael to an HQ unit to isolate him from soldiers he could come into conflict with in the near future. He didn't want him to have any confusion as to where his loyalties lay.

Michael got assigned to basic administrative duties where he was able to utilise his German and, to a lesser degree, Russian language skills which, once their depth became known, attracted the attention of MI3 who quickly snapped him up. He noticed how everybody in MI3 referred to themselves and others as chaps.

This unexpected development concerned Captain Hywel-Jones. He'd underestimated Michael's language skills and now the spooks had him. Damn. He knew he was in deep trouble as he waited for the call telling him how much trouble he was in. If he lost Michael to Military Intelligence that would be a huge blunder on his part. He'd have to give some serious thought to how he could put a spin on the situation otherwise the last three and a half years he'd spent infiltrating the Organisation would have been for nothing.

***

Michael was assigned to the Russian desk of Military Intelligence Liaison – Russia (MIL[R]), who were responsible for monitoring Soviet activities along the whole of the East/West border. This elite group within MI3 were impressed by him after he cracked an encrypted message in his head because, "I had some time on my hands." They'd tried without success for four days to crack it.

The cipher had characteristics which MIL[R] was looking out for. The fact that this young man had cracked a bespoke cipher was noteworthy, they thought. "Noteworthy? Noteworthy? It's bloody astonishing. Give him more of the same to do." Which they did. After forty-eight hours, no similar ciphers were received. They'd been replaced by a broadcast cipher, the origins and nature of which eluded them. It was as though the sender knew the cipher had been cracked and had changed the method.

Michael became immersed in his cipher-cracking duties. As he became more and more involved he became lost in his own thoughts and weeks drifted by. This dream-like state continued until mid-October, just prior to the start of the American-led war games.

***

People nowadays think in terms of MI5 and MI6 when they think of British Secret Service organisations but those establishments were brought about over decades through the amalgamation of dozens of specialist MI units whose origins stretch back to the middle part of the nineteenth century.

***

The call Captain Hywel-Jones was expecting finally came when he was home on weekend leave. Since he now had no family, they knew he would be home alone.

"It's me."

"I'm okay to…"

"I know. I believe congratulations are in order. That was a master stroke placing Frost in Bielefeld; MILR took to him hook, line and sinker. Well done. How did you know that getting him recruited by MI fits perfectly with what I have planned for him?" The caller took credit for Michael's MIL[R] placement, taking him one step nearer to filling his quota of Russian speakers for the listening post.

"To be perfectly honest, I didn't but after he arrived at BAOR I thought it best he work for an MI unit for obvious reasons. Having that type of background will work well for us in the future. It might even get him inside MI6."

"Good thinking, if a little risky, but no risk no reward, eh?" replied the phone voice not totally convinced by the Captain's answer.

"Quite." He needed to change the subject in case he tripped himself up. "As an aside, something I've been meaning to ask: why do we use the ABCD list designations? They seem a little simplistic."

"They're meant to be. On the one hand, those carrying out reviews can easily understand the status of those on the lists and, on the other, ABCD designations are used by MI units around the world. We're playing the old imitation game. In the event that somebody comes across our lists, they will assume we're from MI6 or whoever and in their moment of uncertainty we can disappear. It's happened before and it'll happen again the next time somebody trips over us." The Counsellor was enjoying the sound of his own voice and so lectured for ten minutes before getting back to business. "I'm planning on removing your sleeper status. With your background it won't look odd when MI recruit you, after you're placed in the right area that is. And you will be placed in the right area and the right people will know to watch out for you. You understand what I mean, don't you, Gareth?"

On the other hand you could be feeding me disinformation to see where it turns up, thought Captain Hywel-Jones. "I do indeed. I expect I'll be hearing more from you soonish then?"

"Yes, all in good time. For the time being, get close to your primary targets and study the briefs you'll be receiving on Germany and Northern Ireland. I'm not 100% certain where you'll be placed as we've had a few unfortunate losses recently. Once again, well done on getting Frost on the MI ladder, I'm sure that will look good on his record when we move him fully into our world." The phone line went dead.

It was obvious to the Captain that the Organisation was testing him to check how trustworthy he was; checking to see if the information he'd just received turned up where it shouldn't. As for the voice on the phone telling him that he had plans for Michael, that was a big surprise. *What could they possibly have in store for somebody who isn't even fully on-board yet?* he thought. As he had his thought he believed that whatever it was it wouldn't be good news for Michael. A feeling of guilt ran through him. He could have reported Michael's oddness during list reviews. Deep down he felt Michael simply wasn't equipped to deal with the world of the Organisation. He was keeping quiet about Michael for his own purposes. He felt sickened and ashamed of himself.

***

Captain Hywel-Jones was at a loss to guess just who it was had made plans for Michael. As far as he could tell, Michael wasn't so special and besides, the Organisation had lots of people they could use for just about any task he could think of. He wouldn't have had to look far for the reason why Michael was about to be put in harm's way. He really shouldn't have spoken to Major Finn about Tommy Munroe's death. An Organisation conversation was had and the outcome was not favourable for Private Frost.

***

An increasing frequency of bespoke messages were being intercepted by MIL[R] as though they were reaching some kind of conclusion. Even when parts of messages were decoded they didn't make sense. MIL[R] was confident that its decoding was correct which could only mean they were missing a part of the conversation. Going by the decrypted sections of the messages it appeared that somebody or something was going to be coming over from the East and they were expecting… expecting what? What were they expecting? To be met? To be… they were guessing and the more they guessed the more confusing, bizarre and unlikely their guesses became.

***

When the war games started, Michael's assignment at MIL[R] came to a temporary close and he moved into a role performing translation for the chiefs of staff. Who'd have thought that this little lad from the slums of Liverpool's docklands would end up in the big boys' tent? His posting was nothing to do with chance.

***

The site for the war games was just north east of Göttingen, between the American base at Bad Herzfeld and BAOR HQ Bielefeld. This location was right next to the border with East Germany so the Russians could have a good look at what was going on. It was all a big game. It was a chance to show the Russkies just how much trouble they'd be in if they ever crossed the border to invade West Germany. The Russians though were ambivalent about such events as they knew that NATO's forces were no match for them.

During the Cold War, had the forces of East and West

come into conflict, the Americans and their allies would've been slaughtered due to the sheer weight of numbers of men and armaments the Soviet Union could pour into a theatre of war in the blink of an eye. The forces of the West were a very poor second to the forces of the Soviet Union at the time. NATO needed something to help even things up. A missile heist perhaps.

***

While working for the war games chiefs of staff, Michael became an integral part of the translation group. His language skills had improved enormously since his posting and now he was working alongside native Italian speakers. His French was already excellent so he picked up Italian very quickly. Colleagues were astounded at just how quickly he picked things up. They found it quite creepy though. They didn't dislike Michael but they never sought out his company. Not that he noticed.

During the first eight days of the war games MIL[R] passed copies of the bespoke ciphers to Michael via attaché cases marked 'Top Secret' in red lettering. A note inside one of them said one of the chaps thought he'd identified the other side of the conversation but its origin was proving difficult to tie down. It went on to say that the chaps in MIL[R] were looking forward to welcoming him back as soon as 'those silly games are over'.

***

During a war games chiefs of staff debriefing session, a French Lieutenant made an observation which grated with Michael. The observer gave his report on a scenario outcome of a Red on Blue on White exercise, at the end of which he added an opinion on strategy which Michael fundamentally disagreed with.

The discussion between the Lieutenant and Michael went on for more than a minute when a British General asked, "What's going on? What are you speaking with the Lieutenant about, Private?"

"Sir, the Lieutenant postulated a strategy about the exercise which I cannot agree with."

"Agree with? Surely you mean you're having difficulty in translating?"

"No sir, I can translate what the officer said but what he said I don't agree with and it would not prove useful to explore his thinking." Several officers let out small snorts of derision at Michael's words. "What the Lieutenant said is flawed; the only successful outcomes from similar situations have come from armies prepared to sacrifice the White forces." Michael then provided examples of what he was referring to and stated he could provide more if required.

After whispering something to his assistant the General responded, "Very interesting, Private, but if you could just translate what the Lieutenant says that is all that is required of you."

"Yes sir," replied Michael without harbouring any bad feelings about being put down in the way he had been as things like that just simply didn't register with him.

***

As soon as the debriefing session ended some officers left the room. The majority of those remaining had forgotten what Michael had said but several had not.

"What did you think of that extraordinary outburst by the Private?"

"I wouldn't call it an outburst exactly, he seemed perfectly calm and rational and I found what he said rather interesting and, unless I'm mistaken, entirely accurate."

"But to sacrifice the very people you're supposed to be saving?"

"That wasn't the point the Private was making. He was stating, from a strategic and historical perspective, the outcomes of similar scenarios. He was not saying we should go around sacrificing people willy-nilly. Do you agree, General?"

A German General joined in the conversation. "I do and, as you said, it was rather interesting what the Private had to say. I thought it was uncalled for though. I don't know what he expected to achieve by speaking out in the way he did."

"Are you saying soldiers should not show initiative?" interjected a German Major in almost-accent-less English.

"Not at all, I just think there's a time and a place for that sort of thing and this is not it. I welcome soldiers showing initiative. However, these are war games exercises and the Lieutenant would have learned more had he given his opinion uninterrupted by the Private, then we could have questioned him about his opinions. It wasn't appropriate for a Private to enter into a debate with the Lieutenant, he should simply have translated what he had said without offering an opinion. Don't you agree?"

"I wonder, would we really have taken the time to question the observer about his thoughts on alternate strategies or would we simply have regarded him as a self-promoting upstart? I believe that after his report we would have just warmly thanked him and instantly forgotten about what he'd said; but having the Private comment in the way he did the matter has stuck in our heads. Well, stuck in mine at least."

As the remaining group looked like it was breaking up the officers followed protocol and saluted those who should be saluted and went their separate ways.

An Army conversation

"Where was that Private before he came here?"

"I understand he was seconded from MILR. They've asked if they can have him back after the games."

"Was he with a regiment prior?"

"Yes sir, the First Royal Tank Regiment, sir."

"He's obviously well read on military history. The White sacrifice examples appeared to me to be a blending of Napoleon and Alexander. Unsurprisingly, for a tank soldier, a bit of Monty in there too. Surely he can't be that well read about such things as this at his age? Can he?"

"I could contact his CO for more information, sir? I understand he was allowed entry into the Royal Tank Regiment even though they weren't actually recruiting at the time. He was a cadet with them and so they must have got to know him and thought enough of him to pull a few strings. That's not so unusual, sir. Though, on passing out he didn't actually join the regiment as such, instead he went to Altcar and remained there until his posting to BAOR. Shall I mention anything in particular to his CO at Altcar, sir?"

"No, just ask for background. It seems this Private leads a bit of a charmed life and I'd like to understand why. Keep him on translation duties but emphasise to him that he's only to translate and not anything else. Keep me posted on what you get back from his CO. Carry on."

"Yes sir."

The junior officer was however already intimately familiar with Private Frost's background. Through his Counsellor he'd been advised about Michael's posting in advance. He fed his Counsellor information about the translation incident, which was passed up the line until it got to a point where the lines crossed and was fed down another line to end up with Captain Hywel-Jones's Counsellor and then the Captain himself. This wasn't such an unusual occurrence as hundreds of messages were transmitted hundreds of times a day all across the globe. It was a totally manual system, ripe for improvement when the computer age arrived. The system then though was clunky but simple and effective, though hardly Stalinesque. There aren't many layers in the Organisation so it's easy to keep tabs on situations such as

Private Frost's posting and what happens during them. Several parties were now keeping tabs on Michael.

***

An Organisation conversation

"It's me, I want to talk about Private Frost's most recent incident. Have you had time to consider his next move? Or perhaps I should say your next move? I am extremely nervous about this odd fellow. I was against bringing him in at the start but I was persuaded to act otherwise. I should have followed my instincts. It seems he simply doesn't have anything between his brain and his mouth. Unless you're able to provide me with a good reason why I should keep him on I will cut him loose. He'll be none the wiser about us, particularly after you move on, which I have to tell you is imminent."

"I think we should persist with him until after RMC selection."

Hmm, we could send him to Northern Ireland if it all goes wrong. All sorts of things can happen to a stupid soldier over there, he thought. "Okay, fine, I'll give him until RMC selection and see how he is then."

"I understand MILR want him back when the war games are over. When it's time for RMC selection I'll refuse any requests for the secondment to continue." Captain Hywel-Jones paused to check consent, but typically the voice remained silent. "I'm thinking of allowing him some home leave at Christmas. That will help act as a natural break. Will you support me?"

"I wouldn't go so far as to say I support you. Once he goes for RMC selection then there's no turning back. He either makes it or we cut him loose," said the voice while his head said, *I'll send him to Northern Ireland and deal with him there.* As usual, the call ended without goodbyes.

Following this conversation, Captain Hywel-Jones once

again felt guilty about keeping quiet over his concerns about Michael. He was putting his needs foremost without any regard for Michael's safety or wellbeing. He should cut him loose now and let him get on with his Army life. *It could be a good life for him,* he thought. Despite his misgivings he'd convinced the phone voice to keep faith with Michael and review the situation after the outcome of RMC selection. He hated himself at times but he hated the Organisation more.

***

An Organisation conversation

"I've just had a conversation with Hywel-Jones. He's so slippery. What's with him and that boy Frost?"

"I'm certain he's a doubler."

"There's no doubt about it in my mind. Why are you so keen though to see the boy come to harm? Northern Ireland is a brutal place to send anybody."

"He's wrong for us and he knows too much."

"What does he know?"

"He knows his friend was murdered at Altcar. He said as much to me and now this in Germany. I'm certain MI3 are looking into him."

"MI3? Rubbish. What else is there about him you don't like?"

"He seems to be protected beyond his worth. LeFort once said…"

"And there we have it. It's the old LeFort thing again. That vendetta is more likely to be the end of you than him."

"It's nothing to do with…"

"Don't waste your breath. We've already agreed on Frost. He'll go to Northern Ireland when the time is right. There are one or two there who'll share his fate. I'm late for my next meeting. Goodbye." His next meeting was with his barber.

***

Before the end of the war games the attaché cases from MIL[R] stopped. Going by the contents of the last attaché case they were no nearer to solving the puzzle than when he'd left to join the war games. Hopefully he'd be able to return to MIL[R] soon and resume his duties with them. Unusually, he crossed his fingers at that thought.

CRACKING THE CODE

An Organisation and splinter conversation

"Is it all set?"

"Yes."

"Are there any changes to the plan?"

"None."

"Good. Do you have enough people or do you need me to find you some?"

"We have enough. A couple more Russian speakers are going to be joining us."

"When will you do it?"

"Soon. Perhaps within the next forty-eight to ninety-six hours."

"I see. Still don't trust me?"

"I always say that if you don't need to know then you won't be told and if you don't want somebody to know something then you don't tell them. It's for your own good. You know that."

"Are they under orders to use maximum prejudice if necessary?"

"You mean: are they under orders to kill if necessary." She hated the way her erstwhile co-assignmentee abused the English language at times. "Yes they are but we're going to try and avoid that possibility at all costs. It's bad enough that we're going to steal the property of the peoples of the Soviet Union without killing its citizens into the bargain."

"Hopefully it won't come to that. Vladimir is taking some time away from work as he's not holding up too well. If he gets any worse I'm sure he'll have a heart attack."

"I hope not. That sort of thing is bad for business. You must do all you can to ensure that everything goes smoothly with Mr Grigorovich and he gets to spend his autumn years soaking up the Californian sunshine. If he's sanctioned that will turn others against us all."

"I'll do my best to make sure that he remains in the land of the living."

***

A sealed order arrived for Michael to report to a forward operational unit. When he arrived he recognised Major Finn and the French Captain. They ignored him and he did likewise in return. Following a conversation between another man and the French Captain he left without acknowledging Michael, who didn't think his behaviour strange as he'd acted similarly in the past.

"Sit down, all of you. Some of you don't know yet why you're here. Let me explain. We're going to be carrying out an exercise involving forces disguised as Soviet soldiers. The exercise is designed to test our ability to carry out espionage on Soviet hardware. We'll be operating close to the border with East Germany and, no doubt, the Soviets will be observing how well we do so I want you all to do your utmost to make sure this exercise is a complete success. I hand you over to Major Finn, he'll give you the details of the mission and the parts you'll play in it. Major Finn."

"Thank you, General. First things first, do not discuss this operation with anybody. Not even your COs. Secrecy is paramount in order to maintain the element of surprise. Please note that once the mission has commenced everybody will stay in character, including the men playing the parts of the Soviet forces. To add an element of realism, live ammunition will be issued as once we have relieved the Soviets of their hardware we may have to fight off marauders who might try to relieve us of our prize." Those in the know thought all this dramatic scene-setting ridiculous. Had they understood the circumstances of several of the actors they would not have held that opinion. After going over the plan twice, Major Finn split the men into four groups with each unit assigned a leader who took them through their roles in the ambush. The word ambush had substituted exercise. Following the briefing everybody dispersed after being told where and when to rendezvous. Sealed orders were distributed to some to get them out of their normal duties on the day.

***

The war games were almost over. They were widely regarded as a great success and hadn't been the total cock-up everybody feared they would be with the Americans in charge. Arriving back at MIL[R] Michael walked into his office, sat at his desk and picked up where he'd left off without missing a beat. In his mind it was as though he'd never been away.

His colleagues were extremely glad to have him back as there'd been a significant increase in Soviet activity since the start of the war games. They knew their communications would be heavily monitored and so took the opportunity to send lightly obfuscated highly offensive messages about the allied forces. The majority of the crudest messages were transmitted in plain English, German and even Russian. Many of the messages were quite humorous. All messages were routinely copied between staffs to assist in identifying their originators. These unnecessary communications were bread and butter for MIL[R] as they helped them enormously in the decoding of confidential messages as they got to know the habits, phrases, cadence and idioms used by the people originating the coded messages. All intelligence is useful no matter how insignificant somebody believes their lapses in security to be.

***

The moment Michael sat down, Ronald pointed out to him that Clifford had gone on leave at short notice a week previous. "Something to do with a family emergency or so Victor said."

No wonder the attaché cases stopped, thought Michael. It was all bad timing as far as the rest of MIL[R] was concerned as they were so very busy with all the Soviet chatter to contend with. Following Clifford's departure the East/West conversation had gone into overdrive but had stopped altogether yesterday. They'd planned a review session to go over what they'd learned about the East/West conversation but it was called off by Victor who said MI3 were now running with it. Since that morning there'd been nothing whatsoever from the Soviet side of the fence. Something was going on.

***

Michael made ready to travel to his rendezvous point. He gave his NCO the sealed orders he'd been provided with to allow him to travel and off he went. He left in plenty of time as he had quite some distance to cover and he hated being late.

***

While Michael was on duty at the war games he'd been receiving attaché cases marked 'Top Secret' and containing the latest East/West conversations together with notes from Clifford Coley regarding progress on tracking down the West side of the conversation. The final attaché case Clifford had planned to send him had been intercepted so he never got to know how close Clifford had come to cracking the whole thing wide open.

After working round the clock trying to crack the coded conversation, Clifford Coley had what he thought was a stroke of genius. He took a sequence of words from the East side of the conversation and interspersed them with the words from the West side. In doing so he discovered it wasn't a conversation at all, it was a broadcast. The sender was obviously broadcasting a predetermined coded communication concerning… what? What the hell was it saying? What was it all about? Was it a Russkie joke?

After trying dozens of cipher-cracking sequences it was clear that the words of the two sides of the conversation were some kind of broadcast script. Things started to make sense. The message probably concerned something which had been previously agreed. Several words stuck out; this was all to do with armaments… possibly missiles. So many numbers though. What did they mean? Dates? Locations? Co-ordinates? Words, lines, paragraphs, pages, chapters in a novel? A reference book common to both sides? He had to get help, but where should he go? He'd start with his supervising NCO, Victor. Then at least there'd be more brains on the job as his brain was very tired.

"Are you sure?"

"I'm as certain as I can be, but then again I'm so tired I'm hallucinating so who knows what I'm looking at. That's why I need fresh eyes and more brains on the job. Whatever this is it seems to be coming to completion, a conclusion… finalisation… whatever." Clifford drank from a tall glass of water. It was tepid. "I've been sending Private Frost updates using TS attaché cases, so let's see what he thinks. He's good at this sort of thing, after all it was he who first cracked it before they changed the cipher."

"Maybe we should hold back a bit. You know, get our thinking straight before we go setting hares running. Who else knows about the work you've been doing?"

"Well, nobody really. Except Ronald of course. He got fed up though and stopped a few days ago."

"This all smells like espionage to me. Secret bespoke ciphers, unexplained numbers and the mention of missiles. Maybe the Russkies are planning an attack. After all, at least half of the messages originated in the East but tracking says half of them were transmitted from the West. Our little scribbler might have an accomplice. What do you think?"

"I'm too tired to think. I need some help."

"I agree. Give me what you've got so far and I'll carry on while you get some sleep. I'll wake you if I find anything interesting." Clifford went to his bunk and Victor left the camp to find a public phone.

Two hundred yards outside the main gate was a bar which had a public phone. Victor dialled a long series of numbers, waited for a confirmation tone and then dialled another series of numbers. After receiving his instructions he returned to the camp and got on with tracing the point of origin of the West side of the broadcast. As he was more technical than analytical he managed to obtain a good guesstimate of the location of the transmission. There was only one building in the vicinity that could possibly be the point of origin. After a quick drive out there he was convinced he was on the right track and immediately got back on the phone to his Counsellor.

A splinter conversation

"What do you propose?"

"It's only a matter of time before Coley works things out and if this is what we think it is then there is only one course of action to take."

"Shall I send somebody?"

"Yes. I can't afford to be involved in any way. I'll speak with Coley and suggest he takes a much needed break following his recent exertions. As soon as he's off the base he's yours to deal with. How long before you get somebody here?"

"We already have people close to you. I might send somebody special and take care of LeFort at the same time. I'm certain the Americans and the Organisation are in this together. Call me if the situation changes. My people will let you know when they are ready for Coley. Expect a call within the next four hours."

Victor returned to the MIL[R] offices, which were now deserted. He went through Clifford's files and removed everything connected with the work he'd been doing on the East/West broadcast and placed it all in his own filing cabinets. He was just about to leave the office to wake Clifford when he noticed a TS attaché case pushed under the desk. The address slip was to Private Frost at war games HQ. He opened it and read what Clifford had written about progress on the work he was doing. *Well, that won't do at all,* thought Victor as he tore up the note and placed the TS attaché case back in the rack alongside all the others. *Private Frost will not be receiving any more of these from Private Coley.*

When Victor told Clifford he'd tracked down the source of the West side of the broadcast he was ecstatic with joy. He was not quite so ecstatic however after Victor told him that he'd spoken with MI3 about the intercepts and they'd taken over the case. He said that he was as unhappy about it as Clifford was but there was nothing either of them could do about it. In fact MI3, he told Clifford, were already aware of the broadcasts but thanked him for all his work before confiscating everything and ordering them both not to disclose anything to anybody. Additionally, he said, they were very concerned as to the amount of time Clifford had put in to crack the case and ordered him to take a week's leave. Clifford went into protest mode but Victor said that, reluctantly, he had to agree with MI3 that he needed to take some leave.

"A tired Clifford is not what the service needs" and "after a good rest you can return refreshed and ready to get on with things again".

"When does my leave start?"

"Immediately. They're so concerned about you that they're sending somebody to make sure you obey orders. I'd say you have about an hour to get ready."

"What about Private Frost? I've been keeping him updated on events."

"Don't worry about Private Frost, I'll make sure he's kept informed. I sent him the TS attaché case you had under your desk. I did it before I had my chat with MI3."

"Oh, thanks, Victor, you're a pal. Where will I be leaving from by the way?"

"That all depends on you and where you want to go. If you want to go back home you'll be on the next transport out but if you want to do a bit of travelling and sightseeing in dear old Deutschland then you can be dropped off at a railway station or even driven to your destination if it's close by. Entirely your choice."

As soon as he sat in the rear seat of the taxi he felt a scratch on his leg for which the taxi driver apologised. Seconds later he was passed out cold. The taxi driver looked about before removing a small leather pouch from his jacket pocket. Then, taking two phials of liquid and a syringe, he used the fat hypodermic needle to pierce the top of the first phial and half-filled the syringe. The taxi driver injected Clifford with a new type of sedative followed swiftly by a second injection designed to ensure the experimental drug stabilised in his body. The new drugs combined to put Clifford into a coma which he would only come out of once injected with an antidote drug. The taxi driver propped him up in the corner of the rear seat, holding him in a sitting position with a harness-type seat belt pulled tight across his chest.

Totally comatose, Clifford was driven to an isolated rural building where he was given the antidote injection to bring him round. He was questioned about what he knew of the bespoke coded messages his group had intercepted. He spoke openly about his work on the messages as he didn't really understand very much about them anyway except to say they were a broadcast and not a conversation and he hadn't managed to track down its West side but his supervising NCO, Victor, was looking into it. Or rather he had been looking into it but MI3 had taken over the file and were keeping it to themselves. "Must be big," said Clifford stupidly. "You seem to know a lot about the work I've been doing, you must have a..." He tailed off his talking before he said the word 'spy'.

In the isolated rural building Clifford wasn't being treated badly by his captor. Or rather captors as two others had arrived while he slept. They were eating a rather delicious-smelling meal at a table behind the chair he was tied to. They spoke French most of the time. Clifford's French wasn't bad so he understood most of what was said. He asked them what it was they wanted and told them he was perfectly willing to co-operate fully. He was confident that as he was such a small fish in this pond he would probably be taken and dropped somewhere in the countryside when they were done with him; so, co-operating would get him released most quickly, so he believed. They weren't asking him many questions though. Perhaps they were waiting for somebody else to arrive before the real questioning started. That thought filled him with dread as this inquisitor might be a professional and... he was letting his imagination get the better of him.

That night was very cold so Clifford asked if he could be allowed an extra blanket and perhaps somewhere to lie down as his lower back was seizing up. When he woke the following morning he was lying tied to a cot bed with a couple of blankets and coats over him for warmth but his shoes and socks had been removed. Shortly after breakfast he was jabbed again and that was the last he ever knew. His abductors had misplaced the phial of stabiliser and so, unable to stabilise the sedative, Clifford slipped into a coma. After eventually finding the stabiliser, the men tried to revive him. Over the next couple of days they injected him with various amounts of the sedative followed by the stabiliser and then the antidote. At times he seemed to come round but never quite attained full consciousness. Eventually his heart just gave out. He'd been given too many strong drugs in a short time and it had been too much for his body to take. The kidnappers went into a state of panic. They were supposed to keep hold of Clifford until after the operation had been completed and then drop him off in a country lane for their future use at MIL[R].

The taxi driver drove to a public phone box to make the call to his Counsellor about the mishap with Private Coley. He was ordered to send him back to where he came from.

***

In some woods near a small American camp on the outskirts of Bielefeld a German Shepherd guard dog pulled its handler towards a clump of bushes beyond a slight depression in an open area of ground. When he got closer to the bushes he caught a reflection bouncing off his torch beam. Then another. Then another. Like a row of buttons. It was a row of buttons. He got straight on his radio and called it in.

The area where the guard discovered the body was quickly cordoned off. A military vehicle with a generator was requisitioned to provide the local Bielefeld police investigation team with lights to conduct their grim tasks. The body was photographed insitu and the whole area examined before being removed from the bushes and placed in the centre of the depression in the ground. This was the first body to be discovered that night.

The Bielefeld police liaised with the American and British military police as the body was discovered right outside an American military camp and the dead soldier was British, going by his uniform, though no ID was found on the body or at the scene.

The dead soldier appeared to be around twenty-five years of age with strawberry blonde hair and stood at around five feet eleven inches tall, or one metre and eighty centimetres according to the Bielefeld police scene of crime log. He appeared to have been dead for several days though it was unlikely that he'd lain where he was found during that time, leading to the early presumption that he'd been placed in the bushes so that his body could be discovered. He wasn't wearing shoes or socks. His jacket was buttoned. It was the reflection from the light of the guard's torch bouncing off the buttons which had caught his attention.

Officers from the British camp were summoned to the scene to see if they could identify the body before it was removed to the local mortuary. An out-of-uniform officer recognised the body as that of Clifford Coley, an MIL[R] analyst. He called the camp CO to one side and whispered in his ear that the body was one of his men who had recently taken some leave. Considering the work performed by MIL[R] the CO called his officers together and told them that they were to return to camp and under no circumstances were they to discuss the night's events with anybody. "This situation is highly classified and I will not tolerate idle chatter, gossip or speculation as to what happened to this unfortunate soldier. You are not to discuss tonight's events with anybody. Dismissed."

A British Army conversation

"What was he working on?"
"Oh, the usual stuff, you know."
"Stop the secret squirrel bullshit and tell me what he was working on."
"Apart from his normal intercept duties he was working on some unusual messages along with another Private called Frost."
"And where is Private Frost?"
"That's the thing. As soon as he returned to his desk after

working for the chiefs of staff at the war games he left the camp and I have no idea where he is."

"Were they friends?"

"I believe so. Why, do you think Private Frost might have had something to do with Private Coley's murder?"

"Murder? Oh yes, it might well be murder. We won't know until we question him. If he shows up don't alert him to anything, just let me know. Understood?"

"Of course, anything to help bring Private Coley's murderer to justice." The officer reported to Major Finn that as Private Frost was the prime suspect he would cooperate fully with the investigation into Private Coley's murder.

***

Given the nature of Private Coley's work, the British Secret Service contacted their German counterparts to obtain a total news embargo. They thought it highly likely that Private Coley had met his end at the hands of foreign agents. This meant he would be on ice until after investigations were completed, which could be years. His body might never be released, perhaps ultimately being listed as a missing person, like so many around the globe are every year.

***

Clifford Coley's body was dumped where it had been due to a misunderstanding between the taxi driver and his Counsellor. He was German and his Counsellor French. Hardly surprising there was a breakdown in communications. The Counsellor hadn't wanted to attract unwanted attention and so ordered the return of Private Coley's body to his home town. "Send him back to where he came from." He was, after all, meant to be on home leave. This was a humanitarian gesture on the part of the Counsellor as it meant Private Coley's parents would be able to grieve their dead son. Instead, the body of the Private Coley was never repatriated and his parents went to their graves never knowing what had happened to their lovely boy.

THE SOVIET MISSILE HEIST

At the rendezvous point Michael fell in with the rest of his unit. Their role was simple. They were to dress as Soviet soldiers, flag down a convoy of missile carriers, speak to their leader and convince him that he needed to turn the convoy around and return to base as the road ahead had been compromised by NATO forces. The more the welcoming committee thought about it the more ridiculous it sounded. Still, orders are orders so they had to remain in character throughout.

***

It was an audacious plan conceived by Madame Chairman herself, or so she claimed. Ever on the lookout for opportunities, the Organisation wasn't averse to stealing the assets of one nation, country or power and selling them on to where they'd do the most good, or harm, to another nation, country or power. Anything to keep the international hate-pot bubbling.

Not long after the news broke of the NATO war games, there came a flash of inspiration from Madame Chairman, or so she claimed, which manifested itself as, "Let's get the Soviets to hold counter-war games to coincide with the NATO war games and have them bring their shiny new missiles with them to the party. When they get close to the border between East and West Germany we'll snatch them and sell them on!" Could it be that simple?

In a nutshell, that was the essence of the plan. Simple; but the Devil is in the detail and Madame Chairman is not a detail person, she's an ideas person. She left the detail to others. The Organisation has always maintained that simple plans are best. Less to go wrong. The fly in the ointment of this plan was that the missiles would be surrounded by tens of thousands of Soviet troops and thousands of Soviet tanks. As soon as the missile carriers came under attack they'd simply put out a call for help and that would be that. Game over. But the Organisation wasn't going to be put off. There were hundreds of millions of dollars at stake for use to set religions against religions, neighbours against neighbours and brothers against brothers. They had to go for it. They'd let the CIA make all the running and then they'd step in at the last minute and steal the prize from under their noses. They'd played and won this game before.

***

At the start, everything went according to plan. The NATO war games exercises began right on schedule. The Soviets held their counter-war-games-exercises in response to them. The CIA made their plans to snatch the Soviet missiles and the Organisation had its plan to relieve the CIA of its prize.

***

Just before the war games exercises commenced the Organisation went on high alert.

*

Somebody inside MIL[R] called Michael Frost cracked the code to VVG's bespoke cipher messages. A new and uncrackable code had to be found PDQ. What's more, Mr Frost is known to the Organisation as a potential on list B.

*

Private Frost went on to join the war games exercises as an interpreter working for the joint chiefs of staff at their HQ. While there, he attracted attention to himself by getting involved in an argument over strategy. Attracting attention is never a good thing for someone on the lists.

*

"Could this get any worse?" those doing the planning asked themselves. If it is ever asked, the answer to that question is invariably, "Of course it can."

*

After Private Frost cracked the original code and left to join the war games, somebody called Clifford Coley began working round the clock to crack the new code. He almost succeeded before suddenly going on leave.

*

It is practically certain that Private Coley's supervising NCO is an operative with the French splinter and he was involved in the disappearance and murder of Private Coley.

*

A Major in the Royal Tank Regiment requested that both Private Frost and Private Coley's supervising NCO be sanctioned. His request was denied as his governor has plans for Private Frost, and Private Coley's NCO is a doubler for the Israeli splinter.

*

It was now certain that the French splinter knew of the plan to snatch the Soviet missiles.

***

As soon as Victor learned the meaning behind the messages he informed his French splinter masters who then made plans to steal the missiles following the heist. The Organisation learned of the French splinter's plans from Captain LeFort and one other. Captain LeFort was asked if he could use his influence to dissuade the French splinter from getting involved by promising it a cut. Out of principle it rejects deals involving the Americans or the Russians. The French splinter was confident of a favourable outcome as it'd moved considerable numbers of its forces into north eastern West Germany. Unfortunately for the French splinter it was just that, a splinter, and besides, twenty percent of its operatives are doublers. It would have to be extremely fortunate to get anything at all out of this venture.

***

All the players were in place. VVG had ensured that a detachment of a dozen missile carriers would be at the co-ordinates he'd transmitted in one of his final messages. The CIA ensured that radio jamming would be 'accidentally' extended to the area where the missile carriers were to be snatched from. Also, they deployed experimental state-of-the-art devices designed to render instrumentation ineffective; plus they changed the direction of road signs as the convoy was from the Urals and consequently in totally unfamiliar territory. Right on time the missile convoy arrived at the rendezvous point which was a mere hundred metres from the border with West Germany.

Enter Private Frost's unit. They emerged onto the dirt road from the undergrowth holding Soviet-issue metal mugs filled with hot steaming drinks and holding up the palms of their hands to stop the convoy. They acted casual and natural. And why shouldn't they? Not for a minute did they know they were approaching an actual Soviet missile detachment bristling with fully armed soldiers. Michael, having the best Russian accent, though some thought it Karelian, approached the lead vehicle. He spoke to its driver, telling him to turn the convoy around and head back to base as the road ahead had been compromised by NATO troops. He looked distrustfully at Michael and asked him what unit he was from. He replied that he was from an intelligence unit and had been roped into this job because it was his unit that had decrypted the messages about the NATO troops and, as his CO didn't believe him, his reward was to leave his nice warm office and deliver his message personally. The driver laughed, saying that was typical of bloody officers. Michael offered him and his men a hot drink before they made their return journey. "Why not," he replied.

As the men got out of their vehicles they were quickly overcome by the Special Forces soldiers waiting in ambush for them. It was all over in seconds.

***

A splinter conversation

"It's me."

"I can speak, go ahead."

"I got hold of the details of the new route the convoy is to take after the missiles are stolen, if they are successful, that is."

"Give me the location."

"Eduard has it, he'll call you. The point where our ambush is to take place is clearly marked on the map he has with him."

"What are the orders regarding the Soviet soldiers?"

"I'm told they they're going to try their best not to kill anybody."

"I have been reliably informed that the greeting party is to be sacrificed."

"I wonder who they've upset? Anyway, LeFort got us what he said he'd get us so maybe he'll live a little longer."

"Do you trust him? Do you think the information is real?"

"He'd be stupid to provide us with bad information. He knows what would happen to him and his sister if he did something like that."

"I wouldn't go anywhere near her. She's a bigger killer than him. Last time we…"

"Just to be on the safe side check the information out. I don't want our people coming back with nothing to show for their efforts."

***

A double doubler conversation

"Was the welcoming committee taken care of?"

"What do you mean?"

"How can I put this?" A pause for thought. "There were one or two who've outlived their usefulness and were meant to remain at the scene."

"What?"

"They were not to leave the scene. They were to have been left for the Soviets to find. That's why they had Ukrainian IDs."

"The orders were to ensure that no clues were left behind and I was specifically ordered to ensure that a Private called Frost was ushered away and driven back to his barracks in Bielefeld."

"Who gave you those orders?"

"An officer after the final briefing."

"Captain LeFort?"

"He didn't give his name for obvious reasons and as I've never met him before I can't say whether he's your Captain LeFort or not."

"Is this him?"

"Yes, that's him."

"LeFort. He's gone too far this time. He's gone too far… again."

***

A splinter and guest conversation

"I heard LeFort betrayed you."

"I suspected he might. Don't worry though, we're not waiting where they think we'll be waiting. We have somebody on the inside who's keeping close to him."

"Will you send sentinels to take care of him?"

"There's no need, he'll be taken care of soon enough."

"Where will the ambush take place?"

"That's best kept to those who have a need to know."

"I agree. Good luck."

***

An Organisation and guest conversation

"I urgently need to speak with…"

"It's me. Did you…"

"There's no time to lose. They know. They've changed the ambush location."

"Where…"

"I couldn't find out. Tell LeFort there's somebody close to him that he needs to watch out for. I don't know who it is but I think he'll be killed as soon as they find out what he did."

"Will you be suspected?"

"I think so. I'm going back to Israel. If they want me they can come for me there."

"Thank you, David. Take care. I won't forget this."

Madame Chairman trusted David even though they'd only met once before during a conference with the Israeli splinter. He came across to her as a man of integrity. He had a reputation for doing the right thing. He desired peace between the splinters and with the Organisation. He understood that she must consolidate her position as Madame Chairman and his actions were his way of helping her achieve that. A message was sent ordering the convoy to leave Germany by the original route.

A signal was sent back to London requesting the confirmation key, for obvious reasons. Lisette was the key sender, for obvious reasons. The key was accepted and they reverted to plan A.

***

Immediately following the heist, the stolen missile carriers were driven straight over the East/West border and were away within four minutes of the ambush. *What a smooth operation,* everybody thought, giving themselves imaginary pats on their backs. The convoy and the ground team left East Germany via the same hole punched through the border defences by a tank from the Western side.

***

It wasn't until long after they'd arrived back at the debriefing RVP that an American Special Forces NCO noticed there weren't any missile carriers where he expected them to be. "Maybe they got lost on the way," joked a Major whose laughter wasn't shared by any of the others in the compound. From the time of the ambush to the assault teams arriving back at the RVP was one hour and twenty minutes. They'd been kept waiting a further hour and thirty minutes for the top brass to arrive before the debriefing commenced. It was an hour after the debriefing session when the Special Forces NCO noticed the missile carriers weren't where they were meant to be. By this time, the missile carriers and their lovely shiny new missiles were already on the road out of Germany.

***

The French splinter was waiting at the counter-ambush location along the route they'd been assured the stolen missile convoy would take. The location was perfect. It was just around a sharp bend meaning the vehicles would have to slow down. Just beyond the bend was a wide trail leading off into a forested area, ideal for driving the vehicles into. They'd be under the cover of a thousand trees. There was a sliver of moon giving just enough light to aid the ambushers. The leader of the ambush was already dreaming of the plaudits, and the millions of dollars, coming his way.

Intelligence led the French splinter to believe there would be minimal personnel travelling with the convoy. Twelve drivers and a few guards, so unlikely to be more than twenty in total. Despite their superior numbers and having the element of surprise on their side they didn't want to get involved in a firefight. They felt confident the Organisation's operatives would throw in the towel as soon as the convoy was stopped.

***

It was a long cold night they spent in the woods waiting for a convoy that didn't show. In the small hours a single motorcyclist cruised slowly around the bend in the road at the ambush location.

As it came to a halt on the gravel verge between the forest and the road, four members of the ambush squad emerged from the trees making like they'd been attending to a call of nature.

The motorcyclist dismounted and put the machine up on its stand. "Please, gentlemen, don't go to all the trouble of putting on an act on my behalf. I'm here to deliver a message to your commander." The leather-clad motorcyclist removed her silver, black-visored crash helmet and shook out her waist-length blonde hair. It was a wig but a very good one. The hair shaking out was all that was needed to distract four randy men. She knew men were always randy. She knew that no matter what the circumstances, or the danger, men are always randy and ready for sex. The hair shaking out was her way of distracting them.

"What are you talking about?" replied one of the men, walking toward her with a swagger for the benefit of those hiding in the trees. He moved close to her. That was all she needed.

She grabbed the man by the arm and spun him around, putting an arm lock on him and placing the muzzle of a neat little .22 against his temple. She shouted into the forest, "I am not alone." She lied, "I am here to deliver a message to your commander. I know what you are doing here. The convoy isn't coming this way. It's long gone on its way out of Germany."

"Who are you?" shouted a voice from the forest.

"I don't talk to trees, show yourself." A man emerged from the trees. "Are you the commander?"

"I am. What is your message?"

"I have a message for you from Madame Chairman. I am one of her personal sentinels so you appreciate how important this message must be." The motorcyclist whispered her message into the commander's ear while keeping her .22 pressed hard against his gut.

The commander looked totally deflated after receiving the whispered message. "So, what do we do now?"

"We all stop shivering and go home. Okay? No shooting of

messengers. Okay? I'm going to turn around and ride away. My associates are watching me and if anything bad should happen to me then all hell will break loose."

"You have my word that nothing will happen to you. You are very brave coming here under such circumstances. Madame Chairman is very lucky to have someone like you… or perhaps she doesn't value your life?"

She smiled. "Of course she values my life." Followed by a low hiss-whispered thought as she turned away: "You stupid man."

***

It was vitally important that the French splinter dispersed as soon as possible because the CIA and the American Special Forces were on the lookout for their stolen booty. If they came across the French splinter hiding in the forest then the outcome would have been disastrous and Madame Chairman didn't want that. She didn't want the Count's operatives slaughtered, especially as eight of them were Israeli doublers.

***

The post-mortems, allegations, accusations, counter-allegations and finger pointing started even before the French splinter had finished covering their tracks at the ambush location. They wouldn't be getting the massive payday they thought they were going to get. The post-mortems, allegations, accusations, counter-allegations and finger pointing continued for several days. Order was only finally restored following a call between Madame Chairman and Count Bouvier, the head of the French splinter. She offered the Count a share of the spoils of the missile heist by way of compensation. More than anything, she said, she wanted peace between the Organisation and its splinters which, she insisted, could never be achieved unless all infighting ceased. She wanted to heal the wounds of history and unite the Organisation once again. The Count promised most sincerely that he too wanted the same thing.

***

"Count Bouvier, Maurice, thank you for taking my call."

"It's always a pleasure to speak with you, Madame Chairman," he replied sincerely and truthfully. They had a long-established mutual admiration for one another.

"I know how disappointed you must feel right now. You must realise I had no option after you turned down what I considered to be a very generous offer."

"I didn't like the terms of the offer. You know how I've long despised the Americans and the Russians too. It wasn't your Organisation I was set against, I hope you understand that?"

"I do, Maurice, I genuinely do. But I had no choice. The whole thing was set up by an operative of the American splinter and when the Russian splinter got to know of the project there was no way I could deny them, for obvious reasons."

"It turns my stomach that these criminals are going to be rewarded. They abandoned the mission after Bonaparte. They are traitors to the cause." In truth the Count was being more than a little hypocritical.

"You're aware of my plans to reunite the Organisation and return it to its past glory. If we fight over money of all things, then all my hard work… all our hard work… will have been for nothing. You must realise that, Maurice?"

Not answering Madame Chairman's point, the Count changed the subject. "What about LeFort? I understand it was he who betrayed us."

"If you use words such as 'betray' then it can only sound bad. He's not a bad man. He's liked and trusted by all the splinters and I believe he's possibly the right person to become the first President of a reborn Brotherhood. What he did was for the greater good… need I say any more?"

"Margaret, there has to be another way."

"There might well be but I can't think of one. LeFort is the best chance we have for peace." She paused. "You know what I'm going to ask you, don't you, Maurice?"

"I do."

"Then please promise me that you will not seek revenge or harm…"

"I will forgive LeFort but I cannot forget what he did. No harm will come to him or his family from me or anybody in my splinter. Is that good enough for you, Margaret?"

"It is. I love the way you say my name. I always have."

"There was no need for the Irishman to threaten to kill Hugo."

"He went too far. I apologise." This was news to her.

Madame Chairman now had Captain LeFort right where she wanted him and if he was successful in reuniting the Organisation she knew she'd be running the whole show and he'd be her puppet. She just needed to let a little time go by to heal the wounds before proceeding.

READ HIM HIS RIGHTS

As soon as Michael was dropped off at his barracks he was arrested and taken away by MPs. His driver stopped at the nearest public phone and called Control to let them know what had happened. She wasn't sure what was going on but assumed it must be something to do with the missile heist.

On the drive back to Bielefeld she'd spoken to Michael about the need for total secrecy concerning the Soviet exercise. She said it wasn't something the public needed to know about and the best way to keep it from them was never to speak about it with anybody. Anybody at all.

He asked her if it was really an exercise because he knew that person he spoke with to be Russian. She reminded him that most of the welcoming committee were Russian and asked him what his point was. He replied he didn't have a point in that case and promised not to say anything about the Soviet exercise. She thanked him for his promise.

***

Jurisdiction decided, Michael found himself sitting in a cell in Bielefeld police station. His visions arrived the instant the cell door slammed shut. He kept his eye on the one with the yellow eyes. The others milled around but clearly It was their leader. It was always at the front. The cell door opened after two hours. They'd left Michael alone in his cell to put pressure on him. He didn't feel under any pressure despite the seriousness of the charge read out to him by the Police Sergeant when he'd been booked in. He didn't think in terms of pressure when his mind knew what it knew and it knew he hadn't murdered Private Coley.

Michael endured two hours of what the police thought was a pretty gruelling grilling before a lawyer arrived, telling them they weren't allowed to question her client until she'd had a conference with him. They were led to a private room where the lawyer proceeded to instruct Michael on how to conduct himself while in custody. She was confident his incarceration would be short. Indeed it was. Michael was bailed later that afternoon. Statements were obtained from the chiefs of staff from the war games regarding Michael's whereabouts for the time it was determined Private Coley was murdered. More attention on Michael only strengthened Major Finn's hand.

As Michael and his lawyer exited the police station a car horn sounded. She guided Michael to the car and she said her goodbyes to him. She leaned in through the car window and kissed the driver on the cheek and told him she'd be in touch soon.

"Hello Michael. I hope you are feeling okay after your ordeal."

"Yes thank you, Captain LeFort."

"How did you find your lawyer? I think she's excellent."

"She told me what to do and what not to do when in custody."

"Don't worry, Michael. We'll soon clear up this misunderstanding."

"I'm not worried. I didn't murder Private Coley."

"I believe you, Michael."

"Why did you ignore me at the briefing?"

"I didn't want you to be shown any favouritism," lied the French Captain. "If it were common knowledge that you and I know one another then you wouldn't have got the most out of the exercise."

"I told the woman who drove me back that I thought it wasn't an exercise but she insisted that it was."

"And what do you think?"

"I'm not sure. I'm hungry."

"I imagine you are. I'll take you back to camp. Don't worry about a thing, you'll be allowed to continue with your duties with MILR. Please don't mention today's events or the exercise to anybody. Okay?"

"I promise."

They drove back to the camp in total silence, which suited them both for different reasons.

SERGEANT PEPPER'S

Getting the missiles out of West Germany was simplicity itself. The Organisation knew that from several days before the end of the war games many units would make their way to their home bases early. This was normal practice as it served to break up convoy lengths and not to clog up the roads of the host country, which would be bad PR.

Shortly after the heist, the missile convoy stopped at a farm six miles from the hijack at which a pre-fabricated drive-through workshop had been erected. Each of the stolen vehicles entered the workshop, conveyor belt style, and came out the other end decked out, ironically, as 'Red' forces bearing the insignia of an obscure AA unit. Their outline and cargo were disguised with camouflage webbing. The missile convoy joined the autobahn heading north toward the docks at Hamburg. All along the autobahn they gave and received horn toots and thumbs-up signs to other vehicles. They also received some double-take looks with some vehicles even slowing down for open-window-to-open-window shouting conversations asking what sort of vehicles they were driving as they didn't recognise them.

"They're the new ones from Canada. Everybody'll be driving them soon."

Who was going to stop and challenge a convoy of twelve

NATO decaled vehicles no matter what they looked like? Who would have the balls to do something like that? It wasn't as though the Russkies would report their missiles stolen, now would they? Not publically at least. At government level they would request their property be returned, as to keep it would be theft. The Organisation was confident that once the convoy was on the road and hiding in plain sight they were home free. Who could stop them now? Nobody, that's who.

***

At the docks, a cargo vessel was tied up at the furthest end of a quiet pier after unloading its cheap wooden toys from the People's Republic of China. Military vehicles had been coming and going around Hamburg docks for months so a small convoy wouldn't attract attention. As soon as the first of the missile carriers passed through the dock gates the cargo boat lowered its loading ramp. All twelve vehicles drove straight on and were secured within minutes by the dozens of operatives crewing the boat. Within twenty-five minutes they were underway. A pilot joined the boat to guide it out of Hamburg's busy port. He returned to his launch with the customary lack of recognition familiar to operatives of the Organisation.

The cargo boat made several stops along its return route to China, depositing personnel, equipment and boxed-up cargo containing various parts of the heist booty. The main drop was in France of all places, hiding the bulk of the booty right under the nose of the French splinter. Classic.

***

Following his return to MIL[R] Michael was quizzed about the war games exercises by the chaps, a couple of whom were widely touted as being spies. He answered their questions in his polite, matter-of-fact way which made them curious as to what had really gone on during his hush hush war games assignment. Was he a spy after all?

"Not a chance," was the general consensus as he was regarded as not right in the head somehow. He worked, ate, went to his barracks at night, slept, got up and did it all again. He was like a machine. When not on duty, he was frequently observed sitting on his bunk talking to himself while staring at the blank walls. Had people been aware of what he was seeing while staring at the walls in the barracks they would have been very concerned about his state of mind.

"Hey Michael? How do you fancy coming along to the pub tonight?" asked an MIL[R] chap. He was keen to know more about Michael and getting him sozzled might loosen his tongue. His invitation was not an act of comradery.

"I don't drink. I don't like the taste."

"You can have a coffee then if you don't fancy a beer. C'mon, you need to get out and let off some steam. You never know, you might meet a nice German bird." Soldiers had little luck with the local females as they were sick and tired of the ungentlemanly treatment they often suffered at their hands.

"You should go, Michael," said a familiar voice from behind. "It'll do you good."

"I saw you in the debriefing tent at the war games. Why were you wearing a German Major's uniform?"

"Did you like my disguise?"

"You're wearing your French Captain's uniform now. Did you get a demotion?" The French Captain laughed. He thought Michael had made a joke.

"No, Michael, when I go about my observing tasks I like to remain incognito so reactions to me are… appropriate to my rank. I like to observe things unsanitised. But to get back to the question at hand, you should go to the pub tonight. I'll be there and it'll be nice to catch up with what you've been up," replied the French

Captain despite knowing full well Michael's every move over the past few years.

"And you are?" asked an MIL[R] chap holding out his right hand. The French Captain gave no answer nor did he reach out to shake the offered hand, he just stared in the chap's direction, then in Michael's, turned around and left.

"Well, that was impolite. Typical bloody Frenchie."

"I am not sure he's French."

"He's wearing a French Captain's uniform so I assume he's in the French Army. Isn't it customary for a soldier to be a national of one's own army?"

"Not necessarily. Have you heard of the French Foreign Legion? There are soldiers of many nations who are not nationals of the armies they serve in."

"Perhaps. So how about tonight then? We can paint the town red or whatever."

As soon as they were off duty, a dozen MIL[R] chaps changed into their civvies and marched off in small groups to the newly opened Sergeant Pepper's beer garden. They were laughing and chatting as they made their way along the dimly lit Straßen, stopping occasionally to turn their backs into the wind and cupping their hands to light a cigarette.

"Fancy a ciggie then, Michael?"

"No thank you. I do not smoke."

"Don't drink, don't smoke, what do you do?" Several MIL[R] chaps laughed at the answers to that question running around in their heads.

"Hey Michael, tell me, are you getting yer hole anywhere then?" A few sniggers from the chaps on that one.

"Where would he be getting his hole then, eh? He never goes anywhere. Unless you mean he's shagging old Fruity Boy Williams?" Again, laughing.

"Piss off and leave the lad alone. He's a good Catholic boy and doesn't go in for that sort of thing," teased one chap in an attempt to make light of the situation and get the rest of the MIL[R] chaps off Michael's back. Michael didn't care either way.

When they arrived at Sergeant Pepper's it felt good to get through the heavily curtained door and out of the wind especially as it had just started raining. Bielefeld's rain reminded everybody of Manchester.

"C'mon then, what'll it be. My round." The MIL[R] chap made his way to the bar and got a dozen drinks on a tray and brought them to a table they'd managed to commandeer. "That was lucky gettin' a table so quick. Well done, chaps. Now, I got everybody beer with schnapps chasers, all except Michael, I got him a Coca Cola and a little schnapps for the cold. Cheers." Everybody downed their schnapps and got stuck into their litre glasses of beer. Within minutes of their arrival the whole bar area filled up with soldiers. "There's that bloody rude Frog over there staring at us." At that the whole table turned to look at the French Captain who then beckoned Michael to come and join him.

"What a terrible evening it is. So much rain and wind. You'll notice I'm talking about the weather which I know you British love to do," laughed the French Captain alone. "So, Michael, you did it. You joined the Army. I hoped you would. I think you'll make a great soldier. What is that you're drinking? Schnapps? Let me get you another." The French Captain caught the attention of a beautiful young waitress who took their order. "What a beautiful girl. She's around your age, Michael. I can't say I'd be too happy about her working here if I were her father." The waitress returned with a bottle of red wine and two glasses of schnapps. "Thank you. I haven't seen you here before."

"No... I go university... sorry, my English." Michael and the French Captain spoke to her for a couple of minutes in German.

"Charming young lady. You should see if she has any free time and maybe get to know her better. Salute." The schnapps went down well and despite the Captain saying how terrible German red wine was it seemed to taste okay to Michael who showed little outward signs of the effects of the booze but his head was becoming dangerously disordered.

"Look at those two over there chatting up that waitress. She's gorgeous."

"And out of your league, posh boy," shouted the chaps around the table and laughing. They were having a great night.

The night was proving very interesting as far as the French Captain was concerned. He noted the effect alcohol had on Michael's behaviour and so decided he'd had enough. He ordered two steaks with fries and salad from the pretty young waitress to give Michael's stomach something to soak the booze up.

After their meal, Michael and the French Captain made to leave. A couple of groups of soldiers, who'd been eyeing up the table they were vacating, raced to claim their seats. In the ensuing melee Michael was pushed to the ground. The French Captain picked him up and the waitress came by to see if he was okay.

"Hey gorgeous, I'm not feelin' too good myself so maybe you can come and talk to me for a bit? What do you say?"

"Shut up, Larry, and leave the girl alone. Don't pay him any attention, love, he's from Essex."

"I'm not botherin' you, am I, darlin'?" asked Larry while grabbing the waitress by the elbow and pulling her toward him. Once in close proximity the soldier attempted to kiss the pretty young waitress.

"Young man, if you don't let her alone I'll be forced to teach you some manners," said the French Captain in his best put-on Franglais accent.

"Ooooooooo, listen to the Frog. Get back to Frogland you, or I'll…" That was all the soldier had time to say before Michael acted. It was unheard of for him to instigate a fight but he'd felt a violent rush of aggression and acted on it. His attack was swift and decisive with a cross-shot to the jaw followed by a straight strike with the heel of his hand to the chest of the soldier.

Lucky that wasn't to the point of the nose, thought the French Captain.

When he turned to restrain Michael three soldiers jumped him from behind. In an instant Michael executed his attack. He started by making room for himself by pushing the soldiers with all his might. Others made to join in the imminent scrap but thought better of it once they witnessed Michael in full flow. In less than five seconds he landed more than a dozen punches and kicks and, once finished, he stood stock still in a karate stance over the prostrate soldiers, ready to continue his attack should it be necessary. Without uttering a word the French Captain casually took Michael by the arm and they calmly left the bar without making eye contact with anybody. When in trouble, rely on your training. It's well documented that eye contact is a sign of aggression, plus people who make eye contact are easier to recognise in the future.

The chaps from MIL[R] were open-mouthed speechless at what they'd just witnessed. *How could,* they thought, *that drip Frost do something like that?*

"I've never seen anything like that in my life. Have you?"

"I have. It looked like karate to me. I've seen some Chinese films where they do that sort of thing but I thought it was all faked. Did you see how hard he hit that bloke? Oooh that must have hurt. I thought he was going to start on the rest of them and then it would've really kicked off."

"Let's leave. It's not good for MILR chaps to be involved in stuff like this."

A couple of the more 'serious' MIL[R] chaps sidled up to one another after the fight, whispered a few words between them and left the bar immediately after. There was a pair of eyes there that night keeping watch on the French Captain and they recognised talent when they saw it. Something interesting to report back to her Counsellor but she never got a chance.

***

After the bar closed, the bogus university student made her way along the main road in the opposite direction to Bielefeld University student accommodation. Within a hundred metres a car pulled alongside her; its passenger side window was already wound down. The polite, quiet-spoken man inside the car asked her for directions to the airport. As she leaned in to point in the direction of the airport an eight-inch stiletto dagger entered the underside of her chin just behind the jawline and continued in an upward direction, angled slightly away from the assailant, and into her brain. Death was instantaneous. Their orders were to leave the body at the scene as a message to whichever group had been so foolish as to send an amateur to spy on them. "Pity," said the young Mediterranean-looking man, "I hate to see beauty destroyed."

"Are you some kind of a pouf or what? It's backs to the wall in future when you're around, pal," commented the driver in a soft Irish accent. "Let's go and see who else is around. We'll drop yer man off at the barracks first though."

The young woman, in fact, wasn't an amateur at all. She was older than she appeared, an experienced operative and an accomplished assassin. She'd been caught off guard as she hadn't considered for a moment that her cover had been blown as she'd only been in Bielefeld for four days. Her mission was to make contact with, and then to make herself available to, the French Captain. What had gone wrong? Perhaps somebody alerted the French Captain as to her mission. It could be the Organisation acting to protect a valued ally or a doubler acting on their own initiative. In some cases the homeland Organisation knows about the activities of splinter operatives but allows them to continue, so long as they remain useful.

The only thing we can be certain of is that somebody sold the young woman out as the French Captain was aware of her mission in advance and he ensured that she waited on him in the pub. The young woman wasn't in fact German, she was French, an operative in the French splinter and a KGB doubler. Her orders were to get close to the French Captain and pass back information about the Soviet missile heist as the French splinter had not given up on cutting the Americans and the Russians out of the action. It would have been highly unlikely that the French Captain would have divulged anything significant to the pretty young waitress during pillow talk in which case she was to kill him black widow spider style. Classic French splinter, sex with everything. The Count knew nothing of this initiative.

Due to the lack of physical evidence at the scene those who first arrived to investigate did not suspect foul play. During the autopsy, all that was discovered amongst the mud splatters around her neck and face was an eight-millimetre wide scratch on the underside of her chin. Some of the Mediterranean man's work goes completely undetected, with some deaths being put down to natural causes because the entry wound is so small and the slice through the brain is easily missed by the autopsy. He often literally gets away with murder.

***

During their walk back to Michael's barracks they discussed what had happened in the bar that evening. The Captain's advice to him was to adopt the FBI defence: "Deny everything at all times, no matter what the weight of evidence is against you." He told him that if a senior officer asked about the incident he should just make light of it. "Say it was just a misunderstanding." He recommended that under no circumstances should he answer any questions in detail with his stance being that he was too drunk to recall the evening's events while vowing never to drink again. They discussed the possibility of Michael being brought up on charges but the French Captain said he should "cross that bridge when you come to it".

Michael entered the barracks and stood alone in the dark. He counted to one hundred before going back out into the night. His head was a clamour of voices and visions brought on by the alcohol. He'd heard tell that a walk would clear his head. He remembered little about the events of the evening and nothing at all of his night when he woke at reveille.

***

In the weeks following the war games, life was extremely dull and boring for the chaps at MIL[R]. Nothing was happening at all, everything was silent. Not even any chatter. It was as though the Russkies had shut up shop and shipped off back to the USSR. During the war games they'd been rushed off their feet but now… this… it was driving everybody crazy. "Why don't they send us the usual insults? Anything!" Anything at all to break the boredom.

Being an insular bunch, MIL[R] weren't keeping up to date with BAOR communiqués, including those regarding the annual inter-regimental games. They were, of course, keeping up with any news about the poor young woman who'd been found murdered close to the pub where they'd been drinking on the night they'd seen Michael in action. Each racked their brain as to who could have perpetrated such a dreadful crime. Some speculated that Michael might have had something to do with it as not only had he gone missing later that same night it was discovered that the murder victim was the pretty young blonde waitress he'd got into a fight over.

"Hey, Frost. That girl who was murdered. You remember her. Well, it turns out she was the same girl you had a fight over in the bar. Did you know that?"

"I didn't have a fight over her. I got pushed to the ground and got angry."

"Yeah, but you got the hump when the soldier boys started getting funny with her. In fact it was after one of them…"

"I told you. I got angry because I got pushed to the ground." Michael walked away from the questions. Due to the effect alcohol had on him, he could barely remember the fight, it was as if it had been somebody else who'd been doing the fighting and he was an onlooker. The voices in his head and the increasing frequency of the visions added to his confused state of mind.

***

While the chaps were out of the office preparing for the inter-regimental games, an enormous amount of Soviet communiqués landed on their desks. "This always seems to happen every time we're away from the office," remarked one of the chaps as the beautiful young postroom administrator walked into the office. The chaps fancied her like mad. It amused her to see them drooling over her. She was a Czech citizen married to a German national according to her personnel file. She knew as long as she kept a low profile and all the spy boys were in love with her, her cell would remain safe. She spoke to Michael to wind the other chaps up. He replied but in Russian. She asked him why he was speaking to her in Russian. He said he'd overheard her talking and she spoke with a typical Russian cadence and with flaws such as a lack of prepositions. They spoke together a couple of times afterwards; she always maintained that she was Czech.

***

For decades, the Soviets used beautiful women to infiltrate the world's intelligence agencies. It's a simple ploy but very effective and despite knowing this is how they operate the honey trap seems to work time and time again, even to this very day. You'd have thought by now that countermeasures would have been put in place to mitigate this simplest of ways for spies to get close to intelligence officers and ranking government officials.

The vast majority of people working in British intelligence are just ordinary people, the vast majority of whom perform repetitive, mundane tasks every day of their spy lives. Some of these dreary people work in areas of interest to foreign governments, the Organisation and its splinters which makes them targets for blackmail, bribery and, most of all, receiving the attention they believe they so richly deserve. Individually, these people do not shake the world; in truth, they barely even brush up against it. Around the world there are tens of thousands of secret squirrels imperceptibly micro-adjusting situations in one direction or another before returning them to their original position when the political winds blow in that direction once more. It's not a lot of work to return things to the status quo as they haven't been moved very far anyway.

To spice up their spy lives, staff working for intelligence agencies have been known to purposely get close to people they know they shouldn't be getting close to in order to add excitement to their mundane existences. Perhaps their imaginings get the better of them from time to time, making them giddy and do silly things. Some, of course, have hobbies and pastimes which are career limiting or perhaps career enhancing depending on who you happen to bump into in the steam rooms of Mayfair, Belgravia or Covent Garden. Sexual deviancy has often been the crack foreign agents look to exploit to commit blackmail or get into places they are looking to penetrate.

FROSTY CHRISTMAS

From his earliest years, Michael was noticeably different from other children. When he was a child, his differences were not very apparent and though children can be unspeakably cruel they can be astonishingly tolerant of differences.

As he grew into adulthood, Michael's differences became more and more stark. He wasn't interested in drinking, dancing, football, going out to night clubs or, more noticeably, getting together with girls. This lack of interests meant he stood out from the crowd as his non-participation was easily picked up. This lacking behaviour made people around him suspicious of his nature and unsure of how to deal with him as they had no common ground. Generally speaking, people didn't dislike Michael but the older he got and the more noticeable his differences became the more people wanted to distance themselves from him lest they become tarnished by his peculiarness.

It was detrimental to the Organisation's goal of remaining hidden that Michael kept getting noticed in the ways he was. Some wanted to help him blend in while others wanted to cut him loose. Some wanted him dead. Certain people covered up for Michael for their own purposes because each felt he might be useful to them in the future. Guilt led some to suffer great anguish about what they'd chosen to do, or rather what they'd chosen not to do, about Michael. He could have cut him loose at any time before he got in too deep but they chose not to for their own purposes. Over time, each would pay the price for their deceitfulness.

***

Though Michael seemed content to sit alone on his bunk in the light of day or the dark of night and stare at the blank barrack room walls, battling the terrible visions created by his mind from taking him over, some became concerned for his wellbeing. An operative inside MI3 arranged for him to enrol in self-defence classes at a local American base and a civilian karate club in Bielefeld. It was only a few weeks until his return to the UK for the Christmas holidays and they didn't want him to attract any further attention, especially as RMC selection was just around the corner.

***

As soon as his shift ended, Michael ran to the dojo at the local American camp. After being shown around by the Japanese American sensei, they talked about his experience in the martial arts.

The sensei was interested to hear of Michael's experience with Japanese swords and how he'd adapted his fencing style to incorporate kenjutsu techniques. He suggested Michael join a kenjutsu class that evening. As soon as he picked up the bokuto he felt warm inside. From observation, the sensei could tell Michael was more than just competent with a sword.

After the class was over, the sensei asked Michael more about the sensei in England who'd taught him Japanese swordplay. He told him how he'd watched the Huyton sensei and imitated his moves and how he'd introduced him to the straight katana as his style was European.

"That's very interesting. I myself own a collection of katanas, including a very elegant straight katana which you might like to practise with some time. I hope to see you here again. The club meets three times a week and we have weekend workshops to focus on particular aspects of martial arts. This weekend we're going to be concentrating on kendo. Come along, you might find it interesting."

"See you Saturday." During the evening, the sensei observed Michael watching the people taking part in the various classes and noticed how his body adjusted to what he was observing as though he was trying out things he was watching other people doing.

***

"How was your karate class, Michael?" asked the MI3 operative after he returned to the barracks.

"I didn't do karate. I'll do karate in Bielefeld tomorrow night. Tonight I practised kenjutsu and I'm going to a kendo workshop this weekend."

"Wow, you never fail to amaze me, Michael. What next? Are you going to tell us you can fly?" asked one of the chaps.

"I can't fly. I noticed there are a lot of women on the American base. Some are soldiers and some are officers. I'm not sure what the others do." This was a lot of unsolicited information for Michael to volunteer.

"Women eh? The bloody Yanks have got it all, haven't they? Women, jeeps, nice boots, brilliant uniforms, no cruddy gear for them, only the best. Still, when all's said and done, they're only Americans, poor things, and we must sympathise with them for that fact." Michael didn't get it.

Michael noticing women? thought the MI3 operative. *Maybe he's normal after all. No, he's definitely not normal.*

***

With Michael's time being fully occupied, the last few weeks in Bielefeld before his Christmas leave flew by.

***

"Are you looking forward to going home for Christmas?" asked the French Captain.

Michael had learned that the response to questions of this type was, "Yes I am." Which is exactly what he said.

"When do you leave for England?"

"Late tomorrow. I should be back at my house early on Wednesday morning. Christmas day is Friday."

"When you return to Bielefeld I won't be here, Michael. I have a posting which I can't tell you about right now. I heard about your MILR colleague snooping around in the files of the Australian SAS soldiers. That was a stupid thing for him to do."

"That's what the Major told him."

"Yes, I heard that too. Michael, I spoke with Captain Hywel-Jones earlier and mentioned to him that you'd met and spoken with the Australian SAS soldiers and he's none too happy. If he says anything about it tell him that it was an oversight on my part that led to you meeting them."

"Okay."

"By the way, he's has arranged for you to try for Royal Marines selection. If you're accepted you're likely to be posted to some pretty hostile places and in those places you might meet up with guys like the Aussie SAS soldiers. In those circumstances it's best you don't know one another. Let's say you get captured and you're interrogated or tortured, what you don't know you can't give away. Do you understand me, Michael?"

"Yes, that makes sense." Of course that wasn't the real reason why the Organisation didn't want Michael rubbing shoulders with the Aussie soldiers. For the first time in a long time the French Captain found it distasteful to deceive somebody about the true nature of things. He'd grown to like Michael. He'd liked him since their first meeting at Altcar and if right now he could tell him anything he'd tell him to fail RMC selection and return to the Royal Tank Regiment, enjoy his time there and get on with the rest of his life. He knew though that if he said anything like that it could mean the end for both of them. There was no going back for him and soon there would be no going back for Michael.

***

The flight to England, the coach journey to Liverpool and bus ride to Huyton was just delay after delay. Michael eventually arrived home just after 4 p.m. on Wednesday 23rd December 1970. School had already broken up for the Christmas holidays and waiting for him were Margaret and Thomas. Margaret was now working as a kitchen hand at the local school so she had the same holiday breaks as the children. Queen Rose was nowhere to be seen when Michael arrived home. "What do I want to see him for?" was all she'd said before leaving the house at 9 a.m. that freezing cold morning.

In the time that Michael had been away, Queen Rose had turned into a drama queen, with any little thing setting her off on a moody. She'd become expert at creating situations for her to be the centre of attention. People who behave in this way are usually hiding something and their drama queen antics are merely distractions. Queen Rose was creating a smoke screen to hide the fact that not only was she getting her share of the money Patrick was sending to the family every week, she was also borrowing heavily from Margaret with neither of them telling Patrick nor Thomas about the so-called loans. It was their little secret, anything to keep the drama queen happy.

Even so, this wasn't enough for Queen Rose. She'd taken to pocketing any money she found lying around the house or even her friends' houses. The stage was set for Patrick's little queen to grow into her lifetime role of thief, serial scrounger and pathological, compulsive and congenital liar.

***

Even before Michael got to the front door it flew open and Thomas ran to greet him. He launched into Michael's chest and hugged him as hard as he could.

"I've missed you, our kid, I've really missed you…" Thomas went on for five minutes telling Michael everything he could think of as they slowly edged their way crab style through the front door and into the living room. While the boys were talking, Michael could see Margaret out of the corner of his eye, standing there by the fireplace just watching them together with tears of happiness in her eyes.

The evening was spent filling Michael in on family matters which usually meant catching up on the dead pool. The extended Frost family was very large and as both Margaret and Patrick were the youngest of their respective families there was always some older sibling, aunt, uncle, second whatever thrice removed who had died and so the usual confusing conversations were had about, "Do you remember so and so? Oh, you do? Good. Well he's/she's dead." Margaret was always astonished at how Michael was able to remember all the relatives and the events surrounding their lives. Nobody else she knew could do that.

Queen Rose showed up after the evening meal. "Look what the bleedin' cat's dragged in," was her greeting to Michael.

"Hello Rose, how are you?" Michael had learned that it was polite asking how somebody was.

"Never mind 'ow I am. You know you're not sleepin' in your old room, don't ye? It's my room now, ye know."

"I'm sharing with Thomas."

"Good, now where's me tea?" Taking Queen Rose to one side Margaret asked her not to be so rude as she wanted Michael to have a nice time during his leave. Ten pounds changed hands for the promise of pleasantness during Michael's stay.

"Are you going to meet up with your school mates, son?" asked Margaret.

"I haven't stayed in contact with any of them."

"Why don't you get in touch with Allan Rice or Robby Garcia or Eddie Shearon, you always got on well with them boys."

"I'll see if they're about, if I have time." Margaret knew he wouldn't. She worried so much about Michael not having any friends. The boys at the grammar school were nice to Michael but they weren't close to him. She'd realised long ago that he was different to other children and they found his behaviour off-putting.

"Yeah, see how it goes then, son." There was a loud knock on the door. "Jesus tonight and tomorrow!" exclaimed Margaret nearly jumping out of her skin at the booming knocking at the door which was amplified by the carpetless hallway.

Before they could answer the door the big square face of Timbo Mulhall was at the lounge window. "Let us in, will yez? It's freezin' out 'ere." When he walked into the lounge Timbo grabbed Michael and gave him a play butt on his forehead. "Stitch that," joked Timbo. "Well, 'ow are ye, our kid? 'Ow long are ye 'ome for?"

"Six days."

"Ace. Lots of time for bevvyin'. Let's shoot out to the Farmers' now for a quick one."

"He's not going anywhere tonight, Timothy Mulhall, and don't you go getting him into trouble. He's in the Army now and he can't afford to get into trouble." Timbo, Thomas, Margaret and Michael chatted for hours making arrangements for the following days. Queen Rose took her meal upstairs not wanting to hear anything Michael or 'that jailbird', as she called Timbo, had to say.

***

The boys slept in on Christmas Eve morning. Michael hadn't slept so late in more than a year.

At seven o'clock that night he and Thomas met up with Timbo at the Farmers' Arms. After his schnapps and wine session at Sergeant Pepper's, Michael was staying away from alcohol. It made him aggressive and sent his head seriously out of control.

"C'mon, Michael, one Christmas drink won't hurt ye," urged Timbo but Michael wouldn't be swayed and stuck to lemonade; Thomas though downed a couple of pints with whisky chasers. He knew that Michael disapproved of him drinking at fifteen but "it's Christmas", so anything went. The pub landlord knew Thomas was under age to drink but in those days they turned a blind eye in pubs like the Farmers' Arms because everybody knew everybody and if there was any nonsense your parents got to know and then you were for it.

"Have ye kept yer boxin' up, Michael?" Unusually, Michael spoke at length about the dojo in Bielefeld.

"Good for you, it sounds like your fittin' right in. When ye leave the Army don't come back here, it's dead. There's nothin' goin' on 'ere, cousin, I'm tellin' ye. Get down to that London or somewhere but don't waste yer time comin' back here."

"Piss off, Timbo, tellin' our Michael not to come back to Liverpool. What's it got to do with you anyway?" Only certain relatives could talk to Timbo that way and get away with it.

"Same advice goes for you, cousin. Leave Liverpool as soon as ye can. I'm off to Southampton in February and I tell yez wha', I'm not comin' back 'ere again. No chance."

"What rubbish are you talkin' about now, Timbo?" Baz from the Sparrow Hall Gang had just entered the pub. They'd served time together in Walton nick. "Still hangin' out with yer weird family?" The two men moved away from Thomas and Michael for a little chat together. It was business, or so Timbo said after they'd re-joined him and Thomas at the bar.

"I don't like that Barry Grogan. He duffed me up once," whispered Thomas to Michael.

"Did you beat my brother up?"

"Just messin' about like. Nothin' serious. It was a long time ago anyway. Nothin' to get yer knickers in a twist about, mong boy."

"What did you call 'im?" asked Timbo.

"Just messin' about, Timbo. Jesus, I can't say anything without you or your weird relatives gettin' the 'ump."

"You shouldn't have beaten my little brother up."

"Listen, plums, you wanna watch yerself, I've been to prison. D'ye know what I mean?"

"Baz. I told ye before and I'll tell ye again, our Michael'd burst you with one hand tied behind his back. My advice is for you to keep that hole in the front of yer face shut because it's gonna get ye into trouble."

But Baz wouldn't be told. "Alright then, plums, you and me outside, now."

"Baz mate, it's Christmas Eve and nobody is goin' outside with anybody. I'm tellin' ye. Okay?" With that Baz pushed Timbo out of the way and drew a six-inch flick knife from out of his pocket. The pub went silent as they'd been listening in on the argument and they saw Baz draw the knife.

"Don't be an idiot, son, put the knife away," pleaded the barman but Baz's blood was up. He'd wanted to fight Michael all those years ago. Vendettas between street boys run long and deep. Thomas was terrified but Michael was completely calm.

"Ye know I stabbed somebody, don't ye?" screamed Baz trying to strike fear into Michael's heart but he could see it had no effect. "What's wrong with you? I've got a bleedin' knife here not a… bunch of… daffodils. Do ye think I'm jokin'? Is that why yer not scared? Think I'm jokin' do ye?"

"I'm going to stick your knife in you," was Michael's reply in a quieter than usual monotone voice. Baz knew he had to act before fear gripped him. He came lunging forward, knife in hand. Michael dropped him with a leg sweep. As soon as Baz was face down on the floor Michael jumped on top of him, grabbing the hand with the knife in it. He forced Baz's wrist agonisingly against the joint and then slowly, very slowly he moved his knife-holding hand towards his throat. Baz's eyes were wide with fear.

"Timbo. Timbo. Get yer weird cousin off me. I'm not messin' about, I mean it, get this bleedin' weirdo off me."

In an effort to calm the situation Timbo said, "Michael, whatever ye do, don't stab Baz. I mean it now, cousin. Don't stab Baz. Yer'll be in a cartload of trouble if ye do."

Michael wasn't listening to Timbo or anybody else nor was he aware of anything around him as he was in the grip of his tunnel-vision terrors. All he could see was a writhing apparition morphing between Baz and a scaly creature. Michael moved the tip of the knife to within an inch of the creature's throat before facing It eye to eye. Staring unblinkingly, he pushed the knife into the creature's throat, making a three-quarter-inch-wide slice in the bristly skin under Baz's chin. The cut wasn't very big or very deep but big enough and deep enough to draw a lot of blood. Michael held Baz in a dead-eyed stare. There was no emotion in what he did; he felt no mercy, no pity, no compassion nor empathy. He felt nothing at all. He just did it and as calmly as he sliced Baz he picked himself up off the floor, put on his overcoat, grabbed Thomas by the arm and casually made for the door.

Timbo was aghast at the level of cold-heartedness shown by his cousin. "Michael, ye just stabbed someone and yer actin' like nothin's 'appened. The police will be here in no time. What we're gonna do next is get you and 'im a long way from 'ere." Then to the people on the bar, "Listen, youz lot, if any of yez say anythin' to the police I know who ye are and I'll be back to pay yez a visit so keep yer gobs shut, okay?" Then to Baz, "An' you, if you grass our Michael up I'll find ye and I'll cut yer plums off. Don't you forget, Barry Grogan, I did time for you in Walton nick because none of us grassed yer up when ye stabbed that bloke in town an' now it's payback time. I'm warnin' ye, Baz, yer'd better keep yer gob shut 'cos if yer even whisper our Michael's name… it's up to you." Then to Thomas and Michael, "C'mon, youz two, let's ge' ourra 'ere."

***

The lads made their way in hunch-shouldered silence from the pub, then huddled in an open bus shelter to wait for the next bus to Huyton. Timbo had already decided there was no point running because Michael would get caught sooner or later and as Thomas would be implicated if they ran they headed back to Margaret's house.

Timbo was confident that nobody would grass them up, partly out of the fear of him and partly due to being a grass on a council estate in Huyton was a dangerous thing to be.

"Whatever yez do, don't mention a word of this to yer ma. I gorra say this to ye, Michael, you frightened the life out of me back there. You stuck that knife into Baz's throat without a second thought. Is this what the Army 'as done to ye? Ye even lowered yer head so ye could look 'im in the eye while yet did it. Jesus Christ, Michael, what's goin' on with ye?"

"He hurt Thomas. He deserved it."

"Did the Army teach ye tha', eh?"

"No, I've never done anything like that before."

"I'm pleased to hear it an' now's not the time to start. I know you're different to the rest of us, Michael, but wha' ye probably don't realise is tha' all the family are dead proud of ye. Ye passed yer eleven plus and went to grammar school, ye kept yer nose clean and didn't end up in borstal or jail; ye joined the Army and yer mum says yer doin' great. Yer a great boxer, not as good as me like," grinned Timbo giving Michael a friendly punch in the arm to lighten the mood as he could see the concern in Thomas's eyes.

"So don't be a prick. Keep yerself outta trouble, especially for yer ma's sake."

***

Later that evening Timbo bumped into Baz who was with a few other former members of the Sparrow Hall Gang. They went for a Christmas drink together and swore not to talk about what had happened that night ever again.

***

The brothers and Margaret settled down to watch classic Christmas Eve TV, ate mince pies and drank lemonade. At eleven thirty the lounge door opened and in pranced Queen Rose with three of her friends. As soon as she was through the door she said, "Mum, I've got somethin' to tell ye. Our Michael was in a fight in the Farmers' Arms and he stabbed some lad in the neck an' now he's dead."

Margaret initially thought it was just one of Queen Rose's sick jokes. "What? Are you serious? Michael, do you know what she's on about, son?"

"A bloke called Barry Grogan beat Thomas up and he pulled a knife on me. I took it off him and stuck it in him. He's not dead." Michael seemed to think this sufficient explanation. Margaret started sobbing deeply.

"See what yer've done to Mum now, eh, ye weirdo? Yer've really upset 'er. You shouldn't 'ave come 'ome. Yer not wanted 'ere so sod off back to the Army now or I'm gonna phone the police on ye."

"Listen, Rose, ye can phone the police if ye like but you know what happens to grasses around 'ere, don't ye, girl? If you grass our kid up I'll make sure everyone knows ye did it. I'll tell everyone at yer school too."

"Are you threatenin' me, Tommy? Don't even think about

bleedin' threatenin' me, ye little freak, or I'll tell everyone ye play with yerself in bed."

"Listen, Rose, we're goin' 'ome now, see ye tomorrow," said Rose's best friend. "By the way, if ye grass your Michael up we'll never speak to ye again. Everyone knows Barry Grogan is a div, an' I heard it was 'im who pulled the knife on your Michael an' he got wha' 'e deserved. I'm warnin' ye, Rose, don't you dare grass your Michael up."

A tearful Margaret closed the front door behind Rose's friends, returned to the lounge and threw her arms around Michael, whispering into his ear, "For God's sake, son, please don't ever do anything like that again or you'll end up in jail just like your cousins. Promise me now, son, promise me?" Michael promised. Another classic Christmas in the Frost household.

***

Margaret was up at 7 a.m. preparing the Christmas meal of roast turkey, roast potatoes, sprouts, carrots and gravy. Like most people in Liverpool at the time the Christmas meal was eaten around 1 p.m.

Queen Rose didn't crawl out of her pit until just before the meal was on the table. She took her seat, ate her food and went back to her room in a massive sulk. She didn't like not getting her own way about calling the police about Michael stabbing Barry Grogan. She tried her best to create a bad atmosphere in the house to ruin Christmas for everybody but failed miserably.

Boxing Day, all the family, including Queen Rose, sat watching telly together while various relatives dropped in to see what was going on. Timbo dropped by at five. Margaret took him aside for a word about the fight on Christmas Eve. He set her mind at rest. "It was 'ardly even a scratch, Aunty Marg, honest, he's done worse shavin', an' anyway I went out with 'im later on that night. Honest, Aunty Marg, he's okay; so stop worryin', will ye?"

Margaret wasn't totally convinced but as the police hadn't shown up and Timbo had met up with the lad then all was probably okay.

***

His Christmas leave over, Michael kissed his mum goodbye at the door and she watched his back disappear around the corner, the possibility of never seeing her son ever again not entering her head. And why would it? During one of Queen Rose's more poisonous outbursts, she'd said she hoped he'd end up getting killed in Northern Ireland. She told him that nobody wanted him to visit anymore but they were too polite to say it to his face. She said Patrick hated him and that he'd told her that if she had been born first then they wouldn't have had him and Thomas. Michael understood that if what Rose said ever came out it would hurt the whole family. Unseen, Thomas overheard everything and waited his time to use it.

***

On his return to Bielefeld, Michael sat at his desk and got on with his job. The chaps were talking about what they'd got up to over Christmas. A couple of them asked after Cliff Coley and Victor and were told they'd been transferred. Michael had been prepped not to say anything about the Barry Grogan incident.

***

As soon as his shift was over Michael raced to the American camp. The dojo was open but there was hardly anybody there.

"Come on in, Michael Frost, good to see you. I'm the only sensei here tonight so I guess we'll just do some warming up and then spend a couple of hours doing whatever everybody wants to do. What would you like to do, Michael?"

"You said you have a selection of katanas. Can we use them... p... please?" Still having difficulty with the p word.

"Hey everybody, listen up. Michael here has asked if we can have a session with katanas. Anybody up for that?" Were they ever.

"Good choice, man," said an American soldier slapping Michael on the back a bit harder than he was comfortable with. The sensei took a set of keys from beneath his gi and went to a tall metal locker, springing open both doors in dramatic style.

What they saw before them was an impressive array of what were clearly top notch katanas. Their sayas were of a deep lacquer, high-shine finish in black, dark red or dark green. Several sayas had silk ribbons hanging from them. They were things of startling beauty. The sensei picked a katana from the locker and, grasping it, he fractionally separated it from its saya. Then with a flourish he pulled the katana free. The ha of the blade shone like cracked diamonds in the glare of the dojo's fluorescent lights. The blade was etched with the life journey of the first dragon.

"This is a katana. It is very sharp. Have any of you used a katana before?" Four students, including Michael, raised their hands. "Before you can use my beautiful katanas you need to show me you're competent with a bokuto. You'll find them in the locker at the other end of the dojo; go get one each and come back to the mat." The students sighed thinking it was all just too good to be true that they would actually get to use a real katana.

The sensei asked each of the experienced students to perform some exercises with a katana so he could assess them. After, he felt everybody in the group was capable of wielding a katana without cutting anything they shouldn't.

"Okay. Good. Go get some straw bundles and place them around the mat and I'll demonstrate a few strikes which I'd like you to copy." The helpers placed a half dozen tightly bound straw bundles on weighted stands around the mat. The sensei approached them and as quick as you like he cut the top off each of them and replaced the katana back in its saya. He was unhurried in his actions but they each knew they'd have had no defence had this been a real situation. "I want you to inspect the cuts I made. You should notice that the angle is even and the plane of the cut is flat. That shows good technique. I would now like you to perform a cut on a straw bundle and then examine the plane and angle. Your starting position is with your katana drawn free of its saya. Aim to cut the top off the straw bundle if you can." Each of the students took a katana from the steel locker and approached a straw bundle. Two cut the straw bundles at an angle of about thirty degrees and two parallel with the floor, a much more difficult strike to execute properly. The sensei inspected each cut with each student. "Not bad cuts. Let's move onto combination cuts."

The sensei demonstrated a series of combination cuts. Each student went in turn. They had to move through a corridor of straw bundles attempting to cut the top off each bundle. If Michael could be in seventh heaven he was in it now. He didn't want the session to end. After the sensei called the students together for the warm-down he took Michael and two others to one side and told them that if they wanted to use the katanas again, under his supervision of course, they were just to ask. After he left the dojo that evening, Michael practically levitated all the way back to the barracks.

***

There were less than two weeks to go before Michael was to leave Bielefeld. Normally the internal mechanism for him dealing with time would be racing ahead to his RMC selection but not so this time. Katanas pushed everything to the back of his brain.

For the remaining sessions at the dojo, Michael was first in and last out of every session. The sensei noticed he was very good at mimicking him and mentioned how unusual it was for somebody to be able to mimic movements to the extent he was able to. He asked him about his gift. Michael told him how he'd mimicked people in boxing and fencing. He also told the sensei about the first time he'd held a katana and how it had made him feel inside. Finally, Michael told the sensei that he could mimic movements during actual combat if he saw something that worked well against him.

The sensei was curious to know how far Michael's mimicking could go and so he invited two sword masters to the dojo. The students that evening had come expecting to train using bokuto as usual but instead they were asked to sit around the dojo mat for a demonstration by some specially invited guests.

The sword masters arrived like a whisper. They were dressed totally in black. Their face masks even had black mesh filling the eye gaps. Their katanas were matt black. The only thing that wasn't black was their sclera which reflected through the mesh of their face masks from the lights of the dojo. They moved to the centre of the mat and stood back to back, their katanas angled toward the ground. They behaved like statues. "Students, tonight we have two very special guests who I've invited to give a demonstration on the use of the katana. They need to keep their identities a secret hence their face coverings. I'll be breaking out my katanas for you to use after the demonstration." The densei paused but there were no questions just a sea of stunned faces. "Okay. Most fights involving a katana last less than a minute. They are usually resolved due to a mistake made by one's opponent with the other party making a single decisive strike with the katana. Strikes on human beings from a katana usually result in death through the loss of a limb, or beheading or the severing of a major artery or, more usually, disembowelment. You only have one chance in a katana fight. So, students, it goes without saying that it's most important that you're never on the receiving end of a katana strike." Introduction over, the sensei described the exercises his guests were going to perform and for the next ten minutes the audience sat in stunned silence at the awesome power of the katana in the hands of people who were clearly expert in their use. The demonstration ended with a ballet of slashing katana blades on the straw bundles. The sword masters made virtually no noise whatsoever.

After the demonstration was over the sensei's guests politely bowed and made their way out of the dojo without uttering a word. It was now the students' turn. The sensei asked Michael what he thought. His reply was typical and short. "I have a lot to do to be like them." His eyes were clear and focused as he picked up a bokuto and got to mimicking what he'd observed.

The sensei split the students into groups, one katana for each group to practise their strike techniques. When it came to Michael's turn he wandered head down, round shouldered, to the end of the alley of tightly bound straw bundles and took up the stance he'd observed the sensei's guests taking up. He stood stock still for ten seconds before raising his head. Grasping the tsuka in both hands, he ran at blistering pace down the alley of straw bundles, striking each of them at least once.

His choreography was identical to that of the two sword masters, something only the sensei picked up. The students in Michael's group applauded him which attracted the attention of the other students who asked what all the fuss was about. "C'mon, man, do it again," cried one of the students. Michael did do it again. He did the identical choreography of the first set of strikes. The sensei walked forward and inspected the cuts. They were identical to the first set of cuts. They were perfectly flat and in the same plane, demonstrating excellent technique. "Well done, Michael. Now can all please return to your groups and continue practising."

As he was leaving the dojo the sensei asked Michael if he'd enjoyed the evening. "I have a long way to go to be as good as your guests. When I was considering their movements it became apparent to me that one of them was a woman."

"Absolutely correct. Well detected. See you on Saturday?"

"Yes. I leave on Sunday." Michael left the dojo and returned to the barracks. His sleep that night, as usual, was visited by the same visions and terrors which had haunted his sleeping and waking hours since childhood but they were getting worse and becoming more frequent and he didn't know how much longer he could stand their company. No, not their company; how much longer he could stand their existence. Stand his own existence.

After Michael left the dojo that evening the sensei wrote a letter which he handed to him before he left to return to England. It contained the names and addresses of people in the sensei's martial world who could help him perfect his martial arts. The letter included his thoughts as to what lay behind his gifts and an offer for Michael to contact him any time he needed help from somebody who didn't want anything from him in return. He recognised that Michael was special, if not unique, and he knew from experience that people like him were all too often exploited and are seldom in control of their own destiny.

When he reached the sanctuary of his temple, the sensei swore an oath that he would keep Michael from the harm that he knew would be waiting for him on his path through life. All Michael had to do was reach out to him at any dark time and he'd use his considerable resources to help and protect him. That was the sensei's sacred vow which he sealed with blood and prayers to his ancestors.

THE FORTY-FOUR

This time around, Madame Chairman enjoyed her Christmas break, despite having no family around her. "What a difference a year makes."

***

In her opening address at the AGM she was gracious and feigned modesty. Nearly everybody was worshipping at her feet over the Soviet Missile Heist, as it had become known. She hoped it would become known as Madame Chairman's Soviet Missile Heist. She instructed Lisette to read out congratulatory messages from vacationing governors and splinter leaders as part of the AGM's toast to her. Lisette milked the messages for all they were worth, ad-libbing parts to improve the quality and magnitude of their congratulations.

As she peered down from the top table, the all-powerful Madame Chairman held certain people in the gripping gaze of her ice blue eyes for what must have seemed an eternity to recipients. She conveyed an unspoken message to them. It was up to their consciences or their intentions to decide the meaning of the message.

Immediately after the cheese board, Lisette passed Madame Chairman an envelope which she'd discovered underneath her napkin. It was wrapped in a note instructing her to hand the envelope to Madame Chairman personally. Having inspected the envelope, and decided it presented no danger, she did as the note instructed, shrugging her shoulders when passing it over. Madame Chairman recognised the handwriting. She picked up her glass of champagne and wandered into the ladies' toilet, this time checking to make sure she was alone before locking the door. She was bubbling inside with excitement.

Dear Margaret

Congratulations on a tremendous year. You have made me feel very proud.
    Your success is vindication of my decision to back you.
    There are many challenges ahead but I'm confident you will rise to each of them.
    You deserve a well-earned rest.
    I wish you a Merry Christmas and a successful New Year.

Maximillian

That's it? It was not the note she was expecting. She felt deflated. She felt she deserved more than this.

***

In the months following the second AGM of her reign, Madame Chairman increased the speed of implementing her, or rather Max's, plans. She was beginning to regret agreeing to the terms of her appointment and was starting to resent Max's interfering. She often recalled what the Recorder had said when denying her the thin black tabernacle shroud as a memento of her coronation. He'd said that not even an all-powerful Madame Chairman could keep the black shroud as a memento. When he'd called her that, it sent a shiver spiralling down her spine. All-powerful Madame Chairman. She'd liked it then and she liked it even more now.

The job came with more strings than she now felt she should have accepted. Philosophically, she agreed with many of the conditions imposed on her at the time but that was then and this was now. She agreed to remove the old farts club, and the autocracy of the Chair was to be supplanted by an executive council, her secret inner council. She still agreed with these conditions… in principle. But after she'd been referred to as the all-powerful Madame Chairman she found the images those words conjured up intoxicating.

The old guard had run the Organisation for centuries and they were running rings around her, or so they thought. But not for long, the countdown had started.

***

Max was keeping so close to her that she felt she didn't have his confidence. That perhaps he thought he'd made a mistake by sponsoring her and was already thinking of replacing her. She had to have it out with him. She decided that on his next visit she'd broach the subject during their one-to-one session.

Four days later, Max arrived, unannounced as usual, and, as usual, they went off to a suite he'd booked at the Park Lane Hilton for their one-to-one session. The view overlooking Hyde Park was magnificent.

"Do you like the view, Margaret?"

"I do. I've seen it before though from a couple of floors up. Remember?" she replied frostily.

"I see," replied Max recognising the coolness of her mood. "I think a view is important. Views make the soul soar. Perhaps this is the opportune moment to mention that I've arranged new offices for you overlooking St James's Park. The building has ten floors. I assume you'll be taking the top floor as your own? It has a…"

"Stop. I don't need candy. Let's get straight to it, Max, you're looking over my shoulder and I get the feeling that you're regretting appointing me."

"What? That's nonsense. Whatever gave you that idea?"

"You did. You're always here. Giving me little talks. I never seem to get anything right. You always want things done your way but I'm the boss and I'm here every day so I do what I think is right. Do you want me to call you before I make a decision?"

"I see. I think you misunderstand my motives. You're not the finished article but you soon will be, especially after you remove the old guard. I voted for you because you are the future of the Organisation. In you I see the person who I believe will make the Organisation great once more. Your predecessor couldn't do it but I believe you will. I want you to achieve the vision we share for the Organisation as quickly as possible. Look, I'll back off and let you have space to do things as you see fit. Okay?"

"Thank you, I appreciate that. Now, what did you want to cover this time?"

"I believe the time is right for removing the old guard but perhaps… ?" She could tell by the cadence of his speech, tone of his voice and the movements of his body that it was going to be sex before their little talk this time.

***

She hadn't wanted it to happen but during their time together in Italy she became infatuated with him, with his arrogance and confidence. They became lovers on the second night and continued their affair as she travelled to meet with the splinter leaders. It wasn't unusual for her to be with a man like Max; her husband was considerably older than her, but that was a whole different situation. She was starting to regret their affair. She wanted to break it off but now was not the right time, she thought. Besides, she wasn't having sex with anybody else and she needed to feel wanted or was it wanted to feel needed? It didn't matter which. Also, she really liked sex with Max and before her appointment as Madame Chairman she wondered if they might take things further.

Whenever he turned up, especially out of the blue, it gave her a feeling inside that nobody else had ever given her. She sometimes couldn't wait to get to the hotel; she wanted to lock her office door and… but he always stopped her. He said it made things feel cheap. She agreed and disagreed. She agreed that it was cheap but sometimes she wanted to feel cheap. She disagreed because it was passion driving her lust for him and if the moment passed unfulfilled then it could never be recreated. "How can that be cheap?" They never had sex in her office which was one of her life's regrets at the time. When she had such thoughts she realised she was more like Lisette than she liked to admit.

Max was rich, which always helps, but he was powerful and she found power more sexy than money. He was handsome and in good shape and was an astonishingly good dancer. She'd noticed how men who were good dancers were also good in bed and Max was the best dancer she'd ever met. Her husband wouldn't have minded if she found somebody else but, given the changes in her life recently, that somebody was definitely not going to be Max. But the sex was good.

***

She woke alone in bed from her post-coital nap. Max was just closing the door, perhaps that is what had woken her. Before the bedroom door closed completely she briefly saw a room service trolley. They always had champagne afterwards and by the looks of it there was lots of food on the trolley this time. "How on Earth are we going to eat…" She heard talking and, assuming Max was on the phone or the TV was on, she wandered naked into the lounge.

As she rounded the bedroom door she was shocked to see three other mandarins in the room. They didn't seem surprised to see her which meant that this was either something Max often did or he'd told them they were having an affair. How she hated those hackneyed words. She darted back into the bedroom and got dressed without showering. When she returned to the lounge they were all eating and Max had made up a plate for her of her favourite things. A glass of champagne was fizzing on a small table at the end of the sofa and so she assumed that was her place and sat down in it.

"Madame Chairman." They each greeted her in turn with a slight bow of their heads. She didn't offer up an explanation of what they'd witnessed, though she felt acutely embarrassed.

"Good afternoon... or is it evening? Did you all have a good..." She didn't bother finishing her sentence.

"I was saying to Madame Chairman earlier today that it's time to get on with the changes she agreed as a condition of her appointment. Firstly, the secret inner council is in place. How is it operating?"

"Very well, it..."

"Secondly, we need to discuss the timing of the removal of the old guard. Béat, can you provide us with an update please?"

"Certainly, Max. The majority of replacements for controllers and governors we are responsible for selecting have been identified and Madame Chairman has selected most that she's responsible for choosing. In total we're about seventy-five percent of the way there." Max and Béat had made all their selections many months previous. Their pretence was all part of the game plan. "Here are copies of the lists." Béat handed out sheets of paper with the names of those to be replaced adjacent to those who'd be replacing them. Forty-four names had little crosses next to them. "We should be ready to make our move this coming Christmas. Madame Chairman can make the announcement of the changes at the AGM in December. All

I need do ahead of time is brief the sentinels on their targets." Had she heard Béat correctly?

"I beg your pardon. What did you just say about sentinels and targets?" She was still a little sleepy and wondered if she'd misheard Béat. If he had said what she thought she'd heard him say then it could only mean one thing with sentinels involved.

"I don't understand how I can make it any more clear for you. When you agreed to get rid of the old guard of controllers and governors, what did you think it meant? Some of them need to be got rid of permanently, for obvious reasons. It's only forty-four, that's four percent. It's only four percent."

"There's a huge difference between getting rid of somebody and… what do you mean, it's only four percent? These are human beings we're talking about."

"Please, everybody leave us. Go to my Kensington home, I'll meet you there after I've finished up here."

He has a home in Kensington? she thought. *Then why do we always meet in…* She always suspected he was married, though they'd never spoken about it, but now that the reality of it hit her it stung. Béat and the other two mandarins packed up their papers and left the room.

"Margaret, you yourself have said that a person slighted will seek revenge." She couldn't recall if she had but she recognised the quote. "There are controllers and governors who are just too dangerous to keep alive and they will never accept you or the changes you're about to make. You cannot make the changes and keep them alive. They will return to destroy you."

"There has to be another way. We could retire them in tranches, for example, leaving the more difficult ones until last. If we let them know they are going then many of them will jump anyway. You know, doublers and the like. Many of them are looking forward to their retirement. I'm sure they'll go quietly." She knew she was talking nonsense. "Leave the more difficult ones until last." How could that ever work?

"People like them never really go away. Do they? You know they don't. They leave tendrils behind that act as well as any poison. If there was another way we'd take it. You know this change has to be made and though it will be painful, once it's over then it's over. The Organisation is dying, Margaret, and only you have what it takes to save it." She was convinced that she was the right person to change the Organisation and she believed that if it didn't change it would die.

They talked throughout the night and into the next morning. By the end of their talk she understood that the assassination of the forty-four would go ahead with or without her. She said she needed time to think. Max said she'd had all the time she was going to get and now it was time for action. "They are dead anyway so why sacrifice yourself?" was what he'd said. She took that to mean that she wouldn't be allowed to walk away from being Madame Chairman. She had her sentinels but doubted they'd be enough to protect her. Besides, some of them were bound to be owned by Max and the Mandarins. She steeled herself and said she'd do as they asked and hoped inside that she could find another way before the killing started. Max replied that it wasn't as they'd asked, it was as she'd agreed to do. He was right, it was as she'd agreed to do. There was no going back for her now.

***

As she entered the building in Half Moon Street she passed through several knots of people, some of whom she knew to be on the list of the condemned. They were people over whose murder she would have to preside. They each offered a slight bow of the head as she passed them on her way to her office. As she entered her office she saw Lisette perched one-cheeked on the corner of her desk going through her in-tray.

"I'm allowed to do this sort of thing now I'm on your hush hush council," she joked. "I hope you don't mind me saying so, darling, but you look terrible. Truly terrible. Are you feeling alright?"

"No, Lizzie, I'm not feeling alright but I don't want to talk about it. It's something I have to deal with but I may have to discuss it with you at some point." An eavesdropper wasn't pleased with what she'd heard and would wait to see if this conversation progressed.

Lisette brought them both a coffee. They sat holding hands on a black two-seater leather sofa in the corner of the office. Making small talk, she told Lisette they were on the move to swish new offices overlooking St James's Park. While she was speaking she wrote a short note asking Lisette not to react but she thought the room might be bugged and they would talk properly later.

***

When they did speak later, Madame Chairman left out the bit about slaughtering forty-four human beings. She'd leave that topic for another time.

LYMPSTONE

January 1971

His trip back to England was much better than the one before Christmas. Everything went very smoothly. As there weren't many people travelling, he had lots of room to spread out, relax and enjoy the scenery. Or rather take note of landmarks, which lately he'd started doing habitually.

He arrived in Liverpool late in the afternoon and went straight to Altcar. On arrival he met Sergeant Morgan for a debriefing. The Sergeant told him to get some food inside him and then get a good night's sleep. He couldn't possibly understand what those words meant for Michael. Though not all of the visitors he came across in his sleep meant him harm, none of them was really benign. His waking hours visitors were invariably malevolent. He'd learned to cope with the visions over time but it was getting harder to distinguish them from reality.

***

"Welcome back, Private Frost. How did your work go with MILR? I imagine with your mathematical skills you quite enjoyed all the analysis work, eh?" Michael provided the Captain with a detailed report of what he'd got up to at MIL[R]. "I understand that you got involved with some Australian SAS soldiers. You boxed with them I believe?"

"No sir, I didn't box with the Australian SAS soldiers but I did spar with one of them."

Interesting, thought Captain Hywel-Jones, *no mention of what LeFort told him about telling me that it was an oversight on his part that led him to being placed in contact with the Aussies. He's taking the rap himself. Interesting.*

After the debriefing, Captain Hywel-Jones picked up a thin file. "These are papers concerning selection for the Royal Marines. You'll be tested to your limits and have the opportunity of experiencing something truly unique. If you pass selection and want to remain with the Royal Marines then that is your choice but it goes without saying that you'll be welcomed back here as I believe you'll make an excellent addition to the training staff. Here are your travel orders. You'll report to CTCRM Lympstone on Monday morning. Any questions?"

"No sir."

"The Royal Marines is a meritocracy and there's no reason why you couldn't become an officer. There are no guarantees, Private Frost, so give selection your best shot and see where it takes you. Does that make sense?"

"It does sir."

"Well, Private Frost, if there are no further questions it just leaves me to wish you luck. Dismissed." For the first time they shook hands.

***

Captain Hywel-Jones suffered pangs of guilt similar to those of the French Captain but he needed to build up his own unit of operatives, loyal to him, in order to get closer to the centre. That was his mission. Having people like Michael around him would enable him to provide better intelligence on the Organisation for his MI6 bosses. He knew he was destroying Michael's life by leading him deeper into the Organisation, as once through the portal there was no going back.

***

Arriving at CTCRM late on Sunday afternoon, Michael reported to the main gate and was directed to the building where the PRMC induction briefing would be held the following morning. There were four other candidate potentials there by the time he arrived and twelve more arrived shortly afterwards.

The advice Captain Hywel-Jones gave to Michael was to be the grey man; not getting noticed was the way to get noticed by the selection staff. Classic Special Forces technique. Consequently Michael just blended into the background which was something he was naturally adept at anyway. That night Michael's dream visions were particularly bad and prolonged, meaning he got very little sleep but he was used to surviving on a few hours' sleep and knew how to handle being tired to keep charged up for challenges. It was all in the mind as far as Michael was concerned and his mind was his saviour as well as his tormentor.

***

Bright and early on day one the potentials assembled in a hall where they were given an induction briefing for what to expect over the coming days. Once over they were taken to supplies and handed their kit for the selection exercises. After a quick tour of the camp they were taken back to the hall for numeric, verbal and written tests. They were all thinking, *When is the action going to start?* They didn't have to wait long. As soon as the bell sounded for the end of the tests the potentials assembled in their running gear for two back-to-back, one-and-a-half-mile runs against the clock with each return leg having to be completed faster than the outward leg.

After lunch they assembled once again in their running gear and were taken to the gym where they undertook timed point-to-point beep tests followed by activities they recalled from their school days. The session finished with press-ups, sit-ups and pull-ups with each exercise having a minimum number of repetitions.

The potentials were feeling pretty good about their chances of progressing onto the full RMC course. As good timing would have it, the next scheduled intake was four days after the end of the PRMC. The last exercise of the day was a swimming assessment which involved jumping from a diving board situated ten foot above freezing cold water. After entering the icy water the potentials then had to swim at least twenty-five yards or be classed as a weak swimmer and fail the course altogether. Because the Royal Marines is an amphibious force, operating routinely from the sea, swimming is a vital skill.

At the end of the first day, each potential recruit met with an NCO to discuss whether they remained serious about a career in the Royal Marines. The potentials were quizzed on RMC matters to ensure they understood what the corps stands for: its values and its history. The NCO assigned to Michael was a corporal he'd previously met at Altcar. Because the Corporal already had a high opinion of Michael they had a relaxed discussion, at the end of which he wished him luck for the remainder of the course.

Day two brought a shock to the early morning systems of the potentials. Before breakfast they were put through their paces on the obstacle course with penalties awarded for not following instructions or lagging behind. Obstacles had to be overcome individually and as a team. In addition to the obstacles, the potentials had to complete dozens of circuits consisting of burpees, star jumps, sit-ups, press-ups, pull-ups and squat thrusts. By the end of their morning's efforts they felt as though every one of their muscles was on fire. They knew worse was to come in the endurance test that afternoon. There was the possibility of not making it through to the last day if the minimum criteria were not met.

"I heard the NCOs place bets on who'll fail the endurance course and they actually sabotage you if they have money on you failing. I'm watching out for that Corporal who was on the obstacle course this morning, I think he's got it in for a few of us."

"Where did you hear that? That doesn't sound right to me. If that's what they're up to somebody would say something, wouldn't they?"

"I know the Corporal and he wants people to try their best and I don't think he'd do anything to prevent anybody passing the course," added Michael.

"Where'd you know him from then?"

"Altcar. I was on an exercise with him and a group of other marines and SAS and paratroopers."

"What? Are you sure you weren't dreaming? What was that all about then?"

"It was a civil defence exercise looking at the Army's state of readiness in the event of a nuclear war. It was put on for the Minister of Defence."

"Seriously? That sounds brilliant. How'd it all work out?"

"It was successful and the Minister of Defence congratulated us in a speech he made."

"He's bullshittin'. Look at 'im. Does he look like somebody who'd be involved in somethin' like that?"

"I don't know, Albie, what does somebody have to look like? I mean to say, look at the Corporal at this mornin's obstacle course. He's the top man and he looks just like an ordinary bloke. He's not big or anythin' but can you imagine pickin' a fight with 'im one night in a pub or somethin'? He'd batter ye. Nah, I don't think ye can tell by lookin' at somebody what they're like. I mean to say, look at you, you look like an idiot. Oh wait, you are an idiot." The potentials laughed. It's a good sign when team members take the rise out of each other because it shows they are close. You joke with your mates but you treat your enemies matter of factly.

As they moved off, one potential said to another, "I don't trust that Frost. He's weird and he's in love with himself. Who does he think he is? Minister of Defence! Rubbish."

***

The endurance course was a big step up for the potentials.

The first part of the course was a two-and-a-half-mile run through hilly terrain strewn with obstacles; including pools and flooded tunnels which must be overcome individually and as a team. The NCOs made sure they got nice and wet at the start of the run so they were cold and wringing wet throughout the one and a half hours it lasts. 'Rests' are taken at a quick march in between major obstacles.

At the end of the endurance course the potentials were told they had a 'scenic country run' of four miles back to CTCRM and anybody who failed to complete it faster than the backmarker instructor would fail the whole course. They were dead on their feet but they knew they had to show determination and good humour in all circumstances no matter what. Though nothing was said, they knew they had to complete the run individually and as a team. They left no man behind, doing what was necessary to get everybody over the line ahead of the backmarker instructor. Some were dragged over the line and others carried.

The rest of the afternoon and evening was spent gaining an insight into the state of mind and the business of being a Royal Marines commando. Just before turning in, they were given last-minute orders for a night out under canvas.

During the exercise, potentials undertook all the activities that would be expected of marines under canvas including the mounting of a guard to make sure the area remained secure. They were certain that the NCOs would carry out a midnight raid to keep them on their toes but that wasn't part of PRMC, that would come later, during full selection. The following morning a full kit and weapons inspection revealed a few of the potentials weren't up to standard. They were taken away for a session with their NCOs while the remainder were told they had fifteen minutes before exercises would commence and what they did in the intervening time was up to them. To eat or not to eat? That was the question.

***

Pumped up for day three they were surprised to be ordered to return their kit to the stores and to set about cleaning everywhere with a vengeance. While cleaning was going on, potentials were called out to meet with their assigned NCO and an officer and told whether they'd passed the PRMC. Michael only just passed.

"Sir, I understand there's an intake next week. I was wondering if I could join it."

"Corporal, are there any places available on next week's intake?"

"We have four withdrawals so far, sir."

"Well, Recruit Frost, it seems there's a place for you and so long as your CO has no objections you can start your training to become a Royal Marines commando on Monday. Carry on."

"Thank you, sir, thank you, Corporal. I'll speak with my Sergeant and my CO later today." Michael joined the other potentials for 'operation clean everything'.

"How'd it go? Are you in?"

"Of course he's in. He's the Corporal's boyfriend." They all laughed. "But seriously, how'd it go, Michael? You seemed to run out of steam toward the end of the run yesterday. I thought they might hold that against you." Once again Michael was the victim of his nana's old wives' cure for whooping cough. His lung capacity still wasn't very good and with much more demanding tests to come he was beginning to wonder whether he could make it through full selection.

"All I'll say is I'm off to pick up my boots and socks and I'm back here Monday." Two other potentials joined the intake with Michael.

A Royal Marines commando conversation

"Corporal, that new recruit, Frost, he concerns me. There's something not quite right about him. I assume you've heard the rumours about him? Keep a close eye on him, Corporal."

"Yes sir. His service record is fairly unusual. His Captain pushed him in this direction. To be perfectly honest, sir, with his language and weapons skills, plus he was on special assignment at BAOR, I'd have thought he would have been pushed towards MI. His BAOR service record is heavily redacted which means he was with a spook outfit. It wouldn't surprise me if he is a spook. They're always putting their lads through selection to get them trained up. Still we're all on the same side and that's what counts, eh, Lieutenant?"

"Indeed, Corporal. He may be a spook as you say but let's make a marine out of him to give him his best chance of survival. Carry on, Corporal." The Lieutenant called his Counsellor who passed a message up the line. It came back down the line to Major Finn's Counsellor. Another strike against Michael Frost for attracting attention. This really will not do.

***

As soon as he found a working public telephone, Michael called Captain Hywel-Jones and asked him if he would speak with the camp CO to request a transfer to the Royal Marines as there was a place available for him immediately.

"Very well done, Private Frost, or should I say Recruit Frost of the Royal Marines Commandos? That really is terrific news. I'll speak with the Colonel straight away and have an answer for you by the time you return to barracks. See you tomorrow. Would you like some home leave?"

"No thank you, sir, I'll call and speak with Mum and my lovely little brother." He didn't mention Queen Rose. What she'd said to him before he left to return to Bielefeld hadn't actually hurt him but he knew that if it came out in a family argument then his mum would be deeply upset. "I'll see them after passing selection."

***

As soon as Michael was through the gates at Altcar he went straight to Captain Hywel-Jones's office and knocked on his door. "Enter."

"Sir, Private Frost reporting, sir."

"Stand easy. I've had a word with the Colonel and put in my recommendation and he had no hesitation in approving your transfer, effect immediately you turn up at Lympstone. He's as sorry as I am that you're leaving. He keeps tabs on all soldiers here and he's been impressed by you. As I'm going off base in about an hour I won't be here to say a final goodbye so I'll say it now and wish you the very best of luck. Report to Sergeant Morgan. Dismissed." The Captain raised himself from his chair, leaned forward and shook Michael firmly by the hand.

"Good bye, sir, I hope we meet again."

You can count on it, thought the Captain as Michael saluted, about-faced and marched out of his office.

Leaving the administration building Michael found Sergeant Morgan waiting for him on the parade ground. "I hear you're leaving us, Private Frost? The Royal Tank Regiment not good enough for you then?" the Sergeant joked.

"No, Sergeant, I like the regiment but…"

"I'm only teasing you, ye silly sod. I'm as pleased as punch for you, Private Frost. Well done. We're all proud of you and we know you'll acquit yourself well as a Royal Marine for the honour of the regiment."

The tank crews congratulated Michael by dousing him with gallons of freezing cold water.

***

On Sunday morning Michael went around Altcar saying his final goodbyes before travelling to CTCRM Lympstone. Passing through the gates of Lympstone for this second time would forever change his path through life, setting in motion events that would govern his existence for the next forty-five years before taking him on a final journey to meet his fate.

In front of him he had thirty-two weeks of basic training, the longest of any fighting force in the world.

***

Think of everything you might include in basic training for a soldier and then double it, triple it, quadruple it and then some. The training every Royal Marines commando receives covers everything from troop fighting patrols to attacks and ambushes to underwater escapes from helicopters to fighting in built-up areas to amphibious cliff assaults and much, much more, plus there's more physical exercise than you'd think it possible for any one human being to endure.

With the training clock ticking, Michael was becoming anxious waiting for the swimming and water-related tests and exercises. Everybody told him to concentrate on his technique and not on his strength. One of his fellow recruits took him under his wing. They spent hours and hours in the pool together where Michael observed other people swimming and just as with boxing and swordplay he mimicked the better swimmers, eventually becoming a strong breaststroke swimmer.

Michael's other concern was his lung capacity which historically had impacted on his stamina quite noticeably. The rigorous exercises he was going through worked wonders and he became markedly more able to quickly recover from physical exertion after obstacle and endurance courses. He liked what was happening to him.

***

Over time, the differences between Michael and his fellow recruits became more and more pronounced and it was causing problems. Recruits' feedback on Michael during NCO review sessions was "I don't know if I can trust him" and "he talks to himself all the time" etcetera. Many recruits branded him a homosexual because he didn't do what they did when they went out on the town. In truth he hardly ever socialised, preferring to go to extra classes, especially armed combat classes. They noticed he never spoke about his family or his personal life and this, they thought, was because he had something to hide. Most spoke well of him when it came to the job of being a Marines recruit but they felt he just didn't have their backs.

The main thing they held against Michael occurred during a weekend exercise on Dartmoor. The aim of the exercise was to evade capture and navigate, as a team, through four checkpoints while travelling at night and holing up during daylight hours. On the second night, while making their way to the final checkpoint, the group were being pursued over extremely boggy terrain by men with dogs. They were all exhausted as they hadn't managed to get much sleep and each was carrying a 50lb Bergen. As the men and dogs closed in on them it crossed their minds to ditch their Bergens, find cover and make a fight of it by trapping their pursuers in a crossfire. Not a bad strategy. But they were exhausted and weren't thinking straight and consequently they simply continued on their course hoping to somehow outrun the men and dogs.

The sound of the dogs barking suddenly got a lot nearer. Unexpectedly, from out of the blackness, four dogs, which must have broken free of their handlers, came on the recruits from behind. There were shouts of "dogs, dogs, dogs loose" from the dogs' handlers whilst also shouting at them to lie down and remain completely still and whatever they did they "mustn't hurt the dogs". Fat chance, those things were huge. Being on Dartmoor, the emerging scene brought images of the Hound of the Baskervilles to the minds of some of the better-read recruits. Instead of lying down, Michael walked toward the dogs and as they got near they slowed their pace and stopped barking.

One of the dogs came and sniffed at Michael's boots before moving off into the dark while the others came and lay down on the ground in front of him, looking up adoringly with tongues lolling out of the side of their mouths and their heads tipped to one side. Everybody was astonished at the scene they witnessed by torchlight but when it all sank in they became quite concerned and then scared in the darkness and the stormy weather conjured up by Dartmoor.

The group took a few minutes to gather their wits and their bearings. The pursuers, their dogs and the recruits made their way to rendezvous point four where they were loaded into vehicles and taken back to CTCRM Lympstone. There was very little chatter on the drive back. They didn't know what to make of what they'd witnessed but the events of that night did nothing to enhance Michael's reputation or endear him to his comrades. After that night Michael came under even greater scrutiny as rumours spread that he must have had some kind of chemical on him which incapacitated the dogs, subduing them and putting them into some kind of trance. Nobody, not even Michael, had any explanation for what happened that night on Dartmoor except perhaps it was the dogs' sixth sense about people, and whatever they sensed in Michael pacified them.

***

By the time the recruits entered their twenty-ninth week they were full of confidence that most of them would pass selection and be awarded their green berets.

Entering the final period of training they were all a lot fitter and physically much stronger than they'd ever been at any point in their lives, and especially so Michael. He wasn't big but he was like steel.

During a parade rehearsal, Michael was called out of line and told to accompany a Corporal to the Colonel's office. He could sense something wasn't right by the way the Corporal was walking ahead and not entering into conversation with him. Was it bad news from home? He hadn't seen his family since just before returning to Bielefeld. What could possibly be the matter? Why was he being dragged up before the Colonel? Nobody from the course had been dragged up to see the Colonel before.

They stopped outside the Colonel's office which was guarded by two MPs. The Corporal knocked on the door and waited to be admitted. After an indistinct mumble from inside the room, the MPs opened the door and both men entered the Colonel's office whereupon the Corporal announced, "Recruit Frost, sir, reporting as requested." He did an about-face and stood behind Michael after closing the door to the office and giving the MPs permission to stand down.

"Stand easy, Recruit Frost. Take a seat." The Corporal pulled a wooden chair back from the Colonel's desk for Michael to sit on and for him to stand behind, to be close at hand in the event of trouble. "Before we commence, Recruit Frost I want to say that whatever the outcome here today you are at liberty to request a formal hearing."

"Why am I here? What's going on?"

"Firstly, let me introduce the gentleman sitting behind you." Michael hadn't noticed anybody else in the room when he entered which was most unlike him. "This is Mr Flask, a former

Naval Commander, now with the MoD, and he would like to speak with you about your time at BAOR HQ in Bielefeld."

"Thank you, Colonel, I'll take it from here." The Colonel was visibly put out at the abruptness of the interruption. "Frost, what can you tell me about this person?" Mr Flask slowly placed a black and white photograph on the desk in front of Michael. It was of the pretty blonde female who worked in the MIL[R] building.

"She works in the post room."

"Is that all you know about her, Frost? Is that all you can tell us about her?"

Michael thought for a moment. "Her Russian is excellent. Perhaps she had Russian parents or she studied Russian, she didn't say. She could easily have got work in the translation section. I wondered if she really was a Czech national."

"Did you mention your suspicions to anybody? Your CO perhaps?"

"I didn't have any suspicions. I just noticed her Russian was very good."

"How do you know how good her Russian was, Frost?"

"Because I speak excellent Russian which is why I was seconded onto the Russian desk at MILR."

"Modest, aren't you? Do you speak any other languages, Frost?"

"Yes, I'm fluent in German and French and I'm studying Italian and Spanish. I want to learn Arabic and Mandarin next and then perhaps Magyar or maybe Urdu."

"Why, Frost? Why are you so interested in foreign languages?"

"They interest me. Studying languages occupies my mind."

"Are you a spy, Frost?"

On hearing those words spoken, and as planned, the Corporal took one step back from Michael's chair and placed his hand on his holstered sidearm. The Colonel was noticeably uncomfortable at this development as he felt it was all just too farfetched that this rather odd recruit, who drew attention to himself for all the wrong reasons, could be a spy. Spies are grey. Spies fit in. Spies don't stick out in the way Recruit Frost does. He'd allow things to continue but if matters got out of hand he'd step in and take control of the situation and, if necessary, have Mr Flask escorted from the base. Michael, on the other hand, was the epitome of calmness.

"You seem uncommonly relaxed considering you've just been accused of being a spy and you have a man standing behind you with his hand on his gun. Used to that sort of thing are we, Frost?"

"No, I haven't done anything wrong and I doubt the Corporal would shoot me."

"To make sure he doesn't, I suggest you keep very still in case you're wrong about the Corporal. Where were we? Oh yes. If I can summarise. You know somebody who was about to be arrested for spying for the Soviets. You knew she spoke excellent Russian and in your own words you thought her Russian was so good that it attracted your attention to the point where you doubted whether she was really Czech. Did you ever meet with or speak to Frau Gessler, real name Lyudmila Tarasova?"

"You never mentioned anything to me about the young lady being a spy," muttered the Colonel under his breath.

"Must have slipped my mind. Answer the question, Frost."

"Of course I spoke with her, that's how I found out she spoke Russian; when she delivered mail to my desk."

"Tell me, Frost, do you know of any reason why anybody would want to murder Miss Tarasova?" The Colonel's eyes widened as this was more information Mr Flask hadn't shared with him.

"What's going on here, Flask? You come here and accuse a recruit under my care of spying and then question him about a murder, a detail of your visit which you neglected to share with me. I'm warning you, Flask, any more surprises and I'll have you thrown off the base." At this, the Corporal took another step back from Michael and unclipped the cover of his holster in readiness for removing his sidearm and pointing it at either Mr Flask or Michael as directed by the Colonel.

"What's going on, Colonel, is I have orders to question Mr

Frost and remove him from this base if I deem it necessary in order to facilitate prompt investigation into the murder of Lyudmila Tarasova, a Soviet spy who was working at BAOR HQ. Is that clear enough for you, Colonel?" There being no response from the Colonel, Mr Flask continued, "Frost, I ask you again. Do you know of any reason why anybody would want to murder Miss Tarasova?"

"No." Mr Flask waited for more but nothing more was forthcoming as Michael had answered the question to his satisfaction.

"No? Is that it? Nothing else you'd like to add? Aren't you in the least bit curious to know the circumstances surrounding her murder?"

"No, why would I be?"

"Well, you might be interested to know more if I tell you that your French friend, who masquerades as an army captain amongst other identities, Monsieur LeFort, is implicated in this murder and a copycat murder of a waitress who I believe you know from a place called Sergeant Pepper's. Do you recall the murder of a blonde waitress who was left at the roadside in Bielefeld the very evening you and your French pal had an altercation with a group of soldiers?"

"I read about it in the newspapers."

"Do you recall how she was murdered?"

"The newspaper said she was stabbed in the throat." Under the pressure of questioning, Michael's vision became tunnel-like. He knew what was coming and he hoped he could cope.

"This was an execution-style murder the type of which seems to be the trademark of an individual yet to be identified but who is possibly your French friend. Or at least he knows who it is as perhaps you do too."

"I don't know anything about the murders."

"Are you sure, Frost? Miss Tarasova was murdered in her apartment on your very last day in Bielefeld. She was stabbed with the same type of weapon as the waitress. And of course we know that you were in Bielefeld at the time of both murders. Do you like blondes, Frost? Do they excite you?" Michael hardly heard a word Mr Flask spoke as his tunnel vision became more pronounced. "I hear that you're a dab hand with knives. I hear you're just about the best Royal Marines recruit with a knife there's been here for a very long time. Is that so, Frost?"

Struggling to stay within the reality of the room Michael spoke but was becoming more and more detached from the conversation. He spoke slowly. "I've been studying self-defence for a long time so I…"

Michael stopped talking and through the tunnel of his vision he found himself staring at the creature which had appeared over the left shoulder of the Colonel. He'd seen this creature many times during his life. The first time was when he was lying on the burgundy-coloured velvet sofa with protruding rusty springs in the cellar kitchen of his nana's house while recovering from the joint effects of whooping cough and his nana's old wives' cure. The snarling creature moved slowly right to left, never taking its yellow eyes off Michael for a universal second. He knew it was pointless asking if anybody else could see the creature. When he'd mentioned them as a child it just got him into trouble; his spindly little sticks took the slaps from his frightened parents.

Before Michael spoke for the first time, he thought it was normal to see creatures and that everybody could see them. After his mutism passed he mentioned his visions to his mum and dad and was shocked to discover they couldn't see what was right in front of them. Patrick shouted at him and told him never to mention the creatures ever again. He tried and tried not to talk about them but it was hard for a small child to keep all the horror locked up inside. Over the years he mentioned them less and less until finally he was alone with them. As he grew, he understood that the creatures weren't real but when he was young he couldn't distinguish them as being imaginary and consequently people thought he was disturbed when he openly shouted at them or talked to people about them.

"Are you okay, Recruit Frost? Would you like something to drink? Water? Tea?"

"Frost, what the hell are you up to? What are you looking at? Are you playing games with me?"

"I apologise, I was momentarily distracted but I'm okay now," Michael said despite the creature continuing to prowl around behind the Colonel, always boring into him with Its yellow eyes.

"You were saying, Frost, how you are an expert in self-defence." Which he hadn't said.

"I've studied martial arts and become a competent student."

"Competent student? I hear you're more than competent. I hear you're deadly with bladed weapons. But to go on with what I was saying about the circumstances of the deaths of the waitress and the Soviet spy. They were both murdered with a long thin-bladed weapon, possibly a stiletto. The waitress was stabbed under her chin, the weapon continued into the brain cavity. The Soviet spy was stabbed through the left temple. As with the waitress the blade continued into the brain cavity. Both would have died instantly. Investigations carried out at Bielefeld have linked you and Monsieur LeFort to the murder of the waitress and you to both murders. What have to say for yourself?" The creature was snarling open mauled at Michael, clawing at the air though getting no closer.

"I had nothing to do with the murders. I've known the French Captain since Cadets. I can't believe he would harm anybody."

"A soldier who wouldn't harm anybody? That doesn't even make sense. Your French pal is probably responsible for far worse than involvement in murdering a couple of spy tarts. Oh, didn't I mention that the waitress was a spy too? Is it commonplace, do you think, to have pretty young blonde girls swanning around Bielefeld who are spies and who just happen to be close to people at BAOR, especially the Russian desk? That means you, Frost.

C'mon, Frost, the game's up. You'll feel better if you make a clean breast of it. Tell me everything you know about the spy ring in Bielefeld and the murders of two pretty young blonde spies. Who knows, perhaps you didn't even know they were spies. Perhaps you just like murdering pretty young blonde girls who reject you. I understand the waitress was coming on to your French chum. That must have made you angry, he's old enough to be her father. C'mon, Frost, tell me why you did it."

"I didn't know the women were spies. I didn't murder the Soviet spy and I can't remember anything about the night the waitress was murdered. I'd been drinking and I blacked out and…" The room froze at this admission.

"Colonel, can you dismiss the Corporal please. Don't worry, I've got Mr Frost covered," said Mr Flask patting the grip of a .38 special concealed under his jacket.

"Corporal, leave us."

"Yes sir. Shall I post the guard outside your office?" The Colonel looked at Mr Flask who nodded his head and the Colonel did likewise to the Corporal.

With the Corporal out of the room the atmosphere changed to become quite relaxed. With the relaxation of the atmosphere the creature started to melt away back into Its own world. Mr Flask continued speaking but now quietly and calmly, almost paternally, saying, "You know you're in a whole lot of trouble, don't you, Mr Frost? You know, even if you had nothing to do with those spies or their murders you're going to be arrested and taken back to Bielefeld. I'm afraid this is serious stuff. You'll be locked up while matters are investigated and there's no telling how long the investigations will take. I mean to say, there are always complications when it comes to investigating military personnel being held in a military prison while a civvy criminal investigation is undertaken at the same time. I'd say you're likely to be spending at least a couple of years on remand behind bars before there's even a trial."

The mere mention of being locked up in a cell at the mercy of the creatures was too much for Michael to take and his evaporating tormentor took form again, tearing at the very fabric of the air to get at him. "Of course, that depends on what sort of agreement we can reach today. I can tell you that the Colonel here thinks you're probably innocent, or if not entirely innocent then not as involved as I think you are. But there's always a shadow of doubt in everything, isn't there, Mr Frost?" No response from Michael as he was preoccupied watching the creature. Mr Flask continued, "Well, I say there is. Okay? I'll tell you what I'm prepared to do for you, Mr Frost. I'm prepared to give you an opportunity to take control of your own destiny. I'm going to give you a choice about what happens to you next but bear in mind that once you decide, there's no going back. No going back. Do you understand Mr Frost?" Still no response from Michael. Mr Flask continued regardless. "Somebody with your training, skills and abilities might serve some useful purpose on assignment for Her Majesty's Government while any misunderstandings are cleared up. You could put all the training you've received to good use and I'm sure that once this mess you're in is sorted out you can return here to complete selection and go on to serve as a Royal Marine."

"Yes indeed," said the Colonel whose demeanour too had completely changed since the Corporal had left the room. "You can take up your secondment with Mr Flask, very much as you did with MILR in Germany, and then return here to complete selection, if you wish to that is. Who knows, you might enjoy your secondment so much that you might not want to come back." The Colonel ended his sentence with a nervous little laugh that tailed off toward the end.

"So what's it to be then, Frost? Get dragged off to a military prison or do something useful while this mess gets sorted out? If you're innocent, as you seem to think you are, you won't want to spend time in prison, will you, because... what is it they say, 'there's no smoke without fire'? Time to choose, Frost."

Even though Michael hadn't heard most of what Mr Flask had

said he'd picked up on the basic choice and for him it was a choice of one. He couldn't spend time in prison with only his tormentors for company. "What is your offer?"

"It's simple. You go on secondment to an active unit overseas."

"Where overseas?"

"The final decision needs to be confirmed but let's start close to home. Northern Ireland perhaps. How does that sound?"

"I need to think about it."

"That doesn't work for me, Mr Frost. I need to leave here in the next hour and I'm either taking you with me or you're on your way to a prison in Germany. Time's up, Frost. Choose now."

Michael knew he had no real choice so he simply replied, "Okay."

"Okay what? Okay you're coming with me or okay you're keen to spend time in a cell?"

"I'm going with you."

"Listen carefully while I say this to you, Mr Frost. Once you accept this offer there's no going back. Do you understand me, Mr Frost, when I tell you that there's no going back once we leave this place?"

Listening to Mr Flask saying those words it occurred to Michael he'd heard them before. *No going back*, he thought, *but what is there to go back to or go back for?* Everybody reaches points of no return in their lives so why not take this offer? The creature which had distracted Michael suddenly disappeared and the room was bathed in the yellow glow of the tungsten light bulbs hanging from the ceiling. It was gone until the next time.

"I understand. What do I need to do? Do I need to sign anything? Shall I…"

"You'll be escorted to your locker where you'll retrieve your personal belongings. You'll leave everything to do with Lympstone on your bunk. You'll then be escorted to the main gate where I'll be waiting for you. You'll talk to nobody and nobody will be allowed to talk to you. Is that clear, Frost? Do you understand?"

"I understand."

"Right then, Frost, get on with it."

The Colonel spoke: "If after investigations are complete and it's found that there are no charges for you to face then you're at liberty to return here to complete your selection training to become a Royal Marines commando. Good luck, Recruit Frost."

Mr Flask opened the office door and instructed the two guards to escort Michael to pick up his personal effects from his locker and then take him to the main gate. They were under strict orders that Michael was not to speak with anybody and nobody was to speak to him. The three men walked down the corridor, out of the building and across the parade ground to pick up Michael's personal effects.

"We're done here, Colonel Baxter. I think Frost bought it. I especially liked the comforting thought you gave him that he could come back here to complete his training one day. Nice touch, we don't want him getting all worked up and emotional, now do we? Having something to hope for keeps people nice and compliant. I'd love to stay and chat but I must be on my way. Goodbye Colonel, we will probably never meet again but if we do then we're to ignore one another. Got it?"

"Yes, got it. I doubt the Corporal or the guards picked up on anything untoward so if there's an investigation then all they'll have is me sticking up for Frost. And you, Mr Flask, they'll never find you, will they? If that's even your real name. Goodbye. See yourself out." Mr Flask didn't offer to shake hands with the Colonel nor did he offer Mr Flask a handshake.

***

Walking across the parade ground, Michael was bombarded with questions concerning, "What the hell is going on?" His guards shouted stern orders that nobody was to speak with Private Frost and he wasn't at liberty to speak with them and they should shove off and go about their business.

"What do you reckon is going on there then?" asked one of the recruits theatrically to nobody in particular.

Another recruit was about to offer up his opinion when the Corporal chipped in, "I'll tell you what's going on, Recruit Frost is in it up to his neck. I was standing guard during the questioning he had to face about him being a spy and about the murder of a couple of young blonde women in Germany. They reckon he knifed the two of them."

"What, him? Nah, he's no spy. Who's he supposed to be spying for then?"

"They didn't say but one of the spies he murdered was a Russkie who was pretending to be a Czechoslovakian. They didn't say where the other one was from so I'm guessing he's spying for… do you know, I'm not sure who they said he was spying for but he was working against the Russkies, so he could be working for the Yanks."

"Rubbish. You're saying that an international spy decided to try out for Marines selection after enlisting as tank crew. Where'd he find time to go to spy school then, eh?" The recruits laughed at the Corporal.

"Did you know that he speaks Russian, German and French fluently? And he's learning Italian and Spanish and I think he's doing a bit of Chinese too from what he was saying. Why do you think he needs all them languages if he's not a spy, eh?"

"You got us there, Corporal," replied the recruit in a 'dumbass' voice taking the mickey out of him.

"Yeah, yeah, yeah. I know when people are taking the mick. Do you lot remember the Cambridge spies? Burgess, Philby, Maclean and the other one? They all managed to study to get degrees while spying for the Russians. So anything is possible. If Frost wanted to be a spy then he'd do anything to be a spy and anyway, where'd he learn all those languages, eh? Everybody knows that spies are taught lots of languages," sputtered the Corporal clutching at straws and exaggerating matters in an effort to get the recruits to believe him.

It was important for his personal esteem that they believed him. "I suppose they'll want to get you lot in for questioning next. Better get your thinking caps on otherwise you might be dragged under with Frost. You know how spies never operate alone? Any of you lot could be a spy," shouted the Corporal to the clump of recruits walking away from him.

"Seriously though, lads, what do you reckon? Do you think Frost is a spy?"

"No way. He's too weird to be a spy. It's like I said before he sticks out like dogs' balls and spies are sort of low profile like."

"You seem to know a lot about it, Lenny, you sure you're not a spy," joked one of the recruits making a spy glass gesture as though examining Lenny.

"Stop arsing around, you lot. The Corporal was right about one thing: if Frost is being investigated we're all going to be under suspicion. I'm telling you, it's head down and arse up for me until I'm out of here. Keeping schtum is the order of the day as far as I'm concerned. All I want now is my scran before the next exam."

***

Mr Flask was waiting inside the guard hut at the main gate when Michael appeared through the door. "You took your time, didn't you? C'mon let's get going." Just outside the gate was a black Ford Cortina Mark III with its engine idling. "Put your bag in the boot and sit in the back. Listen, I don't want you puking all over my nice new car so take this." Mr Flask shoved a pill into Michael's hand which he took without argument. The windows of the Cortina had a dark tint so he couldn't see who was in the driving seat. As Michael moved to the rear door of the car, he started to feel woozy and though he knew he was reaching for the car door he couldn't quite reach it. He felt Mr Flask shove him away so that he could open the door and, once opened, he bundled Michael onto the back seat where he was propped up against the opposite back door.

"Where to first?" asked the driver in a soft Irish accent.

"Drive towards North Wales and I'll direct you when we get closer."

"I hope you're not planning on taking us back to the old country. I'm not very welcome there at the moment."

"If we are then we are, so don't you worry about it, pal; you'll be looked after."

"I've heard about the way you look after people so if ye don't mind I'll stay on this side of the water if it's all the same to you."

"Have it your own way. I need to attend to him so pull over at the next layby." Less than a mile up the road the Irishman pulled into a truck-stop and waited for Mr Flask to close the back door of the Cortina before moving off again. Within a few hundred yards of pulling away the Irishman looked in his rear view mirror to see Michael slumped on the back seat and Mr Flask leaning over him.

"Is he dead?"

"No, he's just having a nice little sleep. I topped him up with a little jab of something for the trip."

***

Though Michael couldn't have realised it, he was off the lists and on the register. There was no going back for him now.

CUTTING THE STRINGS

Madame Chairman hadn't shared the details of her deal with the Mandarins with anybody but felt that if she didn't confide in somebody soon she'd lose her mind. "Lisette? How about Lisette?" She knew Lisette was probably the right person to share her burden with even though she didn't entirely trust her. She hadn't shared with her so far because that's what they'd expect her to do. Who could she talk with who she trusted but the Mandarins would never think of watching? It could only be Control.

She'd contact Control as soon as she got to Half Moon Street. No, the building was probably bugged. She realised she was becoming paranoid, *But,* she thought, *not without good reason.* Classic paranoid thinking. Maybe it was and maybe it wasn't without good reason but Lisette had hired an expert weeks previous to check the whole building for bugs and the report came back clean. There were no bugs in Madame Chairman's office nor were any found elsewhere in the building. Peter said he'd stake his reputation on there being no bugs; he'd searched high and low and checked every common and potential hiding place and found nothing. To be on the safe side, and with an office move pending, Lisette decided to keep Peter on as her communications consultant.

Madame Chairman would send Awhah and Cho with a note

inviting Control to come with her to inspect the new office block near St James's Park. Then, if she felt the time was right, and she could hold her nerve, she'd open up to Control about her dilemma.

To cover her tracks she went to Half Moon Street first before quietly slipping out during the morning to meet up with Control. She'd start by telling her that she was thinking about a party to launch the opening of the new offices. As its front was a PR/ad agency and PR/ad agencies are always doing that sort of thing it wouldn't look out of place. Plus it was getting near Christmas so… her pretexts were sounding more and more implausible, even to her.

***

She was working her way through her to-do list before slipping out of the office to meet Control, when she heard a familiar voice outside her office door. It was Rex. *What the hell is he doing here?* she thought. Though she was the boss she didn't have any sway over anything that involved Rex or what he did. He came and went as he pleased and always proffered non-committal answers to her questions. She still didn't know what it was he actually did.

"Is that you out there, Rex?"

"You know it is. Coffee?"

"I'll make it, you go right on in and I'll bring it to you."

"Thank you, Lisette, for inviting people into my office. I'll have one too while you're about it."

"Don't mention it, boss, that's what I'm here for," she replied sarcastically.

"Margaret, I have something important to tell you but let's wait until Lisette has served us our coffees, I'm parched."

"Something important? Does that mean you're finally going to tell me what it is you actually do? I mean to say, I'm only Madame Chairman after all but it's about time I…"

"I said something important to tell you, not something secret."

She wasn't in the mood for his nonsense and warned him so. He looked nonchalant as usual.

After Lisette had served them their coffees and made a little small talk she closed the office door behind her and left them to their discussion.

Rex looked toward the door to see if it was fully closed shut before speaking. "I have some terrible news and it affects you and your position as Madame Chairman."

"Go on." She casually reached under her desk to locate the hatched handle of her .38.

"Max died late yesterday evening. He… here, please, take a tissue." He waited until her sobbing had subsided a little before continuing. He wondered if the tears were genuine. "He wasn't a well man… but we all thought he had at least another decade in him." This was not the time for one of Rex's poor taste jokes.

"How did he die? What was the cause of death?"

"Nothing suspicious. He'd had chronic liver problems for years. It seems he suffered massive organ failure brought on by sepsis. There'll be a post-mortem and as soon as its results are known I'll tell you exactly what they say."

"Where is he?"

"I'm afraid I can't say…"

"Rex, where is he?

"Margaret, you know I can't answer that question for obvious reasons." He sipped his coffee and squinted at the Mongolian horsemen erotic prints on her office walls. "I believe you are aware of the closeness of the vote to elect you Madame Chairman. With Max gone your support is now split fifty-fifty. Some may want to remove you. I'll do what I can but…"

"What if I wish to step down as Madame Chairman?"

"That isn't an option at present; you understand why, I'm sure. I'll do what I can but if things look like they're going badly I'll warn you and then at least you can rally support. Keep your sentinels close at hand."

"Some of them are doublers. Maybe I'm better off not having them close should the worst come to the worst." Rex handed her a list. "What's this?"

"The names of sentinels who are doublers. I recommend you don't do anything about them for the time being but if the vote goes against you then you know what you must do. I have to go. I'll keep in touch." With that Rex left the building.

Her head was in a spin. What should she do? Who could she trust? Lisette, she must trust Lisette. She called her into her office and told her about Max and what Rex had said about her sentinels, showing her the list of names he'd given her. Lisette looked it over. She returned to the second name and remarked that she doubted she was a doubler. Madame Chairman made shushing motions to which Lisette said that Peter had checked everything and there were no bugs, she'd stake his life on it. She said she'd stake her life on the list being phoney. When they went over the list together they were doubtful about half the names on it. Lisette hypothesised that Rex was playing a double game and couldn't be trusted. She believed Lisette could be right and decided to play along with Rex for the time being.

After Lisette returned to her desk she called Madame Chairman on her internal line. "Just had a thought. Don't ask how, but I acquired a couple of rather snazzy chromium-plated Brownings the other week. They might come in handy should somebody decide to take matters into their own hands. I'll give them a good clean and bring them into your office." Madame Chairman thanked Lisette and asked her to put them in her desk drawer as she was off out for the rest of the day. Lisette told her to be careful when she handled the pistols as they'd be loaded. She'd put the safety catch on if she could remember which way it activated. "They'll either both be on or both be off. It wouldn't do to leave one each way, now would it?"

***

Max being gone presented Madame Chairman with an opportunity to change the rules. Make things more to her liking. But he wasn't operating alone, he had the support of four mandarins. If the new mandarin sided with them then at least she'd have the majority behind her but it would mean having to go ahead with killing the forty-four. She understood time was short but she was confident she had enough time to save the forty-four. She shook her head, smiled and gave a single derisory snort while exhaling. Here was she… Madame Chairman… the champion of change… trying to save the lives of the lifelong members of the old farts club. *What next?* she pondered. *Maybe I'll take up the cloth.*

***

Madame Chairman met Control in front of the Organisation's new offices overlooking St James's Park. She hoped to tell her everything now Max was gone. She was intrigued to see what Control's reaction would be to her news and her idea to save the old guard. She hoped she could trust her to keep their discussion to herself. If she felt threatened or unsure she'd… no, she wouldn't do that, she'd pay the price, she'd take her punishment. After all, it was she who'd decided to confide in her and if that was a mistake then Control should not have to pay for it. It would be her mistake and she would pay for it. As far as she was concerned, that's the way things would be from now.

They went straight to the tenth floor as Madame Chairman was eager to see her new suite of executive offices. As they exited the lift there was an area which would be perfect for her new PA, Cressida. Now that Lisette was on her secret inner council she'd decided that Cressida would take her place as her PA. At least she wasn't promiscuous nor over fond of recreational drugs. Lisette carried out her PA duties perfectly but there were some aspects of her character which caused concern, and not only with herself.

Control was experienced enough to know that there was more

to this meeting than just having a look around the new offices. Madame Chairman could have done that with anybody so why her? She thought she'd give things a nudge and so asked Madame Chairman if she had anything particular on her mind that she wanted to discuss with her. Was she unhappy with the way she was carrying out her duties as Control? Madame Chairman said she was far from unhappy with her and seizing the opportunity she took up her courage and went straight into it.

She started by telling Control the news of Max's sad passing. Control asked her if she was being sincere; no, not sincere, was she being serious? She replied that she was and asked her why she'd asked such a question in the way she had. Control elaborated on some of the events which had occurred over the past fifteen years in Half Moon Street. She said she knew Max was part of a group calling itself the Mandarins and, as their leader, he was attempting to gain control of the Organisation. She believed he would have succeeded had it not been for the vigilance of the governors. She recognised that they were a crusty old-fashioned bunch but they wouldn't take nonsense from anybody and so sent the so-called Mandarins packing. Madame Chairman quizzed Control about what she knew of the Mandarins, eventually informing her that they'd appointed her to the Chair. Control felt under pressure, why hadn't Charles shared this with her? She replied that she'd heard rumours that they appointed the Chair but thought them to be a myth. She thought it more likely that governors appointed the Chair.

Madame Chairman asked Control why she used a derogatory tone when mentioning the Mandarins, the so-called Mandarins as she'd referred to them. She replied that everything connected with them seemed to be stained with treachery and deceit. She apologised to Madame Chairman if she felt she was speaking out of turn and that she meant no disrespect to her or her position. Madame Chairman assured her that she valued her frankness and she was in no way speaking out of turn. She said she welcomed her comments and respected her knowledge of matters she had no experience of. As the conversation continued, each felt they'd gained the other's trust. Continuing with their discussion about the Mandarins, they proceeded with the inspection tour of the new offices before going for a coffee to cement their new found fellow feeling, if not friendship.

Over their coffees, Madame Chairman asked Control if she'd heard anything about Max which was connected with her. She said she had and that she hoped it wasn't true. She asked how she could possibly know such a thing. Control replied that Rex had told almost everybody in the building about her affair with Max. Now she understood why some believed that was how she'd got the Chair. Control then asked Madame Chairman if she'd spoken favourably of the Mandarins because of her affair with Max. She thought for a moment before replying that could be the case. They finished their coffees without speaking further.

***

As it wasn't too late she went back to the office instead of going home. "What do I have waiting for me at home?" As she opened the outermost doors to her offices she wasn't surprised to find Lisette still hard at it sitting at her desk.

"What are you still doing here? Don't you have anything better to do or a home to go to?"

"No, but please don't thank me for all the effort I put in or the superb job I do for you. Not to mention looking after you by putting two rather fab chromium-plated Brownings in your desk drawer. They look super. Want to see them?"

"I do but first I need a stiff drink."

"Brandy?"

"Perfect."

"I'll get them," she replied inviting herself to join in the snifter. As Lisette poured the drinks she reached inside her handbag to retrieve a blue bottle with a rubber teat fixed to the cap and attached to a glass pipette tube inside the bottle. She squeezed the rubber teat to fill it, unscrewed the cap from the bottle and put two drops of clear liquid into each glass. She hesitated before deciding three drops in one of them would do a better job. "Cheers."

"Cheers, Lizzie. Hmmm, that's better. Now let's go and see those guns." She swigged her entire glass empty and slammed it down on the desk.

They raced like giddy, excited children into Madame Chairman's office. Lisette pulled open the desk drawer and grabbed both pistols, offering one to Madame Chairman.

"Check the weight. Check the balance. Aren't they just the most beautiful pair you have ever seen. Let's check ourselves out in the mirror holding them. I'm going to be holding mine like this." She struck a pose. They both sputtered a laugh, spraying brandy spittle everywhere.

"Lizzie, what if somebody comes in and sees us acting like idiots?"

"Then we'll shoot them right between the eyes," she joked and laughed.

They stood back to back, guns held upright in front of them, admiring themselves in the large, gilt-framed, over-mantel mirror. They looked like they were straight out of a poster for a James Bond movie. The bevelled edges of the mirror somehow seemed brighter and more rainbow bejewelled than usual. The gilt moulding of the frame flowed like liquid gold. Everything appeared more vital to them.

"You know, Lizzie, Max's death could be my salvation." Madame Chairman divulged the details of how she'd been deceived by Max and the Mandarins. She hesitated to tell her about having to off forty-four governors as part of the terms she'd accepted. Lisette's reply was very critical. She said that she must have been so eager to get the top job not to see something like that coming a mile off. She had to agree with her. "I was blinded by ambition and the thought of having all that power, but now I have a chance to put things right and do things my way. The right way. The fair way."

"Hold on now. You don't think that this will all just go away because Max is dead? Just like that?" She snapped her fingers together but they made no sound, "C'mon, Margaret, that will never happen."

"What do you suggest?"

"I'm thinking you shouldn't jump too soon. If you look, even for a second, like you're not going along with them then you're a dead woman. This place is full of doublers and I suspect at least two of your so-called secret inner council are spies who are feeding everything back to their bosses, whoever they might be. We need a plan. Tell you what though, and don't think badly of me for saying this, there are some who need to go… permanently… if you know what I mean?"

"I'm ashamed to say I've had similar thoughts. After they first told me about assassinating the forty-four, the second thought that jumped into my head, after I'd got over the initial shock of course…"

"Of course, darling."

"…was that I'd be glad to see the back of Sir Geoffrey Hamilton-Cross and his cronies. Am I a terrible human being, Lizzie?"

"Yes, but you're forgiven. I'm joking. I'm joking," she replied, laughing at her boss's hurt expression.

"Let's see who've been naughty boys and girls. Let's see who's been using my Organisation for their purposes. Let's see who's been empire building and intriguing. Let's see who the conspirators are who've been corrupting my Organisation. Then we'll make our own list."

"And then what?"

"We'll deal with them."

"We'll deal with them? Who's this 'we' by the way?"

"You're right as usual, Lizzie. I'll deal with them. The all-powerful Madame Chairman will deal with them. She'll deal with them all." The more she spoke of or thought of her self-proclaimed title the more she liked it. The All-Powerful-Madame-Chairman.

***

They worked tirelessly for three days solid sifting through the archives; checking, validating; until they arrived at a final list. They'd given the benefit of the doubt where they could. During their investigations, Lisette was in charge of sustenance. Twice a day she added a couple of drops of the clear liquid from the blue bottle to Madame Chairman's coffees.

The final list had eighteen names on it. They were shocked and appalled and resolved to look at the list again before the deed had to be done. At the top of the list was Sir Geoffrey Hamilton-Cross. There was no going back for him.

As they were collecting up the paperwork, to deposit it once again into the archives, Lisette suggested a celebratory brandy.

"That will go down a treat!"

"I'll pour us a large one each." This time adding eight drops of the clear liquid from the blue bottle.

"Lisette darling, have you noticed anything funny about that mirror over there?"

"No. Why? What's wrong with it?"

"It's beautiful. The rainbows are beautiful. Can you see the rainbows?"

***

"It must be done."

"Yes, it must."

"When will you do it?"

"After the AGM."

"Are you sure you can trust Control?"

"Yes, I'm sure."

"If you're found out they will show no mercy."

"Yes, I know."

"What a year it's been, darling. At the first AGM you shouldn't have… but no, no regrets."

"No, you're right as usual. The dressing down I gave to Geoffrey Hamilton-Bloody-Cross set everybody against me. I shouldn't have done it. I think they're scared of me, Lizzie."

"Yes, but you pulled off the biggest heist of all time and now you're getting ready for your next great challenge. Timing is important."

"Yes, timing is important."

"At the AGM then?"

"Yes, at the AGM."

"All who look upon you will love you."

"Yes, they shall love me."

"And you will pity them in their weakness."

"Yes, I shall pity them."

"Max is dead and the others are nothing without him. They'll run for cover. You'll be the all-powerful Madame Chairman. Just like you always wanted."

"Yes, just like I always wanted."

"Sleep darling, sleep. It'll be our time soon."

End of the first instalment.

EPILOGUE – AFTER THE HEIST

The final accounts for the Soviet Missile Heist were in. They looked healthier than expected thanks to some tough negotiating by Madame Chairman. There was no shortage of potential customers.

Since the six-day war, when the Israelis ruled the skies flying their American jets, the Arab nations realised their Soviet jets weren't up to the job. They wanted to reset the balance of power in their favour and the shiny new Soviet SAMs were just the ticket. Many Arab nations were pro-Soviet or they played the two-faced game between the USA and the USSR in order to gain whatever advantage they could over Israel, their unloved and unwanted neighbour. The Soviets provided their Arab friends with old technology, at least two generations behind their latest technology. Classic USSR friendship.

Disposing of the missiles, the Organisation is concerned not to swing the balance of power too far in any one direction as to do so could produce undesirable outcomes. No, no, no, that won't do at all. That's not what the Organisation is about. To go about its business it must remain unnoticed and so to occupy mankind it creates societal divisions, religious and inter-cultural disorder and economic imbalance through the backing of conflicting political, industrial, financial and trades union organisations as well as backing certain extremist groups to pull society this way and that which has the effect of keeping people watching each other instead of lifting their heads to notice the work of the Organisation. The Soviet missiles would greatly help the Organisation with its work and replenish its depleted coffers.

***

In order to maximise ROI, the Organisation broke up the Soviet missiles, their technology, their guidance systems, their warheads and their carriers into various lots for sale.

It was not just going to hand over complete weapons systems. Peoples, or nations, who just acquire things do not appreciate them. The worthwhile things in life must be worked for. Therefore the Organisation in arranging its lots for sale made sure that there was no possibility of anybody simply plugging in their shiny new missiles and firing them. No, no, no, that wouldn't do at all. A sudden burst of weapons advancement like that would shatter the balance of power, especially between the lower order nations. The balance of power must only be allowed to change slowly otherwise all-out war is inevitable. Besides, if the Organisation sold complete working missile systems on the open market the Soviets would simply put pressure on the buyers to return their property to them and nobody wanted that, especially not some high-ranking Soviet officials in the Kremlin. Therefore the lots for sale were centred on technology acquisition rather than the hardware itself and were structured in such a way as to give the purchasers a teeny-tiny leg up on the weapons race ladder. That's it. That's all. That was the only deal on offer. This approach enabled long-term revenue streams as the Organisation supplied consultants to help their customers get their investments into the air and flying toward the objects of their loathing.

The missile technology sale was conducted menu style. The nations of the eastern Mediterranean were offered SAM and short-range ICBM technology. Where to offload the medium-range ICBM technology was proving problematic from a few perspectives. It wasn't in the interests of the Organisation to start WWIII. Problematic, that is, until the Chinese, the Soviets and the Americans came to the table. The Soviet stance initially was simply to demand their property be returned to the peoples of the USSR. All of it. With nothing whatsoever missing. No negotiation. Doublers operating inside the Kremlin helped dilute these demands and the leadership ultimately accepted they were in a bidding war with the other two superpowers and that was it. Like it or not, that was the situation. Buying back their own property was of no interest to the Soviets for obvious reasons.

Ever alive to opportunities for long-term revenue streams, the Organisation sold half the SAM technology to a consortium of Arab nations at a bargain price plus a modest share of their oil revenues for ten years. This deal was later amended to reduce the share of oil revenues in favour of a split between oil and real estate. The Organisation became perpetual real estate partners. The Arabs were delighted. And why not? Oil was just a happenstance of their geography which had turned them into nations of billionaires. Property they purchased as a result of their oil revenue was thought of in likewise terms. Besides, the Arabs liked having the Organisation, whoever they were, as partners. How naïve of them. The remainder of the SAM technology was sold to the USA and China at a knockdown price. Favours beget favours. The Israelis were provided with SAM and short-range ICBMs through the back door by the USA after it was cut into a deal for ICBM missile systems which is how the USA succeeded in catching up with, and then passing, the Soviets in ballistic missile technology before the end of 1972. It's oh so much easier to improve on an idea than to have the original thought.

All in all, the Soviet Missile Heist, as it became known, was an outstandingly great success for the Organisation. The venture netted them hundreds of millions of dollars, plus they were receiving massive amounts of oil and real estate revenues from their Arab BFFs and their consultants were burrowing in like ticks into the very fabric of the infrastructure of each nation who bought into the deal.

To ensure there was no escalation of hostilities, the missile technology was spread out nice and evenly amongst Arab and non-Arab nations. Neighbour was set against neighbour. Brother was set against brother. Religion was set against religion. They each became so preoccupied watching what their so-called enemies, and some of their so-called friends, were doing that they had no time to lift their heads and look around to see what was really going on. This is exactly how the Organisation likes things to be. Classic Organisation, spreading fear, uncertainty and doubt wherever and whenever it can so it can remain in the shadows.

But what about the poor old Soviets? What was in it for them? After all they'd been the victim in all this. They were looked after by the Organisation when it silently partnered the setup of a new dark pools stock exchange trading in the latest technologies. For the next two decades the Organisation hooked the Soviet Union up to purchase equity, via the back door, in many Western IT and R&D companies. This would prove to be the best bit of business the Soviets ever did as nobody predicted the explosive expansion of technology into every part of every walk of life.

Nasdrovia.

EPILOGUE - MICHAEL'S STORY

The manner in which Michael Frost was inducted into the Organisation was ugly but wasn't so unusual. By whatever means, newbies are marginalised and isolated from society in such a way that it's simple for the Organisation to gain control over them. Some don't actually know, or ever even discover, who they're really working for or whose interests they're serving and so it will be, for the time being at least, for Michael Frost. He may never be told who he's really working for. Any details are so thin they have no tradeable value. Some newbies don't live long enough to discover who they're working for.

Unlike most operatives, Michael will not receive his orders via a counsellor. He will be slowly, almost imperceptibly, dragged deeper and deeper into the depths of the Organisation with every little thing he does for it. The details of everything operatives do are recorded and reported upwards, as it is with all levels: date, time, place, outcome, photographs, participants etcetera. The reason for this is obvious. Apart from good intelligence gathering, if anybody in the service of the Organisation considers, even for a second, betraying it they will be buried under a ton weight of evidence of their illegal or treacherous activities. Then, following an investigation by law enforcement, the former servant will be dealt with by local judiciary before disappearing into one penal system or another. Never to emerge again due to a contrived death, or accident as they're commonly called.

***

And so, toward the back end of August 1971 Michael Frost made his way onto the register of the Organisation. His designation had not been fully decided but he would start, as did many newbies, as an operative. That same day, around the globe, eight others 'officially joined the Organisation'.